Red Sky at Morning

Melissa Good

Yellow Rose Books

a Division of

RENAISSANCE ALLIANCE PUBLISHING, INC.

Nederland, Texas

ISBN 1-930928-81-5

First Printing 2002

9 8 7 6 5 4 3 2 1

Cover design by Mary D. Brooks

Published by:

Renaissance Alliance Publishing, Inc.
PMB 238, 8691 9th Avenue
Port Arthur, Texas 77642-8025

Find us on the World Wide Web at
http://www.rapbooks.biz

Printed in the United States of America

This is for Mike. He'd appreciate the yacht.

Chapter
One

The hotel lobby was full of people: men in business suits, and women in equally well-tailored suits of their own. The plush carpet muted the conversation, but the buzz tickled the senses as the crowd shifted and moved, sophisticated glances meeting and mouths tensing into polite smiles.

Behind the long, marble-topped front desk, two reservations agents observed the cocktail party with mildly bored expressions. "I hate these parties," one confided. "They're so stupid."

Her companion shrugged. "They're all right. At least, this bunch is okay. They tip. That convention we had in last week...shoulda ended up at the Motel Six."

"You got that right." The female clerk fiddled with her terminal, then leaned on the counter and sighed. "How much longer?"

"Two hours." The dark-haired man leaned on the counter next to her, watching the crowd. "Uh-oh..."

"What?" The woman peered in the direction of his gaze. "Oh." She rolled her eyes. Entering the hotel's elegant glass and brass revolving door was someone obviously out of place in the lobby full of expensive, chic clothing.

The sweatshirted, blue-jeaned figure edged its way through the party, collecting stares along the way, headed unmistakably for the desk. Rips sliced the denim above the knees and complemented the hiking boots that scuffed across the thick carpet.

"Water fountain," the man guessed.

"Bathroom," the woman countered.

"Directions."

"Change for a dollar."

They both smiled sweetly as the scruffy figure came to the desk and rested long, powerful hands on the polished surface.

"Yes...ma'am?" the male clerk inquired. "Something we can do for you?" His tone indicated polite doubt.

One of the hands lifted and removed the sunglasses hiding a pair of remarkably piercing eyes, which now drilled right through him. A dark, perfectly shaped eyebrow lifted wryly as the woman answered, "Roberts. I have a reservation." It was a low voice, but distinct, with the faintest hint of the South in it.

The male clerk blinked. "Um..." He rattled a few keys, then managed to get the name typed in, aware of his co-worker peering avidly over his shoulder. To his immense surprise, the name obediently returned an actual reservation, of which he studied the details. "Yes...yes, Ms. Roberts. We've got it right here. Um...do you have any luggage?"

"Just this." The woman hefted a weathered leather overnight bag slung casually over one shoulder. She took the key the clerk handed over. "Elevators?"

"Over to the right there, ma'am." The man's tone had altered to one of tense respect. "Is there anything we can send up for you?"

Dar turned and surveyed the crowd, some of whom were eyeing her disreputably ripped jeans with distaste. "Aspirin." She enunciated the word carefully, then turned and made her way to the sleek elevators, ducking inside one and punching her floor. The doors closed lazily, trapping her in a small brass coffin smelling of polish, but at least it was quiet.

The two clerks watched her leave, then glanced at each other. The man shook his head. "Son of a bitch."

"That's their CIO?" The woman stared at the computer screen. "She's got the VIP suite?" She looked up at the now closed elevator. "Holy shit."

Dar sighed and leaned back against the wall, swallowing as her ears popped with the rising of the car. She already regretted agreeing to present the company's quarterly results at their stockholders' meeting here in New York City, all the more so because it was so close to the Thanksgiving holiday, and that meant crowded planes, and crowded airports, and lots and lots of traffic.

Dar closed her eyes. *And small elevators.* She felt a familiar queasiness start in her stomach and concentrated on taking long, deep breaths, clenching her hands around the straps of her bag and the laptop case over her other shoulder. Add that to the sinus headache she always got when flying in the winter, and the dry heat, and by the time the damned elevator grudgingly allowed her out, her body was tense and shaking, making her nauseous.

The hallway was also small, and she edged down it, finding

her room and opening the door, moving forward into a plush, thankfully acceptably large room, and letting the heavy partition shut behind her. She dropped her bags down on the huge bed and collapsed into the nearby chair, her head falling back to rest on the soft leather. "Alastair, I'm going to get you for this."

As though in psychic response, her cell phone rang. With a silent curse, Dar removed it from its clip on her belt and opened it. "Yeah?"

"Well, well, good afternoon, Dar." Her boss's voice sounded calmly cheerful. "Where are you?"

"The hotel," Dar replied, keeping her eyes closed. "Finally. We circled for over two hours before they let us land at LaGuardia." She exhaled. "Damn weather."

"Well..."

"Damned Northeast. Why the hell can't we have these meetings in Houston?"

"Now, Dar." Alastair's voice grew placating. "It won't take that long. Besides, I thought you liked to travel."

Dar thought about the hours spent inside the crowded plane, pressing in on nerves newly sensitized by an accident weeks earlier that had reawakened a latent claustrophobia Dar had thought she'd conquered years back. "Not as much as I used to," she admitted, having been surprised by the level of discomfort she'd had to endure. "Maybe I'm just coming down with something. Anyway, did you need anything, or are you just calling to bust my chops?"

Alastair McLean, the CEO of ILS, chuckled. "That sounds more like you. Actually, I wanted to invite you to dinner. There's a nice place just across the road from here...good Italian."

Dar let her eyes flick around the room, aware suddenly of its silence.

"I realize I'm not as interesting company as Ms. Stuart is, but..." Alastair coaxed. "C'mon, Dar, I promise I won't talk football at you."

Just hearing Kerry's name brought a smile to Dar's face. Her friend, lover, and roommate was stuck back in Miami, consolidating a large deal with one of their major clients. "All right," she finally replied. "You're not bringing the whole board, are you?"

A snort. "No, I wouldn't waste the clam sauce. Just you and me, Dar," Alastair reassured her. "I'll drop by your room at six, all right?"

Dar eyed the clock. It was barely four, and that gave her time to shower and relax a little. "Sounds good." She let a smile cross her face. "See you then, Alastair." She closed the phone and relaxed a little, stifling a yawn with the back of her hand. "Damn." The hand lifted and rubbed her eyes. "I need some coffee." The hotel phone was nearby, but her body resisted moving, content to remain nestled in the leather chair, now nicely warmed and comfortable.

She slumped there limply for a moment, then lifted her cell phone and thumbed a number into it without looking. Dar lifted the instrument to her ear and listened to its buzzing ring. Once, twice...then the noise stopped and a soft grunt issued down the line, bringing a smile to Dar's face.

"Hello?" Kerry's voice sounded almost breathless.

"Avoiding the elevators?" Dar queried.

"Oh." Kerry exhaled, then apparently stopped moving. "How'd you guess? They just called me down to the tenth floor, and I thought I'd jog back up." The sound of a door opening and closing, then the echo of the stairwell vanished, replaced with a soft hum. "Where are you? Did you just get there? How was the flight?"

Dar pictured her lover striding down the hall, with that distinctive, sexy walk, and her nose wrinkled in pleasure. "Hotel, yes, pain in my ass," she replied succinctly. "Just thought I'd check in. We hit weather over Virginia."

"I know," Kerry answered over the sound of a door closing. Now the hum was gone, and it was quiet. "I, um...tracked your flight."

Dar stretched out her long legs and felt her muscles relax. "Oh, you did, huh?"

"Yes, I did." Kerry's voice dropped a little, taking on a hint of huskiness. "I worry about you, y'know."

Mmm. Dar smiled at the ceiling. "Well, I made it here. Alastair's taking me out to dinner, then I'm gonna get some sleep. The meeting starts at eight tomorrow."

"Ew," Kerry replied. "I've got that group meeting at the church tonight, then Colleen and Ray are meeting me and we're going to walk down the beach and see what trouble we can get into."

Uh-oh. Dar imagined the possible results. "Be careful, okay?" she advised her lover.

"You too." Kerry replied seriously. "That city can be a scary place."

Dar smiled. "I will. Talk to you tomorrow, okay?"

"Okay." Kerry was smiling too, easily heard in her voice. "I love you."

"I love you, too." Dar exhaled contentedly. "Night."

"Night." Kerry listened until the call ended with a slight click, then regarded the phone for a moment before she leaned back in her comfortable desk chair and tapped her pen on her notepad. Her desk was neat and clean, the LCD screen and her phone on one side, her inbox, notepad, and the small wood-framed picture on the other. Idly, she reached out and lifted the picture, smiling at the beautiful face gazing out at her. "Don't you be getting lost down any subway tunnels, cutie pie," she instructed the picture. "We've got holiday plans in a few days."

Thanksgiving. Kerry set the picture down and started straightening out her things in preparation for leaving. Her very first real Thanksgiving, where she was in charge and had decided what they'd do and who they'd invite. She'd decided on a turkey and a party, and Dar had amiably agreed, having never experienced the occasion as a host herself. She'd gotten her turkey—an enormous, frozen thing—and all the trimmings, and Colleen had volunteered to come over early that morning and help with the cooking.

Dar's parents would be there. Kerry smiled as she picked up her laptop, slipped it into the leather shoulder bag she carried, and clipped her cell phone to her belt. She heard a light knock and looked up as the door opened and her secretary Mayte peeked in. "Hey."

The slim young Latina girl smiled at her. "You go home, yes?"

"Not exactly," Kerry answered easily. "I've got a meeting to go to, then some socializing to do. What about you?"

"I have my group tonight," Mayte replied. "I was going to ask, if it is not too much trouble, if I could get a ride with you just past the bus stop."

"Absolutely." Kerry circled the desk. "C'mon, we'll beat the traffic." She motioned the girl out before her and they left the office, walking together down the hall. They were both dressed with casual elegance, and Kerry was amused to note that Mayte had taken to carefully studying Kerry's own choices of silk shirts and well-tailored slacks and had chosen items as close as she could without copying Kerry's selections outright.

As they entered the elevator, Kerry straightened her shoulders in reflex, drawing the eyes of the occupants already inside, her wine-colored shirt with its tiny embroidered flowers contrasting neatly with her pale hair and fair complexion. "Evening." Kerry returned the quiet murmurs with a brief smile, acknowledging the slightly uncomfortable silence from the marketing clerks who were years older than she was and probably aggravated beyond words that someone who looked just about Mayte's age of low twenty-something had been promoted to vice president, regardless of what her qualifications were.

Or, she admitted wryly, they could also be fundamentalists who disapproved of her very publicly known alternative lifestyle. The doors opened on the bottom floor and the other women moved out quickly, heading across the huge brass and marble lobby toward the front doors of the building.

"Ms. Kerry?" Mayte murmured as they followed more slowly. "I do not think those ladies like you."

"Nope." Kerry gave the security guard a smile and received one in return as they exited the building. "There are people out there that don't." She led Mayte over to the dark green Mustang convertible and unlocked the doors, popping her hatch to set her laptop bag down inside. Then she got in and fastened her seat belt, watching her assistant do the same. "You know how it is."

Mayte was quiet as Kerry started the car and backed it from its spot. The space next to her was conspicuously empty in the full lot, having been filled with Dar's Lexus until the CIO had left for the airport. An irrational desire to have left right along with her flared suddenly, but Kerry suppressed it and turned her attention to the traffic as she pulled out of the parking lot.

"Did *la jefa* get to New York all right?" Mayte inquired shyly. "Mamá was worried; she said there was a big storm somewhere."

"Yeah." Kerry nodded. "She called me just before we left. It took them forever to land, but she's there, safe and sound." Her brow contracted. "I should have called your mother and told her. I know she was concerned." She turned west, and winced as the sun invaded the car. "Whoops." One hand fished into the center console and emerged with her sunglasses, which she put on, cutting the brilliance and restoring her vision.

"I will tell her when I get home," Mayte reassured her. "I think you were worried too... you did not eat your lunch."

Hmm. Kerry's nose wrinkled. *Busted.* "Well, everything turned out okay, so I'll just make up for it at dinner." She chuckled, then considered her choice of streets. "Listen, I have to go downtown anyway—why don't I just drop you off at home?" she offered. "No sense in you having to grab a bus at this hour." Normally, Mayte rode home with her mother, María, who was Dar's assistant, but the older woman had left early for a doctor's appointment after Dar had gone to the airport.

"You don't have to do that." Mayte looked shyly pleased at the offer, though. "You're so busy."

"Nah." Kerry produced a grin. "Besides, after what I've

heard about the Metro buses, I'd be a nervous wreck until I saw you again tomorrow morning." She pulled out onto the highway decisively, almost cutting off a huge truck as she ducked nimbly across two lanes of traffic.

"Oh. *Sí.*" Mayte closed her eyes resolutely and grabbed for the overhead handle. "I am feeling much safer already."

It was, after all, New York City, and here she was, dining out at night, with the CEO of one of the largest IS firms in the world. Dar crossed her ankles and reviewed the dark fabric covering her legs. *At least he gets the jeans without the rips.* She gazed across the table at her boss, who was watching her with a bemused expression. "Am I ruining your image?"

Alastair laughed. "Who, me? Just because half the people in here know who I am and are dying of curiosity as to where I picked up the beautiful vagrant I'm eating dinner with?" He poked a fork at Dar's sweatshirt sleeve. "They'll find out soon enough."

Dar returned the chuckle. "Sorry. I would have changed, but I fell asleep after you called and barely had time to get my head on straight before you knocked." She stretched and picked up a fragrant garlic stick, nibbling its end appreciatively. "I was at the office at four a.m. Needed to get that new contract squared away before I left."

"Ouch." Alastair winced. "How's that going?"

"Not bad," the dark-haired woman replied. "I've got a meeting scheduled next week with the top brass down at Southeast Command...that's where Gerry wanted me to start."

"Close to home."

"Mm," Dar acknowledged. "They've been getting a pile of complaints about the training programs down there. He wants me to go in and do a complete systems and processes evaluation." She carefully ignored her salad and dipped the breadstick into the spicy Italian soup. "Gonna be a little strange. One of the bases he wants me to review is the one I mostly grew up on."

Footsteps closed in, and they both looked up to see a sharply dressed man standing at the tableside. "Hello, Al." The man had a slight accent, but it was hard to tell exactly what kind. "I was hoping I'd get a chance to see you before the meeting." He flicked a lazy glance over Dar's body, and the corner of his mouth twitched. "Sorry. Am I interrupting something?"

Dar considered the repercussions of stabbing him with her fork and weighed the amusement value of hearing the scream versus the certain lawsuit she'd have to deal with. She sighed and just continued eating. The food was excellent, and she'd missed both breakfast and lunch, which hadn't helped the headache flying had given her. "Nah, go ahead. I'm just his new intern," she commented lightly, sucking in a strand of spaghetti.

Alastair exhaled and hid a smile behind his hand. "Good evening, Bob. Sit down, will ya? What can I do for you?" Bob Trancet was the head of corporate sales for the New York office, which handled a good deal of their international business as well.

The tall man sat down and folded his hands, ignoring Dar now. He was clean-cut and good looking, with silvered black hair and a strong profile. His athletic body was balanced, and he had a very self-assured air. "Nothing major. I was just hoping to put a bug in your ear about a possible new alliance. Datacom contacted me today and started sniffing around the edges of suggesting they want us to take over their network ops."

"Really?" Alastair propped his chin up on one fist. "They're big competitors of ours in some places."

"Mm. But they can't compete with the new network, and they know it." Bob smirked. "They're talking strategic partnership now—trading off them selling our net in exchange for us getting a lot of their South American stuff."

"Not worth it," Dar commented, biting a meatball in half. "They've got twenty-year-old infrastructure, and it'll cost us over a million bucks to upgrade their nodes to our spec."

There was absolute silence for a moment, giving Dar some peace and quiet in which to slurp her pasta.

"Spunky intern," Bob remarked dryly. "But all of a sudden, I'm realizing that voice is familiar." He waited for Dar to lift her eyes and met them with a twinkle of amusement. "I finally get to meet the infamous Dar Roberts. That was outstandingly stupid of me, wasn't it? I should have figured it out from the start." He held out a hand, which Dar reached over and clasped. "Intern, eh?"

Dar smiled at him, and their eyes fenced briefly, two very strong wills gently testing each other. She could feel the intense magnetism he was putting out, and as his glance drifted over her and showed a distinct admiration, her ego pricked its little bat ears right up. "Well," she drawled, "it was better than the other obvious conclusion."

He grinned right back. "Better for who? That would have done wonders for Al's reputation."

Glancing between the two, Alastair cleared his throat. "I hadn't realized you'd never met Dar, Bob. I know you've spoken on the phone, though."

"No, no." Bob slowly shook his head, still apparently fascinated by Dar. "Never had the pleasure; and I do mean pleasure."

Dar took a breath and went back to consuming her dinner. "If Datacom wants to deal, they have to pay for their own upgrades before we sign anything. I don't want them bottlenecking us," she stated, then sighed as her cell phone rang. "Yeah?"

"Dar, it's Mark. We've got a situation."

Figures. "Hang on." Dar stood and tucked her napkin under her plate. "Be right back." She edged around where Bob was sitting and headed for the door, out of the noise, where she could hear better.

Alastair took a sip of his wine and gazed drolly at his long-time associate. "Put your tongue back in your mouth, will ya?"

"Son of a bitch." Bob laughed, shaking a finger at him. "You told me she was smart, tough, and stubborn. How come you never mentioned she was gorgeous?" His eyes stayed pinned on the tall, lanky figure leaning against the door outside, phone pressed to her ear. "That is a serious hunk of woman, Al."

Alastair rolled his eyes. "You never change," he snorted. "Wipe your chin. You're drooling."

"Hell yes, I am!" Bob asserted. "That's one sexy item I intend to get a closer look at."

Alastair held a hand up. "She's taken."

"Bullshit. Nobody owns her—not in this lifetime, bucko." Bob shook his head firmly. "Don't get so serious, Al. I just want to have a drink with her, not get married."

Alastair threw his trump card. "Bob, she's gay."

"And? Your point is what?" his chief salesman replied. "Who cares? I sure don't." He balled up the napkin he'd been playing with and straightened. "I'll just in—hey!"

Alastair had reached across the table and fastened one hand on his wrist. Now he bore down and pulled, a suddenly serious, intent look on his face. "You listen to me, mister. Don't fuck with her."

A tiny pocket of shocked stillness surrounded them. Bob blinked and stared at his boss, nonplussed. "Hey, c'mon, Al," he said, softly. "Take it easy."

"I mean it," the CEO stated flatly.

The younger man drew in a breath and held out his other hand, palm up, in a gesture of conciliation. "Okay, okay, boss. I hear you." He gathered his composure and sat back as Alastair released him. "Is it okay if I just talk to her? She's very bright, and I'd really like to spend a few minutes doing that."

A finger pointed at him. "If you go a step further than that, I will personally fire your ass. Understand?"

"Understood," Bob acknowledged quietly, as Dar reentered the restaurant, moving back toward them and taking her seat. Alert blue eyes flicked first to Alastair, then to him, and he got the curious sensation of being analyzed like a faulty piece of code by the raw, potent intelligence lurking just behind Dar's now watchful gaze.

"Trouble, Dar?" Alastair took a gulp of his wine and swirled the remainder around his glass. "Didn't think we had that much going on this week."

"Ah." Dar twirled a forkful of spaghetti and munched on it, swallowing before she answered. "It's that damned conversion in Chicago. They've been trying to tie in that big ATM pipeline up to Canada for two weeks, and every time they do it, they take down half the Midwest." She took a sip of her own wine. "I may have to send a team out there."

"Lousy time to be traveling," Bob ventured. "Holidays and all."

"Mm," Dar agreed, meeting his gaze. "Comes with the territory, though. My people know that. Work comes first." She finished off her meatballs and sat back, crossing an arm over her chest as she sipped the wine. The problem was aggravating, for sure, and she wasn't entirely convinced she wasn't going to have to go there in person to take care of it.

Which truly, truly sucked.

"Hey, Dar?"

She looked up to find Bob leaning forward with a look of friendly interest on his face. "Mm?" Something had gone on between him and Alastair, that much she knew, but what that was...

Probably didn't involve her. "Something on your mind?"

The corner of his mouth twitched. "Get to the city much?"

That surprised her. "No. I try to not cross the Mason-Dixon unless I have to," she replied dryly, giving Alastair a look. "Why?"

Bob folded his hands together. Dar noticed they were nice, strong ones, with well-tended nails and just a hint of callus along the top of his index fingers. "I'm pretty proud of the place. I've lived here since I was shorter than the fire hydrants outside. Will you let me give you a quick tour?"

Dar considered the request. "If you put an itinerary together for tomorrow night, sure," she agreed amiably. "It's been a long day." He was attractive, and a sharp businessman, and it never hurt to build a few bridges when one had the chance to. Especially with the sales and marketing side of the house, with which she tended to be forever at cross-purposes.

"You're on." Bob grinned, then pushed back from the table and stood up. "Al, it's been a pleasure as always." He inclined his head. "See you at the soiree tomorrow." His eyes shifted. "And you, as well, I hear, Madame. Looking forward to hearing the presentation." With a slight bow, he turned and threaded his way through the now truly busy restaurant, disappearing into the New York night once he cleared the door.

The small group sat in a circle, in chairs so mismatched they seemed like the work of a designer with a definitely twisted streak. All in attendance were young, most in their late teens, save the woman seated cross-legged in the large overstuffed chair nearest the door.

"Okay, Barbara, what makes you think he's got it out for you?" Kerry asked quietly, setting her mind to the problems of these troubled youngsters—halfway between children and adults, and dealing with an emerging sexuality they weren't sure they understood; weren't really sure they wanted, for that matter. At their age, at this stage in their lives, being different meant outcast in so many poignant ways.

She shared her counseling duties with two other older women, and found she enjoyed her time with the group. It meant having to listen to and deal with problems vastly different from the ones she normally handled, and reminded her all over again that her own acceptance of her lifestyle had been far smoother than any number of other people's. Right now, the youngest member of the discussion group, Barbara Gonzales, had confessed that she thought her boss at Burger King had figured out she was gay, and was trying to get rid of her because of it.

"I don't know." The slim brown-haired girl wrapped an arm around one knee. "He changed my shift. Now me makes me do all the hard stuff, like figuring out how much bread and meat to order for the next week, and making me check out the bathrooms, and stuff like that."

"Hmm." Kerry sat back, aware of the girl's eyes on her. "Did you ask him why he did that?"

A shrug. "No. I just figured it was because he saw me and Sally in the freezer that one time. We were so stupid about that."

Kerry reflected. "Do you do a good job?"

"I guess. The customers like me, I get stuff done, and I'm always on time, and all that stuff."

"Well, he could be coming down on you, but there is another possibility," Kerry told her. "He might be trying to nudge you toward a more responsible position in the restaurant."

Barbara blinked at her, obviously never having even considered it. "Huh?"

"If I were a fast-food manager," Kerry speculated, "and I had
a position I needed to fill, say, an assistant manager or a shift
leader, I'd find someone who was trustworthy—who was prompt,
and neat, and got the job done—and give them a little more
responsibility every day to see how they handled it."

"You would?" Casey cocked her head, which was covered in
an explosion of dark curls.

"Sure." Kerry smiled. "Asking Barbara to do the ordering
projections and supervising the cleaning of the bathrooms seems
to me to be an indication that the man trusts her and maybe wants
to see if she's ready to be promoted." Her eyes twinkled at Barbara, who was staring open-mouthed at her. "Tell you what. Think
of it that way for a week and try to look at everything he does positively, instead of negatively. See what happens."

Barbara pushed a lock of hair behind an ear. "Wow! Okay,
yeah, I guess I could do that," she mused. "Maybe I could, like,
iron my shirts and stuff. See if he notices." She smiled, and her
whole face lit up. "Thanks, Kerry, you're so cool."

Kerry stood up and circled her chair, leaning on the back and
gazing at them. "Sometimes, it's easy to get into the mode where
you think everyone's against you, or that your sexual preference
automatically makes you a victim. It's not true." She paused and
considered. "Not that it doesn't happen; of course it does. We all
watch the news or have had stuff happen, so you know it does." A
brief smile touched her lips. "But not always."

"You're pretty out at work, aren't you?" Casey asked, curiously.

Kerry nodded.

"Do you get shit for that?" The girls watched her, intensely
interested in her answer. Kerry tended to turn talk away from her
life to theirs, and they were always digging for little nuggets about
her personal side. They knew she worked for a big company, and
that she was gay, and not a whole lot more. Most of them hadn't
even met Dar, since the group had formed after the last picnic her
lover had attended.

"Sometimes, there are people who find out, and they don't
like it." Kerry allowed. "But mostly, I just do my job, and they
don't really care."

"Your boss doesn't care?"

She couldn't help the smile. "No. Definitely not."

"Cool." Casey nodded. "Maybe I'll get me a job there, then.

They sound all right."

Kerry reviewed the stocky young woman, whose dark hair was dyed in three shades of purple to match the six different kinds of earring stones and contrast with the tattoos dancing across her neck. "Sure," she agreed mildly. "Give me your résumé, and I'll give it to personnel."

Just the look on Mariana's face would be more than worth it.

"All right." Casey stayed by her as the rest of the group filed out. "You're pretty cool, for an old lady."

Kerry's eyebrows lifted. "Just how ancient do you think I am?" she asked, putting her hands on her hips and feigning outrage. "I only have three gray hairs, you know."

Casey grinned, then dropped her eyes bashfully. "I know. I was just ragging you. It must be so cool to have it all so together like you do."

Hmm. Yeah, as a matter of fact, it was pretty darn cool. "I've been really lucky," she admitted. "I've had good opportunities given to me, and I've managed to find someone I want to spend the rest of my life with. I thank God for that every day, believe me, Casey."

The teen glanced down, folding her arms with a distinct air of discomfort at that. "So, when do we get to meet this mystery woman of yours? You keep talking about her. She sounds pretty hot."

Kerry turned and gestured to the door. "C'mon, I've got to lock up. You'll get to meet Dar at the party next week. You'll like her; she's really nice." Well, nice wasn't really what Dar was, but...

Casey walked out, then watched her lock the door to the back room of the church. They strolled together up the narrow aisle, past the rostrum, and up the two short stairs to the main door of the building. Kerry held the heavy portal open, then let it shut behind them and locked it with the key she'd been given. The other girls were waiting outside, giving her shy looks.

"Hey." Casey was, apparently, elected the spokeswoman this week. "We're goin' for a beer. You want to come?"

For a moment, Kerry was tempted. Being the center of this sort of adolescent attention was very new and very strange for her, and she felt the urge to explore it more thoroughly. However, plans were plans, and she suspected the invitation would be repeated.

Frequently. "Not tonight, guys; I promised I'd meet some friends down on the beach. But thanks for asking." Kerry smiled warmly at them. "Go on and have a good time, but be careful, okay?" No sense in her pointing out most of them were underage, since she knew they'd just have Casey, the only one who had military ID, buy the beer for them. The youngster had enlisted and lasted exactly two weeks in the Marines, then opted out, but she'd kept the ID.

She watched them saunter off, then she turned and headed for her car, which was parked nearby, checking her watch as she walked. She had a half-hour until her meeting-up time with Colleen and Ray, which would give her more than enough leeway to get down to the beach and the waiting sushi dive. Her stomach started growling at the thought, and the skipped lunch and breakfast suddenly made her light-headed.

"Damn." Fortunately, she was next to her car, and a quick grab at the doorframe of the Mustang let her keep her balance. "Guess the ascetic fasting gig isn't for me." She got the door open and sat down, waiting for the dizzy feeling to fade. After a moment, it did, and she closed the door and started the car. "Soon." She patted her stomach. "Hang in there, kiddo, teriyaki chicken is straight ahead."

As she stared into the mirror with a scowl, Dar twitched her collar straight for the fourth time. Not that there was anything wrong with the burgundy silk business suit; the soft folds draped nicely over her tall frame, sleeves cut specifically to her measure, coming neatly past her wrists. The skirt was just above her knees, and with her tan, she could have gotten away without wearing hose. But she hadn't, dutifully donning the smoky dark nylons Kerry had tucked into her bag.

"C'mon, Dar," she repeated to her reflection. "Just pretend it's a staff meeting." With over a thousand people. Dar picked up the towel she'd used after her shower and wiped the sweat off her palms. She'd never admit to anyone just how much she hated public, really public speaking. She hadn't even told Kerry about it. But here, alone in her hotel room, barely an hour before she had to address the stockholders, she could admit to herself that she was scared senseless.

"Jackass." She glowered into the pale blue eyes in the mirror. A knock sounded on the door, and she almost hit the popcorn ceiling before she gave herself a shake and stalked toward the entrance. She opened the door to find a plant wanting admittance. "Hello?"

Brown eyes peeked out from between the stems of some extremely gorgeous roses. "Ms. Roberts? This came for you."

Dar surveyed the arrangement and felt her eyebrows lift. She
backed up. "C'mon in." She watched the bellman carefully put the
basket on the room's small table, then back away cautiously.
"Thanks." Dar had taken a bill from her wallet and she now
handed it to him, ignoring his departure as she explored her new
decoration.

It was way too cute and classy for Alastair, she decided,
plucking a small teddy bear from the center. "And he wouldn't
send you, now would he?" She sniffed one of the blooms, which
was large and perfect, then realized some of the roses weren't real.
Curiously, she touched one, then unwrapped the foil top to reveal
rich, milky-looking chocolate. "Ah." Cheerfully, she took a bite,
then fished around until she rooted out the small card. She opened
it and peered at the writing, not really needing the confirmation of
the sender.

Hey, sweetie.
Give them heck.
I love you.
K

"Aw." Dar felt her entire body warm, a gentle flush that
chased away the chills she'd been feeling not five minutes earlier.
"You're something else, you know that?" She took another bite of
chocolate and considered the roses, then selected one and carefully broke its stem off just below the bloom. A few steps took her
to her overnight bag, and she fished inside it, coming up with a
safety pin and neatly pinning the rose on her lapel.

Her eyes then fell on the tiny teddy, and she very briefly considered tucking it into her pocket, a sudden smile appearing when
she imagined the collective reaction of the stockholders if they
saw the little toy peeking out of her jacket. "Oh no...no, Dar, that
would just blow that little old reputation of yours right out the
window and into the Hudson River." But she laughed, the light
sound echoing softly in the room.

She went over to where her breakfast lay mostly untasted on
the bedside table and selected a croissant, cutting it open and covering it with butter and jelly. She ate that and washed it down with
a swallow of coffee, then clicked off the television that had been
playing soundlessly in the background and took one last look in
the mirror.

Chin up, shoulders back. Dar straightened and felt her usual
confident attitude drop over her in a comforting sensation. She
picked up her slim leather portfolio and headed out the door,

hearing it close behind her as she walked down the carpeted hall-way, her medium-heeled shoes sinking just slightly into the pile.

The elevator had many nicely dressed people in it. Most of them glanced at her as she entered, and most of the guys sucked in their guts. Dar graced them with a smile, but kept silent, folding her hands over her folder with its distinctive company logo stamped in leather on the outside.

The trip down seemed to last forever, in that elongated awk-wardness that elevators often produce. But they did finally make it, and Dar exited the small space, moving into the lobby toward the convention center, where large groups of men and women were gathered near the double doors.

"Dar!"

She turned and waited for Alastair to catch up to her. The CEO was dressed in a dark blue suit and red tie, and he smiled at Dar as he took her by the elbow. "Morning."

"Morning, morning." Alastair ushered her through the door and up one broad aisle toward the podium. "Sleep well?"

"Fine," Dar replied as they moved up to the table set on the elevated stage. "Did we get the—ah." She laid her portfolio down and took over the keyboard of the laptop on the table, rattling the keys with a sense of comforting familiarity. "Good," she mur-mured, reviewing the data flashing across the LED screen. The system was hooked to an overhead projector, which would allow her to show the stockholders real-time data moving across their new network. "Looks good."

Alastair glanced at the figures. "You'd know." He patted her shoulder. "I'm going to get everyone settled, then I'll introduce you. Hey, nice rose."

"Thanks." Dar glanced at it. "And thanks for dinner last night. Damn good pasta."

"Almost as good as the company." Alastair returned the com-pliment courteously. "And speaking of which, don't let Bob run you ragged tonight, all right? He loves this town and loves to show it off, but he gets a little too enthusiastic about its vices some-times."

Dar looked up from her data and cocked her head. "Is that a warning?" She watched her boss nod. "All right. I'll keep that in mind. Now c'mon, let's get this show on the road." She concen-trated on setting up the networking monitors and ignored Alastair's walking over to the podium.

"Ladies and gentleman?" The CEO laid his hands confidently on the wood surface. "If you'd like to take your seats, we'll get started."

The crowd bustled into place, scrapes and scuffs overwhelming the conversation as people settled into the comfortable chairs. Almost immediately, a young red-haired man stood up and raised his hand. "Mr. McLean?"

Alastair looked over at him. "Yes? Thomas Bantelberg, isn't it?"

The man blinked a moment, obviously not expecting the CEO to recognize him. "Yes. Listen, we're all really interested in the new network. We don't want to hear a bunch of corporate BS today, if you don't mind." Several people laughed, but more nodded and faced forward.

"Well," Alastair leaned on the podium, "you know, I had a feeling everyone was going to feel like that." He had their attention, and the room settled down, everyone listening to him intently. "These stockholder meetings are usually pretty dry, huh?" A round of polite laughter. "I know how much the industry has been talking about our new infrastructure, and I thought that it would be a strong topic of conversation at this meeting." He straightened. "You all have questions like is it what it's advertised to be, and how are we going to use it, right?"

Nods.

"Well, good." Alastair rubbed his hands briskly. "Because I can't tell you any of that."

Silence.

"So I brought someone here to do the corporate presentation who can." He glanced over at Dar, who had finished fiddling with her hardware and was quietly waiting. "Ladies and gentlemen, I'd like to present to you our chief information officer and the designer of the new network, Dar Roberts."

Dar forced her legs into motion and gave her boss a curt nod as he relinquished the podium.

Then she wondered what all the noise was. Startled, her eyes lifted to see the entire crowd standing up, yelling and waving at her. She looked at Alastair in alarm, only to see the CEO hiding a smirk behind one hand. Only then did she realize that what she was facing was a standing ovation.

Jesus. Now what?

Finally, they shut up and she was able to collect herself, waiting for everyone to sit down before she opened her mouth. Then she shut it again, because she had no idea what to say to the huge, faceless mob, whose attention was now focused on her with fierce intentness.

Well, she had to say something before they all fell asleep, didn't she? "The agenda requires me to spend some time at this point outlining the basic plan and infrastructure of why we implemented a new network," Dar finally said. "But I'd bet you'd rather just see it, right?"

There was a moment's silence, beating against her face, then a laugh. *Ah. That was good.* "Right." Dar clicked on the overhead and behind her, a slim gray screen exploded into life. "This is the deal..."

"Ooh, I thought she was going to choke there." Kerry had her chin on her fists and her eyes glued to the IDLN broadcast of her lover explaining in terse detail the advantages of their new net.

"Mm...." Duks was sitting on her desk, and Mark was leaning next to her. "Public speaking is not an easy thing for Dar, I do not think."

"Nice suit," Mark commented. "Crowd likes her."

Kerry watched Dar's body language, which to her seemed almost painfully stiff. After a few minutes, though, her lover relaxed a little. "That's better, she's loosening up some."

"Yeah," the MIS chief agreed. "Boy, she looks nervous. Never thought I'd see that."

"C'mon, honey," Kerry whispered to the screen, crossing her fingers and willing Dar to calm down. For a brief instant, the blue eyes lifted from the crowd and glanced right at the IDLN transmit camera, and they were eye to eye; then Dar went back to her information, scrolling expertly through a series of benchmarks and displaying a test of the new network's capabilities. "Atta girl." She noticed the rose pinned to her boss's jacket and smiled.

"What's she doing now...oh." Mark leaned forward. "Showing off that new hub. Yeah, lookit that." They watched Dar shift traffic effortlessly from one port to the other, providing seamless fallback for the accounts on that particular system. "Cool."

Dar finished her displays, then turned and laid her hands on the podium, much more at ease now. "Any questions?" The rich, powerful voice rolled out over the crowd. A moment's silence, then a forest of hands went up. Dar seemed to find this funny, the corners of her mouth twitching as she leaned on the wooden surface. "All right. You first." She pointed, and the questions began.

"She likes that better." Kerry nodded. "Questions she can deal with. She has to do that every day." And certainly, her lover was handling them, becoming more confident as Kerry watched, moving out away from the protection of the podium, illustrating her answers with quick, precise motions of her hands. Kerry sighed. "God, she's gorgeous." She became aware of an awkward silence and glanced up to see Mark and Duks making strange faces at her. "Sorry, but she is."

"Yeah, I know, but..." Mark scratched his jaw. "It's just so weird hearing that...um..."

"From another woman?" Kerry asked wryly.

"Yeah."

"Sorry."

"It's okay." Mark shrugged and laughed. "I needed some horizon broadening today."

They turned back to the screen and watched as Dar took another step forward, her personality visibly emerging as she fielded tough questions, displaying an impressive knowledge of their industry.

"Yeah, you go." Kerry smiled as the crowd applauded. "Rock 'em."

"Ugh." Dar flopped down onto her back and stared up at the ceiling, flexing toes newly freed from their leather entrapment. "Well, that wasn't so bad, I guess." Her cell phone rang and she lifted it, stretching as she put it to her ear. "Yes?"

"You rock."

"Oh, I do, do I?" Dar responded with a lazy smile, glad to have the entire affair behind her. "I didn't sound too much like a walking geek tank?"

"No way," Kerry laughed. "We all watched it on IDLN. But my God, Dar, your face when they gave you that ovation...I thought you were going to swallow your pager."

"Erf." Dar threw an arm over her eyes. "Caught me by surprise; but it ended up pretty good. Those West Indies investors are sharp. They had some good questions."

"You had some great answers." Kerry leaned back in her chair and propped a knee up against her desk. "Listen, I did call you to say hi and congratulations and all that..."

"But?" Dar drawled through the phone.

"But," Kerry agreed, "we've got a real problem in Chicago, Dar. I think I'm going to have to go out there." She heard the sigh. "Tonight." Another sigh. "Col said she'd watch Chino, since Mom and Dad are in Bermuda." They were both silent for a bit. "I don't think it'll take long."

"You promised me turkey," Dar protested with a hint of a verbal pout. "Tell Redmond to stuff itself."

Kerry gazed fondly at her speakerphone. "We've still got two days before Thanksgiving, Dar. C'mon, I'll be back tomorrow night at the latest. Besides, you're the one who said you could deal with Egg McMuffins if you had to," she reminded her boss.

"That was before you mentioned marshmallow-stuffed sweet potatoes," Dar retorted, then sighed. "I know, I know. I was reviewing that mess myself. I thought I might have to make a trip out there, but you're really better at handling those people than I am."

"Thank you." Kerry preened silently, tipping back and enjoying the twilight outside. "What're your plans for tonight?"

There was a momentary pause on the other end. "Bob Trancet wants to show me the town," Dar answered. "But after Alastair warned me off today, I'm not sure I want to be shown." Another pause. "Hey."

"Mm?" Kerry was rolling Dar's words over in her mind.

"Thanks for the roses, the chocolate, and the teddy bear."

A smile grew. "I saw your jacket; it looked pretty." Kerry turned her head to one side and regarded the phone. "Hey, isn't he the guy there was the big scandal about over Fourth of July?" she asked curiously. "Him and a secretary, or something, in the Xerox room?"

"Yeah," Dar admitted. "He wears his gonads on his lapel, all right."

Kerry almost spit her tonsils out her nose. She clapped a hand over her mouth and reached for her cup of tea, half choking with laughter. "Dar, don't do that," she spluttered. "I didn't need that mental image; I really, really didn't."

Dar chuckled softly. "Sorry. Maybe I'll just force him into dinner here at the hotel. I'm pretty tired after all that crap today. When's your flight?"

"Nine." Kerry stifled a yawn. "Wish it were landing in LaGuardia." She rolled her head to one side. "God, this is ridiculous."

"What is?"

"Me feeling like a spoiled little brat denied her candy because you're not here," Kerry responded wryly. "Dar, this is not normal. I want you to go to Doctor Steve when you get back, so he can figure out what you put out that has me so damned hooked on you." She paused. "Stop smirking."

"I wasn't."

"You most certainly were." Kerry reached out and ran a fingertip along the speakerphone. "Am I embarrassing you?"

"No." Dar's voice dropped a note. "Flattering me."

"Mm." Kerry's eyes half closed, and she exhaled. "Well, I guess I'd better get going. I want to get to the airport a little early." She stifled another yawn. "At least I can sleep on the plane. You go and have fun with Mr. Happy Gonads, okay?"

"Oh yeah. A blast," Dar mused. "Hey, have a good flight, okay? Give me a call when you get to your hotel."

"I will," Kerry promised. "Later, sweetie."

"Later." Dar hung up the phone and set it on her mostly bare chest. She'd stripped out of her silk suit almost as fast as the damn shoes, and was in her half-slip and bra, the air conditioning raising tiny goose bumps over her exposed belly. She rubbed her chilled skin, then sat up, using one hand to work a kink out of her neck. She got up and trudged over to the dresser, yanking a shirt out of her bag and tugging it on over her head.

"Okay." Dar addressed her now rumpled reflection, blowing a bit of dark hair out of her eyes with a quick puff of air. "Dinner, a drink in the bar, and we're outta there." She took off her slip and exchanged it for a pair of jeans, then tucked the shirt in and buckled the belt. "Might as well get some work done while I'm hanging around waiting."

Minutes later, she was sprawled over the bed with her laptop resting on her legs, reviewing her mail and the two system status reports Mark had sent down. An e-mail opened, and she reviewed it. "Kiss my ass." She typed in a response and sent it back, then opened a second. "Bite me." Another mail winged its way back. Then she opened the third, reading it several times, then cocking her head to one side to watch the tiny gopher graphic dance along its edge sideways. "Ooh. Cool, you got the toes working," she praised Kerry in absentia.

Then she leaned closer and squinted at the small creature, who seemed to have acquired spectacles from somewhere. "Ah." A chagrined look crossed her face as Dar nodded in wry acknowledgement. Kerry had been nudging her for a month to get her eyes checked, and so far, she'd found a lot of different excuses not to. "Cute, Ker, very cute," she replied to the e-mail, blithely ignoring the addition.

Chapter
Two

Kerry settled back in her seat and debated whether or not to take out her laptop. When she traveled alone, she was always conscious of who was sitting next to her—idle eyes that might take in whatever her laptop screen had on display—and while the chances of her being seated next to a competitor were fairly slim, she never knew.

Her seatmate this trip was a bookish-looking young man with heavy glasses and an academic air about him. She spared a moment to imagine what his profession might be, a game she often played with herself while traveling. *Professor? Probably not old enough. Research scientist? Maybe.* The man solved her musings a moment later, when he tugged a pad from a notebook and started scribing lines on it in a familiar programming language.

Kerry smiled and leaned back. *Figures. Another nerd.* She lazily eyed the dark window, observing the clearly not twinkling stars outside. She leaned a hand against the glass to shade the light and peered out, amazed as always at the complete explosion of lights spread so thickly across the sky. Below her stretched only dark land, an occasional brief island of light indicating a city. Far off in the horizon they were traveling toward, she could see a line of darkness shot through with lightning that had to be the storm front the Weather Channel had promised.

A slight clank caught her attention, and she turned her head to see the stewardess standing there, waiting to take her dinner order. "I'll take the filet, thanks." Kerry gave the woman a brief smile. "And if you have a beer?"

"Heineken all right?" The woman wrote down the order. "Be right back. And you, sir?" Kerry's seatmate ordered the filet as well, with a whiskey and soda. That was interesting, Kerry thought, as she folded her hands over her stomach and stretched her legs out, crossing them at the ankles. Whiskey and soda always sounded like something her father would order, not someone of her own generation or younger.

"Do...you fly much?" the young man asked diffidently.

"Unfortunately, more than I'd like to," Kerry replied politely. "It's not for pleasure."

"Oh." The man wiped his hand off on his neatly pressed wool pants leg and held it out. "Josh Abbot. I just started working for Intelsat, and this is my second trip in a week. I'm not sure I like it."

Kerry took his hand and returned the grip. "Kerry Stuart. I work for ILS."

He brightened. "Really? Wow! So you're headed to Chicago for the snafu with that new data center, huh?"

Blond eyebrows shot up past Kerry's hairline. "I wasn't aware we'd released that to the press," she commented.

Josh at least had the grace to blush. "No, well, I...um..." He looked up in startlement as the stewardess offered him a hot towel, taking it mechanically and looking at it as if it was a small dead white animal. "I heard my boss talking about it. I'm sorry; I should have watched my mouth."

Kerry took her towel and carefully washed each finger with it, considering her options. "Well, it's a small industry, right?" She gave the man a reassuring smile. "Who's your boss?"

Josh chewed his lower lip unhappily. "Is he going to get in trouble?"

The green eyes facing him twinkled a little. "How intimidating do I look?" Kerry chuckled. "No. He won't get in trouble."

With a sigh of relief, Josh glibly coughed up the name of his boss, his boss's boss—who'd told his boss—and the secretary who worked for the boss's boss who was married to an ILS admin fairly high up in their sales department. *José, you are so dead meat.* Kerry decided, handing her now cooled towel back to the stewardess. "It's not as bad as it sounds, really...just some incompatibility with infrastructure."

"Oh." Josh nodded. "So, you're going to go fix that?" He gazed at Kerry with new interest. "You one of their tech people?"

"Something like that," Kerry agreed solemnly. "You're a programmer?"

He nodded again. "Yeah. I just graduated from Georgia Tech. I'm working on this neat new application for the control of our sats, so they can squeeze more bandwidth out of them." He held up his pad. "I kinda hit a snag, though. I'm not really sure how to write this one little routine."

Kerry gave him a suggestion. "Try that. It's what we use on our big routers." She sat back as her dinner was delivered, opening her lap tray and spreading the provided linen napkin neatly across her thighs. *Hmm.* She reviewed the tray the stewardess set down. It contained a plate with a petit filet mignon on it in some kind of nice smelling burgundy sauce, and what looked very much like a decent sized blob of whipped mashed potatoes. And a broccoli floret, for those who had inescapable attacks of food guilt. Kerry solemnly consumed the broccoli, then turned her attention to the steaming beef.

"Wow, that works. Cool." Josh laughed. "Hey, Ms. Stuart, are you married?"

Kerry's hands stopped in mid-cut. "Why?" She gave him a look.

"You wanna be? I think I love you," Josh burbled contentedly, making scratch marks on his pad.

A sigh slipped out. "Sorry, I'm taken." Kerry resumed cutting her meat and took a bite.

"Yeah, yeah, but do they appreciate you for your mind, like I would?" Josh seemed totally absorbed in his program now, hardly aware of what he was saying. "Or are they just out after that pretty face?" His tie drooped into his burgundy sauce, but the sartorial accessory could have been a cobra for all he'd noticed.

"Well..." Kerry drawled, taking a swig of her beer, "my girlfriend thinks I'm sexy, but says she married me for my brains."

"Damn. Just my luck." Josh scribbled a few more symbols, then stopped cold, blinked, and turned his head slowly to look over at her. "Did you just say what I think you just said?"

Kerry nodded and smiled, curious to see what his reaction would be. She wasn't generally so out there about her relationship, but since they were 35,000 feet up, and he was proposing...

"Ever consider a threesome?"

Ooh. It was Kerry's turn to be surprised. *Imagine that. I thought he was a pinhead.* "No," she laughed, "but that's a great answer." They grinned at each other, and Josh sat back, putting his pad away and starting in on his food. After the stewardess removed their trays, they talked about programming, comparing techniques until Kerry was suddenly distracted by a flash just outside.

"Whoa." She had turned to peer out the window when the plane dropped out from under her and rocked to one side, sending people and crockery flying. Kerry felt her stomach flip as the craft leveled, then a scary vibration started, and the plane rocked from side to side as lightning flashed past the window.

Oh boy.

"Hang on, everyone!" the lead stewardess yelled. "Hang on!"

"So," Bob strolled along next to Dar, having coaxed her out for a short walk near the hotel, "you don't like cities, huh?"

Dar dodged a stumbling man who was singing to himself and moved smoothly up onto the sidewalk. "Not particularly. We don't have a city in Miami, just a banking and government center surrounded by suburbs."

"Ah." Bob spread his arms out. "C'mon, you can't beat this atmosphere. This is the most exciting, most vibrant city on earth." He pointed. "Look at that building. Isn't it incredible?"

Dar obediently tilted her head and reviewed the building in question. It was large, yes, and the twenties architecture was eye-catching, but... "You know what I hate about cities, Bob?"

"What?"

"They smell." Dar rubbed her nose. "And as big as these damn buildings are, all the rooms in them are smaller than my bathroom at home."

Bob put his hands on his hips and regarded her. "Boy, you really know how to take the wind out of a guy's sails, you know that, Dar Roberts?" His face curled into a rueful smile. "Here I am, trying to paint a lovely, romantic vision of my favorite place, and all you can think of is a few measly scents and floor space?"

Dar shrugged one leather-covered shoulder. "I'm not really the romantic type," she drawled. "Will you settle for dinner and a drink with a nice view?" She pointed to a second-floor dining room that overlooked the busy street.

"Oh, that place?" Bob waved her off. "C'mon, you're more adventurous than that, I bet. Here's where I was going to take you. It's a great little place. Fantastic food." He pointed her toward a tiny stairwell in a dark corner that led below street level. Dar stopped cold and felt him run into her back. "Hey!" Bob bounced off, surprised. "What's wrong?"

"That goes underground," Dar stated flatly.

Bob glanced at it, nonplussed. "Well, sure. It's in the basement."

"I don't do basements." Cool blue eyes flicked to his face.

"What do you mean, you don't do basements? What the heck do you do at home when you have to go below the bottom floor, Dar?" Bob seemed thunderstruck.

"I swim. We have no basements in Miami," Dar told him crisply. "If you think you're gonna get me to go down those stairs, think again." There was a pause. "And before you think again, I bet Alastair never mentioned my interest in martial arts."

"Whoa, whoa, whoa, take it easy, lady." Bob held up both hands and laughed. "Okay, I got the message. C'mon... I know a good hot dog stand out on Fifth Avenue that's got a great view and no enclosed walls." He put a careful hand on Dar's back and guided her back toward the street. "And no, he never did mention that, as a matter of fact."

Dar relaxed a little and spared him a half grin.

"He never says much about you at all, you know...just that you have more brains than is really safe for one person, and you take the word 'attitude' to a new level of meaning." Bob chuckled. "You willing to be more forthcoming than that?"

"No," Dar replied coolly. "When I talk about my personal life, I usually get the specifics thrown back in my face at a staff meeting sometime. No, thanks."

Bob sighed. "All business. Your reputation's completely intact on that front." He gave her a resigned grin. "How about a burger and fries?"

"Lead on." Satisfied with the acceptance of her ground rules, Dar put her hands behind her back and strolled after the sales executive, watching the stream of people crowding the street.

They walked down a set of shallow stairs and ended up in an outdoor café, small tables on a patio that faced Rockefeller Center.

Dar eyed the handwritten menu and chose a sandwich and French fries, giving Bob an agreeable nod when he suggested a bottle of wine to go with it. She let her eyes drift across the scene, taking in the noise and the lights and the people going by. Now they, she acknowledged frankly, were interesting, and very different from what she was used to in Miami. The voices around her were different as well, sharper and more staccato.

"Dar?"

Dar turned and graciously bestowed her attention on her host. "Sorry, did you ask me something?"

They talked about business for a while as they munched their way through the very good sandwiches and half of the wine. Dar managed to relax a little, aware that the almost overwhelming intensity she'd felt from her co-worker the previous night was muted, and he was, to her surprise, on his very best behavior.

She remembered Alastair's warning and wondered. Her hand shifted, swirling the sweet, heavy white wine in its glass, and she took a sip, enjoying the taste she seldom indulged in. "Did you see the presentation today?"

Bob laughed, leaning back and crossing an ankle over his knee. "Definitely unconventional, I'll give you that, Dar. Most of the time, I sleep through three-quarters of Al's speeches. I know them by heart. We did this for the quarter, we were supposed to do that, we took this charge, made that bonus..." Bob swallowed a mouthful of wine. "Not like he comes in and says, well folks, this quarter we lost the farm, don'cha know."

"Not if I can help it, no." Dar smiled. "It's my job to make sure he doesn't ever have to."

The sales exec nodded thoughtfully. "That's true, and boy, does he rely on that," he said. "You're one key player."

Dar shrugged. "I do what I have to do."

He chuckled. "And God help any of us that get in your way. You've pinned my ears back a time or two."

"Nothing personal." Dar's eyes twinkled slightly.

"Hmm." Bob cleared his throat and changed the subject. "You definitely perked up the stockers, that's for sure." Her dinner companion let his eyes, finally, wander over her. "You're much nicer to look at than Al is, and you know your stuff. Nice work with those offshore investors. They were trying to nail you."

"I've faced a lot worse." Dar paused as she felt a chill run down her back. It was the oddest feeling, and she just barely resisted the urge to look behind her. Abruptly, her stomach tightened, and she felt a knot form in her guts. *What in the hell?*

"Dar?" Bob caught the change and sat up. "You okay?"

No. Dar felt the blood drain from her face, and her heart started pounding. *Was it the wine?* She set the glass down. "Yeah, I'm all right..." Her throat went dry, and she felt a surge of anxiety almost make her start shivering. "I think."

Bob put his glass down and reached over, touching her shoulder carefully. "You're pretty pale. Maybe you should put your head down."

"No." Dar suddenly had the urge to be up and moving, an animal reflex fed by nervous energy that made her thighs twitch and tighten. The fear now gripped her guts, and she was afraid she was going to throw up. "Listen, maybe I had something that didn't agree with me..."

"I'll get a cab." Bob stood decisively and walked to the curb, snapping his fingers expertly. He motioned the waiter over with his other hand and handed him a bill, then walked back over to where Dar was just standing up. "Let's go. I'll get you back to the hotel."

"It's all right—" Dar started to protest.

"Lady, your well-being is important enough to make Alastair P. McLean say the word 'fuck' to me," the sales exec told her firmly. "You are going to let me get you back to your room, and I'll call in a doctor if I have to."

It would have almost been funny if Dar hadn't felt like her insides were clawing their way up, eager to erupt from every body orifice she had. "Okay." She let herself be bundled into the cab and concentrated on taking deep breaths, trying not to throw up.

Kerry hung on to the seat arms, one hand jerking free to tighten the seatbelt she'd prudently left fastened across her lap. Josh sat beside her, gasping as the plane bucked in the air, his fingers white with the strain of clutching the leather cushions.

"Folks," the captain's voice sounded strained, but calm, "I know it's pretty scary back there right now, but you all just hang on, and we'll be through this in a bit. Storm front caught us by surprise tonight, so just hold on tight and keep calm."

Okay. Kerry's heart was hammering so hard, she could barely hear the man's voice. Her entire body was tense with fear, and she closed her eyes as the plane dropped unexpectedly, making her weightless for long, long seconds. Then the sensation stopped abruptly, and the plane lurched, tipping on its side and shuddering.

She had to focus on something, so she chose the most vivid thing in her life, clamping her jaw down tight as she pictured her lover's face, trying to let the image fill her mind's eye and push out the horror all around her.

The shaking went on for a lifetime. She heard things fall in the galley and the flight attendants cursing, then soft, faint echoes of some kind of alarm behind the closed door of the cockpit.

The fear was almost choking her.

And then it stopped.

The violent shaking settled to the odd bump, and the labored sound of the engines evened out, still sounding rough but no longer giving the plane sickening surges of speed and slacking.

Slowly, Kerry opened one eye, then the other. Her dinner was chatting with her tonsils, and she hoped like crazy that no one was going to ask her to either think or speak until it decided if it was going to go any higher or not.

She looked out the window, and her heart almost stopped again. They were between two layers of roiling gray clouds, ducking between shooting streaks of lightning, a moment's peace between two slices of hell.

Dar thanked Bob, reassured him for the tenth time that she'd be all right, then closed the hotel room door and escaped into the peaceful silence within.

It was dark in the room, and she only turned on one small light before she trudged across the carpet and collapsed on the bed, her body curling instinctively into a ball as she lay there trying to figure out what the hell had happened to her. For the moment, she was merely sick to her stomach and had a pounding tension headache. The frantic anxiety had faded, leaving only a knot in her gut that simply refused to loosen.

"What in the hell was that?" Dar spoke aloud, her voice slightly hoarse. "What's wrong with me?" She was scared, she admitted to herself, vague snippets from popular magazine articles about anxiety attacks flashing into her memory. Stories about people who couldn't even leave their houses. "No." Dar let her eyes close and she rested, forcing herself to breathe slowly and calmly. "That is not what's wrong with me. I won't put up with that."

After a few moments of simply lying there, she pushed herself upright and got to her feet, glancing at the clock as she did so. Instinctively, her hand went for her cell phone, and she opened it, dialing a number by heart and listening to the ring.

Voice mail. Dar's brow creased, then she shrugged. "Guess you forgot to turn this back on, huh?" she spoke into the phone. "Listen, something weird just happened to me. I..." Dar hesitated. "I'd like to talk to you about it. Give me a call as soon as you get this, okay?" A pause. "Okay. Talk to you later." She closed the phone, then went over to the desk and sat down, activating her laptop and telling it to make a network connection.

A few clicks later, the light from the laptop's active matrix screen lit her features with a ghostly glow, her face still as her eyes flicked back and forth, reading data. Another click, then she entered Kerry's flight number and hit enter.

En route—delayed.

"Delayed." A thousand thoughts sped through Dar's mind. "Why?"

Suddenly, her guts clenched again and she doubled over, grabbing the edge of the table as a wave of fear almost swamped her. It forced a tiny cry from her throat, and she took a deep breath and held it, forcing the emotions down as she struggled to regain control.

It was tough, but she managed to do it. After wiping the sweat off her fingers, she refreshed the screen, watching the words refuse to change. She looked at the clock and calculated times. Then she picked up her cell phone and dialed a number.

It rang. A voice picked up, relatively cheerful given the time of night. "I need status on one of your flights. It's listed as delayed." Dar spoke slowly and clearly. "I need to know why it's delayed, and you're going to tell me specifically, or I'll go up your chain of command until I wake up someone high enough to come down to that center you're sitting in and use a fire hose to make you give me the information." Pause. "Is that clear?"

Dead silence. "Yes, ma'am," the voice finally spluttered. "Can I have the flight number?"

Dar gave it, aware of a shiver working its way through her.

There was quiet, save for the distinctive clicking of a keyboard. "Okay...um...Ms..."

"Roberts," Dar provided softly.

"Right...Okay, well, from what I can see here, that flight hit some bad weather over Virginia...um..."

"Specifically," Dar reminded her.

The clerk sighed. "Ma'am—"

"I am the chief information officer of ILS. I can, if I have to, break into your reservations system and get the information myself, but it's going to take longer, and I'm not in the mood. So just tell me," Dar bit the words out, "what...is...the...problem?"

"It's not—well, they've got some damage to the aircraft, but the captain thinks he can land it okay. The problem is they've got to go through another storm first. They're trying to land in DC."

Dar clamped an arm across her stomach and bit the inside of her lip. She had to take several breaths before she could speak. "Okay. Thanks."

"Ma'am?"

Dar just closed the phone, and let her head drop forward to rest against the laptop's cool edge.

Kerry wrapped her arms around the pillow she had in her lap and just kept her eyes closed as the plane rocked and yawed its way through the clouds. She could feel little shudders running through the frame of the aircraft, and she managed to compose a tiny prayer, which she sent outward, asking for nothing more than to hear Dar's voice again.

That was all.

She felt a touch on her hand, and she jerked her head up to

see Josh looking back at her, his face white as a sheet and looking very young. She managed a smile for him. "We're gonna be okay."

"I know you're an old, married lady, but can I hang onto your hand?" Josh asked. "I'm so scared, I think I just saw my left testicle float past my earlobe."

That forced a breath of laughter from Kerry, and she reached over, clasping his hand with her own. "Sure."

"Folks..." The pilot's voice drew their attention. "Here's the situation. We got hit by lightning and lost one of our engines, but don't get excited. We have three."

"Easy for him to say," Josh muttered.

"We were trying to make it out to Chicago, but there's a really big front ahead of us in that direction," the pilot went on. "Washington is already closed, so we're gonna swing out east and try to get into New York."

New York. Kerry hung onto that one tiny sliver of very good news. New York was where Dar was, and right now she very, very much wanted to be there.

"But we've got to get through this storm cell to do that. It's going to be a little scary, but you all hang on, and we'll get you down all right."

"A little?" Kerry felt like throwing up. "I wonder how long it'll take?"

One of the flight attendants, harried, coffee-stained, and exhausted, heard her. "Thirty minutes."

"Thanks." Kerry gave her a grateful smile. "Have you ever been through this before?"

The attendant, a slim, middle-aged woman with salt-and-pepper hair and an interesting face, nodded briefly. "Twice. Every time, I swear I'm retiring."

Kerry felt an uncomfortable pressure building in her ears, and she sighed, hugging her pillow with one arm and keeping a grip on Josh with the other. The plane began to rock violently again, and the murmur of voices, which had risen, fell again to silence. The cabin lights flickered off, leaving only the indirect lighting on, and the lightning outside brought lurid flashes of silver darting unexpectedly into the cabin.

"I hate this," Josh whispered. "I'm quitting the minute I get on the ground, I swear. I'll go into business with my Uncle Al back home."

Glad of the distraction, Kerry licked her lips. "What does he do?"

"Pizza parlor," Josh yelped, as a bang sounded and the plane tilted to one side. "Oh, my God."

Kerry exhaled, keeping her eyes glued on the window. The clouds were so thick and dark outside, she could only see the edges when lightning flared within them, or when the faint lights from the plane's leading wing edge broke free of the clinging mist.

It was like being inside a bag, rolling down a mountain. She couldn't see anything, she had no sense of where the ground was...

Kerry felt like crying. The fear was so overwhelming, it made her want to scream, but she bit down on the inside of her lip and simply bore it—time running so slowly it was as if every minute was lasting an hour. Fifteen of them passed before something else changed.

The nose lifted, then plunged to one side, throwing the stewardesses. It hung at that angle for an eternity, then slowly straightened out and jerked downward. Kerry started shivering.

The plane kept rocking and bucking, so unstable it made her dizzy as her sense of balance fought to compensate for the movement. Suddenly, she felt a difference in pressure, and she jumped, looking up and half expecting the panel to drop masks at her.

But it didn't.

"Depressurized the cabin," the flight attendant called to her seatmate. "We must be below 10,000 feet."

"Is that good or bad?" Josh asked nervously.

No one answered him.

They all almost screamed when the engine sound changed and the plane slowed, its wallowing becoming far more apparent. Then another sound, a louder one, and Kerry just barely kept herself from total panic by realizing the sound was the landing gear extending. That meant—her frazzled mind clung to the rationale—that meant the noise before that was the air spoilers, slowing the plane for landing.

Right? She never remembered them being that loud, though.

The plane yawed and wobbled, the nose dipping, then the speed cutting back drastically. Outside, she could still only see clouds. She stared at them, willing them to part and show her something other than muddy darkness around the plane. "C'mon...c'mon..."

Lower and lower, until Kerry was sure they were going to crash. She closed her eyes and thought of Dar and fiercely told herself that when she got to heaven—because God damn it, that's where she was going—she'd be so careful to watch over Dar, and make sure she was never alone.

She bowed her head.

Then the darkness on the other side of the window dissolved—into rain, and lashing wind, and the lights of a big city, flashing by quickly as the big plane stumbled and rocked its way onto the runway, landing to one side, bouncing, then landing again, this time solidly on all of its wheels.

The engines reversed, and the blur of the lights turned into the solid outlines of a terminal, then exploded into color as a cadre of emergency vehicles whizzed around them, circling the plane as it limped its way toward the buildings.

Kerry felt all the tension rush out of her, leaving her limp in her seat and completely exhausted. Not even the rattle of sleet against the window stirred her as she simply closed her eyes and gave a quiet, heartfelt thanks.

The plane rocked to a halt. Kerry reached for her cell phone.

It was hypnotic. Dar stayed crouched over her laptop, continually hitting the refresh button and attempting to change the indicator on the page by sheer force of will. "Change, damn you," she whispered under her breath, slamming the button on the mouse for the thousandth time.

And it did. The page redrew, and the Delayed status morphed before her startled eyes to Arrived—Newark.

"Newark." Dar blinked. She clicked on it again and watched the same results occur. Again. Same thing. Her shoulder muscles relaxed and she slumped over the desk. Then she sucked in a breath and closed her hand around the cell phone and started to lift it. It rang as she did so, causing her whole body to jerk in shocked surprise. The cell phone went flying and Dar dove after it, tripping over the laptop's cable and sprawling across the carpet in an undignified tumble.

Her head struck the bedside table and she yelped, but her fingers found the buzzing phone and she managed to get it open and to her ear without further injury. "Yeah?"

"Sweetheart, you have no idea what I've just been through."

Dar rolled onto her back and sucked the voice in, every muscle going completely slack in utter relief. "Uh?"

Kerry sighed into the phone. "We just landed. We hit this huge storm, and the plane was rocking all over the place, and we lost an engine, and I think my stomach's going to resign and find a better job somewhere else after that ride down."

Dar placed a hand over her own belly and blinked. "Yeah. I know what you mean," she murmured softly into the phone. "Glad you're okay."

"I've never been so scared in my life." Kerry's voice was shaking.

"I bet," Dar murmured. "I bet it felt like your heart was coming out your ears." She rubbed one of hers, then let the hand fall to the carpet limply.

"Yeah," Kerry sighed. "I'm still shaking."

Dar lifted the errant paw again and watched it tremble. "Hmm." She let it drop with a thump. "Ow."

"What's wrong?" Kerry asked. "We're stuck in here for a few minutes. They're trying to get the jetway working. It's all iced, I think."

"I bumped my head," Dar told her. "So, you're in New Jersey?" She had hardly a notion of what she was saying, merely pushing words out to fill the quiet. "You didn't get hurt or anything, did you?"

"No." Kerry sighed. "Just scared. I want off this airplane; and I hope I am stuck overnight, because let me tell you—I'm not anxious to get on another one of them."

"Mm...yeah. I can understand that. Boy," Dar exhaled, "wish I'd been there with you."

Kerry was very quiet for a moment, and when she did start speaking, there was a distinct catch in her voice. "I wish you were, too. Just before we landed, I..." Kerry stopped, then went on. "I was so scared."

Dar rolled onto her side and curled her hands around the phone, wanting to reach right through it. Maybe she could squeeze through if she really tried hard. "Sorry you had such a rotten time, Ker. Hang in there, okay? I'll come get you."

A shaky sigh answered her. "You okay? You sound kinda washed out."

Like a limp dishrag. Dar now had an excellent insight into that hoary old saying. "I'm fine, just tired; and I think this damn New York food knocked my system for a loop."

"Oh. Where'd you end..." Kerry paused. "They got the door open; I need to get out of here. Sweetie, I'll give you a call back as soon as I figure out where I am."

"Sure. Talk to you soon," Dar answered. "I love you."

"I love you, too." Kerry's voice, finally, sounded a smile at her. "I can't wait to see you."

Dar let the phone drop onto the carpet and just lay there for a moment. Then she rolled to her feet and grabbed the phone in one hand and her sneakers with the other. The operator came on. "I need to go to the airport."

"Which airport, ma'am?"

"The one in New Jersey."

"Newark?"

Dar spared the receiver a disgusted look. "Is that in New Jersey?"

"Yes, ma'am."

"Then that's the one." Dar got her sneaker on and was tugging the laces one-handed. "I need to go now."

"Ma'am, there are no planes leaving at this time of night. We'd have to call for a special driver."

Dar sucked in a breath and counted to ten. "Then call one," she ground out. "Now."

The airport was in chaos. Kerry eased to one side of the jetway and pressed her back against the wall, letting the flow of people from the plane push past her. The storm had closed a lot of air routes, and the place was packed with stranded, angry travelers.

Her fellow travelers clustered around an airline representative. Most of them were upset and still shaken, and the voices Kerry heard were strident and loud.

Her own knees were shaking. She trudged over and sat down in the one vacant seat near the gate podium, letting her briefcase drop between her feet as she rested her elbows on her thighs. She was sure everyone was frantic to get rerouted or obtain free accommodations or demand compensation from the airline.

Kerry didn't need any of that. She was simply glad to be on the ground in one piece. She folded her hands together and leaned her head against them, taking a moment for a few whispered words of gratitude to the Lord who had surely been watching over her.

A hand on her shoulder made her jerk and look up. "Oh." She straightened as an airline rep knelt next to her. "Hi."

"Are you all right, ma'am?" the woman asked kindly. "I know you had a rough trip in."

Kerry glanced behind her, where their plane was now surrounded by emergency vehicles and flashing lights. "You could say that." She managed a smile. "I'm just waiting for the crush to disperse over there." Her eyes went to the crowd around the other representatives.

The woman patted Kerry's briefcase, glancing at the small platinum tag attached to the case buckle, then back up at Kerry. "Why don't you come with me, and we'll get you taken care of," she suggested casually.

In the maelstrom inside the airport, with all the upset people and canceled flights, the last thing Kerry would have thought of would have been to claim privilege. However, since it was being offered, she wasn't about to turn it down. "Sure. I'd love that." She stood and picked up the case, following the rep as she eased through the crowd and worked her way past the other irate customers.

Kerry caught sight of Josh just as she cleared the crowd. He was waiting his turn rather forlornly, and he gave her a weak smile as their eyes met. "Looks like we're getting floor space," he commented. "No flights out until tomorrow."

"I wasn't in the mood to be on another one anyway," Kerry admitted. "Chicago can wait."

"Not for me." Josh shook his head. "I meant it. I'm going home."

Kerry fished in her pocket and pulled out one of her business cards, which she handed to him. "If you really decide to quit, give me a call."

He glanced at the card, then looked more closely at the title, his eyebrows jerking up in a way that was comical. His eyes widened and he looked back at her. Kerry winked at him, gave him a pat on the side, then turned and continued after the fidgeting attendant.

"Nice-looking guy," the attendant commented.

"Yeah," Kerry agreed, distracted by the speakers echoing loudly around them.

"Did you want to bring him along? We could squeeze him in with you if you—"

"Huh?" Kerry's head snapped back, realizing what the woman was saying. "Oh, um, no. No, thanks." She ran a hand through her hair. "He's not my type."

"Oh." The woman glanced behind them. "Maybe I'll go back and get him later then." She gave Kerry a wicked grin. "If you don't mind."

Kerry nodded amusedly. "Be my guest."

They ducked down a small, unmarked hallway, and the woman unlocked a plain door with her keycard, pulling it open and allowing a gust of cool, brandy-scented air to hit Kerry in the face. "Go on in and relax."

Kerry stepped inside the Platinum Fliers Club door and was glad to hear it close behind her. She trudged to the courtesy desk and set her briefcase down, pulling out her wallet and handing her club card to the woman behind the desk. It was quiet inside the club, though many travelers were already taking sanctuary there, and she could hear the faint clink of glasses from the bar and a soft murmur of voices around the bank of modem-jack equipped cubes.

"Thank you, Ms. Stuart." The woman gazed kindly at her. "Were you on the flight to Chicago?"

Kerry nodded.

"Would you like a drink?"

Kerry nodded again.

"C'mon." The woman rose and took her briefcase, motioning her to follow. "You going to need a hotel room?"

"No." Kerry found herself smiling. "Someone's picking me up." The urge, at that moment, to see Dar's face was so overwhelming, it almost made her cry.

Dar resisted the growing urge to just tell the driver to shut up. He wasn't a bad sort, but he'd started talking to her the minute she'd gotten into the Lincoln, and all her attempts at not providing any conversational feedback had gone completely unheeded.

"You been here before?"

"Yes." Dar leaned her head against the glass window and watched the dark buildings go by.

"You like New York?"

"No."

"Aw, really? Hey, it's not so bad. People say stuff about the crime and stuff like that, but it's really a great place." The driver got into a groove. "We got lots of stuff to see; you been to the Statue of Liberty?"

"Yes."

"See? That's a great place, and Ellis Island, too. You been out there since they redone it?"

"No."

"You should go. It's great stuff. You been to the Empire State Building?"

"Yes."

"That's some place, huh?"

"It's got rats."

"Huh?" The driver turned to look at her, despite the fact that they were driving over a very large bridge.

"Rats." Dar muttered. "They eat the damn cables." She willed the car to move faster.

"Oh, well, you know, we got them all over," the driver apologized. "They live here too, y'know?" He turned around and weaved his way through the traffic. After a moment of blessed, pensive silence, he spoke up again. "You an exterminator?"

Dar looked at the back of his head, willing it to explode. "No."

"Oh. I figured maybe you were, since you knew about them rats," the driver commented. "My cousin Vinnie's an exterminator. They make good money, y'know?"

The traffic was thinning out now, and they made better time. Dar saw a sign for the Newark airport, and she felt her pulse pick up. Before she'd left, she'd swallowed a few aspirin to try and kill the headache Kerry's scare had given her, but the back of her head still throbbed.

The car pulled up to the terminal entrance a minute later, and she gladly got out, pulling up the zipper on her leather jacket. She leaned on the window and handed the driver the fare, giving him a dour stare in the bargain. "Thanks."

"No problem! NO problem." The man grinned at her. "Hey, you goin' back to the city?" He asked. "You ain't got no luggage, so I figure you gotta be picking somebody up, right? You want me to wait for you?"

Dar glanced around, gauging the lateness of the hour against the annoying nature of her friend the driver. "Yeah, all right," she decided. "Wait here." She turned and headed for the terminal, breaking into a jog as she dodged the stream of people heading in the opposite direction.

The terminal felt overheated. Dar unzipped her jacket the minute she cleared the doors and plowed through the crowd inside, heading for the security gate in front of the terminal she knew Kerry had to be in. Impatiently, she dropped her cell phone and pager into the small bucket, then walked through the metal detector as the guard waved her casually by.

She grabbed the electronics and moved on, pausing in the center of the terminal and looking around in mild dismay. It was a zoo. There were people piled everywhere, and angry, tired faces seemed to fill every available space. Dar pulled out her cell phone and flipped it open, then closed it again as a thought occurred to her.

She turned on her heel and headed toward a bank of elevators.

Kerry curled herself up into a ball in the comfortable leather chair. She had one hand clasped around a glass of cognac, and she sipped slowly from it as the tension in her body very gradually unwound. All around her were trapped travelers, most on cell phones, none of them happy people.

She was facing away from the entrance to the club, looking out the plate-glass windows at the busy terminal on the level below. Suddenly her senses prickled and she felt a tingling sensation between her shoulder blades. Instinctively, she turned in her chair and looked up.

And there was Dar, her tall frame outlined in leather and denim, walking toward her through the crowd. Kerry put down her glass and untangled herself, nearly tripping as she stood up and reached for Dar's already outstretched arms. "Oof." Off balance, she landed in an embrace that fairly lifted her off her feet anyway. "Oh, boy, am I glad to see you."

Dar simply hugged her in silence.

"They just brought my bag up," Kerry murmured.

"So I see." Dar eyed the leather overnighter. She sniffed curiously. "What was in the glass?"

Kerry licked her lips. "Cognac," she admitted. "I was tied up in knots from that damn landing."

Dar rubbed her back. "Did it work?"

"No." Kerry peeked up. "But you did. I feel great now." She smiled. "Thanks for coming after me. I realized after we hung up I could have just taken a cab to your hotel."

"Bah." Dar picked up Kerry's bag. "And had me miss a ride with a prize New York cab driver? C'mon." She put her arm over Kerry's shoulders as Kerry retrieved her briefcase. "Let's get out of here."

Kerry blew out a breath. "I guess I can keep tabs on the flights from the hotel," she said. "So I know when I have to come back here."

Dar glanced at her. "Uh-huh. Let's worry about that later." She steered Kerry toward the door, ignoring the envious looks from those obviously destined to spend the night right where they were.

Dar scribbled her name on the room service bill, then shooed the waiter out, shutting the heavy door behind him. She turned and regarded Kerry in silence for a moment, and then walked over to the tray on the table. The blond woman was curled up in one of the leather chairs, propping up her head with one hand as she gazed out the windows at the city lights.

"Ker?" Dar picked up a cup of hot chocolate and walked over to her, holding it out invitingly.

"Mm...thanks." Kerry accepted it, turning in the chair to face Dar as she sat down next to her. "I think my insides have stopped shaking, at least." She raked her fingers through her hair and sighed. "God, I've never been so scared in my life, Dar. It was horrible."

Dar pulled her knees up and circled them with one arm, sipping on the glass of milk she held in her free hand. "Yeah. I..." She hesitated, and then shook her head. "I'm glad you made it out all right."

Kerry watched her over the rim of her cup. "I picked up my voice mail. What was it you wanted to talk to me about?" she said, changing the subject. "You sounded weird."

Dar got up and walked over to the table, selecting a shrimp chip and scooping up some crab dip with it. She put it into her mouth and chewed slowly, aware of the curious eyes on her back. Her attack of nerves had now taken on another, even stranger cast, and she wasn't sure she wanted to talk about it. "Ah...I just had a strange idea and I wanted to run it by you," she answered casually. "Nothing important."

There was a rustle of fabric and leather, then the soft sounds of bare feet on carpet before a warm hand touched her back. Taking a breath, Dar turned and faced Kerry.

"Well...it's important enough for you to lie to me about it," Kerry stated with quiet bluntness. "And I, um...don't think you've ever done that to me before." She laid both hands against Dar's stomach and leaned into her. "Honey, don't do this to me right now. I can't handle it."

Dar inhaled sharply, responding to the look in Kerry's eyes. "It's not...what you think. I just— Right before I called you, I had this...this fit," she said. "It was like I was going nuts or something."

Kerry's expression altered into one of mild alarm. "A fit?"

Upset, Dar sat down on the arm of the nearby chair and ran her hand through her hair. "It was like a—a panic attack or... But I've never had that before, and I know I'm not..."

Kerry slid between her lover's knees and let her forearms rest on Dar's shoulders. "Were you scared?"

Dar nodded unhappily.

Kerry took out her cell phone and examined the memory. Her brow creased. "When did it happen?" she asked suddenly. "Do you remember what time?"

"Um...after eight, I guess. Quarter after, something like that." Dar shrugged.

"Quarter after?" Kerry said. "Quarter after eight?"

"Yeah." Dar nodded. "Why?"

Kerry's gaze went inward for a long moment. "That's just the time the plane got into trouble," she murmured. "And I was scared poopless." She looked up into Dar's eyes, searching them. "Did you know?"

Dar frowned. "Kerry, I'm not a psychic," she protested. "I'm not even a good guesser."

"No, I know." Kerry leaned her forehead against her lover's. "It's just a very strange coincidence, don't you think? I mean, there I am, up in an airplane, nearly out of my mind I'm so scared, and thinking about you, and here you are..."

"Urmf," Dar grunted. "That is weird." She considered in silence for a bit. "Hell, I'd rather think it was that than I was going nuts, though," she admitted. "I thought maybe I was starting to lose it."

Kerry rubbed her thumb along Dar's scalp, just behind her ear. "Have you ever had a panic attack?"

"No."

"I didn't think so. You're just not the type." Kerry managed a chuckle. "Though I know you've been a little stressed lately."

"Mm." Dar circled Kerry's waist with both arms and pulled her close.

"Now, I'll admit to having several panic attacks on that plane. All I could think of was never seeing you again," Kerry whispered into her ear. "And I wasn't nearly ready for that." She put her head down on Dar's shoulder, a perceptible catch in her voice on the last few words.

Dar's nerves had settled now that she had an odd, though infinitely preferable alternative to her recent fears. She dismissed the concern and concentrated on soothing Kerry, rubbing her back with gentle fingers. "Oh, sweetheart," she murmured, feeling the jerks as Kerry started crying. "It's okay."

Kerry buried her face against Dar's shoulder and simply let it all out as Dar rocked them both in a careful rhythm. She finally ended up with a headache but a lot less stress wound up in her body, and she rested against Dar for a while after the tears had dried. "Wow," she sniffled. "Sorry. I got you wet."

"No problem." Dar gave her a kiss on the forehead. "I'm glad I was here for you. Okay now?" She rubbed the back of Kerry's neck and felt the tension relax under her fingers as Kerry let her head fall to rest against Dar's shoulder.

"Yeah, now." The blond woman circled Dar with both arms and hugged her. "Maybe I'll get lucky and that storm'll never stop."

Dar returned the hug, her eyes studying the outside darkness thoughtfully.

Kerry leaned back against the wall, letting the fragrant steam fill her lungs. One thing about the Marriott, she acknowledged; they always had nice hot showers. She let the pounding spray thrum along her back, easing the headache she still had even after a good night's sleep.

In Dar's presence. Kerry exhaled. She'd called the airport and found that the airways were open again. A flight was available for her at noon. She'd booked it, but with a reluctant heart and a sense of trepidation she tried hard to hide from her lover.

You're not a baby, stop acting like one, she told herself sternly, picking up Dar's tube of body wash and squeezing some into her hand.

A blast of cool air made her pause, then smile as Dar joined her in the shower. The clouds of steam parted and writhed around the tall, tanned form, and instead of putting the gel on herself, Kerry applied it to her showermate. "Hi."

"Hi." Dar amiably reciprocated, scrubbing the back of Kerry's shoulders. "Weather's cleared."

Kerry swallowed. "I know." She drew in a breath. "I...um...booked a noon flight out to Chicago," she said. "Hope I have better luck than I did last night."

Hands cupped her face and she had to look up to meet pale blue eyes peering down at her through the mist.

"You don't sound thrilled," Dar commented.

"I'm not," Kerry admitted softly. She hesitated a long moment, and hated herself for the weakness. "Dar, can I ask you a favor? As my boss?"

Dar looked down at herself, then at Kerry. She smiled.

"I'm serious."

"Sure," Dar answered.

"You know I never ask you to butt in."

"You never do."

Kerry studied the angular profile watching her, knowing the words would be a disappointment. "I'm asking," she said. "Can you fix it so I don't have to go out there?"

Dar considered the request very seriously. The situation needed resolution. She couldn't go because her Navy project was about to start and it was, definitely, Kerry's responsibility. She looked down into Kerry's eyes and saw the shame there, and the awareness of what she was asking.

And lurking in the shadows, a lingering fear. "Yes, I can fix it," Dar replied easily. "Just leave it to me." She took Kerry's hands and squeezed them. "You'll come home on my flight today."

Kerry leaned against her, almost dizzy with relief and more than a touch of guilt. "I'm sorry."

Dar simply embraced her. "Don't worry about it." And in a strange sort of way, she felt glad that Kerry could come to her, knowing what she was asking, and still ask it, knowing that Dar would take care of it for her.

Which she would. Dar straightened, considering the problem. In her own way.

Chapter
Three

The hotel's restaurant was busy when Dar threaded her way through the business crowd to a table near the rear windows. Already seated, Alastair spotted her and waved, and she lifted a hand and waved back. "Morning." She gave Bob a brisk nod. "Thanks for the lift last night."

Bob returned the nod. "You look a lot more chipper this morning. Was it the food or the company?" he asked with a wry grin.

"Neither." Dar sat down. "Migraine. Delayed reaction from the meeting."

"Ah." Bob nodded.

"Damned nasty things." Alastair appeared relieved. "Glad it was nothing serious, though. Coffee?"

"Definitely." Dar flipped open the menu and studied it.

"Heard from Chicago last night, Dar." Alastair leaned forward. "Doesn't look good. Johnston sounds panicky." He took a sip of luridly orange juice. "I heard Kerry was on her way there."

Dar stared at the menu for a moment, then blinked. "She was." The tall executive made her decision. "I've decided to bring the Chicago team down our way instead."

Alastair cocked his head to one side. "Oh, really?"

"Thanksgiving week?" Bob also sounded surprised.

"Yep." Dar kept her eyes on the breakfast selections. "How's the Benedict here, Alastair? Any good?"

Her boss was caught off guard. He fiddled with his napkin, then leaned back in his chair and hitched up a knee, cupping his hand around the gray flannel surface. "Never had it, really. Listen, Dar...do you really think pulling the whole team out is a good idea?"

"Yes." Dar put her menu down and met his eyes. "There's been a big foul-up there. If I send someone in, it's on their turf and it'll take me a week to get to the bottom of it. Bring them in to Miami, and I'll have it turned around in twenty-four hours. You pick."

Bob sniffed reflectively. "Got a point there. Sometimes it takes coming out of the forest to see the trees," he said. "Sounds like they're buried in crap."

"Eh." Alastair grunted. "Could be, could be. All right, Dar. It's your ballgame, after all." He motioned to the waiter. "Benedict, was it? Wheat toast?"

"White." Dar gave the waiter a thin smile. "And a half stack of pancakes. Thanks." She handed over her menu and sat back, lifting her newly poured cup of coffee and sipping at it. She glanced around at the full room, returning nods and smiles from some of the investors she'd met the day before. "Nice crowd."

"They certainly liked you." Alastair chuckled. "Haven't had so many people come up and ask me questions in six years, none of them about the balance sheets for a change." He gave his CIO a smile. "Even the board members had to come and suck up to me. I really enjoyed that, Paladar...I really did."

"I bet." Dar smiled, toasting him with her coffee. Then she pulled out her cell phone and flipped it open. "Now let me give Chicago the bad news."

Bob leaned back in his chair and munched on a biscuit. "Weather they've been having, not sure it's gonna be that bad, Dar. Now if someone would offer **me** a week in Miami in winter..." He gave Alastair a look. "But noooo...I get to fly to Cleveland from here."

"Be thankful," Alastair told him crisply. "It coulda been worse. Bracken's been asking me to get him a top salesman out to North Dakota."

Dar chuckled as she waited for the phone to connect. After a moment, it did. "Morning, Clarice. Dar Roberts here."

A moment's silence was followed by a small gasp. "Oh, hello, Dar! I wasn't expecting you! Here we thought we'd be seeing your new VP, but I hear the flight was delayed."

"Canceled," Dar told her. "So get your team together and book a ride down to Miami. I'm not wasting a minute more of Kerry's time on your impending cluster." Her voice took on an edge. "Our offices, tomorrow morning."

"But—"

"No buts. Move it!" Dar barked.

Clarice sighed. "Yes, ma'am."

Dar closed her phone and returned it to its clip, then finished her coffee, basking in the crowd's covert attention.

Kerry settled into her leather seat next to Dar, buckling her seat belt and tugging her sweater straight. She knew she'd have to strip it off the minute they landed, but it was soft and pretty, and the plane's air conditioning was chilly so she was glad Dar had bought it for her on a whim.

She was still feeling pretty small, like she was running away from her responsibilities. *But you knew you'd feel like that, and you did it anyway. So, suck it up and get over it, Kerrison.* She leaned on the console between their seats and glanced at Dar. "Was Clarice upset?"

Dar shrugged one shoulder. "I didn't give her time to express her opinion one way or the other," she told her partner. "I just told her to get her and her team's asses on a plane and be in Miami tomorrow morning."

"Mm." Kerry pursed her lips. "You know—"

"Ah ah." Dar tapped her on the bridge of the nose. "No second-guessing. It's better this way, at any rate, because you won't have to deal with them being territorial. You'll have them at your mercy from the get-go."

Kerry winced. "That sounds so manipulative."

"Kerry, they're endangering a forty-million-dollar contract," Dar reminded her. "Don't feel sorry for them. I don't."

True. "I know. I just want to get their side of it before I start hammering on them," Kerry told her. "I'm really surprised at Clarice. I thought she was very sharp the last project she worked." She shook her head. "Wonder what went wrong?"

Dar shrugged. "She's always been stubborn."

Kerry's ears perked. "Have you known her long? You never talked about her before."

Something occurred to Dar. It made her sit up straight and open her eyes wide as she remembered what had precipitated Clarice's transfer to the Midwest. Slowly she turned and regarded Kerry, nibbling the inside of her lip. "Um...there's something you'd better know about before you meet Clarice."

Kerry looked up from reading the emergency card in her seat pocket. "Hmm? What?" She studied Dar's face closely. "Don't tell me she's a phobe."

I wish. Dar shook her head. "She shares our lifestyle," she admitted. "Pretty openly."

"Ah." Kerry frowned, then she glanced back at Dar. There

was a distinct hint of "uh-oh" right around her lover's pretty blue eyes, and it made her pause and think hard. She knew Dar had been involved several times before they'd met, but... "Um...you two weren't..."

"No."

Kerry exhaled in relief. That kind of complication wasn't something she'd bargained for.

"But she really, really wanted to be," Dar added, lowering her voice and looking around. "And she was pretty persistent."

Kerry leaned closer, intrigued. "And?"

"Wasn't my type."

"Ah." The blond woman nodded. "So...what's the problem?"

Dar assumed a sheepish expression. "I pulled the old 'no relationships in the office' rule on her to get her to leave me alone."

Kerry stared at her for a minute, then let her face drop into her hand. "Oh, Jesus," she muttered.

Dar cleared her throat, giving the flight attendant a wan smile. "Sorry," she whispered into Kerry's ear. "I'm sure you'll be able to handle it."

Kerry looked up at her from between her fingers, then covered her eyes again and sighed. "Paybacks," she uttered. "They always getcha."

Kerry leaned against the wall in the copy room and tried to ignore just how much the machine's whining noise was annoying her. She wondered what would happen if she gave in and kicked the thing, but the presence of two of the more gossip-prone marketing assistants made her cross her ankles instead.

Okay, Kerry. Take a deep breath and pretend you don't have cramps from hell, woke up late, and have an ex-admirer of Dar's to deal with in twenty minutes.

"Okay, all yours." Candy gave Kerry one of her sweeter smiles and took her papers with her as she and her crony sauntered out.

"Thanks," Kerry muttered, pushing off from the wall and putting her agenda on the machine before starting it up. She could have asked Mayte to do this, of course, but her assistant was busy getting the conference room ready and pulling down network diagrams to the transparency printer. Besides, walking around usually got her cranky body to loosen up a little, something she fervently hoped happened before she had to start her meeting.

Sometimes, she reflected, *being female and fertile sucks large piggy wonks*. The machine finished its work, and she removed her still-warm copies from the sorter and stapled them, then tucked them under her arm as she made her way back to her office.

Mayte was still gone, so she left the collated papers on her assistant's desk before she went into her office, closing the door behind her as she entered the sunlit space. Her brows lifted as she spotted a small cluster of items she was sure she hadn't left on her desk surrounding her favorite cup, which was now gently steaming. "Oho...what have we here?"

She circled the desk and sat down in her leather chair, tucking one leg up under her to try and ease the cramping. Resting on the desk were several things, each with a note. First, her cup, scented with a hint of spicy raspberry, then four wrapped chocolates, then a bottle. "Try this first..." She took a sip of the tea. "Then try these..." She unwrapped a chocolate and popped it into her mouth. "Then this." She held up the bottle of powerful painkillers. "If all that fails, call me."

Kerry chuckled around her mouthful and took a swallow of the tea to wash it down. "Thank you, Doctor Dar." She didn't really expect either tea or candy to work, and she'd already taken a handful of painkillers, but the thought of Dar in here, meticulously arranging her action plan and writing her notes, brought a smile to Kerry's face and allowed her to forget her misery for a short while.

A very short while. Her intercom buzzed. "Ms. Kerry? They are waiting for you in the conference," Mayte's soft voice floated into the air.

Kerry sighed and unwrapped another chocolate. "I'll be right there, Mayte."

"Dar?"

"Yes?"

"Commander Albert is here to see you," María replied quietly.

"Send him in." Dar finished signing the last of a stack of requests and closed the folder, tossing it in her out bin and putting the top back onto her fountain pen. Kerry had given her the elegant teakwood instrument, and she played with it for a minute, admiring the fine grain before she set it down and folded her hands.

María opened the door and stood back, allowing her guest to enter. In walked a tall, muscular man in his mid thirties, every crease in his uniform razor sharp and precise. Dar had about ten or fifteen seconds as he crossed the room to decide how to play her side of the encounter and decided, as she stood and took the offered hand, to let the commander make the first move. "Commander. Thank you for coming down here."

"That would be up, ma'am," the man answered crisply. "I did as I was ordered to do."

Oh boy. Dar resumed her seat. "Please, sit down." She waited for her guest to comply. "I understand you're going to be the Navy's liaison officer for this new project, and I wanted to have a word with you before we got started."

"Ma'am, I don't know what you've been told, but in my opinion, this project is a waste of both our times," Commander Albert stated flatly. "I'd just as soon it stopped right here, to save us all the hassle."

"Commander, that's not your decision to make," Dar replied mildly. "Nor is it mine, for that matter. The government, for its own reasons, has decided to contract us to do this, and if you want it stopped, you're going to have to appeal up your chain of command to do it."

"With all due respect, ma'am, we do not need a civilian efficiency expert coming in and telling us how to run the Navy."

"With all due respect, Commander, that's not what your government hired," Dar said. "I'm a systems analyst. I could give a crap how you run the Navy. What they asked me to do is analyze your systems and controls structures and recommend technological enhancements."

"Our systems work just fine." Albert's jaw twitched.

Dar sat back. "Then it'll be a very short project, won't it?" She felt almost a sense of amusement as she studied the sharp profile. "Listen, Commander, you're making three assumptions that are going to get you into trouble, so you might want to just reverse your course right now."

"Excuse me, ma'am?" he replied stiffly.

"One, you're assuming I don't know an obstructionist when I meet one. Two, you're assuming I need your cooperation to do this little job; and three, you're assuming I'm a stranger to the Navy." Dar stood up. "I'll meet you out at the base Friday morning. I think we've wasted enough of each other's time today."

Commander Albert stood and gave her a short nod. "Ma'am." He turned and walked to the door, opening it and slipping through without ever looking back at her.

Dar sat back down and shook her head. "Gerry, I'm going to get you for this." She pulled out her Palm Pilot and scribbled a few notes on it, adding her new contact's name. She looked up as her intercom buzzed again. "Yes?"

"Dar." Kerry's voice, though calm, held a distinct edge to it. "I think we need some high-level situational administration here."

Ah. My ass-kicking skills are in demand. "Be right there," she told Kerry. "Take five." She released the intercom and stood, circling her desk and heading for the door. "Definitely not a good day."

Kerry rested her weight on her elbows and cradled the mug in her hands, slowly sipping from it. Across the table, Clarice Keown, a strikingly attractive black woman, was arguing with Mitchell Grafberg, a member of the Midwest team that had been responsible for administering the account over which they were currently fighting.

God. Kerry counted the seconds. She hadn't seen this much finger-pointing since the last time someone had knocked over the water cooler and shorted out the Xerox machine. It wasn't that she didn't know what the problem was—she did, and in fact, all of them knew it. The account had been botched from day one, and the bandwidth designed for it was simply not enough. Adding to it would be at ILS's expense and would take far too much time, and no one wanted to be responsible for making that decision.

Well, actually, Kerry had already made it. The point was, no one wanted to be the reason she'd had to. She'd been a little surprised at Clarice, who was sharp, and funny, and whom she liked, because the regional director was the main roadblock. She flatly refused to accept that her team had goofed and was simply going around in circles with arguments, trying to justify the bill Dar was surely going to slap right onto her desk.

The outer door opened and closed, and the room was suddenly full of Dar Roberts, who swooped down on the table and circled it like a huge hunting hawk before settling neatly at Kerry's side. Her entrance stopped the argument in its tracks, and now everyone's attention was focused on Dar's sleek form.

Dar gave them all a level, serious glare before turning and cocking her head at Kerry. "Well?"

"There was a significant underbudgeting of resources for the account," Kerry stated. "That miscalculation allowed the bid to undercut the other offers, and it was awarded based on false data."

The bridge of Dar's nose wrinkled expressively.

"I've just had to order two additional T1 pipes and six new routers to make up the shortfall," Kerry went on. "Which we won't be able to bill back for. I'm looking at additional leveraging with other accounts in the area."

Dar grunted.

Kerry correctly interpreted this to mean she'd done the right thing, but the cost was giving Dar a hive.

"So you needed me here to do what?" Dar asked. "Seems like you've got a handle on the disaster without me sticking my nose in."

"There was a breakdown in processes," Kerry reminded her. "And, unfortunately, I can't fix the breakdown because we can't seem to come to an agreement over where, exactly, the gap is."

"Oh." Dar nodded, then reviewed the table. "I get it. No one wants the blame, is that it?"

Clarice leaned forward. "Dar, it's not anything to do with blame, okay? I still think it was a valid bid. The customer didn't tell us enough for us to know different."

"Bullshit," Dar snapped back. "The customer doesn't know his ass from a hole in the wall—that's why they hired us. It's our job to make sure we know what their business is, Clarice, and if we don't know enough to ask the right questions, then we end up in situations like this." She slammed her hand on the table, and everyone jumped.

Except Kerry. She'd felt the shift in the body next to her, and figured it would either be a table slap or a jump to the feet. Since Dar's thigh didn't move, she chose the slap and was expecting it.

"Kerry's going to save your ass, and I agree with her decision, but somewhere down the line, she's got to stand up and explain why Ops's budget is in a deficit because we had to take on the expense of your screw-up," Dar went on. "So you'd better figure out where your hole is and close it, or I will."

Everyone was quiet for a minute. Clarice finally exhaled. "All right. We'll take care of it."

"Good. Because if it happens again, I'm not going to worry about whose fault it was, I'll just fire all of you," Dar snapped back, her voice low and electric, then building to an impressive volume that almost made Kerry wince. "Is that clearly understood?"

In the silence that followed, Kerry could clearly hear the air conditioner cycling on and off.

Clarice broke the stillness. "Understood."

"Good." Dar's manner shifted abruptly to calm cordiality. "There's a Midwest regional sales meeting going on down on ten. You might want to stop in there. I know José wanted to talk to you." She cleared her throat, then absently picked up Kerry's cup and took a sip of her tea.

Kerry was careful not to react. She kept a bland, interested look on her face and studied her pen. "I think we might even be able to push up the due date on those extra T1s. The local up there owes me a favor."

"Good," Dar said again, putting the cup down and standing up. "Ladies and gentlemen." She gave them a nod and strode out, leaving a Dar-sized awkwardness behind her.

"All right. Now that we've got that cleared up," Kerry pushed back from the table and stood, "anything else we need to clarify?" She was met with silence. "Great. I've got a conference call I'm due on in ten minutes. I'll keep you advised on the status of those circuits." She gathered up her papers and tucked them under an arm, then picked up her cup and made her way to the door, pushing her way through it and letting it close behind her.

Dar heard the steps catching up to her in the hallway, and she debated making a sharp right turn into the restroom. Then Clarice called her name and she regretfully abandoned the thought and stopped, turning and giving the black woman an inquiring look.

"Got a few minutes?"

Patience, Dar. Take a deep breath and imagine Kerry teaching you to crochet. "Sure," Dar replied, then fell silent, putting the burden of the conversation back on Clarice.

"Somewhere more private than the central lobby?" There was a note of nervous amusement in Clarice's voice. "Your office, maybe?"

"C'mon." Dar turned and led the way along the hall, pulling the door to her outer office open and holding it as Clarice passed in front of her. María looked up as they entered, and her gaze slipped past Clarice's shoulder and met Dar's in wry amusement. The poor secretary had found herself in a most awkward position, having had to field the love-struck woman's inquires into Dar's personal tastes and preferences, and had retreated into a bland, Cuban incomprehension on many occasions.

"That is how I knew about you and Kerrisita," María had told her once. "I did not have to tell her anything, Dar. When I saw her first time fixing you the coffee, the right way? I knew."

Dar considered that as she followed Clarice into her inner office, realizing that should have signaled to her the difference between Kerry and all her former interests. Kerry alone hadn't fenced around with her, done the dance, played the game. She'd walked in and simply claimed Dar, lock, stock and barrel, as though she'd had some inalienable right to do so.

Hmm. Dar set her interesting revelation aside as she sat down behind her desk and crossed her arms on it. "All right, what can I do for you?"

"So, how are you, Dar?" Clarice asked, seating herself cautiously.

"Never been better," Dar replied with complete honestly. "What do you want?"

"Haven't changed, huh? Straight to the point." Clarice cleared her throat. "Well, you remember my mom?"

"Mm." Dar nodded. Clarice's mother lived in Coral Gables, and she'd always thought the two were close.

"She's getting on, and the doctor doesn't want her living alone anymore. She wants me to come back here and live with her. So I was wondering if there was anything in the company available for me." She paused. "Here."

Oh. Something simple for a change. Dar sat back and propped a knee up against the edge of her desk, looking up at the ceiling as she brought to mind a list of openings in operations in the area. Her peripheral vision told her Clarice was watching her with a look that mixed curiosity and something else. "There might be one or two things, but I'll have to check with Kerry," Dar replied. "It's her ballpark, unless you want to change divisions. When are you looking at making the move?"

Clarice exhaled, obviously relieved. "As soon as I can. Listen, I'm sorry about this whole mess-up, Dar." She got the words out in a rush. "Paul's new, and he's young, but he really did sound like he knew what he was doing, and I—"

"Don't apologize to me," Dar cut her off. "Do yourself a favor and don't cover up for him. Everyone takes the heat for their own mistakes, remember?"

Clarice pursed her lips and exhaled. "You sure haven't changed much at all."

That got an amused quirk of Dar's lips. "You expected me to? Hope you weren't holding your breath," she remarked. "There's a reason everyone would rather deal with Kerry."

A shift. "Yeah, she's pretty sharp," Clarice said. "Where'd she come from?"

Dar sensed a ruffle in the waters. "She was part of an account we consolidated down here," she said. "I'll send her a note, tell her you're looking to relocate."

"Thanks." Clarice stood up. "I'll go talk to her myself. I just wanted to make sure you didn't have a problem with it. Maybe she'll have a minute now."

"I'm sure she'll find time," Dar answered.

"Hmm...She's really efficient, that's true," Clarice said. "I can see I have a lot to learn from her." She turned and walked out, closing the door behind her with a distinct snick.

Dar gazed plaintively at her ceiling. She was reaching over to hit her intercom button when her inner door cracked itself open and a blond head poked inside. "Ah. I was just about to call you."

Kerry entered and closed the door behind her, running the fingers of her right hand through her hair as she made her way across the office. "We got the overseas links to the UK straightened out," she announced. "And they were able to get permission for that new link station in India."

"Good." Dar laced her fingers together behind her head and leaned back. "Clarice was on her way to see you. She wants to move back here." Dar considered. "And I think she's heard about us."

"Sweetie, you drinking my tea in a meeting doesn't really help hide that." Kerry perched on the edge of Dar's desk and let her hands rest on her knee. "Not that you weren't welcome to it."

"Damn." Dar exhaled. "I did do that, didn't I? Oh well." She laughed softly. "Have you had lunch yet? Want to go downstairs?"

"Is that an invitation from my boss?" Kerry answered playfully. "No, I haven't; and I'd love to, since all I've had so far today is a handful of chocolate kisses."

"Good." Dar stood up. "I'll be down at the base Friday and all next week, eating God only knows what." She slipped on her jacket and straightened it, smoothing the line of the crisply tailored skirt in the same motion. "C'mon. I think they have pot roast today."

"Is that going to be a little weird for you?" Kerry asked, as they walked out the door and through the outer office. María was already at lunch, and the room was, for once, quiet. "Going back there, I mean, not the pot roast."

"A little," Dar admitted. "I've got a lot of memories invested in that place, both good and bad."

Kerry waited until they were on the elevator before she spoke again. "Can I come down there with you one of the days, just to see it? I'm curious."

"Hgrm." Dar held the door open for her. "It wasn't exactly the nicest place in the world to grow up, Ker. Mostly sand, palmetto scrub, and mosquitoes."

They strolled across the lobby, passing several people headed in the same direction who called out greetings. "Is that a no, then?" Kerry asked. "I mean, if you'd rather I didn't, that's okay, Dar. I think you know enough of how I feel about your upbringing to know you've got nothing to be embarrassed about."

The noise in the lunchroom stalled further conversation, and they got in line after exchanging hellos with Mark and Duks, who had snuck in just ahead of them. Dar took the opportunity to capture a chocolate mousse hiding behind two pieces of fruitcake and listen to the chatter. She'd been frequenting the lunchroom more often the last few months—not as regularly as every day, but at least once a week, so her presence no longer drew outright stares and whispers.

She still found it easy to imagine the covert attention, though. But she'd been dealing with that since her first overall promotion to regional manager, and by now, it was more an amusing way to pass the minutes than anything else. Or play with their minds. Dar reached out an idle hand and arranged a lock of Kerry's blond hair, getting a raised eyebrow from her lover. She tweaked the hair, and Kerry turned her head, a smile pulling at the corners of her mouth. "I'd love you to come on down to the base with me."

"Next Friday good?" Kerry asked, the corners of her eyes crinkling in amusement. "I've got stuff scheduled the rest of the week."

"Fine." Dar turned her attention to the cafeteria server. "Pot roast, potatoes, gravy on the side." She watched the lady assemble the plate, looking up inquiringly with her spoon over the two choices of vegetables. Dar merely raised an eyebrow at her and received her plate, naked of green invaders. "Thank you." She followed Kerry over to the large round table where Duks, Mark, Mariana, and several others were already seated, discussing a movie that had just opened the previous week.

"You seen it, DR?" Mark asked as they sat down. "Your kinda flick, I thought."

"Why? Did it exceed the severed body part quotient of *Aliens?*" Kerry asked, making everyone chuckle. "During dinner the other night, we were watching *Braveheart* on disc, and boy was I glad we weren't having steak."

"Hey!" Dar objected. "It was your pick, remember? Not mine. I wanted to watch *The Ancient Secrets of Rome*, but no..."

Another laugh went around the table, easy and unforced. Dar dipped her roast into her gravy contentedly, enjoying the banter as Duks and Kerry started arguing over the historical accuracy of the picture. She listened to Kerry's laugh and watched the smiles go around the table, and it occurred to her quite suddenly that for once she was damned happy with her life.

She paused in mid-bite, just to savor the knowledge. Then she washed her mouthful down with a sip of milk and pretended she didn't see Kerry stealing a spoonful of her mousse. "Hey."

Everyone turned to look at her.

"You all interested in going out on the water next weekend? We can do a cookout on the beach, that kinda thing," Dar said. She'd caught Kerry flat-footed by surprise, she knew, and the way Kerry's expression read, she half expected her lover to reach over and check her for fever.

Mark accepted instantly. "Sure. Sounds great."

"Yes, I agree," Mariana recovered. "Thanks, Dar. What a great idea."

"Absolutely." Duks nodded solemnly. "I will bring the beer."

Dar sucked on her milk, enjoying the sensation she'd caused. It was the first time, she acknowledged, that she'd instigated a party, usually leaving Kerry to do the social arrangements for them. *Well*, she decided, *it was about damn time.*

Yeah.

The cool breeze blew across the patio, ruffling the soft cotton of Dar's pants leg as she pushed against the stone wall with one bare foot, rocking them gently in the net swing chair they'd recently installed. It was just big enough for two people, providing those two people really liked each other, and a comfortable way to sit and watch the moonlight travel across the water. Kerry was curled up in her arms, and they both held glasses of sweet white wine for sipping.

"You surprised me today," Kerry murmured.

"With the party?"

"Mm."

Dar had her eyes closed. "Good surprise or bad surprise?"

"That's not a serious question, is it?" Kerry asked. "Of course it was a great surprise, and a great idea, by the way."

"Good." Dar rested her cheek against Kerry's head. "I sort of figured anything that involved water, boats, sun, food, and beer would be okay with you." She felt Kerry's body shake as she laughed. "I'm just warning you, if you and Mark decide to have a belching competition again, I'm gonna tape it, convert it to an mpeg, and broadcast it companywide on Monday."

Kerry laughed harder, almost spilling her wine. "You wouldn't."

Dar chuckled. "You wanna stake your dignity on that?" She put her glass down on the table next to them and put both her arms around Kerry. "Feeling any better, by the way?"

Kerry let her chuckles wind down into a sigh. "Yeah, thanks for asking." She put her now empty glass down next to Dar's and folded her hands over her lover's. She caught a hint of smoke in the air from the beach club, mixed with the salt tang of the sea, and decided life just couldn't get too much better than this. "Clarice made an appointment to come see me after Thanksgiving."

"Mm."

"She kept making pointed comments, I kept ignoring them." Kerry yawned a bit. "I think I found her something in product development, though."

"If she gets too obnoxious, let me know," Dar rumbled. "I don't want her taking potshots at you."

Kerry tilted her head to observe the angular profile above her. "I can handle her, Dar. It's not her fault she picked my personal property to get a crush on."

Both of Dar's eyebrows lifted. "Hmm. Maybe we'd better go back to that leather place and get me a leash and collar," she suggested with a smile. "I could get your name on it in rhinestones. What do you think?"

"I dare you." Kerry regretted the words the instant they came out of her mouth. "Oh, no, wait—forget I said that, Dar. Just erase it from your... Don't you look at me like that!" Kerry reached up and tweaked Dar's nose. "Stop it! Just don't you even think about it."

Dar pouted. "You don't think I'd look good as a love slave?"

Kerry's nostrils flared. "Ooh." She blinked. "Now there's an image."

They both started laughing. "Dar, you're a lot of things, but submissive isn't one of them," Kerry told her fondly. "Putting a collar on you would be like tying a bow on the tail of a tiger." She grinned. "Pretty, but definitely not functional."

Dar gave her a little squeeze. "I'd do it for you," she said. "Because you do own me, body and soul. You know that, right?"

"I do?" Kerry murmured.

Dar nodded.

"What an incredible gift that is." The words were a mere whisper. "Especially since I think you know I feel the same way." Kerry ran a delicate fingertip over Dar's lips. "I'll take good care of you, Dar. I promise."

A faint smile appeared. "I know." Dar captured the finger with her lips, then kissed the tip of it. "You know what I realized today?"

"What?"

"What a joy life can be," Dar answered softly. "And how lucky I am."

Kerry couldn't answer. She felt the tears well up and she

pressed her face into Dar's shirt, unable to articulate an emotion so powerful it almost stopped her breathing. *This feeling,* her mind whispered to her, *this is what love is.* It was like a reassuring hand stroking her head. *This gift comes straight from God, and no words of any man can tell me it doesn't.*

It was like being washed clean.

Kerry just started crying openly, hugging the supportive, but very bewildered Dar.

Maybe she'd find words later to explain.

"Need some help getting that bird out of the oven, Ker?" Dar called into the kitchen, giving the guests seated in their living room a wry grin. "It's bigger than she is."

"It is *not!*" Kerry yelled back, having heard her.

Everyone chuckled. Dar was in the single leather chair with her father and mother on the couch across from her and Colleen and Ray on the loveseat.

"Ah'll go give it a heave," Dar's father announced, getting up and stretching out his six-foot-four-inch frame. The ex-SEAL ambled around the end of the couch and headed for the kitchen.

"Andy, no nibbling," Cecilia Roberts called after him. The diminutive silver-blond woman gave the rest of the guests a wry look. "Not that it'll help. I used to lose halves of whole meat-loaves that way."

Dar chuckled.

"I thought that you were the vegetarian, Mrs. Roberts?" Ray asked.

"I am. That's why she's laughing." Ceci pointed to her daughter. "She'd take the other half and leave me with a bowl of peas."

Dar eased one denim-covered knee over the arm of the chair she was in, and cocked her head in agreement as another round of chuckles sounded.

"My da does the same," Colleen chuckled. The redheaded woman, Kerry's oldest friend in Florida, was from an Irish family with a very extended household. "I have to stop by there tonight, or I'll never be hearing the end of it." She turned to Dar. "How was your trip to the Big Apple, Dar?"

"Went all right," the tall, dark-haired woman said. She sniffed the air as the combined scent of turkey and cinnamon penetrated the living room. "New York's not my favorite town, but the stockholders were happy; and I got in and out fast."

"Kerry came back with you?" Ceci asked. "I thought she went out to Chicago."

Dar got up and stretched, the intriguing smells from the kitchen luring her over. "She ran into weather on the flight up...had some plane problems. They landed in Newark." Her head poked around the corner of the kitchen doorway. "Ready?"

Kerry looked up from spooning whipped sweet potatoes into a bowl. She had on a Dilbert apron, and she met Dar's eyes with a grin. "Why? Are you hungry?"

Pale blue orbs darted to Andrew Roberts, then back to Kerry's face. "Yes."

"Right nice-looking bird," he drawled. "Never saw one with slippers on before, though." He fingered the white frilly caps on the turkey's leg bones. The bird itself was done to a nice golden brown, and a mound of stuffing spilled out over its breastbone and tumbled down onto the plate. "Good job, kumquat."

"Yeah," Dar agreed, licking her lips. Chino poked her head between Dar's knees and investigated as well, wagging her tail hopefully.

Kerry regarded them fondly, a proud grin appearing on her face. For her first turkey, it sure had turned out better than she'd dreamed. "Okay, let's get it to the table, then. I'll bring this stuff." She indicated the side dishes.

Andrew took possession of the turkey tray, lifting its bulk with little effort and heading for the dining room. Dar sidled over and took a fingerful of sweet potatoes, sticking it into her mouth before relieving Kerry of the bowl. "Mmm."

"Know what?" Kerry sucked on the end of her spoon. "I am pretty darn impressed with myself here."

Dar leaned over and gave her partner a kiss on the lips. "I am totally not surprised."

Kerry leaned against her. "Thanks... At least I managed to be competent at one thing this week." Her lingering guilt resurfaced unexpectedly.

Dar straightened and gave her a stern look. "Ah ah ah. I told you. No second-guessing, Kerrison," she warned. "It worked out better this way, and we both know it." She gave Kerry another kiss, then headed for the dining room, tugging Kerry along after her by the apron strings. "After all, I got my sweet potatoes, didn't I?"

Yeah. Kerry surveyed the group oohing and aahing over her turkey. *Maybe it did all work out for the best after all.*

Chapter
Four

Dar woke just before the alarm went off and silenced it before it had a chance to ring. It was still dark outside, and by the scant starlight coming in the window, she could just barely make out Kerry's features, peaceful in sleep.

For a moment, Dar debated not waking her up. They'd meant to go to bed early, since she knew she had to leave for the base first thing, but somehow they'd ended up watching a Croc Hunter special, and before she knew it, two a.m. was staring them in the face.

Whoops. Dar rubbed her eyes, wishing she could close them and go back to sleep.

The movement, however, woke Kerry, and she gazed up at her with half-opened eyes, a smile sketching its way across her face. "Can I come with you?" she said.

Dar spoke at the same time. "You want to come with me today?"

They both stopped and blinked.

"Wow," Kerry remarked mildly. "The invisible psychic fiber hub's up and passing packets, huh?"

A laugh escaped from Dar. "I guess." She rolled over onto her back and stretched. "I was just thinking I'd like to have an outside opinion while I go through there. I know I'm biased." Was that just an excuse to have Kerry along, though? Dar examined the thought carefully and decided it could go either way, but the fact that she wasn't impartial was incontrovertible.

Kerry reviewed her schedule. "Well, I've got a marketing meeting I can reschedule, two conference calls that are just follow-up, and some small odds and ends. Yeah, I can clear my day," she decided. "And, come to think of it, since you're going to be allocating my resources right and left to Uncle Sam, I think I'd better be there to see how much trouble you're going to get me into."

Dar turned her head and regarded the dimly visible profile in amusement, remembering the agony Kerry had gone through not so very long ago and wondering if she was qualified to do the job Dar was asking her to. Since her promotion, Kerry had blossomed into the position, exceeding even Dar's admittedly biased but high expectations for her. She felt briefly like a mother bird watching its offspring soar proudly. "You don't seriously think I'd overextend you, do you?"

A soft chuckle came out of the darkness. "No. C'mon, Dar. You know our systems and infrastructure better than anyone else, including me. I was just kidding."

"Mm. You're pretty close," Dar told her. "I'd say, if I had to judge both of us, you're doing a better job than I was as VP."

There was absolute dead silence from the other side of the waterbed for several long heartbeats. "I think my brain just exploded," Kerry finally spluttered.

"Good thing this is a waterbed, then." Dar rolled up out of it and stood. "C'mon. I know I need the run this morning or I'm not going to be awake enough to drive south."

"Start the coffee. I'll just suck up my neurons and be right with you."

"You've got it," Dar agreed before heading out of the bedroom and through the living room with Chino frisking at her heels. She opened the back door for the dog, then started the coffee running. By the time she turned around, a sleepy Kerry was trudging into the kitchen. "That was quick...use the vacuum?"

"Sucked them up with a straw." Kerry pulled open the refrigerator and removed a jug full of juice, sloshing it around a few times before she popped the top open and poured herself a large glass full. "Can we stop talking about brains while I drink this? It's got pulp in it."

Dar slid both arms around her and rested her cheek against Kerry's head. "Sure." She listened to the soft, distinct sounds of swallowing as their bodies touched through two thin layers of cotton and swore she could feel the cold juice as it traveled into Kerry's stomach, under where her hands were resting. She rubbed the spot, and Kerry gurgled as a chuckle interfered with her drinking. "Ah ah ah...don't you dare bring that in here."

Kerry glanced over to see Chino in the doorway, a big stick in her mouth and a guilty expression on her face. "Honey, where's your toy? Where's Hippo? Play with that instead, okay?"

Chino dropped her find immediately and dashed off, to return with a stuffed fleecy animal in the vague shape of a hippopotamus. "Growf." She dropped it expectantly at Kerry's feet.

"Oh. So now I guess you expect me to play with you?" Kerry put the glass on the counter and her hands on her hips. "How about you running with me and mommy Dar, hmm? That should tire you out." She reached behind her and patted Dar's thigh. "I'll get your gear, if you fix the coffee."

Dar released her. "Go for it." She nudged Kerry toward the door and busied herself in pouring.

As luck would have it, they hit rain halfway to the base. "Figures." Dar drummed the fingers of her right hand on the padded console next to her. "Hope you like mud."

Kerry looked up from her laptop, which she'd been busy working on. "Mud?" She regarded her pristine, nicely starched white shirt. "You did tell me not to wear this, didn't you?" Her eyes studied the wash of heavy rain hitting the windshield, then a smile appeared. "But you know, this reminds me of the first time I rode in your car."

Dar's lips twisted into a wry smile. "I'm sure that's not one of your fondest memories."

"Au contraire," Kerry objected. "It most certainly is, Dar. That was the start of everything; that was one of the biggest turning points in my life. You know that."

It was quiet except for the rattle of Kerry's keyboard for a little while, as Dar indulged herself in memories as she drove. "You know what I remember the most from that night?" she commented, after about fifteen minutes.

"Huh?" Kerry looked at her. "Oh, no. What?"

"Getting home, sitting down on the couch, and not being able to stop thinking about you."

Kerry tilted her head back and smiled. "Oh yeah." She sighed. "If you'll remember, I sent you an e-mail at one a.m. I hate to tell you, because I know you'll laugh, but I slept in your sweatshirt that night," she admitted.

Dar did, in fact, laugh. "Did you?"

"Yeah. I really liked the way it smelled." Kerry leaned over and sniffed Dar's shoulder, emitting a low hum of approval. "I'm not sure I remember what BS I fed myself to explain that." She paused. "Actually, I don't think I even bothered trying."

"I woke up the next morning, hired you, then conked out with the laptop sitting on my chest," Dar recalled. "I got your mail asking about the clothing and answered it before I was actually awake."

"Ah. That explains the shopping," Kerry teased. "You have no idea how nervous I was waiting for you in the mall."

"I was pretty rattled, too," her lover murmured, steering carefully around a large puddle. "I'm not exactly a social butterfly."

Kerry nodded. "I know. You were fidgeting during dinner." She remembered watching Dar's long fingers play restlessly with the table tents. "But I felt really comfortable being with you," she added. "Especially after you shared your dessert with me."

Dar laughed. "Oh, so that was the big icebreaker, huh? I should have known."

Kerry shook a finger at her. "Now that I know you the way I do, I know you sharing a plate with someone is a big deal, Dar, not to mention you actually gave me a bite of your dinner."

"Mm." Dar's face took on a curious expression. "I should have realized right then." She slowed the car. "Okay, hang on. Here we go."

Kerry closed her laptop and tucked it into her briefcase as they turned into the base, the road blocked by gates and an impressive set of armed guards. "Dar, that man has no neck."

"Don't start me on inter-service jokes, okay?" Dar muttered as she pulled the Lexus forward. "Damn place hasn't changed much." She waited for the car ahead of her to be admitted, then drove on.

"I don't think the military is known for being avant-garde, hon." Kerry watched with interest as Dar rolled down the window and slipped on her attitude like a pair of sunglasses.

"I have an appointment with Commander Albert," Dar stated in a crisp, no-nonsense tone as she handed over her identification badge.

The guard studied the badge, then studied Dar as though comparing the picture. Then he consulted a plastic-covered clipboard. His eyes lifted, and he peered into the Lexus. "Commander Albert is expecting one person, ma'am."

"Lucky him, he gets two," Dar replied. "This is my associate, Kerrison Stuart." She offered him Kerry's badge, which the blond woman had helpfully passed over.

"I don't have clearance for her, ma'am," the guard said.

By sheer will, Dar kept herself from smirking. "Then I guess we'll be blocking your gate until you get it or turning around and going back to Miami and billing you for our time," she said. "What's your name again? Williams, is it?"

"Ma'am, this is a secure base, and we don't give people clearance just because they show up at the gate," the guard replied stiffly. "I think you need to understand."

"Son," Dar leaned on the doorframe, "I used to eat breakfast every day with someone a lot scarier than you, so put your attitude up in your side pocket and either let me in or tell me you won't, and I'll do what I need to do."

The man stared at her for a moment, then retreated into his hut. Dar leaned back and crossed her arms, shaking her head slightly. "Some things just really never change," she sighed.

"I don't think I can quite picture you doing this, Dar," Kerry observed. "Though you'd look really cute in those uniforms." She fell silent as the guard returned, a look on his face that made her think he'd been sucking key limes in the interim.

"These are your passes, ma'am." He handed their identification cards back to Dar, along with two clip-on badges. "Wear them at all times when you're on the base."

"All right." Dar took one, and gave Kerry hers. "Thanks."

"Commander Albert is in the Huntingdon building. Drive straight through the gates here, turn left, turn right, turn left, second stop on the right." He opened the gate, and ducked his head in a semirespectful salute.

Dar finished putting her badge on. "That's the long way," she gave him a grim smile, "but thanks."

Kerry waved at the guard. "*Do svidaniya,*" she told him cheerfully as Dar drove past. Then she settled back into her seat and looked around curiously as they made their way along a rather weather-beaten road. It was so different than she'd expected, Kerry mused, taking in the long rows of sturdy, plain concrete buildings. Everything was neatly kept, and there were columns of men and women doing various military type things— like running and chanting, drilling in a nearby field—and some were just walking about.

To one side, through a stretch of tall trees, she spotted a large cluster of small houses. She glanced at Dar and saw her lover's eyes on them as well, a curious mix of regret and nostalgia on her face. "Was that home?"

"Yeah." Dar gave her head a little shake and returned her attention to the road. "Wasn't much. I think my room was the size of the back of this car." She fell silent for a beat. "I spent my first...five, six years here, I guess; then we moved up to Virginia. Year or two after that to North Carolina, two years later to Baton Rouge, then we came back here for a while."

"Sort of tough on you, moving to different schools all the time, hmm?" Kerry half turned in her seat, watching Dar's profile. "Making new friends and all."

Dar laughed shortly. "That was the least of my worries." She

turned down a side street. "I never bothered much with friends."
She parked the Lexus and turned her head. "You ready for this?"

"Me?" Kerry allowed an easy laugh to escape. "Dar, you forget how I grew up. It would take more than a bunch of hunky sailors and Marines to spook me." She put a hand on Dar's arm.
"Thanks for asking me to come along, though. I'm glad I'm here."

Dar smiled. "Me, too." She gathered up her briefcase and
opened the door. "C'mon. Let's go see what trouble we can get
into."

Kerry followed her as they walked along the sidewalk and
turned in to go up a short flight of steps to a guarded doorway.
She tried again to imagine Dar as one of these stern, earnest, professional warriors.

Ow. It made her brain hurt. She gave the guard a smile and
passed through the portal to another world.

Dar's nose twitched as she walked along the hallway, memories gently buffeting her from all sides. The air was thick with
familiar scents: wool and brass and wood polish, and floor wax
she knew came in gray five-gallon cans. The merest hint of gun oil
trickled through, tickling her senses and bringing a faint smile to
her face.

It was quiet as they passed closed doorways, the faint clatter
of honest-to-goodness typewriters leaking through but not much
more. Kerry gave her a look. "Multipart forms," Dar murmured.
"Eight layers at least, sometimes ten."

"Ew." Kerry winced. "They ever consider donating part of the
government's operating budget to saving the rainforests?"

"Mm." Dar led the way up a flight of double stairs that swept
up to a landing, with a door guarded by an armed Marine. "I tried
to convince them to go thermal, but they held onto those Selec-
trics like they were worth actual money and wouldn't give them
up." She gave the Marine a brisk nod and turned past him into a
smaller, closer hallway with doors on either side.

"Dar?" Kerry watched her bemusedly. "When was the last
time you were here?"

Dar thought about it. "Jesus...has it been ten years?" She
shook her head and took a left, then put a hand on the first right-
hand door and pulled it open. "I can't believe it."

Kerry glanced at the doorplate, which said "Computer Operations—Do Not Enter."

"You're telling me they haven't moved anything in ten years?"

Dar looked at the plate, then at her. "Ten years? Kerry, there are some government offices that haven't changed in over two hundred. C'mon." She followed her lover into a suite of offices that had a darker shade of carpet and colder air.

Now it was Kerry's turn to twitch her nose. "That's not mimeograph fluid I smell, is it?"

Dar chuckled, walking past her toward an office with a thick wooden doorframe and a scarred wooden door.

Perched outside it was a small desk, occupied by a dour-looking woman with curly dark hair and an attitude three times larger than she was. She intercepted them as they walked forward. "Ms. Roberts?"

Dar regarded her soberly. "Yes."

"Commander Albert is in a meeting. He asked me to fill in for him," the woman stated flatly. "My name is Perkins, and I'm the data center manager." She stood up. "We have a full schedule, so if you'd like to give me a list of what you want, I'll see what I can do."

Dar flicked her eyes over the much shorter woman, then simply walked past her, heading down a small corridor toward a set of double doors.

"Ma'am?" The data center manager bolted after her. "Ma'am, that area's off limits."

Dar just kept walking, stiffarming the doors open and letting them close behind her, almost slapping her pursuer in the face. Kerry sighed and followed, catching one door as their naval guide blasted through them. Inside was a large room filled with mainframes, some of which, she realized, were perilously close to being an older vintage than she was.

"Ms. Roberts, I need to ask you to leave, or I'll have to call the guard," the data center manager stated fiercely.

"Go ahead." Dar turned abruptly and faced her, showing her edgier side. "You call the guard, I call the Pentagon." She took out her cell phone and opened it. "Because frankly, Lieutenant, I've had about enough BS for one morning, and I just got here."

"This is a secure area," Perkins shot back. "You are a civilian, and this is off limits; I don't care how many generals you know." Pause. "Ma'am."

"Look." Kerry eased between them. "Lieutenant Perkins, I know this is seriously messing up your day." She smiled kindly at her. "And I know that Commander Albert probably told you to be as big a pain the ass to us as possible, but that's okay, because Dar and I are used to that."

The lieutenant eyed her warily.

"Most of the time when we're doing this, the people we're

working with are scared silly we're going to fire them, and sometimes we do," Kerry went on. "But you'd do us and yourself a favor if you'd just relax and let us do our jobs. Things will go much faster, and we'll be out of your hair before you know it."

The woman stiffened a little, bringing her head just slightly above Kerry's. "We have a job to do here. Everything works, and we don't need a couple of outsiders coming in and changing things," she replied. "I don't have time to explain these systems to you. So why don't you do yourselves a favor and just get the hell out of here."

"Because we're being paid to be here, just like you are," Kerry explained gently. "And frankly, Lieutenant, you don't have to explain anything to us. Between Ms. Roberts and myself, we've got enough certifications to plaster every square inch of the walls in here, so why don't you just go over there and sit down and stay out of our way."

The three junior operators in the room had become silent, radar-eared statues, staring at their screens and watching the reflections of the three women behind them.

Dar put her briefcase down and unzipped it. "If we're done with the first round of jousting, I'm gonna get the analyzer up and connected and start running first- and second-level tests." She pulled out a coil of network cable and booted up her laptop. "If you'd like to do something other than stand there gaping, Lieutenant, you can get me a list of subsystems and running job streams."

Without a word, the woman turned and walked out, letting the doors swish shut behind her with a vindictive sound.

"I'll take that as a no." Dar continued her task. She looked around and caught one of the console ops staring at her, a look of mixed awe and admiration on his face. "Would you like to run that for me?"

The sailor grinned at her wholeheartedly. "Yes, ma'am, I would."

Dar grinned back and winked at him. "Smart boy."

The other console operator turned in her seat and folded her arms over the back of it. "Who are you people?" She was a willowy thin woman with straight russet hair and an innocent face. Her voice was soft, and thickly Southern.

Kerry, who was closest to her, held out a hand. "Kerry Stuart, and that's my boss, Dar Roberts." She shook the red-haired woman's hand with a firm grip. "Our company's been asked to come in and see what we can do to make your lives easier."

"You just did," the third operator drawled softly. "Lieut's been on the warpath all week, driving us half crazy."

"Well, that's probably our fault," Kerry told him. "I know your leadership isn't too happy we're here, because they think we're going to find all kinds of things they're going to get blamed for. But that's not what our plan is."

"It's not?" the girl asked.

"Nope." Dar studied the results on her laptop screen. "The government's looking to spend some money here, we're gonna help them." Her brow creased.

"Why're they all freaking out, then?" the towheaded man closest to Dar asked.

The lines of data flashed before her eyes. "You know, that's a good question." Dar looked up at Kerry.

"People get comfortable with things, Dar. They don't like change," her lover reminded her. "Even if the change is good."

"Mm." Dar finished her capture and closed her laptop. "That's all I need here for now. Let's see if we can get into the command and control center." She gave the operators a half wave. "We'll be back."

Kerry heard the whispers and muffled laughs as they left, and she shook her head. She had a feeling this was going to be an uphill battle all the way.

And they were wearing roller blades.

Dar put her briefcase down on the scarred wooden conference table and sat, folding her hands together. Kerry took a seat to her right, and the two Navy officers settled opposite them. "We've finished our initial review," Dar said. "I've identified three main systems that need replacement of hardware, and I'm going to recommend installation of a new infrastructure to support that."

Albert and Perkins exchanged glances, but didn't comment. Kerry could almost read their minds, which were buzzing along the lines of 'not as bad as we thought.' "I'll have the proposal transmitted to the Pentagon by tomorrow," she told her boss. "And an estimated timeline for install."

"All right," Commander Albert said. "You can coordinate with Lieutenant Perkins for that."

Dar nodded. "That was the easy part."

Both officers stiffened. "You're not finished?" Albert hazarded.

"No." Dar met his eyes. "General Easton has forwarded us status and analysis reports on the existing processes you have in place here for training and implementation. He wants them reviewed."

Kerry thought the two of them were going to implode, right there at the table. She'd never seen someone turn that red that fast, and her eyes widened a little as the veins appeared on the side of the commander's temples. "It'll go faster if you just cooperate," she told them. "He's not saying you don't do a good job here, he just wants to see if there's a way to make things easier and better." She leaned forward. "Sometimes you need an outside pair of eyes to look at things—you get too close to the situation otherwise. Really."

"Lieutenant, Ms. Stuart, would you excuse us please." The commander bit off his words.

Kerry glanced at Dar, who cocked an eyebrow at her, then she stood and pushed her chair in. "I'll go find some coffee." She waited for the glowering lieutenant to join her, then walked out of the room, closing the door behind them. "Would you like to tell me where it is, or do I have to go ask the Marines?"

The woman was grimly silent for a beat, then her shoulders perceptibly relaxed and she shook her head. "Follow me."

As they strolled along the corridor, Kerry took the opportunity to study their erstwhile adversary more closely. They were about the same size, she realized, and more or less the same age. She'd also detected something familiar in the dark-haired woman's speech. "Where in the Midwest are you from, Lieutenant?"

Brown eyes flicked to her in wary attention. "Ann Arbor."

Kerry nodded. "You sounded local. I'm from Saugatuck." They stopped at a coffee station and busied themselves in silence for a moment as they poured cups. Kerry was aware she was being covertly watched, and it made her ears twitch. "Want to sit down for a minute while they finish yelling at each other?"

Without answering, the other woman led the way to a utilitarian table with two bench seats. She put her coffee down and straddled one, resting her elbows on the table and keeping her gaze firmly fixed on the beaten formica top.

Kerry took the seat opposite and composed her thoughts briefly. "We're not as bad as you think."

"Do you know how often we have to go through this?" Perkins lifted her head and glared. "Everyone thinks they know how to do our jobs, so they come waltzing in here, change things all around, and two months later we've got to go back to doing it the old way because it's the one that works."

Kerry's eyebrows lifted. "They send in consultants every two months?"

"No." The other woman sighed. "Every goddamned newly made admiral they put in charge of this place."

"Oh." Kerry took a sip of the coffee and held back a wince at the pungent strength of it. She was abruptly reminded of Andrew Roberts's affection for tar sludge, and now knew where he got it. "Well, we're not admirals."

"No, you're even more clueless about what we do," Perkins snapped.

"That can be a plus," Kerry answered mildly. "And as far as I'm concerned, yes, you're right, I'm clueless about the Navy. But I've got a good understanding of the government and how it works, because my father's a senator."

The lieutenant grunted, tensing muscular forearms as she lifted her cup.

"Dar, on the other hand, couldn't care less about the government, but she's got a good understanding of the Navy," Kerry told her, hiding a smile as the other woman's head jerked up in surprise. "She was born here, on this base."

One of Perkin's eyebrows lifted, very much like Dar's often did. "She's a Navy brat?"

"Yep," Kerry agreed. "She sure is. Her father just retired, as a matter of fact." *Should have told them that first*, her mind analyzed. *Might have made the day a lot more pleasant.* "So between the two of us, we're not that clueless."

"Commander Albert know that?" the lieutenant asked. "About her?"

"I don't think so, no. Not unless Dar mentioned it before, and I don't think she did," Kerry replied. "Why?"

For the first time, a smile appeared on the other woman's face. "Just wondered."

Dar went to the window and looked out, ignoring the man behind her who was yelling into his telephone. She let her eyes wander over the familiar confines of the inner courtyard, noting the new sheds and walkways that dotted the grassy area. A smile appeared on her face as she eyed a thick hedge, remembering times spent huddled inside the center of it in a tiny space she'd dug out for herself, hidden from adult eyes.

How many hours had she spent in there? In the leafy warmth, green filtered sunlight trickling through the leaves and spilling over the ragged pages of whatever book she'd been poring over that week. Reading had opened the world to her, a love she shared with her father, but a skill only reluctantly displayed to her peers on the base.

There were no points for being a bookworm in her childhood

world.

So she'd saved her books for that little private space, absorbing the words greedily, reading years ahead of her age from almost the very start.

The phone slammed down behind her, and she reluctantly left her memories behind and turned, leaning back against the windowsill. "Done?" Albert looked about as frustrated as anyone Dar had ever seen. His face was beet red, and there was a small tic jerking the side of his mouth upward in disconcerting rhythm. "Look, Commander—"

"No. You. Look," he got out from between gritted teeth. "I am not going to have some half-assed civilians coming in here and telling me how to run my operation." He slapped his desk. "The base commander's on his way here, and let me tell you, lady, he's not going to put up with it either."

Dar exhaled. "Commander, I think you're overreacting," she told him.

"No, ma'am, I am not," the naval officer shot back. "To have you come in here and evaluate our computers, well, I don't like it, but no doubt you know your business." He pointed at her. "But the Navy's my business, and madam, I don't need you telling me how to do it."

Dar sighed and shook her head. "This is a waste of time."

"That's what I've said all along," Albert responded. "That's what I told the base commander, and he agrees with me."

They heard heavy footsteps approaching, and then a low gruff voice that seemed more a growl than anything else. "That's the commander now." Albert looked relieved. "He'll get this straightened out."

Dar folded her arms and watched as the door swung open, admitting a very tall, extremely burly man with thick, grizzled silver hair and a full, well-trimmed beard.

"All right," the newcomer boomed as he closed the door behind him with a solid crack. "Let's just get this cleared up right—Son of a fucking bitch." His eyes had fallen on Dar, and he stopped in mid-motion.

Albert glanced between his commander and Dar. "Sir?"

Dar blinked as a surprised smile spread across her face. "Uncle Jeff."

The man covered the space between them with startling rapidity and engulfed Dar in a pair of very large arms, hugging her and lifting her completely off her feet. "Son of a bitch. Son of a bitch. I can't believe it." He gave her a squeeze, then released her and took her by the shoulders, studying her intently. "Tadpole, what

the hell are you doing here?" he rumbled, then glanced at the
dumbfounded Commander Albert. "Oh, hell... Don't tell me
you're the posse the Pentagon sicced on me?"

"'Fraid so." Dar caught her breath, her mind still spinning
with the shock of being reunited with a long-lost part of her past.
"I didn't know they'd put you in charge of this place."

"Lord God, yeah. Three months back," Jeff Ainsbright said.
"Look at you... Damned if you didn't grow up gorgeous!" He
cupped her cheek with an easy familiarity. "I can't believe it."

The door behind them opened, and Dar was aware of Kerry
and the lieutenant entering, her peripheral vision catching the
shift in body language as Kerry absorbed the stranger in the room
with his hands all over Dar. She gave her lover a reassuring smile
and caught her eye, then met the tall commander's gaze. "Feels
like it's been forever since I saw you. Wish I'd known you were in
charge here; we could have avoided a lot of yelling."

Jeff pulled her into a hug again. "Tadpole, if I'd known you
were behind this, I'd have just handed the keys off to you and gone
fishing."

Dar watched Kerry bite the inside of her lip to prevent a
smirk from appearing. "Well, that's not what I was hired for," she
told the tall man. "We're just here to give our best advice."

"Damn straight," the base commander agreed, putting his
hands on her shoulders. "Albert, you give this lady whatever she
wants, whenever she wants it, however she decides she needs it
sliced and diced, you got me?"

"S-sir?"

"What part of that was in something other than English?" Jeff
growled, turning his head to glare at the younger man. "Or are
you developing a hearing problem?"

"No, sir." Albert braced. "But I'd like to remind the commander of the discussion we had—"

"Forget it," the answer came back. "I've got a whole different
picture now. So you tell your staff to cooperate, or I'll have every
last one of you scrubbing the heads with a box of Navy issue
Kleenex, understand?"

"Yes, sir." Commander Albert got the words out from
between clenched teeth.

"Good." Jeff turned and slung a long arm around Dar's
shoulders. "C'mon, lemme give you the top brass tour. Well, hello
there, young lady." The commander found a slim blond woman
planted firmly in his path.

Dar cleared her throat gently. "This is my associate, Kerry
Stuart. Kerry, this is Jeff Ainsbright. He's an old friend of the fam-

ily."

Kerry stuck a hand out. "Sir, it's good to meet you."

"Same here, Ms. Stuart." Jeff cordially enveloped her hand in his much larger one and shook it. "Let me take you both to lunch. I think we've got meatloaf today. You still like meatloaf, Tadpole?" He gave Dar a grin. "C'mon."

"Sounds good to me," Dar agreed, allowing herself to be hauled through the door while guiding Kerry before her, leaving a glowering silence behind them.

Commander Albert waited until the footsteps had receded down the hall, then he looked at his data center manager. "Son of a bitch."

Lieutenant Perkins grunted. "This could be trouble."

"Yeah." The muscular blond man tapped a pencil on his desk. "Get me a report on Roberts. Find out who the fuck she is, will you? I never figured her for military."

"She's a brat." Perkins picked up a pad and scribbled on it. "She's from here. Shouldn't be too hard to figure out who she is. Her dad was Navy."

"Find out." Albert nodded. "Find out everything you can. This could fuck up the whole project."

"Big time," the woman agreed. "She ain't stupid. Neither is the other one, what's her name? Stuart."

"Hmm." Her boss pursed his lips. "See what you can get on her, too." He exhaled in consternation. "We could be in trouble. I need to call Scrooge."

"Give him my regards." Perkins took her pad and left, closing the office door behind her.

Kerry found herself seated at a comfortable, if Spartan table in the noisy cafeteria, listening to her partner and the commander catch up on old times. She cut neat squares of meatloaf and nibbled them, surprised at the agreeable taste. A rakish smile spread across Dar's face as the commander talked, and Kerry smiled too, charmed at the uncharacteristic, almost adolescent expression it gave her lover.

"So, what's old Gerry's beef, Dar?" Jeff asked around a mouthful of mashed potatoes. "He got a surplus he needs to spend somewhere?"

"Nah," Dar replied. "From what he told me, it's more a matter of the Joint Chiefs getting crap about making sure the military keeps ahead of the private sector in technology." She took a swallow from her glass of milk. "They told him to make sure it happened, he figured he'd hire me to do it and save himself some time and heartache."

"And me." Jeff grinned, poking his fork in her direction. "I was fixing to toss your civilian butt off my base, y'know, 'til I walked in that office and found out who it was that was putting a mine in old Albert's pants."

Dar sighed. "I should have just come to see you first." She gave Kerry a rueful look. "It would have saved both of us some time and half a bottle of aspirin."

They ate in silence for a few moments, then Jeff leaned forward, fiddling with his knife a bit. "How's your daddy doing?" he asked in a curiously gentle voice. "I tried to track him down after I heard they'd found him over there, but I never could put a finger on him."

"He's fine," Dar reassured him. "He and Mom are living on a boat nearby my place, if you can believe it."

"Aw." Jeff smiled. "He got back with your mamma? Damn, I am so glad to hear that, Dar. It about killed him to leave that last time with her so mad." He stopped awkwardly and glanced at Kerry. "Pardon me, Dar. I didn't mean to bring all that up here."

"It's okay." Dar's blue eyes twinkled gently. "Kerry knows my parents very well."

"That's right." Kerry spoke up for the first time. "We have their phone number if you'd like it. I bet D—Mr. Roberts would love to hear from you."

"I bet he'd kick your butt for calling him mister." The commander laughed. "I'd love it. Hey, Dar, listen, Chuckie's coming in this weekend. Why don't we all get together and have a night out? I know he'd love to see you, and me and Sue would give up a month's pay to see Andrew and Cec."

Ah. Dar's memory pricked her suddenly as she recalled Charles Ainsbright, Jeff's son who was her age and growing up was one of her closer friends. Tall, cute Chuckie, with his blond crew cut and snub nose, who had wanted nothing more than to captain a Navy ship. "He finally get his command?"

"You bet your ass." Jeff beamed. "Wait 'til I tell him you're here. He's gonna float home. He still talks about you."

Oh boy. "It'll be good to see him," Dar allowed. "I'll see what I can arrange for Friday, how's that? I think Mom and Dad'll be glad to come down."

"Great." Jeff placed his utensils precisely onto the plate he'd scraped clean. "Tadpole, you let me know if the pinheads down in ops give you any trouble, all right? I've got a staff meeting I have to go kick some asses at. You about done here for today?"

"I think so," Dar nodded. "I was just going to show Kerry around the place."

"Good deal." The commander gave Kerry a friendly nod, then walked past and clapped Dar on the shoulder. "See you later, Dar. Drive safe, y'hear?"

"Thanks, Uncle Jeff," Dar replied, turning her head to watch him make his way through the tables, threading through a forest of salutes and stiffening bodies as he headed out the door. Then she turned her head to see curious green eyes watching her. "Hmm. That was a surprise."

"Mm, yeah, I gathered." Kerry cupped her chin in one hand. "He seems nice, though."

Dar leaned back and exhaled, scratching her neck with one hand. "He is. And his wife's a sweetheart. They were pretty good friends of my folks. Dad and Jeff used to fish together at night."

"Uh-huh...and Chuckie?" Kerry teased, having noted the faint blush that colored Dar's face at the mention of the name. "Sounds like he liked you."

Dar's face scrunched up into a half-amused, half-embarrassed scowl. "Yeeeahh...he um..."

"Another crush?" Kerry laughed.

"Not exactly," her lover admitted. "My first boyfriend. He was my high school prom date."

Kerry's blond brows shot up in silent amazement.

"I was young and still pretty clueless." Dar folded her arms and sighed. "But we had a good time together," she added. "I know my folks'll be glad to see them."

Kerry sipped her ice tea thoughtfully. "He's pretty Republican, isn't he?"

Dar nodded, her lips twitching.

"Want me to find something else to do that night?" Kerry offered with quiet grace.

Dar gazed sightlessly at the center of the table for a long moment, her brow wrinkled slightly in thought. Then she drew in a breath and met Kerry's eyes. "No. I really don't."

"Fair enough." Kerry accepted the answer. "C'mon, as long as I'm here, I want to see this BX thing you mentioned and get some souvenirs," she changed the subject. "Maybe a cap, since I've got enough Navy sweatshirts to outfit the entire Florida Marlin baseball team."

"You got it." Dar stood, and they put their trays away, then left the cafeteria, aware of the curious eyes that followed them.

"Good morning, Ms. Kerry." Mayte looked up as Kerry entered her office, giving her boss a bright smile. "Did it go okay Friday?"

"Sort of," Kerry replied, pausing before Mayte's desk. "It started off pretty rocky, but it turns out the officer in charge of the base is an old friend of Dar's, so things smoothed out after lunch." Remarkably so, in fact. Dar had gotten all the data she needed or asked for, and they'd departed early, heading back up the long, lonely road home while the sun was still a decent angle in the sky.

That meant they'd had time for a nice long workout in the gym, a walk on the beach, and dinner at the club before Dar sat down to digest the information they'd gleaned. Kerry stretched her shoulders out a little, still tight from the climbing wall, and wished briefly she could repeat the day. "What's going on here this morning?"

"You have marketing sessions at nine and ten and the operations meeting at one," Mayte answered promptly. "Mrs. Anderson, from the new company where we are buying cable, is to be here at three."

Kerry exhaled. "Okay." She spared a moment of envy for Dar, who had ambled out early dressed in jeans and hiking boots, then tucked her laptop case under her arm and headed for her desk. "Can you print me the meeting minutes for this afternoon and remind me what we're fighting with marketing about this week?"

"Of course." Mayte's voice floated after her. "Would you like some *cafecita?* I was just about to get some."

"Yes," Kerry called back. "I'd kill for a large *café con leche.* Thanks."

It was quiet then, for a bit, and she settled down in her large leather chair, its cool surface warming against her legs as she nudged her computer on and investigated the inbox on her desk. "What have we here?" she mused, pulling over a folder and flipping it open. "Ah." Requisitions for new computers for the accounting department. After a moment's study, she nodded and picked up her pen, checking the totals carefully and signing off on the papers.

Duks didn't ask for new hardware often. She'd talked to him last month about the depreciation on the systems they'd last bought for his department, and he showed a studied reluctance to changing what he viewed as perfectly acceptable workplace tools. Kerry had disagreed, considering 386 DX systems that still ran Windows 3.11 to be something along the lines of what she'd use as a door stop.

But Duks had said no.

So, Kerry had reviewed the accounting software they were using and called the vendor, discovering a new, upgraded version with lots of nifty new features and reports they just couldn't live without. She'd told Duks, and he'd agreed. "Great," she'd said. "Now you can put in your order for new systems, because this software only runs on a Pentium III."

"Heh." Kerry put the folder into her outbox. "Accountants...fastest way to their hearts is through their report writers." She turned and opened her mail program, watching as the screen filled quickly with black lines of new messages, a good percentage with red exclamation points next to them. She sighed and propped her chin up on her fist, waiting for the download to end.

Lieutenant Perkins tucked a folder under one arm and knocked lightly on the door. She paused to listen for a reply, then opened the door and slipped inside. She crossed the wooden floor quickly and put the folder down on her boss's desk, her eyes meeting his as he sat behind it. "I found her."

Albert raised an eyebrow. "And?"

"Not good." The lieutenant shook her head. "Take a look, sir." She waited for Albert to open the folder. "Her actual name is Paladar Roberts. Her father was in for twenty years; he just retired a few months ago. She was born here, spent fifteen years on and off on the base. Left after she graduated from UM." She paused. "BS in Computer Science, tops in her class. Been with ILS ever since."

"Mmph." Albert studied the contents of the folders, flipping through transcripts and documentation. "Wonder why she never...Oh. Did you see these ASVAB scores?"

"Yeah. Did you see what program she was qualifying for?"

His eyes flicked over the papers. "Aha. Wanted to follow in Daddy's footsteps, but he was a SEAL. I get it. She's probably got a grudge the size of a flat top." He chuckled dryly. "She seems the type."

"She passed the physical," Perkins commented.

"Mm." Her commander prowled through the papers, then selected a black-and-white photo, examining it curiously. An adolescent Dar Roberts stared dourly back at him, dark hair half obscuring the pale eyes, her lean body encased in a tight sleeveless black shirt and well-used fatigue pants. "Scary." He flipped the picture over to her.

Perkins picked it up and studied it. "Very." She tossed it back. "What are we going to do about her?"

The commander sorted through the papers. "Can we keep her out of the inside systems?"

A shake of her head. "Probably not. Based on the questions I was getting, I'm going to guess she actually knows her way around a programming language. I could try to throw a pile of code at her, but I don't know how long that would hold her up."

"Give it a try." Commander Albert sighed. "I'll see what else I can do. Get everything you can and stick it behind the number six firewall. We need to find something to distract her." He closed the folder and pushed it back across the desk. "The timing just sucks."

"You told Scrooge you had it under control," Perkins reminded him in a worried tone.

"That was before I found out she grew up with Dudley Do-Right's kid," he snapped back. "I didn't figure it'd be a problem getting her thrown out of here. Now we have to find another way." He sighed. "What about the other one?"

"We got lucky there." The lieutenant smiled. "She's Roger Stuart's daughter."

Their eyes met. "No shit?" The commander's eyebrows lifted.

"No shit, no, sir," Perkins said. "I thought you'd be glad to hear that."

Albert leaned back in his chair, and laced his fingers behind his head. "I guess we don't need to worry about her, then. I don't think she's coming back here anyway." He exhaled. "But that might be the leverage I need... I'll have to call Scrooge. He'll know if we can use it."

She was early. The guard let her in without comment this time, and Dar drove slowly through the base, allowing her memories to surface without interruption this time. She parked at the far end of the lot and got out, locking the doors to the Lexus with a negligent flick, then turned around and leaned against the side of the car, just letting her gaze travel across the scene.

Damn. It looked different, but in some ways, the same. The buildings had been altered, new construction changing the outlines subtly, and everything had fresh coats of paint on it. But as she stood there and looked, older images floated before her eyes; and without much conscious thought, she started walking toward the neatly trimmed pathway that wound its way around the base.

Of course, there was activity. Unlike most of the rest of the city, the day here started before dawn, and she listened to the familiar chants as groups of men and women jogged by her, some sparing a curious glance as they moved past. Dar regarded their backs thoughtfully and wondered for the hundredth time if she'd have ever had the internal fortitude to get through training if she'd chosen to join the Navy after all.

Physically, she knew she could have. She'd been all whipcord and iron back then, strong and tough and more than up to whatever demands the Navy would have chosen to dump on her shoulders. Even now—Dar glanced down and considered her tall form with a touch of conceit—even after all the years of desk-bound work and a plush lifestyle she'd never imagined back then, even now if she really pushed, she could probably force herself through the basic course.

On sheer stubbornness, if nothing else, she wryly conceded.

Mentally, though? Dar sighed, pausing and leaning against the fence to peer at the tiny houses just beyond it. She had the self-discipline, but she hadn't had the ability to accept taking orders from anyone just because they had a stripe on their arm or a collar insignia. *Not then*, and, her lips pursed into a slight smile, *certainly not now.*

Her eyes found that one small house, third one on the fourth block. She examined the neatly painted outside, then she circled the fence and walked down the sidewalk, stopping as she came even with the front door. It appeared vacant, and she walked up the small driveway into the carport, putting out a hand and touching the cement brick surface. It felt rough under her fingertips, and a familiar scent of dust and sun-warmed tar filled her nose as the breeze puffed through the enclosure.

Home.

She walked through and out the back into the yard, over to a ficus tree still firmly entrenched near the side of the house. Her eyes lifted and found the old, rotting bits of wood held by rusty nails that once, long ago, might have been the outlines of a tree house. She looked between the branches into a blank window, seeing the faint outlines of a plain, small room inside that had once been hers.

It felt very strange. Dar leaned against the tree and tried to remember what it was like being a small child looking out of that window. She found she couldn't. Too much time had passed, and she was too different a person now to feel a link here.

Hell. Her face tensed into a scowl. She hadn't even wanted to bring Kerry here to see this. Not that her lover would have laughed; in fact, Kerry would have been interested, as she was in everything Dar had to tell her about her childhood. She wasn't ashamed of the house, either. It was just that it was so unremarkable a place, and she could no longer feel any kind of connection to it.

With a sigh, Dar pushed back from the tree, then she glanced up and craned her neck, shifting a hand to part a thick branch full of leaves. Her eyes fell on her own initials carved into the bark of the tree, and even after all these years, plainly visible.

Then her brow furrowed, and she leaned forward, blinking as her eyes tried to make sense of the freshly cut markings right next to her old ones.

Kerry's initials. Dar's jaw dropped in open shock. When in the hell had she... Then Dar recalled the long stretch of time her lover had been gone on one of their breaks from the endless data gathering. She'd returned, cheerfully claiming a walk to clear her head. Dar remembered the smell of warm skin as Kerry had brushed against her, and now knew where it had come from. A silly smile appeared on her face as she gazed up at the letters.

Friday's date, with a plus sign joining the old and the new, all carved into the gray bark in slightly awkward, but competent letters. Without looking, she fished her cell phone from its holder clipped to her belt and speed-dialed a number. She waited for a voice to answer, then she closed her eyes. "You are the most incredible person I've ever known." She heard the slight intake of breath. "I love you."

Then she closed the phone and tucked it back into its holder and walked away from the house, headed back toward her waiting job, humming softly.

Kerry glanced at the roomful of marketing executives, all intently focused on her, and folded her phone back up. "That was a...um...a status report." She smiled weakly, knowing her face was a red as a boiled beet. "I'm sorry, what were you saying about fourth-quarter projections?"

Eleanor cleared her throat. "We were talking about the emerging South American IT market."

"Right." Kerry rubbed her face. "Sorry. Go on."

"Ah, boy." Kerry put her cup down and filled it with hot water, waiting for her tea to steep. The break room was quiet, and she leaned against the counter reading the message board with idle curiosity.

She decided she liked the board in Operations better. It usually had good Dilbert cartoons posted on it.

"Well, hello."

Kerry turned, to find Clarice entering the room. "Hello," she responded cordially. "Getting settled in?"

The slim, black woman poured herself a cup of coffee in a bright pink mug. "Yes, I certainly am. It's nice to be back home," she replied. "Thanks for making it so easy for me."

Kerry smiled. "No problem."

"In fact, I think I have a much better handle on things in Chicago now that I can see the whole picture," Clarice continued. "I'm working with Paul to try and get things settled."

Kerry stirred her tea and turned, leaning against the counter. "I'm glad to hear it. I know it was kind of a rough week, but I'm sure you can get it all worked out. I heard from the account manager out there this morning—he feels a lot better about the client relationship now."

Clarice leaned on the counter as well, studying Kerry. "Well, sometimes things just do happen for a reason, don't they? Who'd have guessed a little winter storm could end up causing all these changes."

A hint of a smile crossed Kerry's face. "Storms sometimes do that," she agreed. "Excuse me," she went on politely. "I've got a conference call I'm late for."

"Oh, please, don't mind me!" Clarice said. "Work comes first, and we sure don't want to mix work and pleasure, now do we?" She gave Kerry a big smile and eased out ahead of her, strolling down the hallway and not looking back.

"Urgurf." Kerry winced, catching the edge in the words. Not the way she'd wanted the conversation to go. After Clarice's initial volley, which she'd ignored, she'd hoped the woman would just let bygones go.

Apparently not.

"Or maybe, Kerrison, you're just being too sensitive, and she just was using a common expression," Kerry told herself as she opened the door to her office and entered its cool peace. "Don't go looking for trouble. You live with it, remember?"

Dar's words on the phone came back to her and she dismissed Clarice's, chuckling softly as she headed for her desk.

Chapter
Five

Dar leaned back in the hard wooden chair and rubbed her eyes, closing them for a moment as she reloaded data for the hundredth time. She listened for the hard drive to stop spinning, then sighed and rocked forward, scanning the results with a tiny scowl on her face.

"Damn it." She checked and rechecked the figures. "Something's just not adding up." Dar paged through the reports strewn over the desk and shook her head. She'd taken the performance data of the base first and dumped it into her analyzer, letting the custom-built scripts she'd written sort through the columns of figures, matching dollars spent with viable product—in this case, qualified personnel who were assigned out to various Navy installations around the world.

Something just wasn't matching. Her scripts kept returning errors, finding discrepancies between the list of expenses and the lists of demands for payment, and so far she hadn't been able to put her finger on the reason. It was almost as though parts of the data were misplaced, not missing, because the end result balanced, but in the wrong areas—so that the orderly progression of bookkeeping went every which direction.

Hmm. Dar scratched her jaw. Maybe that was why her data parse on the base hadn't brought back snips of relevant data, like who the new base commander was. Her eyebrows hiked and she dove into her briefcase, retrieving the case study she'd done before starting the project. Impatiently she flipped through the already ruffle-edged papers, her eyes darting back and forth until she found the spot she was looking for. "Ah."

She leaned back and rested the report on her knee as a warm draft of air entered through the window and stirred the pages,

bringing with it a scent of freshly cut grass and the sound of rugged chanting. Dar had requested, politely, a small office space for
her use, and Commander Albert and Lieutenant Perkins had,
equally politely, led her to this tiny room with its single scarred
wooden desk and unpadded chair.

And no air conditioning. Dar had given them both a smile,
then simply taken off her denim overshirt, leaving her comfortable
in a very light tank top as she sat down and kept them standing
there, answering questions in their full uniforms until they'd both
turned red as beets and started sweating.

Dar chuckled to herself and glanced out the window, watching a training group go through an obstacle course, clawing their
way up a tall wooden wall and flipping over with strained grunts
she could hear all the way where she was sitting. It wasn't too different from when she and the rest of the base brats used to sneak
over after dinner and try the course themselves, ending up with
splinters and cuts as they struggled along.

She remembered the first time she'd made it all the way
through, at age fourteen. Almost without a scratch until she came
to the last hurdle, the rope ladder she'd swarmed up, sweating and
almost yelling with exultation as she grabbed the top and flung
herself over.

*Completely forgetting the ditch on the other side. Ow. Dar
winced, even all these years later, and reached down to rub her
ankle, which she'd twisted so badly she almost didn't make it
home. Fortunately, her daddy had spotted her limping down the
sidewalk and pulled over in their sturdy pickup halfway there.*

*Andrew Roberts's rugged, crew-cut head poked out the win-
dow of the pickup. "What in the hell happened t'you, young
lady?"*

*Dar grabbed the doorframe gratefully and hung on, catching
her breath. "Nothin'...I just fell offa something."*

*Andrew leaned closer. "Were you over at that monkey pit?"
he accused.*

*Dar chewed her lip. Lying to her father was never a good
idea. She'd learned that the hard way. "Yeah."*

*"After I told you not to go there?" The low growl made her
flinch.*

*"Yeah." She looked back up into his face. "Got through this
time." She wasn't able to help grinning, just a little, but she
stopped at the scowl on his face.*

*"You are just a pile of trouble, ain'tcha, Paladar?" Andrew
shook his head. "Git your ass into this here truck."*

So she did, limping around the front and getting in on the other side, glad of the chance to sit down and get off her aching ankle, as he pulled away from the curb and started down their street. It took her a moment to realize it when he passed the house and kept going, and she gave him a startled look. "Where're we going?"

"Git you some ice for that leg and some water to wash the mud off yer face," her father told her. "'Cause I ain't bringing you in the house looking like that, little girl. Your mother'd kill me."

Dar scowled and looked down at her mud-stained hands, her momentary happiness fading. They'd only recently returned to Florida, and the adjustment back had been tough for her. Friends were very few and far between, and Andrew was facing another six-month tour in just a few weeks.

"'Sides...you can't eat ice cream with all that dirt down there," Andrew muttered.

Dar looked at him sideways.

"Figure anyone stubborn enough to get through that monkey pit deserves an ice cream cone, don't you?" Andrew stopped at a stop sign and turned, reaching over and wiping a bit of mud off Dar's cheek. "I know I went and got me one first time I got my butt through it." He patted her face. "Good job, Dardar. That's a tough thing you done."

Dar smiled so hard it hurt, making her forget her ankle completely. "Thanks, Daddy."

Hmm. Dar licked her lips thoughtfully. *Ice cream. Now there's a thought.* She decided to take a side trip during lunch, and resettled her attention on the report she held. The date was current—as of two weeks ago, as she'd thought—but the name of the base commander she knew now was wrong.

So what else was wrong, and why? Dar switched to the laptop and typed in a query. It came back, this time with the correct information. Was the reporting that far behind, and she just got caught in the lag? She checked another bit of data and frowned. *Okay, that came up all right now, too.* So maybe she did get caught between updates. "All right, let me just run these suckers all over again." She typed in a request and watched a long bar start across her screen. "Note to self. Self, upgrade this damn base to 100 Base-T before you do anything else. Jesus. At ten I could walk to the blasted server and get this faster."

Her cell phone buzzed and she flipped it open. "Yeah?"

"Morning, boss." Mark's voice came through. "You left me a voice mail to call ya, so here I am."

"I need a T1." Dar flipped through another set of reports as she talked. "Even a fractional would do if we can't get a full. I'm gonna need the big boxes to run the specs on this place, and they don't have a pipe big enough for me to hook into."

"Hang on. I'm GPSing you," Mark muttered. "Yeah, yeah, yeah, shut up. Stop with the error messages, willya...Ah, shit, Dar. You're in bumfuck."

"I am not," Dar protested.

"You most certainly the heck are, boss. The nearest CO to you is freaking Marathon," Mark replied. "I'd have to piggyback on the National Defense circuits. BellSouth's not gonna go for it, that's for sure. They don't have crap anywhere in the area." He paused. "What in the hell are you doing out there in the scrub, anyway?"

Dar felt stung; irrationally, she realized, but stung nonetheless. "I'm on a project out at the Naval base here," she answered slowly. "The one I grew up on."

There was a very awkward silence on the phone. "Uh...sorry, Dar," Mark finally stuttered. "I didn't mean to dis the place."

Dar sighed. "It's okay." She glanced around. "It is bumfuck."

"Well, it must be a pretty cool slice of bumfuck if you're from there," Mark rallied gamely. "But I gotta tell you, even if I cross my legs and squeeze, I can't really imagine you as a kid."

No. Dar tossed the report onto the desk. "That's probably a good thing," she told her MIS chief. "When can I get my T1?"

A silence filled with clicking followed. "Best I can do is Thursday."

Dar's eyebrows lifted. "After all that griping? You're a damn fraud, Mark."

Mark chuckled softly. "Yeah, well, I was checking the commercial availability; I went back and checked the governmental. They've got a big POP not far from there. We can zap in a pipe there. I'll ship you down a Cisco and a mini hub."

"Good," Dar responded. "When it gets a completion, I want to hook up and suck everything in their main systems out and over to the mainframes. I ran an analysis on my laptop, but there's something not jibing, and I don't have the CPU cycles to rip it apart."

"Sounds good to me—Oh, hey." Mark's voice altered and warmed. "I was just talking to the big kahuna."

"The big kahuna who nearly got my ass nailed to the table in a marketing meeting? That big kahuna?" Kerry's voice echoed through the circuit. "Gimme that phone." There was a fumbling noise. "Paladar Katherine Roberts."

"Uh-oh." Dar started laughing. "You sound like my mother."

"You are so busted." Kerry joined her in laughter. "Oh my God, Dar...you knocked me for a such a loop in that meeting. How's it going?"

"Eh." Dar reviewed the report now running on the laptop's screen. "All right, I guess. There's so much to do, I can't decide where to start." She sent the report to print. "How's it going there?"

"Well," Kerry exhaled, an audible rushing sound, "I've got a session with José in about an hour. Wish me luck." She perched on Mark's desk and winked at him, "Other than that, it's been fine, with the slight exception of me being rendered speechless earlier. What was that all about?"

"Someone's initials," Dar replied succinctly.

Kerry smiled. "Oh," she murmured. "Yeah. I don't know what got into me. I got to use the Leatherman you got me, though." She'd circled the small house and tried to imagine her lover and her family living in it. "Well, I've got to get to my meeting. Here's Mark back. See you later at home?"

"You bet."

Kerry handed the phone back and stood, picking up the handful of requisitions she'd come to collect. She gave Mark a pat on the back and walked through the MIS command center with its semicircular desks and racks of seriously blinking lights. Just as she hit the door an alarm went off, and she paused, looking back over her shoulder to where two techs were scrambling toward a monitor. "What is it?"

"Shit." One tech slapped buttons, then glanced up. "Sorry, ma'am."

Kerry returned to the desk and peered over it. "What's going on?"

"Crap...crap...crap...We just lost the Southeast." The other tech was furiously rattling his keyboard, and now Mark approached, leaning over them. "Mark, something big just took a dump over Georgia." He looked at Kerry. "You know what that means."

Kerry grinned cheerfully. "Hot darn. It means I get to cancel my meeting." She set her papers down and rolled her sleeves up. "Okay...Mark, you start checking the access routers; I'll call Bell-South."

Dar made her way through the labyrinth of corridors and pushed open Commander Albert's door without ceremony or even a knock. She found him just getting off a call, and she paused, giving him a look. "You wanted a conference?"

Albert took in a breath visibly and released it. "Okay, look." He held out both hands. "Can I raise a truce pennant here?"

'Bout goddamned time. Dar folded her arms, but relaxed her posture at the same time. "Depends on what your terms are," she said. "This can be just as tough as you want it to be."

"Okay." The man sat down and motioned her to do the same. "Look, Ms. Roberts, I really don't mean to be such a bastard, but..." He paused.

"But I'm stomping all over your territory with spike heels," Dar finished for him. "You think I don't know that? Listen, Commander, if I were in your shoes, I'd be just as pissed off as you are, believe me."

Albert relaxed a little. "Have you ever been? In my shoes?"

Dar considered the question. "Not really, no," she admitted. "My company was taken over by ILS, but I was just a programmer then. I remember resenting the hell out of having to explain to clueless githeads what my code was, though." She crossed an ankle over her knee. "So I do understand, but you need to understand that I'm not your enemy."

He watched her closely. "You were hired to do this, I know that."

Dar nodded. "That's right. The brass is looking for two things. One, to make themselves look good by hiring the biggest, most well-known IS firm around to come in and evaluate them; and two, they're wanting justification to spend billions in improving infrastructure. If it comes to a question, they point to our analysis, and it's right there, in black and white."

Albert grunted, his brows twitching in thought.

"So, do yourself a favor, Commander, just let me do what they're paying me a fortune for, okay?" Dar said.

He leaned forward and rested his elbows on the desk surface, clasping his hands together lightly. "All right, Ms. Roberts. I'm just going to get my butt chewed up one side and down the other if I don't." He exhaled. "So, do you have everything you want? Lieutenant Perkins told me you were pulling down statistics most of the day."

Dar got up and walked to the window, resting both hands against the sill and peering out the dusty panes. "That's right." She watched a squad of men carrying huge logs move past. "But I've got programs to analyze all that. I want to start looking at facilities, firsthand." She turned, and faced him. "You can let me wander by myself, or give me someone who can answer questions."

A faint grin crossed the commander's face. "I think we can arrange for a guide, Ms. Roberts." He hit a button on his desk. "I was anticipating the issue." His voice got louder. "Send in Chief Daniel."

After a moment the door opened, admitting a short, very stocky woman, her ginger hair peppered lightly with gray. She gave Dar a brief glance, then turned her attention to Albert. "Sir?"

"This is our Senior Operations Staff, CPO Daniel, Ms. Roberts. She's in charge of implementing and supervising all our overall processes." He gave the newcomer a brief nod. "Chief, this is Ms. Roberts. She's here on orders from Washington to do an evaluation on us and recommend improvements," the commander said pleasantly. "Please take her where she wants to go and answer any questions."

In her spare moments Dar often played a little mental game where she tried to match people up with what breed of dog they would be if they suddenly morphed before her eyes. She'd often amused herself in meetings by imagining Eleanor as an Afghan hound, discussing sales with José the sheepdog, for instance. She'd even drawn a sketch of it, which had sent Kerry into a fit of hysterics and made her leave the room.

The bulldog in a naval uniform gave Dar a once-over, then nodded briefly. "Yes, sir, I'll be glad to do that. Would you like to start now, ma'am? It's a big base."

"Absolutely," Dar responded, recognizing the aggressive stance with an internal sigh. "Let's start where they come in. After you?" She gestured toward the door. "Thank you, Commander."

"My pleasure." Albert gave her a pleasant, albeit vicious smile. "Let me know if there's anything else I can do."

Dar followed the woman out of the office and organized her resources for this new challenge. Given how Albert had phrased her assignment, calculated to offend the petty officer as much as possible without actually coming out and accusing her of not doing her job, she had to wonder which one of them he disliked more.

She eyed the shorter woman plowing along beside her.

"Would ma'am like to stop at Supply and pick up a pad and pencil?" Daniel asked suddenly. "I'm sure you'll have notes to take."

"No, thanks," Dar replied mildly. "I usually work at a macro level. I leave the micro details to the people who actually implement the designs." *Hmm. What would Kerry do?* Dar sorted through her options. "Look, Chief, I've got no intention of spending days wading through your attitude. Let's go get a cup of coffee and get the fistfight out of the way, then maybe we can get something done."

The petty officer stopped and turned and studied her with a ferocious intentness. She had a strong presence and an air of fierce competence that almost matched Dar's own. "I don't know what your real purpose is here, ma'am, but I'm not one of those data center fluffheads who wander around with printouts tucked up their butts all day. I have a job to do, and I do a damn good one. So, if you want to tell me what your agenda is, maybe I can save us both time and sweat."

"Problem is, I don't have one," Dar replied. "So if you're doing a good job, you've got nothing to worry about, right?"

"What makes you think you can walk in here and judge us?" Daniel moved a step closer. "You think I have an attitude? What did you expect, an outsider coming in here like this, walking into a world you can't possibly understand?"

"Chief—"

"You think we don't know what you people out there think of the military? You think it's easy always getting that attitude from people who couldn't last through a day of basic training, who think we're a bunch of mindless idiots?" Daniel stabbed a finger at Dar. "Don't talk to me about attitude, lady."

Dar cocked her head. "You like the Navy, Chief?"

That threw the petty officer right off her track. "What?"

"Do you like the Navy? You're a career in, right?"

Warily, Daniel backed off a pace. "It's a job," she answered slowly. "You take a lot of shit, but it's like a family. I've gotten used to it. Why?"

Unaccountably, Dar smiled. "You just gave me an answer to a question I've been asking myself since I was eighteen. Thanks." A flock of "what ifs" took off and left her shoulders lighter. "You're right, Chief. I am an outsider." Now she met the shorter woman's eyes. "You need to choose whether you want me to be a hostile or a friendly one."

They stared at each other in silence.

"Okay, so how are you guys today?" Kerry pulled both legs up under her and sat cross-legged, leaning on the arm of her chair as she regarded her small group of teens. "Did you have a good Thanksgiving?"

Five sets of eyes rolled. "I hate holidays," Lena groaned. "We

had the whole family—my grandparents, the cousins—everyone at
our house. I had to dress up. It sucked." The tiny blond girl made
a face.

Kerry chuckled. "Oh yeah. I remember those days," she said.
"Thanksgiving was always big at my parents' house. We had thirty
or forty people there sometimes."

"Did you like it?" Lena asked doubtfully.

Kerry thought about that. "Sometimes," she answered.
"When I was really young, I did, because all my cousins would
come over, and we were too little for anything really formal.
They'd let us loose in the solarium with a couple of the nannies,
and we'd have a ball."

"Ooh." Erisa pushed a lock of dark hair back off her forehead. "You were, like, super rich, huh?"

"My parents are well off, yes," Kerry replied.

"So, what did you do for Thanksgiving?" Lena asked. "Did
you cook that turkey you got?"

How did we end up talking about me? Kerry wondered. "Yes,
I did, and it turned out better than I expected."

Casey sat up. "Just you and your SO?" Everyone's ears
perked up visibly, and they watched Kerry with interest.

"And my in-laws." *Time to change the subject.* "Anyone seen
Barbara? She usually doesn't miss a group meeting."

"Oh, yeah, I forgot to tell you." Lena slapped her head.
"Shit, man, my brain is, like, not even here. I went by there on my
way. She got promoted." She snapped her fingers. "Like, to an
assistant manager, you know? She had to work a little late
tonight."

"That rocks." Erisa clapped her hands. "So, like, Kerry, I
guess you were right, you know?"

Kerry smiled. "I guess I was," she agreed. "I'm glad to hear
that. It's good to know that Barbara took a chance, and she really
got something out of it." Her body shifted and she straightened up
a little. "That's a good message. Sometimes you do have to take
risks, and those risks turn out to be some of the best things in your
life."

"I dunno." Lena sighed. "For two days I had to listen to my
folks tell me how I should get a boyfriend. They're so clueless, I
mean, like...hello. Those are not pictures of Leonardo Dumbasa-
Fishio on my wall, okay?" She twisted her limbs in the chair, moving into a position that made Kerry wonder if she had bones or
plastic rods in her body. "You think they'd know, you know? Do I
have to paint, like, my whole room in friggin' rainbow stripes?"

"They'd probably think you were just doing that retro seventies thing," Casey snorted. "My freaking father finally caught a clue when I dumped a box of friggin' condoms he'd left in my room in his cereal bowl and told him I wasn't innerested in letting anything that fit in them fit in me."

Kerry bit back a snort of laughter. "What did he say?"

Casey shrugged, and laughed without humor. "He said thank fucking God. At least I wouldn't go out and get stupid and pregnant, and make him pay for it."

"Yo...he'd rather you be gay than a slut, right?" Lena remarked. "My folks would rather I be dead than gay."

Kerry sobered. "You don't know that."

"Sure I do." The slim blond looked directly at her. "My mom told me that, right to my face, after she watched some fucking Oprah shit about gay kids." She snorted. "She said if she ever found out I was gay, she'd shut me up in my room and gas me."

Holy crap. Kerry took a breath to steady herself. "I don't think she meant that," she reassured the girl. "Parents say things like that to scare their kids sometimes."

Lena shrugged. "Yeah, maybe, but I know why so many gay kids pretend they ain't. You get so sick of people thinking you're just so fucked up."

"Yeah." Elina nodded. "I was thinking the other day, is it even worth it?"

Kerry sat up and put both feet on the ground, clasping her hands between her knees as she leaned forward. "Listen." She spoke slowly and quietly. "My parents don't like me being gay, either, and that hurts, because I love my family very much." She sorted through her feelings. "I hated having to make a choice between them and the truth about myself."

"They just don't get it," Elina remarked softly. "It's like they don't understand it, so they have to hate it."

Kerry nodded. "That's true, and believe me, I was scared after I realized I was going to have to face that. I didn't want them to hate me." She paused and collected her thoughts. "You know, I never knew what it would be like to fall in love. So when I fell in love with Dar, it was all so much of a surprise to me—how good it felt, and what an amazingly powerful emotion love is."

They all looked at each other, then back at her.

"It's worth it," Kerry stated simply. "I wouldn't give up Dar for all the money, or the approval of my parents, or anything else in the world."

There was utter silence, and she glanced from face to face as they stared. "C'mon, it wasn't that profound," Kerry chuckled, then realized they weren't staring at her, they were staring past her. She turned her head to find Dar leaning in the doorway, her arms folded and a quiet, pleased smile on her face. "Ah. It's you."

"Yes, it is," Dar agreed.

Kerry was aware she was blushing. "C'mon in. Guys, this is Dar."

The tall, dark-haired woman entered and circled Kerry's chair, perching on an arm of it as she regarded the circle of young faces. "Hi," she greeted them briefly, then turned her attention to her victim. "You're late."

Kerry found herself flailing bewilderedly in that sea of blue. "I am? For what?"

"You have an appointment with me, some of my stone crab friends, and a tall bottle," Dar told her, watching the startled delight creep into Kerry's features. "With lots of bubbles in it." She turned her head and peered at the girls. "You'll excuse her, right?"

Five heads nodded.

"Good." Dar turned her attention back to Kerry. "Well?" She held a hand out, palm up, and lifted an eyebrow. Kerry put her own hand out and clasped it, their fingers curling warmly around each other's. Dar stood and tugged and waited for Kerry to join her.

"Um..." Kerry faced her group, who were now smiling and giggling at her. "I guess I'll see you guys next week, huh?" She flashed them a rueful grin. "See? She's definitely a keeper."

The two women walked out of the meeting room and out through the church, still clasping hands, respecting the peaceful silence until they pushed the large outer door open and went from the slightly close air into a cool fall night and a gusty breeze tinged heavily with salt. "Wow." Kerry turned her head to regard the profile outlined in stars next to her. "That was a surprise."

Dar nodded. "I know. I had a tough day and ended up getting through it by planning the night with you," she admitted. "C'mon...let's go count stars."

Kerry smiled and turned her face to the wind as they walked toward the small seaside restaurant nearby, its table candles fluttering in the breeze. Her hand felt warm in Dar's, and the concrete sidewalk seemed to turn into a soft cloud.

The ocean rolled in nearby, a rhythmic shush and roar followed by a faint tinkle of shells. Dar and Kerry were sitting braced against a tree with their legs extended out on sand still holding the day's warmth. Or, to be more precise, Dar was leaning against the tree and Kerry was leaning against Dar, seated between her lover's legs in a blissfully comfortable sprawl.

"So, I'm a keeper, huh?" Dar drawled, a hint of a chuckle in her voice.

"You bet your boots, Dixiecup." Kerry lifted one of the hands clasped loosely around her waist and kissed it. "How long were you in that doorway, anyhow?"

"Not long," Dar said. "I heard what that little blond-haired girl said, then what you said back."

Kerry exhaled. "I can't believe her mother said that. How could a parent be that..." She paused and reflected. "You know, I don't think even my parents would have said something like that to me."

"You think the mother was serious?" Dar sounded doubtful. "That sounded like one of those 'if you don't behave, I'm going to cut your hands off' kind of parental things."

"That's what I thought too, then," Kerry agreed. "But the more I think about it, the more I wonder why someone would say that to a child, even if it wasn't serious."

"Well," Dar shifted a little, then gave Kerry a squeeze, "I don't know. You get frustrated, I guess. When I look back on when I was younger, I know my mother said things to me that came from her being so at a loss with how to deal with things that I did." She paused. "I think maybe you want your kids to be perfect, so when they're not, and you can see all the things you want to be different in them, it gets you crazy." Another pause. "But even when she said things, I never remember feeling afraid of her."

"No, but if you're really upset about something, and scared, you take things like that to heart, Dar." Kerry sighed. "When I had my confrontation with my parents, at least I was an adult. I knew who I was, and I was old enough to have developed a mind of my own."

Dar chuckled. "I'd certainly agree with that statement."

Kerry stuck her tongue out at her. An instant later, she found it caught between Dar's teeth as it was gently nibbled and tasted, then lips brushed hers and disappeared, restoring the view of the ocean to her. "Ooh." Kerry enjoyed the tingling. "That was erotic." She turned her head. "Can we do it again?"

"Only if you're interested in making the front page of the Lifestyles section of the *Herald*." Dar indicated the strolling passersby. "On the other hand, I know a hot tub that might be willing to look the other way for us."

"Eeoorwl." Kerry emitted a contented gurgle and stretched. "I could go for that. You can tell me more about this petty person who's giving you such a migraine. Do I need to come down to the base again and have a chat with her?"

Dar stood, tugging Kerry up with her, and they started back toward the church parking lot. "No. The chief's all right. At least she knows what she's doing and understands base ops. I just get the feeling she'd like to bump me into the two-hundred-pound hamburger grinders and give herself a mark for reducing chow costs," she said. "I feel like I'm walking around with a slightly rabid dog trotting around after me, ready to clamp on at any second."

"Hmm." Kerry's nose wrinkled up as she smiled. "I think that's how people feel about you sometimes, you know."

A sigh. "I know."

"Not really nice, huh?" The green eyes twinkled.

Dar gave her a look. "Are you laughing at me?"

Kerry pulled her closer, tucking her hand around Dar's arm. "I'm not laughing at you. I was just thinking that it must be strange for you to be faced with the kind of challenge that you usually present to other people." She felt Dar sigh again. "Why don't you try making friends with her? I'm sure you two have something in common."

They approached Kerry's car, and she used the remote to unlock the door, then muffled a smile as Dar opened it for her. She got in and paused as her lover leaned on the window and watched her get settled. "Meet you at the ferry?"

"Drive careful," Dar told her, then closed the door. She walked around the back of the Mustang and got into her own car, starting it and pulling out after Kerry onto the main street. They drove along the beach road and turned right onto the causeway that led home, navigating the relatively sparse traffic in tandem. They reached the first bridge and rolled over it, reaching the top and starting down the other side.

It took Dar's mind a frantic second to confirm that the headlights coming toward them were really in the wrong lane, a half-ton of truck barreling down toward Kerry, who was starting to react, throwing her wheel hard to the left and sending the Mustang bolting toward the green center island.

For a second, Dar froze, her eyes caught in the glaring headlights bearing down on both of them. Then she reacted with pure instinct, gunning the engine of the Lexus and roaring past Kerry, putting herself between the oncoming four-by-four and the skidding Mustang as she slid into a sideways block.

The oncoming blue vehicle jerked to the right, then suddenly made a hard turn, skimming Dar's front bumper as it clawed its way over the center island and bounced into the eastbound lanes, missing a taxi by a hair and roaring off down toward the beach.

Dar slowly unclenched her fingers from the steering wheel and pushed back, her heart slamming so hard in her chest it threatened to squeeze between her ribs and escape. She jerked the door open and tumbled out of the car, hanging on to the edge of the window for a long moment as her shaking legs refused to hold her up. Then she took a breath and forced herself into a run to where Kerry's car was half up onto the center island, her engine off and her headlights shining wanly into the tropical foliage.

The door opened as Dar reached it, and she yanked impatiently, dropping to her knees beside the seat as Kerry leaned halfway out. "Hey." She hugged Kerry to her in mindless relief, feeling the shaky breath as Kerry buried her face against Dar's neck. "You okay?"

"Yeah." Kerry nodded. "Just scared the holy pooters out of me."

"Me, too."

Kerry released her and got out of the car, leaning on Dar's shoulder as she glanced around and examined the damage. Though the other car hadn't touched her, climbing onto the center island had done evil things to a car not intended as a four-wheel-drive vehicle. "Erf."

Dar got to her feet and regarded the apparently broken axle. "Well, that's it."

Kerry was leaning against the side of the car. "That's what?" She turned and gave her lover a puzzled look. "I'm sure they can fix this."

"You're getting a new car," Dar responded matter-of-factly. "If that thing had hit you, this would have folded like a used piece of tin foil."

"Oh, I don't know about that, Dar. It always seemed pr—" Kerry got a good look at Dar's face, and cut her sentence off in mid-word. "Well, I was thinking about a new one the other day. Maybe it's a good idea." She walked over and leaned against her partner. "Can we call a tow for this, and go home?"

"Good idea." Dar took out her cell phone as they walked toward the balefully crouching Lexus, its hazard lights flashing as traffic drove cautiously around it. "We can go car shopping on the web when we get there."

Kerry let out a slightly hysterical chuckle. "Honey, we don't have to do that. Besides, I think I want to check out one of these for myself." She patted the SUV. "It's nice and solid, right?"

Dar glanced up from her conversation. "I was thinking maybe

a Hummer." She went back to the phone and gave directions.

"A what?"

"Unless maybe Dad could get a Humvee." Dar closed the phone, tapping it against her chin thoughtfully, her face completely serious. "He probably could."

Kerry knocked on her chest. "Hello? Earth to Dar? I'm not driving an armed personnel carrier around Miami, so I hope you're joking."

Dar nudged her into the car, then closed the door and got in on the driver's side. "Deny that it wouldn't be handy in afternoon traffic." She started the car and moved cautiously into drive. "Maybe a tank."

"Dar."

"What? They come in surplus, and Dad loves tinkering with the engines."

"Dar!"

"Hell to park, though."

"You are joking, right?"

Pale blue eyes regarded her as they waited in line for the ferry. "Yes." Dar finally smiled. "I tend to say stupid things when I lose my mind."

Kerry lifted a hand and they interlaced fingers, a gesture that always brought a sense of warm familiarity to both of them. "Well, I was completely safe. I had this huge Lexus between me and the kamikaze wackos. They'd have probably bounced off and ended up in Biscayne Bay." She was rewarded by another smile. "Crazy people."

Dar nodded, leaning back in her seat in quiet relief. The draining of the adrenaline that had raced through her body left her almost sleepy, and she didn't feel like moving, not even when the ferry docked and she had to maneuver the Lexus onto its lightly shifting deck. She kept her eyes half-closed and rubbed Kerry's fingers with her thumb as they rode over to the island. Then she turned and gazed at Kerry's profile. "You sure a Hummer's out of the question?"

"Dar."

"They come in nice colors."

"Blue, gray, and green." Kerry regarded her amusedly. "And black. I'd like something a little lighter."

"Hmph." Dar leaned her knee against the steering wheel. "The tank comes in desert camo. That's light."

"Dar," Kerry started laughing, "would you just cut that out? I'm not getting a tank."

They were both quiet for a few minutes.

"Can you imagine the gas mileage those things get?" Kerry finally spoke up. "It'd cost a fortune."

"No problem. I'll give you a raise to cover it," Dar responded instantly. They looked at each other, then they both burst out laughing in relief. "Think of the impression you'd give, pulling up to a consolidation in THAT," Dar got out.

Kerry just kept laughing.

Chapter
Six

Thunder rolled sullenly in over the ocean, lightning flashes outlining the whitecaps that scurried up the beach and ruffled the water's dark surface.

Most of the island was still dark, the condos squatting on the edge of the land silent and brooding, their windows blank and featureless in the predawn hours.

From one outward facing window, however, a faint light poured. Anyone insane enough to be walking out along the beach in the storm would have seen a profile outlined in it as someone stood inside the dry, safe building watching the surge of the waves.

"Wow." Kerry leaned against the counter, feeling the cool surface through the thin cotton of her T-shirt. "Glad I'm not out there." She turned her head as the toaster released four slices of fragrant cinnamon raisin toast. "Ah." A moment later the toast was resting on plates and she was spreading softened butter over it. They were so used to waking up early that even today, when their usual morning run was out of the question, they both were up and rambling around the condo.

Dar was in her study catching up on mail, and Kerry set the plates of toast and scrambled eggs, along with two glasses of orange juice and coffee, onto a tray before heading in that direction. For a moment she paused in the doorway to watch her lover, hard at work behind her desk, before she continued on and set the tray down on the small table nearby. "Anything catastrophic?"

"Hmm?" Dar looked up, her face outlined in luridly ghostly phosphor light. "I got a compliment on you from Intratech. Whatever you did with BellSouth yesterday got them back up and running."

"Really?" Kerry looked pleased. She set the plate of toast and eggs down, then handed Dar her orange juice. "Bottoms up."

Dar took the glass and leaned back, hitching her knee up to rest against the desk's edge as she sipped at the brightly colored beverage. "Nasty out there, eh?"

Kerry took a seat on the couch and tucked her legs up under her, leaning on the broad padded arm as she selected a slice of toast and nibbled on it. "Very. I hope it calms down before we have to get out of here."

Dar looked thoughtfully at the window as a lightning strike hit somewhere close, causing a wicked cracking sound. She picked up the phone on her desk and dialed a number, listening for several seconds before it was answered. "Morning, John. This is Dar Roberts. How's it looking?" She cocked her head as the lightly accented voice answered, then grunted. "That's what I thought. Thanks." She hung up and eyed Kerry. "Ferry's not operating."

"Oh, gosh. You mean we're stuck here?" Kerry asked ingenuously. "I'm devastated."

Dar smiled. "I can see that. I'm not sure the company would feel the same way, though." She gazed at her inbox. "I can just imagine what yours looks like if I've got three pages."

"Eek." Kerry got up and circled the desk to peer at Dar's screen. "Well, some of those are from yesterday, Dar. I cleared my box before I left work last night." She scanned the headers. "Some of them are duplicates of mine, too, I can tell you what h—Dar?" Teeth were nibbling on her hip, and she glanced down to see mischievous blue eyes peeking up at her. "Do you give a poo about the mail?"

"No," Dar responded cheerfully. "I just wanted you to come over here," she chuckled. "It's not like either of us can do anything about the weather, Ker."

Kerry leaned over and kissed Dar's head. "That's true. I'll call Ops, though. We might have staffing issues if people can't get to work, and I think I just heard they've got power outages in the southwest." She felt Dar's arm circle her leg. "Hey, after that, maybe we can go car shopping."

One of Dar's arms moved, and her hand curled around her mouse, clicking on a closed window and opening it. "Funny you should say that." The new window revealed the Lexus website, snazzy and sleek looking with various models of the automaker's wares appearing and disappearing. "Look what I found."

"Ooh." Kerry nudged her. "Move back so I can sit down."

Obligingly, Dar scooted back in the huge leather chair and gave Kerry room to perch on the edge of it, wrapping herself around her lover's body and peering over her shoulder as she took possession of the mouse. "It's pretty cool. You can choose your model, pick a color, tell it what you want inside, and send an order to the nearest dealership." She paused. "And get it delivered."

A grin split Kerry's face as she pointed and clicked. "Now this is my idea of car shopping." She nodded in approval. "There we are...the little SUV."

"It's cute," Dar commented. "Like you."

Kerry paused, and glanced over her shoulder so they were nose to nose. "Thank you. I'm glad we're not mentioning the Hummer this morning."

Dar's nose twitched, and then wrinkled up into a grin. "They don't have as neat a website."

Kerry bit her playfully, then returned her attention to the screen. "Let's see...pick a color first. Hmm." She scrolled through the possibilities. "Crimson, green, blue, black, white, silver, or gold. What do you think, Dar? The black is kinda snazzy."

"Not in Florida. I'm not into poached partner," Dar remarked. "Go light."

"Okay." Kerry clicked. "How about white?"

"Not living out here. You'd be washing it every day."

Kerry eyed her. "Is this why you ended up with that gold color?" She resumed clicking. "Oh, I like the blue, Dar. I don't care if it's dark. I've got a dark car now, and it's not so bad." She admired her choice. "Yeah, I like that."

"Hmm." Dar cocked her head.

"Now, what's next... Ah, interior." Kerry reviewed her choices. "Oh, leather, definitely." She selected it. "I've really gotten into this stuff since I've met you."

One of Dar's eyebrows lifted sharply. "Me? Why?"

"Leather car seats, leather couches, that leather vest, those leather boots you got me," Kerry murmured. "I have nightmares of being visited by PETA sometimes and having to escape out the back." She clicked on the added options. "Hmm...what do we have here? Heated seats? No thanks."

Dar was still snickering over her comments. "I never thought about that. I just like the feel of leather, especially in stuff I've gotta sit on."

Kerry laughed softly. "Me, too." She paused and gave her lover an assessing look. "Hmm. Could I talk you into a pair of leather pants?"

"Sure." Dar settled both arms around Kerry. "As long as you wear them," she amended quickly, hearing the chortle. "I had a pair, long time back. I only wore them once."

Kerry paused, and turned again. "Once?"

Dar nodded. "They squeak," she explained. "I scared the crap out of myself every time I moved." She felt Kerry start to laugh and she held on as her lover dissolved into helpless chuckles. "Ahem. Weren't we discussing heated seats?"

"Mine's plenty warm." Kerry gave her a sultry, over-the-shoulder smirk. "Oh, you mean for the car. Right." She returned her attention to the screen. "CD player, check. Sunroof, check. Four wheel drive, check. Extra electrical package, check."

"It'll be nice when they do integrated satellite cellular," Dar commented. "And put in a laptop mount." She peered over Kerry's shoulder. "Air bags and ABS? Good."

"Yep." Kerry reviewed her selections, then had the website provide her with a three-dimensional view. "Looks good. I like it." She investigated further. "Lease, you think? Yeah... Okay, here we go." She sent in her request and added a digital wallet and signature with her personal information. "Oh yeah, I like this, Dar. Much more fun than getting a car the old-fashioned way."

"Oh, I don't know." Dar freed a hand and took a swallow of coffee. "It's sort of exciting to go to the dealership...in a sleazy, carnival kinda way." She chewed on her toast. "I remember the first new car I got. I'd been saving up for months, and I just decided to go one night, and not tell my parents."

"Oh boy." Kerry took a bite of the toast held so invitingly nearby. "What'd you get?"

"I traded in an eighty-five Malibu." Dar smiled in memory. "It was paid off, so that, plus the down payment I had, pretty much guaranteed me just about anything I wanted on the lot. I felt like a kid in a toy store."

Kerry pulled the plate over and started sharing forkfuls of eggs with Dar. "Uh-huh."

"I looked at little ones, big ones, musta driven that salesman nuts," the dark-haired woman said. "It was such a weird feeling. I finally narrowed it down to a choice between this little sports car number that was really cute and a pickup truck."

"A pickup truck?" Kerry fed her some eggs.

"Mm. I was such a little redneck," Dar admitted. "Besides, Daddy had a pickup truck." She leaned back and drained her juice glass. "So I ended up with a charcoal gray pickup with racing stripes and a roll bar."

"And fuzzy dice?" Kerry muffled a smile. "Hey, don't give me that look. I used to have a pair of trolls hanging from my rearview mirror. I had to settle for something a lot more conservative, though. My parents allocated cars to us every year, whatever manufacturer was trying to woo my father." She got up and retrieved her own coffee, standing before the window and gazing out. "The first time I got to pick my own car was when I moved down here." A smile crossed her face. "I was so damn sick of teak panels and snooty hood ornaments. I remember passing by a Ford dealership and seeing the new Mustangs, and boy...I was right there." She laughed. "Vroom vroom...a convertible muscle car. Damn, that felt good to drive off the lot in." Kerry sighed. "I felt like such a rebel. My parents almost had a heart attack when I told them." She turned and looked at Dar. "How did your folks react?"

Dar grinned. "Well, it was one of the few decisions I'd made that we all agreed on," she related. "It was an extended cab, with space in the back for Mom, so I became the official driver in the family. Dad loved the truck, and Mom loved not having him drive, so for once, we were all on the same page."

Kerry tried to imagine what it would have been like to have had that kind of relationship with her parents. She couldn't do it. Her mother had been horrified when she'd told her about the Mustang, and her father had told her in no uncertain terms that the car would be left behind when she came home from Miami. Thoughtfully, Kerry wondered if it was at that moment she'd decided she wasn't ever going back. Certainly she'd gone a little over the line after that, staying out and breaking all the rules she'd lived under for such a long time.

She'd actually been lucky, now that she looked back on that wild period. She could have gotten herself into a lot of real trouble and not just ended up suffering a few hangovers and barely remembered near misses, the last of which had scared her so badly it finally knocked some sense into her. She'd been more careful after that, but she was still aware of that potential wild side, something she doubted she wanted Dar to ever see.

"Well. I'm going to go work on my inbox, so I don't feel completely guilty about being trapped here in my underwear with you." She winked at Dar. "Come visit me?"

Dar responded with a frank grin, visible in Kerry's mind's eye as she left the study and headed upstairs with Chino trotting at her heels.

"Jesus." Kerry tugged her hood closer and bolted for the front door of ILS, crossing from the drenched air into the climate-controlled lobby with a sense of being slapped in the face with the chill. As she hit the tile, she lost her footing and slid, yanked to a halt by the frantic grip of the security guard as she passed the station. "Whoa! Thanks."

"No problem, Ms. Stuart." The guard patted her arm. "Careful there; it's the Lord's own rivers raining out there."

"No kidding." Kerry shook herself, scattering droplets of water over the tile, which she correctly assumed would be easier to clean than the carpet upstairs. "Much more of this, and we'll have to close the parking lot. The water's up to some hubcaps out there." She turned, getting a brief glimpse of Dar's taillights as she turned out of the lot and headed south. "Hope Dar doesn't run into trouble driving." She glanced at her watch and sighed, turning to walk across the cold lobby toward the elevators. The rain had let up a little, the winds abated just enough to allow the ferry to commence operation, and they'd reluctantly decided that playing hooky from work the week after they'd both been gone for days was probably not the best idea in the world.

Rats. Kerry punched the elevator button and waited. It wasn't that she didn't like her job; she did. The door opened and she entered, turning and hitting the button for the fourteenth floor. She just liked spending time with Dar more, that was all.

"Morning, Ms. Kerry." The doors had opened at the tenth floor, and Brent edged on behind a rubber-wheeled AV cart.

"Morning, Brent," Kerry replied politely. Brent had been avoiding her for a few months, since the night he'd found out about her and Dar's relationship. She suspected he didn't approve of her lifestyle, and she felt a little sad about that, since she'd developed a fondness for the young tech. "Who's that for?"

Brent had been staring intently at the wall, and now he glanced briefly at her. "Requisition 23343, ma'am." He returned his eyes to the wall.

"Well," Kerry exhaled, "I hope the requisition enjoys it." The doors opened and she held them while Brent moved the cart off the elevator. "Did the equipment for Accounting come in?"

"I don't know, ma'am. Thank you, ma'am." Brent turned and wheeled his cart away, keeping his head down as he walked.

Kerry made a mental note to talk to Mark about his tech, then headed for her office. She heard raised voices halfway down the hall and raked a hand through her still-damp hair as she readied herself for another fractious day.

The camp was positively gray when Dar got there. The heavy rain had turned the ground into a slough of sheeting ripples of water, broken by heavily rutted areas of mud where marching recruits and multi-ton vehicles had passed.

The guard didn't even blink at her this time, he just waved her through; and she navigated the puddles cautiously as she made her way into the main parking lot. "What a mess." She regarded the steady rain with a critical eye, glad she'd brought her all-weather gear. She pulled up her hood and fastened the front clasps, then opened the door and slid out, her booted feet sending a respectable splash out in all directions. "Glad I remembered these, too." She closed the door and started toward the command building, ripples moving away from her toward the edge of the lot as she walked.

The Marine beside the door opened it as she approached, and she gave him a nod as she went inside the building, taking in a breath of the brass-scented air with a renewed twinge of nostalgia. She took the stairs up two at a time and walked briskly through the upper hall entrance, turning right and crashing headlong into Chief Daniel, who had been headed just as quickly in the other direction.

Dar hopped back a step, reaching out in pure instinct as the shorter woman bounced off her and slammed against the wall. "Hey. Sorry about that."

The chief ripped her arm out of Dar's grasp and glared at her. "You really should watch where you're going, ma'am."

"Well, I would, but my eyeballs don't extend out on stalks and reach around corners," Dar replied. "And I left my handheld radar at home. So, either accept my apology, or just get the hell out of my way."

The chief wrestled her best stiff upper lip into position and dusted herself off. "We didn't expect to see you here today."

"I bet." Dar smiled engagingly at her. "We left off at Battle Operations yesterday, didn't we?"

The chief's jaw jerked and her lips twitched, but she merely extended a hand in the direction she'd been originally going. "After you."

They passed through the halls, going through offices, then the chief turned and went through a door into a stairwell. "It's on the top floor," she informed Dar with a brief smile. "We don't have elevators." The chief started up the stairs without further words, and Dar shook her head and rolled her eyes before she followed.

The six flights served to give her a nice little workout, and she was in a better mood by the time she beat the chief to the door at the top of the stairs and pulled it open, sweeping her arm forward in a courtly flourish. "After you."

The chief eyed her narrowly, then sighed and walked past into the hall.

Dar undid the catches on her trench coat and let the edges flap free as she strode down the center of the woven carpet floor. On either side of her, the walls were lined with bulletin boards, and this area had the look of a working space. It was more Spartan than the floors below, and she could just detect the scent of sweat and old wool on the air. The boards held notices of classes and rotations; she caught glimpses of platoon names and the personnel assigned to them, uniformly typewritten with a first initial and surname. She smiled at a brief memory of when she was very young, running up here and searching for her father's name, hoping against hope he'd been assigned to a base unit and not a ship for the next six months.

She'd usually been disappointed. But every once in a while, there'd been a break, and she'd gone back home in giddy high spirits, looking forward to six months of piggyback rides and Saturday morning games in the backyard.

"Ms. Roberts."

The chief's voice broke into her memories and she looked up to face the sailor's dour expression. "Yes?"

"I don't care what you think about what you see in here, do not voice your opinion in front of the recruits or my sailors." The ginger-haired woman's jaw moved. "Is that clear?"

Dar let her wonder what her response was going to be for a few seconds. "Agreed," she finally replied. "Even if it's a good opinion." She met the chief's eyes steadily. "Let's go."

They passed through the doors and entered into another world. Here, the quiet hallways were left behind, and a bustle of activity surrounded them, consisting chiefly of moving bodies in blue denim with serious faces. To one side, a small group of recruits was getting bawled out, their bodies stiffened against the tirade and their eyes strictly to the front. To their left, a row of closed gray painted doors with rubber seals on them called to mind the watertight doors on a ship and, Dar knew, enclosed simulators.

They kept walking, past the open doors of a large open room where a class in hand-to-hand was being taught, the hoarse yells and dull splats of bodies hitting the floor distinctive in the air.

"Chief!" a male voice hollered from just in front of them. A young man with bright red hair was leaning half out a doorway and gesturing to Dar's reluctant guide. "That damn sim program's down again!"

"Wait here," the chief ordered, heading in that direction.

Dar ignored the order, following the sailor with a look of mild amusement.

Chief Daniel stopped and turned. "Don't you ever do what you're told, Ms. Roberts?"

"No." Dar walked past her and ducked around the redheaded sailor. "One of the major reasons I never joined the Navy." She evaded a hurrying tech carrying a piece of hardware and let a brief grin cross her face. "This place hasn't changed." Three men were gathered around a computer console, and as she watched, one reared back and slapped the side of it in frustration. She walked up behind them and peered over their shoulders as the chief hurried up on the other side. Lines of code were scrolling across the screen, and Dar studied them, head cocked just slightly to one side, blue eyes intent.

"What's the problem?" The chief pushed one of the sailors out of the way and sat down, punching buttons rapidly. "Did you reset it?"

"Twice," the displaced sailor told her. "Stupid thing keeps going out. Piece of crap."

The chief managed to get the display to steady, and she started a reset of the equipment. "Is there anyone in this thing? I don't want to cycle it if I'm gonna douse a furkin' admiral or something."

"No. It's empty." The sailor glanced over the equipment into the simulator through a one-way mirrored window. "We took the class out the second time it dumped and told 'em to dry off."

"All right. Let me just..." the chief muttered.

"Hold it." Dar's voice cut through the crowd suddenly. She moved the sailor in front of her aside and leaned over the chief, ignoring the look of outrage. "Move."

"Ma'am, now you just—"

Dar's tone deepened and went cold, snapping with an authority they hadn't heard from her yet. "I said move!"

Purely by instinct, the chief obeyed, sliding out of the chair as Dar dropped into it, her eyes on the screen as her fingers sped over the keys with practiced sureness.

"What are you doing?" the chief demanded.

Dar didn't answer. She was too busy wracking her brain for codes and logic as she called up the simulator's program and studied it, her brows knitting tightly as she searched the lines of green letters and symbols.

"Ms. Roberts, what are you doing!" the chief yelled, almost into Dar's ear. "You do not have the authority to be touching this equipment."

Dar called up another screen. "Someone's altered the program." She moved the system into an editing mode and started to make changes. "Someone who didn't have half a damn clue as to what the hell they were doing."

The chief's eyes almost came out of her head. "Hold it. I said, hold, ma'am. That is a state-of-the-art system and you can't just—"

"Sure I can." Dar's hands moved in a blur. "State of the art? Gimme a break, Chief. Figures the Navy'd still be using a system prototype designed by a half-baked sixteen-year-old code jockey with an affinity for COBOL." She made a last change, then saved and recompiled the program. "There." She reset the system with a set of keystrokes and watched as it reinitialized. She was rewarded with a steady login screen and a slate of green lights, which flickered across the top of the machine with a set of satisfied clicks. "Hoo yah," Dar muttered softly, for the first time in a very, very long time. She got startled looks from the sailors, but she ignored them as she stood up and relinquished the terminal. "All yours."

"Ms. Roberts," the chief's voice was very cold, "a word with you over there, please." She turned and walked into the nearest simulator and waited for Dar to follow her, then she shut the door and spun the wheel, locking them both inside.

It was an engine room, Dar realized as the door slammed shut and she felt the air compress around her. Her pulse jumped and she went still, grabbing hold of the sudden panic that gripped her guts. "Was that necessary?"

The chief studied her intently for a moment. "Who in the hell do you think you are?" she barked, advancing on Dar and making the small space even smaller. "I thought I told you to keep your mouth shut in there!"

Dar felt her temper rising. "Back off, Chief," she warned, edging away from the angry woman.

"I most certainly will not back off." Daniel poked her sharply. "I've about had it up to here with you, Roberts, and I am not going to put up with one more minute of your kiss-my-ass attitude!" Her voice got louder, ringing off the metal floor and walls as she backed Dar against the wall.

The room closed in on Dar, and a wash of blood and energy swept over her, warming her skin with startling rapidity. "Back off!" she repeated, her voice dropping pitch.

"You listen to me! You either decide to keep your damn mouth shut," Chief Daniel forged on, "or I'll—"

She never really saw it coming. One moment her civilian victim was pressed against the wall, the next moment the chief was on the ground, her skull ringing with the contact against the grill floor, with Dar Roberts's forearm pressing against her chin and a pair of wild blue eyes boring into her like searchlights.

The chief was no coward, but she'd seen that look before, and she had the sense to realize the dangerous situation she'd initiated was rapidly getting beyond her control, so she did the only prudent thing left to her. She let her body go limp, secure in her own tough condition but not stupid enough to challenge the youth and strength she felt crouched over her.

"Back off," Dar whispered, seeing red for the first time in a long time.

"All right," Chief Daniel answered, just as quietly. "Easy." Slowly, the pressure on her throat lessened, and Dar eased back away from her, the taller woman's body rising to a balanced stance, her hands balled lightly into fists that looked fully capable of doing some damage. It was not the reaction she'd been expecting, having figured Dar for the loudmouthed type that turned into a puffball when blown on hard enough. Her angular features, now settled in darkly savage lines, struck a sudden chord of familiarity but the chief knew she didn't have time to figure out where from. "Okay, just relax, all right?"

Dar leaned back against the console, the intense surge of adrenaline still making her heart race and causing faint twitches to shiver up and down her arms and legs. It was the closest she'd come to losing control in half a lifetime, and it scared her a little, to know just how easily the chief had triggered that. "That was a very stupid thing to do," she told the sailor, who slowly sat up and was rubbing her head. "I'm not one of your recruits, and if you ever do that again, I'll knock you right through that damn bulkhead, you got me?"

"Think you could?" the chief asked softly.

"Yes," Dar answered with utter sureness. "When my daddy taught me to fight, he made sure of that."

Daniel studied her for a long moment, then she sighed and got up, rubbing her elbow where it had slammed against the floor. She turned a console chair around and sat on it, resting her arms on the back and gazing at Dar. "All right." She nodded slowly. "I thought we had an understanding that you wouldn't spout off in front of my staff."

Dar let her hands rest on her thighs, her heart finally slowing to its normal pace. "I said I wouldn't give an opinion." She skirted the issue. "I didn't."

The chief snorted. "Saying a kid designed the sim wasn't an opinion? Bullshit."

"I was the kid," Dar replied simply. Then she got up and walked over to the hatch, taking a breath before she spun the wheel and released the catches, allowing it to swing inward. The air outside rushed in, and she stepped out of the simulator with a sense of relief to face round, wide eyes that rapidly found other objects to look at.

Then she realized they'd all been watching everything on the monitors. Without a word, she walked past them and into the hallway, desperate for a moment of peace and quiet and a cup of Navy coffee.

The operations meeting had been underway for ten minutes or so before Kerry entered, giving everyone a brief, distracted nod before she took her seat at the head of the table and ran her eyes over a freshly printed agenda. The staff all started warbling at once.

"Kerry, that circuit you were escalating came in."

"We've got six mainframes stuck in customs in Mexico. Midwest OPS wants to know if you can help."

"The coffee machine just exploded."

Kerry's head jerked up at the last statement, and she peered across the table at Enid Petrofax, the MIS coordinator. "What?"

Enid scratched her jaw nervously. "Didn't you hear the bang? The machine just exploded. We've got espresso grounds from the main door to the bathroom."

Everyone was silent, exchanging startled glances. "Ah." Kerry sat back. "Well, have we called the company? How in the hell could that thing explode? I realize it's steam powered, but good grief!"

"Well." Mark had entered and was now approaching the table, his entire shirt front covered in dark brown liquid and grounds. "I gotta tell ya, that was the stupidest thing I ever saw." He held up a piece of round metal. "Damn hot chocolate top musta fallen in the espresso handle. It blocked the steam."

"Ew." Kerry winced.

"That wasn't the stupid part." Mark glared dourly around the table. "We need to find out what technognorp kept pressing the brew button when nothing was coming out."

Kerry covered her eyes. "Oh, good grief." She peeked between her fingers at the muddy-looking MIS chief. "Mark, go change. Enid, call Laurenzo Brothers if you haven't already, and put a note out to the building to remind them we're a technology company and should act like it."

"Yes, ma'am." Enid made a note on her pad. "María already called Laurenzo Brothers. She's got a cousin that works there."

"Unbelievable." Kerry shook her head. "Okay, now...what was that about Mexico? Those aren't the mainframes for the university project in Illinois, are they?"

John Byers, their Midwest operations manager, nodded glumly. "Yeah. Next you're going to ask me how they ended up in Mexico, right? I wish I knew. All I can get from IBM is that they were on one of our POs that had that as a freight address." He paused and reviewed his notes. "I asked them to fax me a copy of it, but the bottom line is, they want a ton of money to release them out of customs and onto the plane to Chicago."

Kerry leaned back, wishing she didn't have the headache she did. The weather, she suspected, was the root cause. "Okay." She steepled her fingers and rested her lips against the tips of them, trying to figure out what Dar would do.

Something tricky, she was sure, because handing over thousands of dollars into government fingers wasn't something Dar would have liked. *Hmm.* She was aware of everyone's eyes on her, curious and intent, especially Clarice's at the other end of the table.

What would Dar do?

"Okay. This is what you're going to do." Kerry took a breath. "What's the closest account we've got down there?"

"Tijuana International," Stacia Brennon supplied, her voice curious. "Why?"

Kerry got up and paced, something she knew her partner loved to do. "Call up the delivery executive for that account. Tell him to take delivery of those mainframes." She paused and turned, leaning her hands on the back of Mark's empty chair. "Then write up an inter-divisional transfer between the South American SBU and the Educational, and have FedEx International pick them up on our inter-company account."

"Ooh," Stacia smiled, "I like it."

John Byers chuckled. "Me, too. Stace, you want to call Pedro? I'll get FedEx on the line." His eyes twinkled as he glanced back at Kerry. "Very slick, chief."

Kerry smiled and walked back around to her seat, dropping into it and stretching her legs out under the table as she cradled her tea mug in both hands. She'd hoped the herbal stuff would settle her stomach, which had been in churning upset most of the morning, but so far it hadn't, and Kerry hoped she wasn't coming down with something. "I had a good teacher."

Chuckles traveled around the table. "That's what we hear."

Clarice smiled sweetly at her. "Looks like Dar picked a wonderful successor."

Yeesh. Kerry smiled back at her. "Thank you. I like to think so." She glanced up as Mark reentered the room, then reviewed the rest of the agenda. "Okay, what's next? Mark, did we get all of the equipment requests in for first quarter?"

Clarice looked back down at her notes with a smirk, ignoring Mark as he circled around her and took his seat again.

Kerry's nails drummed softly on her pad.

"Hey, Ker, you up for lunch?" Mark caught up to her in the hallway on the way back to their offices. "They've got some decent-looking fried chicken down there today."

Kerry winced and laid a hand over her stomach. "Ergh...I don't think I'm up to that. I'll go down and have a cup of soup with you, though." She punched the elevator button. "My guts have been in knots since before the meeting."

"Flu, maybe?" Mark hazarded. "Been going around, I hear."

"Maybe," Kerry agreed, as they entered the elevator and let the doors close. A thought occurred to her, and she shifted her portfolio under her left arm and removed her cell phone from its clip with her other hand. As they reached the bottom floor and exited out of the elevator into the huge lobby, she hit the auto dialer and held the phone to her ear.

It rang an unusual number of times before it was answered and she heard Dar's voice, a slightly hoarse note in it that immediately worried her. "Hi."

"Hey." The note modulated and deepened, sounding relieved even through the cellular connection. "What's up? Problems there?"

"Um." Kerry wracked her brains for a reason to be calling. "Well...ah...I just need to know..." She stopped and took a breath. "Would you believe I just wanted to hear your voice?" She lowered her own and gave the two passing admins a smile. "Mark, can you grab a table?"

"Sure." The MIS chief waved at her. "Say hi to the boss for me." He disappeared into the cafeteria, leaving Kerry in relative isolation.

"Sorry." Kerry returned her attention to the phone and moved toward the plate-glass wall. "Anyway, it was silly. How are you?"

A sigh came down the line. "Tough morning," Dar said. "I think I went over the line for a few minutes."

Uh-oh. Kerry found a bench and sat on it, ignoring the passing crowds on their way to lunch. "What happened? The petty person get to you? I knew I should have come down there and booted her in the behind." Her guts started to ease up a little, and she took a deeper breath. "No wonder my insides are in knots."

There was a little silence. "Are they?" Dar asked. "Really?"

"Yeah," Kerry said. "Have been for a while. Between that and the headache I've got, I thought I was coming down with something. Are you all right?"

"Pretty much. I found a bottle of iced tea and a balcony. I've been standing out here for about ten minutes just watching it rain," Dar answered. "I think I've got your headache's twin sister. Damn, I haven't lost it like that in years, Ker."

"Did you yell at her?" Kerry returned the waved greeting from Duks.

"No." A sigh sounded. "She backed me into corner and started bawling me out. One poke too many, I guess. I took her down and nearly ripped her head off."

Kerry stared at the phone in shocked silence. Apparently Dar realized it, because her next words were rushed, almost stammered.

"It just happened so fast... I don't know what she thought she was trying to do, but I—"

"Wait a minute," Kerry interrupted. "Just hold it there."

Dar fell silent.

"She poked you?" The blond woman's voice rose. "She laid a finger on you? Who in the hell does she think she is? That's bullshit, Dar!"

"Um..."

"Jesus! You should call that general buddy of yours and get her butt transferred to the bottom of Hoover Dam!" Kerry went on. "Son of a bitch!"

"Ker, take it easy." Dar's voice had calmed. "I took care of it. I pretty much think she won't try that again."

"Damn straight she won't," Kerry snorted. "Boy, wait 'til I see her."

Dar laughed softly. "Oh, sweetheart, you just made my day," she said. "Thank you."

"I haven't done anything yet," Kerry muttered in protest. "Dipwad."

"Why don't you get some warm milk and go lay down on the couch in my office for a little while?" Dar was still chuckling. "I'm figuring on taking off from here in couple of hours. There isn't much I can do without the T1; and frankly, I think I'm going to find more when I get everything sucked down and into the analyzers."

Kerry imagined the plush comfort of the couch upstairs and smiled. "Actually, I feel better now," she admitted. "But be careful, okay? I keep having nightmares of you being buried under the billowing clouds of testosterone out there."

"I will. Talk to you later, cute stuff."

"All right," Kerry replied. "Love you."

"Love you, too."

Kerry folded the phone and juggled it in her hands as she leaned back, definitely feeling the knots unraveling in her stomach. Her headache was still there, but the tension she'd felt all morning was dissipating. She stood up and stowed her phone, then tugged her sleeves a bit straighter and made her way into the cafeteria.

Dar braced her boots against the lower railing on the small porch she'd rediscovered near the back end of the training area. There was a small hard bench built against the wall, and just enough cover to avoid being soaked by the still-heavy rain outside.

Ah, Kerrison. Dar sighed silently. *What in the hell would I do without you?* She'd been thumping herself over her reaction to Chief Daniel, but now she sat back and considered it more objectively. The woman had locked them into a closed place and come at her in a threatening manner, aggressively shoving her back against a bulkhead.

What was the chief expecting to happen? Had she really expected Dar to break down and blubber or something? Dar folded her arms across her chest. Maybe that's what Daniel had been looking for, to see how far she could push Dar before Dar pushed back.

Or.

Maybe she'd been hoping Dar would take a swing at her, and give her grounds to force the base commander to take action.

Hmm. In that case, her response had been appropriate, with just enough force to prove her point and not enough aggression to get her in trouble. *Hey.* Dar rubbed her jaw and had to laugh. *Only took thirty years for you to figure out how to balance **that** act. Way to go, Dardar!*

With a sigh, she stood up and grabbed her bottle of peach iced tea, draining it before she made her way back through the small door and into the corner cul-de-sac that it opened onto. Once upon a time it had been a larger suite, and the porch a perk of some big shot's corner office, but time, and changing needs, had forced the Navy to throw up wood and plasterboard walls to divide up the space.

Dar put a hand on one of the worn wooden doorways and gazed down the hall, debating over what to do next. Her decision was made, however, when Chief Daniel swung out of Operations Center and spotted her, turning on her heel and heading toward Dar with a determined look.

Dar chose to remain where she was, and she leaned against the doorframe, folding her arms and watching the other woman approach. "Interested in round two?" she asked as Daniel came within close earshot. A ghostly Kerry poked at her and she squirmed. "Or would you rather just go have lunch?"

Chief Daniel opened her mouth to answer, held it open for a moment, then closed it and released her breath with a sigh.

"C'mon. I'll buy." Dar straightened up. "We're both grown-ups. Let's act like it."

Clearly, the chief had been caught by surprise. She hesitated for a long beat, then lifted both hands a little and let them fall. "What the hell. All right, Ms. Roberts. You're giving me a pain the size of an aircraft carrier, so I might as well get a meal out of it. Lead on."

They found a table in the back of the mess and sat down with trays of open-faced turkey sandwiches. Dar opened her carton of milk and drank directly from it, watching her reluctant lunch partner mess with a pile of lettuce and tomatoes.

"So." Chief Daniel neatly sliced her salad into manageable chunks. "You're Big Andy's kid."

Dar cocked her head to one side. "Yes, I am."

The shorter woman looked up, meeting her eyes. "You could have said that right off."

"Why?" Dar shot back. "Shouldn't make a damn bit of a difference."

Daniel snorted and shook her head. "Can the bullshit, lady. It matters, and you know it does. Did you think you'd have an advantage by acting like a clueless outsider?" She picked up her glass of iced tea and took a sip. "Here I think I've got some dumb civ making my life miserable, and it turns out I've been hauling around some damn smartass Navy brat."

"Oh. You mean I could have skipped the howitzer-up-the-ass attitude if I'd told you up front I grew up here?" Dar inquired. "Maybe you should have done your homework, Chief. I have a file on you an inch thick."

The chief stopped eating and put her silverware down, staring at Dar with a look completely devoid of humor. "What in the hell do you mean by that?"

Dar merely watched her, sucking idly on her milk. She waited for the veins to start emerging on the ginger-haired woman's temples, then she finally replied. "Relax. There's nothing outstandingly scary in it." She actually didn't have that much, but the reaction she'd gotten from the comment made her itch to have Mark search further.

Daniel sat there, breathing hard for a moment. "You're a real son of a bitch, aren't you?"

A charming smile appeared on Dar's face. "I can be." She paused. "If I'm forced into it." One finger pointed at the sailor. "So be smart, and don't." She set the milk down and picked up her fork, spearing a bit of mashed potatoes and tasting them.

"Sure you weren't adopted?" the chief shot back.

The corner of Dar's lips quirked. "I've looked in a mirror enough times to know I wasn't." She took a bite of turkey. "But feel free to ask my dad if you want."

Hazel eyes narrowed, and the chief bit down on her fork with a vicious scrape of teeth on metal. Then her face relaxed, and she snorted softly. "No, thanks. I don't want my fingers pulled off if he hears I laid one of them on his precious offspring." Her eyes searched the angular, intense features across the table, strange and familiar at the same time. She felt like kicking herself for not realizing who this bitch was before, then she felt like kicking the damn commander for not telling her. *Bastard.* She bet he and Perkins were laughing their asses off at her.

And what was in that file? The chief was uncomfortably aware of the sharp intelligence behind those blue-tinted ice chips that were watching her. Evaluating her. Daniel swallowed and reviewed her options. She knew Andrew Roberts and had a healthy respect for him, but she now realized his often spoken of only child was a danger of a much higher degree.

What the hell was she going to do?

The loudspeaker's crackle almost made her jump, and she looked up at the speaker just as Dar did, the younger woman's head tilting to one side as she listened.

"Attention, attention all personnel. We have just received notification that flooding has closed both Card Sound Road and US 1. Be advised that all deliveries to and from the mainland have been canceled until further notice. If you were scheduled to be transported north today, please see your unit commander immediately."

Groans rose around them. Daniel snorted and recovered a bit of her balance at the perceptible annoyance in Dar's expression. "Guess you're stuck here. Just our luck." Possibilities, though, started occurring to her.

Dar sighed, ignoring her sarcasm. "I knew I should have stayed in bed this morning." She removed her cell phone from its clip and dialed a number, holding the phone to her ear and turning away slightly.

Yeah, Chief Daniel mused. *Maybe you should have.*

Chapter
Seven

"Ugh." Kerry dropped into her chair and leaned back, releasing a huge sigh and closing her eyes briefly. Very briefly, since her intercom buzzed a second later. "Yes?"

"Ms. Kerry, my mother says to tell you that they have closed the roads that are going to the Keys." Mayte's voice held a hint of anxiety. "She is worried about Ms. Roberts."

Oh, crap, Kerry cursed to herself. "She said she was trying to get out of there early, Mayte. I'll call her. I hope she's almost back here by now." She reached for her phone and almost dropped it as it rang at the same moment. "Gah—whoops. Hello?"

"Hi." Dar's voice sounded resigned. "Guess where I'm stuck."

Kerry winced in pure reflex. "I just heard about the roads. That totally sucks large rocks, Dar."

"I know," Dar said. "I took care of getting you a ride home, though."

Jesus. I forgot I needed one. Kerry mentally slapped herself. "Honey, you didn't have to do that. I'm sure I could beg a ride from someone here." It was, however, a typically Dar thing for her to do, given her partner's meticulous attention to details. "But thank you."

"Well," Dar chuckled softly, "don't thank me just yet. It's my dad who's coming to get you."

Eeerup. Kerry winced. "Ah. Did you think my life was lacking some excitement today or something?" she replied. "Maybe he'll let me drive. You think?"

"You can ask. He generally caves in to whatever you want," Dar answered. "Just like I do," she added, with a verbal twinkle in her tone. "Hey, I think I'm making some progress with the chief. I tried to do what you'd have done."

Still distracted by the prospect of being picked up by Andrew, Kerry almost didn't respond. "Uh...oh, did you? What did you do?"

"Took her to lunch."

Kerry smiled. "Good girl."

"Then I told her if she didn't behave, I'd have to really get nasty."

"Oh." Kerry covered her eyes and laughed silently. "Gotta work on that part, huh?"

"Eh." Dar sighed. "Maybe it won't be so bad down here. A couple of the guys I grew up with just tracked me down. They wanna take me out to the local bar and trade no-shit stories for a while. They found me a bed just in case the roads don't open back up."

"You have your kit, right? I know I repacked it after the trip to the Keys." Kerry drummed her fingers on her desk. "Don't take a chance, okay? If the weather's bad, just stick around down there. I'd kinda be worried if I knew you were driving up Card Sound at night." She paused. "I'll miss you, though. I was looking forward to a hug tonight."

A few beats of silence followed, then Dar cleared her throat. "I'll make it up to you tomorrow, I promise. Okay?"

"Okay," Kerry agreed. "Call me later and let me know what's up. I think I'm done with all my meetings today; now I just have a mailbox to wade through." She glanced at her monitor. "Dar, how did you deal with all this crap everyone sends?"

"Simple. Take everything that isn't immediate operations and reply with 'Could you please clarify why you're asking me this?'" Dar told her. "I guarantee ninety percent of them won't come back."

"Really?"

"Really."

Kerry grinned and examined the ceiling over her head. "Thanks, boss. I'll do that."

"Any time," Dar said. "Talk to you later."

Kerry closed the phone and put it down, indulging in a few moments of daydreaming as she folded her hands over her stomach and swiveled her chair a little. "What a character," she finally murmured with a helpless chuckle. Her intercom buzzed again, and she regarded it balefully for a moment before she answered. "Yes?"

"Ms. Kerry?"

"I just talked to Dar, Mayte. I'll call your mom. She's okay, she's just stuck down at the base for now," Kerry responded.

"*Sí, gracias*, but there is a phone call for you, from the car place."

Car place? Kerry's brow furrowed, then cleared. "Oh. Right. I'll take it. Thanks, Mayte." She released the intercom and hit the phone line. "Kerry Stuart speaking."

"Ms. Stuart? This is Laura Margoles from Beach Lexus. You sent in a vehicle request using the Internet this morning?"

"That's right," Kerry confirmed.

"Great." The woman's voice was cheerful and friendly. "We had what you wanted right in stock. I've got your paperwork done; when would you like to pick up the car?"

"Really? Just like that?" Kerry was surprised. "Leather and everything?"

"Absolutely!" Laura stated. "They're detailing the car now, in fact. Shining it up and making sure everything's in perfect condition for you."

Kerry turned in her chair and reviewed the rain lashing at her window. "They're washing the car? Have you looked outside?"

"Has to be nice and clean before we turn it over." Laura's enthusiasm didn't miss a beat. "Would you like to stop by after work? We're open until seven."

"All right." Kerry grinned, finding herself anticipating the new acquisition. "See you before then."

"Excellent! Looking forward to it, Ms. Stuart. Have a great day!" Laura warbled happily.

"Sure. You, too." Kerry hung up, bemused. She regarded her quiet office for a moment, then idly spun herself around in her chair a few times. "Vroom vroom."

Kerry had sent Mayte home earlier with María, and by the time she finished up her inbox, a quiet had settled over the building. She clicked on the last message to send it, then sat back and cupped her hands around her tea mug, sucking down the strawberry scented liquid as she watched her mail program transfer all her finished mail to storage folders.

A relaxed strain of music was coming from her PC speakers, which were tuned to an Internet radio station that mostly played New Age Celtic music. She flexed her bare feet under her desk and sighed, glad the long day was over.

A soft knock sounded. "C'mon in." Kerry looked up, a smile already crossing her face as the door opened and Andrew Roberts's familiar head poked inside. "Hey, Dad." She got up and trotted across the carpeted floor as Andrew entered. Her father-in-law was wearing a dark blue rain jacket with its hood up, and he pushed the hood back and unzipped the jacket as she threw her arms around him in an unhesitating hug. "Ooh...it's good to see you."

Unseen by Kerry, a smile crossed the ex Navy SEAL's scarred face as Andrew returned the embrace. "Well there, kumquat. It's good t'see you, too."

Topping Dar's slightly over six-foot height by almost five inches, Andrew towered over Kerry by almost a foot, and his large, broad-shouldered and still-muscular body had the same solid feel. She loosened her grasp and gazed up at him, catching the grin before he could discard it. Eyes the same shade as her lover's twinkled back at her, set in a face that, despite its very masculine ruggedness, still brought Dar to mind in its planed cheekbones and angular shape. "Thanks for coming to rescue me."

Andrew snorted softly. "Since Dar saw fit to go and abandon you, I figured it'd be a good idea."

"She didn't abandon me." Kerry gave him a friendly poke. "She's stuck down on that base. I don't envy her; but on the bright side, it gives me a chance to spend some time with one of my favorite people."

"You are just a sweet-talking young lady," Dar's father drawled. "C'mon, 'fore we have to paddle on out of this here office."

Kerry released him, and went back to her desk to retrieve her shoes. "I have to make a stop before home, if that's okay." She shut down her PC as Andrew wandered around her office peering at the décor curiously. "My new car's ready."

"That so?" Andrew asked curiously. "Dar told me you got yourself into a pickle last night and banged up that little bitty thing of yours."

"Some crazy person driving down the wrong side of the road on the causeway, thanks." Kerry zipped up her briefcase and shouldered it. "Did Dar tell you she got herself and that brute of an SUV of hers between the nutcase and me?" She fastened her jacket and turned her desk lamp off.

"No, she did not." Andrew tried hard to hide a dazzlingly proud smile, and failed completely.

"Figures." Kerry took him by the arm and led him out of the office. "C'mon, we'll get my new buggy, then I'll treat you to dinner. How's that?"

Andrew allowed himself to be escorted to the elevator, shrugging his hood up into place as Kerry hit the button to call it. "I do believe I can do any of that there treating that's required, young lady," he replied, following her into the elevator.

"We'll see about that," Kerry teased as the doors closed.

Interested eyes watched the empty space for a few seconds, then footsteps retreated back down the hallway, disappearing behind the solid sound of a wooden door closing.

The bar was old, and mostly wood, and featured an honest-to-goodness jukebox that was currently droning out something from the country western side of the record catalog. Dar tipped back in her chair and took a sip of her beer, gazing across the table's surface at the five men gathered around it.

Damn, it's been a long time. Dar let her eyes linger on her old friends. They were all the same age, more or less, as she was, and some things hadn't changed much. Mike and Ricardo still looked like GI Joe dolls, complete with buzz cuts and bodybuilder physiques. Duds and John were still inseparable, two lanky, spare men with straight blond-brown hair and Southern drawls.

And Chuckie, of course. Dar let a faint smile cross her face. Chuckie had actually gotten better looking over the years. He'd left the gawkiness of his late teens behind and grown into a six-foot-plus body with nice, broad shoulders and an athletic waistline. Tucked into his Navy captain's uniform, he cut a very impressive figure and Dar had no problem cheerfully acknowledging that to herself.

"So, now what is it you're doing, Dar?" Chuckie turned and leaned on his chair arm, gazing into her eyes with his twinkling gray ones. "I hear you're turning the base upside down."

"Making trouble, like usual," Dar replied, with a chuckle. "The Pentagon hired me to go tell the Navy how to do its job better."

"Ooh." The five men chorused a groan. "No shit?" Chuckie laughed. "They didn't, did they?"

"They did." Dar lifted her beer and took a sip. "Mother of ironies, huh?"

"Son of a bitch." Mike rocked back and forth on uneven chair legs. "The brass on base must be ready to have a heart attack." He poked a finger at Dar. "I still remember the day you redone the base telecom and sent all them private notes of the CO's to the staff fax machine."

Heh. Dar snickered. "I remember that, too. Guy was an idiot to be using base mail to send love notes to that girl he picked up in Chicago."

"Yep. You were a hell raiser, for sure," Mike chuckled. "Bet you still are."

"That's what they say," Dar demurred. "Only now they pay me for it," she added.

Chuckie cocked his head curiously. "You're still working for ILS, right?" He waited for Dar to nod. "So, what kind of money do they pay for what you do?" He noticed Dar's lifted eyebrow. "Round numbers, I mean. We always figured you'd do all right, because you got more brains than half the earth, but for real, Dar...did you end up kicking ass?"

Dar glanced around the weather-beaten bar and caught the interested looks from her old pals. They'd all done well in the Navy, and all of them, even Mike, had grudgingly admitted to being career sailors. "Well," she took a swig of beer and rolled the beverage around in her mouth before swallowing. "I'm the chief information officer of the largest IS company in the world. My base is seven figures, if that's what you're asking."

They all looked at each other, then back at her. There was a moment of stunned silence.

"Well." Chuckie rubbed his jaw. "God damn."

Dar smiled. "So I guess I'm buying then, huh?" she remarked dryly. "See? You shoulda dragged me out to someplace nicer."

"Son of a bitch." Mike started laughing. "Son of a bitch. You're actually one of them corporate big shots?"

"'Fraid so," Dar agreed solemnly. "Got me a big office, floor-to-ceiling glass windows, teakwood desk, the whole nine yards," she told them. "Everyone running around scared to death of me, you name it."

"Wow." Chuckie shook his head. "I can believe the last part, 'cause you can be a scary individual when you wanna be, old buddy, but thinking of you in an ivory tower's givin' me a headache." He slapped Dar's knee lightly, then poked the spot. "You don't spend all your time behind that desk though, d'ya? You don't look much like a cream puff."

"No more than you do." Dar let a mildly evil grin touch her lips as she curled a foot around the leg of his chair and jerked hard, nearly sending him sprawling backward. "Spending your time sitting in that nice comfy chair on the bridge."

"Uh-oh...here we go." Mike burst into laughter. "I knew it was just a matter of time. The two of you ain't changed for shit."

"You—" Chuckie grabbed for the edge of the table to keep from tipping over, but the surface moved, sending the two mugs of beer on it flying. "Yow...sonofa—"

"Hey!" Mike yelped and leaped to his feet, only barely avoiding being soaked. "Cut that out, bilgebrain." He pointed a finger at Chuckie. "Don't you start, either. You never have gotten over getting your ass kicked in that obstacle course the night we all graduated."

Chuckie snorted. "Get out of here. I don't even remember that."

"I do," Dar drawled, with an even more evil grin. "But since I was the one doing the kicking, I guess that's natural." Oh, she certainly did remember that night. They'd had a beer or two way too many, and she'd been just at the very top edge of her best physical conditioning, seriously intent on getting herself into BUDS training and only too happy to prove that to any other Navy brat who questioned her. Twenty of them had straggled out of their graduation party, and bets had started flying.

"That was then," Chuckie reminded her pointedly.

The words came out before she had a chance to think about them. "C'mon, Chuckie, I could still kick your ass on that course."

Now he grinned. "Oh yeah? How much you wanna bet?"

Mike groaned. "Oh no...not again. For Pete's sake, you two! You're furking adults now!"

"Hundred bucks!" Chuckie leaned forward eagerly. "C'mon."

She was out of her mind, Dar dimly realized as she watched herself rise to the challenge, almost as though seeing someone else do it. "How about a thousand?" she drawled softly. "C'mon, tough guy. See if you can lift anything but binoculars now." A tiny voice cleared its throat internally. *Hope you know what you're doing, big shot, or you're gonna be picking splinters out of your ass for a week.* "How about it, Chuckie?"

His eyes glinted and his well-shaped nostrils flared. "You got it. Let's go. I got a lot of things I could do with a thousand bucks."

Dar set her bottle down and stood. "After you?" She held a hand up and pointed to the door. She gave the rest of the group, who were muttering and shaking their heads, a smile. "C'mon, guys. After this, I'll treat for dinner. How 'bout it?"

"You ain't gonna be in any condition to treat anyone," Chuckie warned with a big grin.

"Save your breath." Dar booted him in the butt before he could move, then booted him again when he tried to evade her. "You're gonna need it."

"Hey!" Chuckie slapped at her leg with his uniform hat. "Cut that out, or I'll...I'll..."

"What? Tell my daddy?" Dar was enjoying herself thoroughly. "Last time you did that, I got a banana split out of it."

"Wench." Chuckie started laughing. "God damn you, you're such a wild weasel... Ow!" He slapped at Dar's boot again, which had just impacted his butt. "I am gonna push your ass so far down in that mud, you'll have to call a deep-sea diver to go find you."

"Careful, hairball," Duds rumbled softly. "If'n that deep-sea diver's her daddy, your ass is gonna be flying over the mess hall by morning."

They all laughed and jostled out the door into a still-drizzling evening. "How is yer old man doin', Dar?" Mike asked, lowering his voice a little and getting serious. "Man, I was glad they got him back."

Dar exhaled. "He's fine," she replied. "He and Mom got this fifty-some-foot Bertram, and they're having a blast on it. They've been out to Bermuda twice, and I can't remember ever seeing him so happy."

"Wow." Mike smiled. "That's way cool."

"He got a boat?" Duds asked curiously. "Man, that musta been some pension...or did you get that for him?"

Dar smiled and ran a hand through her now damp hair. "What do you think?"

Duds laughed. "Daddy's girl all the way, that's for damn sure. C'mon, let's get this damn thing over with. I'm hungry!"

"You're always hungry, mouth on wheels," Chuckie chided, giving him a backslap in the belly. "That's why you're outgrowing your uniform. Lookit that."

"Cut that out!" Duds nudged him. "Leave my buttons alone, y'pervert."

"Butthead."

Dar sucked in a wet breath, overcome with a wash of giddy enjoyment, looking ahead to the dark, mud-spattered challenge in front of her. So it was crazy.

That was all right.

Everyone had to have a crazy night now and then, right?

Kerry leaned back in the seat of the stolid gray pickup truck Andrew was navigating through the flooded streets. She had her seatbelt securely fastened around her body, and her feet were braced solidly against the floor, steadying her as the truck moved.

Andrew wasn't really a bad driver, she'd decided, just an impatient one; and little things such as sidewalks and divider islands proved little or no impediment to his progress in getting from point A to point B in the quickest possible manner. "Nice truck, Dad." She patted the fabric seat. "I like it. Dar was telling me about the one she had when she was younger."

Forced by convention to stop at a red light, Andrew sat back and folded his arms. "Ceci tried for some days to get me to agree to drive in one of them Beetle cars."

Kerry raised an eyebrow.

"Well, young lady, that is exactly how I felt about it, too," the ex-SEAL drawled. "Them are the ugliest things I ever did see; and there was no how, no way I was going to be sitting inside one of them, much less drive it."

"I couldn't picture that." Kerry shook her head. "It would be like you having a moped, or Dar drinking skim milk."

"She hates that," Andrew agreed. "Even when she was a tot, Cec used to try and get her to drink it, and she'd toss her bottle 'cross the kitchen."

"I know." Kerry closed her eyes as the light changed and Andrew used the opportunity to cross three lanes between four other cars. "I suggested it once." She paused. "Only because I worry about her cholesterol, and mine; but I got a lecture about cows, and water, and the fact that if she wanted to drink white chlorinated liquid, she'd just add food coloring to the tap."

Andrew snorted. "She's particular 'bout a few things. That's one of 'em," he admitted. "Got that one from me, I do believe."

"Gee, what a surprise." Kerry peeked at him and grinned tolerantly. "Anyway, I got her to stop having chocolate chip cookies for breakfast, so I figure I'm ahead of the game."

Andrew peered through the raindrops and spotted his target. He aimed the truck toward the entrance and proceeded accordingly. "She's a healthy kid," he stated. "Always was. Worst thing she ever did get was them chicken pox. Lord, that was a mess."

"I heard you got them, too." Kerry smiled at him, pretending she didn't see the trucks bearing down on them as Andrew crossed the intersection. The pickup darted into the parking lot of the Lexus dealership just in time, though she imagined she could feel the draft of the eighteen-wheeler crossing behind them. They pulled into an empty spot, and she released her safety belt with a sense of relief.

Andrew leaned on his steering wheel and peered out the window, observing the rows of shiny, if rain spattered, new cars. "You getting one of these damn things, too?" His voice was surprised.

"Sort of." Kerry pointed. "See? That's the one Dar has."

"Uh-huh." Andrew nodded.

"That's the one I'm getting." She indicated a row to the left.

"Sonofabiscuit. Ain't that cute," her father-in-law chuckled softly. "All bitty and spunky looking. Figures."

Kerry gave his arm a poke. "Hey, at least it's not a Beetle." She opened the door. "C'mon, this won't take long, and I'm hungry." She got out and grabbed for the doorframe as a wave of dizziness passed over her. "Whoa."

Andrew circled the front of the truck and put a hand on her shoulder. "You all right?"

Kerry leaned against the metal frame and took a deep breath, waiting for the world to stop spinning. "Yeah. Like a doof I skipped lunch, and I know better." Her vision cleared and she shook her head. "Low blood sugar runs in my family. I usually keep granola bars around but I ran out, and I meant to stop this morning."

"That ain't a good thing." Andrew stuck his head inside the truck and rummaged in a bag behind the seat. "Here." He handed Kerry a banana. "Forgot I had those damn things."

Kerry peeled the fruit and took a bite, a little disturbed by the shaking of her hands. "Maybe I was just overstressed today," she joked faintly, aware of Andrew's concerned expression. "I had some really confrontational meetings, and I was a little worried about Dar driving down there in this weather." She swallowed a few mouthfuls and was relieved when the shakiness faded.

"I do believe we might need to be worrying about you," Andrew stated. "You're white as Caesar's ghost, Kerry. Sit down here."

"No, it's okay," Kerry reassured him. "I feel a lot better, honestly." She finished her banana and neatly folded the skin, then leaned forward and kissed him on the cheek. "Thanks, Dad."

Andrew blushed, faintly visible in the lamplight bathing them. "That was a lotta fuss for a little old banana," he muttered. "You sure you don't want something else? Maybe an orange, or whatever the hell else Ceci stuck in the back of this here truck?"

Kerry smiled. "Does Dar know how lucky she is?"

"Huh?"

"I don't think she does." Kerry pushed away from the truck and straightened her sleeves, then tossed the banana peel into a nearby garbage can. "Let's go get my new wheels." She slid her hand around Andrew's arm and walked with him toward the showroom, where she could see dim forms of hopeful salesmen lurking in wait.

The door opened as they reached it, and she stepped inside the cool, well-lit showroom to be greeted by a very nice-looking young man in a neatly fitted suit and tie. "Hi." Kerry smiled at him. "I've got an appointment. I'm supposed to pick up a car?"

The sound of staccato heels made their heads turn to see a

woman with dark, frosted hair walking toward them, a warm smile on her face. "Ms. Stuart?"

"That's right," Kerry replied.

"Excellent. If you'd step over here to my desk and sign these papers, I'll have your car brought 'round." She glanced at Andrew. "Can I get your husband some coffee?"

Kerry thought her father-in-law's grizzled eyebrows were going to pop right off his head and stick in the drop ceiling. "Sure," she agreed cheerfully. "C'mon, honey, sit down here."

"Excuse me," Andrew barked. "This here young lady is not mah wife." He pinned the saleswoman with a fierce glare. "What do ah look like to you, some kinda candy-assed cradle robber?"

The woman's jaw dropped, and she looked from Kerry to Andrew in bewilderment. "I'm very sorry sir," she stammered. "I know I shouldn't assume...I just thought...Well, excuse me. I'm very sorry." She put the papers down. "Ma'am, if you could just sign these?"

"Sure." Kerry sat down and slid the stack over, picking up a pen. The saleswoman scurried quickly away.

Andrew snorted and sat down next to her. "Mah God."

Kerry giggled. "You're really funny."

"That was most certainly not funny, young lady."

She turned her head. "How old are you?" Kerry watched the blue eyes blink a few times. "Well?"

Andrew sat up straighter. "Ah am forty-eight years old." He paused. "Why?"

Kerry leaned closer to him. "'Cause I'm almost thirty," she whispered. "It's not that far-fetched, Dad." She went back to signing her papers, getting through half of them before she heard Andrew sigh.

"You're right, kumquat," he said. "Mah kid has not one clue as to how lucky she is."

Kerry felt her face ease into a smile as she finished, putting the pen down and glancing up as the saleswoman came back. "All done."

"Here you go." The woman handed her a set of keys and pointed to where the shadowy form of her new car was just pulling up outside the door. "And again, I'm really sorry, sir."

Andrew sighed and stood. "That's all right."

They walked to the door and pushed it open. "You going to kick the tires for me, Dad?" Kerry teased. "Dar wanted me to get a—what are those called? A Hummer."

Andrew snorted. "Fer what?" He circled the new car curiously. "Damn things steer like a Greyhound bus, and you can't park them for nothin'." He opened a door and peeked inside. "Leather, would you look at that? Mah kid is definitely rubbing off on you."

Kerry opened the driver side door and sniffed appreciatively. "Oh yes," she chortled. "C'mon, let's take it for a test ride. There's a good restaurant right down the block."

Andrew slid into the passenger seat, which he adjusted to make room for his long legs. "Ain't one of them raw fish stores, is it?"

"Um..."

A dark brow cocked. "Tell you what, I'll go eat them raw fishies if you let me drive on the way back."

"Oh boy."

"Sonofabitch!"

Dar heard the gasping croak behind her as she reached the last wooden wall and lunged forward, crouching down and releasing her body upward to stretch out and grab the top rail, pulling upward before she could crash against the hard surface. Her boots scraped, then caught a purchase, and she powered up and over the top, releasing her hold and letting herself fall down toward a murky, mud-covered surface.

Behind her, she could hear Chuckie grunt as he hit the top of the wall, but then her boots were hitting the ground and she almost sprawled forward, barely catching her balance before she hopped forward and starting running toward the ropes.

Climbing ropes—one of the toughest things for anyone, especially a woman, to do. Dar wiped her palms on her thighs just before she reached them, then took a breath, ruefully acknowledging that she certainly wasn't a teenager anymore before she leaped and caught the rope, feeling the wet, scratchy hemp bite into her hands. Her legs responded in old memory, curling around the rope beneath her and tightening, supporting her weight as she reached up for a second handhold.

Well. Dar felt the spatters of rain hit her and heard the clank of the rope next to her as Chuckie tried to catch up. It wasn't as hard as she had feared. She powered up the rope and released one hand to slap the bell on top, then slid neatly down, wincing a little as the rough hemp stung her hands. She hit the ground and ducked around the edge of the climbing pit, bolting across the uneven ground and leaping over the water that separated the obstacles from the last, long hundred yards every tired, sore recruit had to run over at top speed. Dar heard Chuckie finally hit the bell and slither down after her, but she knew she was home free.

Running was something she was very used to, something her body, stressed by this unusual tasking long forgotten, was accustomed to doing on a daily basis. She tucked her fingers into a half fist, leaned forward into a powerful, even stride, and just ran.

"Shit," she heard Chuckie groan behind her, and it made her laugh; and the hoots of the other men suddenly rolled around her as they spotted her clearing the end of the pits and heading toward the finish. She tucked her head down and bolted, feeling a crazy surge of energy as the wind brushed her hair back and the rain stung her face.

The trees that marked the end flashed by, and she slowed, bouncing to a halt and into the welcoming arms of the four waiting sailors, who caught her and slapped her back, laughing and razzing Chuckie, who finally made it past with a curse.

Dar could feel her heart pounding from the exertion, and it certainly hadn't been nearly as good a performance as the last time she'd done it, but... She chuckled as she watched Chuckie lean over, holding his belly, his face a visible crimson even in the low light. "Gotta lay off the damn beer, Chuck." She put her hands on her hips, glad beyond measure she'd kept up the sessions in the gym, and the running, and the martial arts, if for no other reason than to be able to stand here on this mud-covered patch of ground with a bunch of her old friends and look better than they did.

Erf. Dar winced. *That was damned egotistical, wasn't it?*

"Hot damn, Dar." Mike clapped a long arm over her shoulders. "You are still one hot mother, y'know that? How about marrying me?"

Dar laughed. "I thought you had a girlfriend?" She poked him. "Or at least that's what you were bragging about in that bar..."

"Well, I didn't hear you say you was married," he joked back. "So I figured I got a chance."

It was a strange feeling. Dar took a breath and released it. She'd been straightforward and out regarding her sexuality for so long, she'd forgotten what it felt like to be around people who had no idea, and to whom it would matter.

To whom it would matter to her if they knew. Dar felt her euphoric mood evaporate, and she took a mental step back and tried to figure out what to do. Her nature disliked unneeded lies, but a part of her was enjoying this unexpected reacceptance into an old world and resisted the estrangement she knew would be caused by acknowledging her lifestyle.

"Asshole. You ain't got no chance," Duds snorted. "Dar's got way better taste than you."

Dar managed a smile, then she walked over to where Chuckie was still recovering. "Hey." She bumped him lightly. "You all right?"

Her old boyfriend straightened, then blew out a breath. "Other than having my goddamned ego dragged over a bed of nails and my bank account emptied? I'm great." His lips twisted. "Will you take a check?"

"Don't worry about it." Dar shook her head slightly. "It was worth the kick just to see if I could still do it."

"Wench." Chuckie's face relaxed a little as he realized Dar was serious. "Just for that, you're gonna take us out to the steak-house." He pointed toward the parking lot. "Now that I proved ship captains do spend too much time sitting on their butts, let's go."

The four others strolled ahead, leaving Chuckie and Dar to walk together toward the parked cars. "Wench." The Naval officer gave her a look. "I'm gonna have to explain to half the base why I got Band-Aids all over my hands from that damn course tomor-row." He held up his hands, visibly scuffed and scraped in the streetlamp light.

"Me, too," Dar admitted, holding up her own hands in evi-dence. "I don't get much in the way of calluses pounding a key-board."

"Ah." Chuckie sighed. "We're getting too old for this."

Dar chuckled. "Yeah." She flexed her hands, wincing a little.

They were both quiet for a few strides. "Ass kicking or not, it's good to see you, Dar," Chuckie finally said softly. "Got some good memories of us."

"So do I," Dar replied. "Your letters to me in college used to crack me up." She reflected on those long past times. "I'm sorry we lost touch."

Chuckie shrugged one shoulder. "We knew we would. That was two real different worlds we were going off into." He glanced at Dar. "I knew I didn't end up doing too bad; always wondered where you ended up. Might have figured you to be some top brass somewhere."

"I used to wonder if I'd made the right choice." Dar inhaled, and looked around. "Now I know I did, but..." She shook her head. "Definitely had second thoughts." She raised her voice. "Hey, head over to the third row. I'll drive."

"Don't trust Mike?" Chuckie laughed. "He's not half as bad a driver as your daddy ever was."

"No. I figure I'm the only one who's likely to have room for all of us," she said dryly. "Unless you ended up getting a Suburban. Did you?"

"Hell no," Chuckie snorted.

'That's what I thought." Dar angled her steps toward the Lexus. "C'mon, I figure it's going to take my shock absorbers to handle you herd of steers anyway."

"Ooh..." Her old friend laughed. "I think you hang out with us just so you can feel petite, in that case." He bumped Dar's shoulder with his own. "Hey," his voice dropped a little, "you going with someone right now, Dar?"

The approach came around a blind corner and surprised her. "Yeah," she managed to answer, on an uneven breath. "Yeah, I am. Why?"

He shrugged. "Just asking," Chuckie said. "I'm between ships, if you catch my drift, and I thought if you were too, maybe we could hook up, for old time's sake."

Dar realized she had about ten seconds before they caught up with the four others waiting. She lifted a hand and unlocked her doors. "Not a chance." She softened the words with a smile. "I'm very taken...and very happy about it."

"Ah well." Chuckie returned the smile. "Just the way my luck's been running. What've we got here?" He turned his attention to the car. "Good Lord, do you mean to tell me you drive a damn Lexus?"

"Yep." Dar opened the driver's side door and watched them pile in. "Hey, one of you guys has to get in the far back. You can't all fit in there."

"Heh," Mike chuckled. "Wanna bet? You forget what service we're in, Dardar." The back seat was filled to the brim with squished sailors. "More room in here than in a Polaris. Get driving."

Dar rolled her eyes, but slid behind the wheel and started the engine. "Why do I get the feeling I'm gonna regret this?" She felt the car rock as the men in back started singing and moving back and forth.

"C'mon, Dar, sing with us. I know you can," Duds chortled. "What do you do with some drunken sailors..."

Dar sighed as she pulled out of the parking slot, but joined in anyway, filled with a very mixed set of emotions. It had been a day far too full of conflict, and she found herself sure of only one single thing.

Five sailors and fifteen beers equaled the tonal quality of six dozen sets of dogs' toenails on a chalkboard.

Jesus. Dar hoped she survived the short drive to the steak-house.

Kerry yawned as she collected her steaming mug of hot choc-olate and wandered back into the living room. Chino butted the back of her knees and almost made her trip, the animal very glad to see at least one half of her family after the long day. "Hey, cut that out," Kerry chided the dog. "You aren't the one who's going to have to clean this tile if I spill chocolate all over it."

"Gruff." Chino pounced on her hippo and brought it over, crouching down and shaking it, begging for some play time.

"Okay, let me put this down," Kerry laughed, setting aside her cup and grabbing the toy. "Go get it...g'wan." She tossed the stuffed animal to the other side of the apartment and watched Chino scramble after it, her toenails sliding on the hard surface.

"Bring it here." Kerry sat down on the couch and tugged the toy free of Chino's very white teeth, throwing it over past the din-ing room table as the retriever acted true to her breed and fetched it. "Good girl." She played with the dog for a while, taking a moment in between tosses to turn on the television and stretch her body out along the couch with a sense of relief.

It had been a very long day, with a surprisingly nice ending. Kerry smiled, remembering the hour spent patiently coaxing Andrew into sharing her sushi in the little sushi dive on the beach she and Dar loved to go to.

Mental note, Kerry, she reminded herself. *Don't take SEALs to sushi bars unless you want to know things about the fish you're eating that would make the plots for excellent sci-fi movies.* He'd finally settled on the cooked variety of sashimi and some stir-fry chicken, leaving Kerry to her more adventurous raw tidbits. They'd shared some sake, though, and she'd enjoyed the evening very much, listening to stories of Dar's harum-scarum youth and hearing the note of unconscious pride in Andrew's voice even when recounting the goriest details.

Kerry leaned back against the leather surface, tensing and relaxing her muscles as she idly watched Steve Irwin cavort across the screen, hugging a crocodile to him and enthusing over its toothy good looks. "What a whack job," she commented. "Did you know he has his own toy set now, Chino? Should I get you one? You want to chew Steve's head off?"

"Gruff." Chino tossed the slightly soggy hippo up to land on Kerry's side.

"I'll take that as a no." Kerry tossed the toy again, then slid down and put her head on the couch arm, allowing her eyes to close briefly as she considered the tasks she had left to do that evening. A wash was due, and she had those reports to go over, and there was that project Dar had left her.

Kerry let one eye open and regard the room, then she closed it again. Or she could just take a nap here on the couch, which was nice and warm and comfortable. Maybe she could compromise, she reasoned, snoozing until Dar called, which would definitely wake her up.

Yeah. That was a good idea. She reached over and picked up her cell phone, which was on the coffee table, and brought it closer, resting her hand on it as she allowed the sleepy feeling to take over and relax her, easing away the last of the lingering headache that had aggravated her all day long.

It was very quiet as Dar pulled into her parking spot, sliding in next to a shiny new smaller version of the car she was driving. She got out and closed the door gently, then ran a hand over the dark blue paint of Kerry's new car. "Nice," she approved, peering inside before making her way up the small flight of stairs to the door.

It had been a nice dinner, if loud, and they'd made it back to the base just after midnight. She'd let her friends out, then sat there for over ten minutes, wondering why she didn't just get out herself and go to the bunk they'd assigned her.

Finally, she'd gotten out of the Lexus, and instead of going toward the building, she'd walked back over to the guardhouse and asked them if the roads had opened.

They had.

Dar had walked back to the car, gotten inside, and left, choosing the drive back to Miami in the early hours over staying on the base, hardly knowing why she'd take the long trek when the Navy bed could hardly be that uncomfortable.

The feeling of relief as she keyed in the lock convinced her it had been a good decision, though; not that she'd really doubted it. She opened the door and slid inside, stopping in surprise as she spotted the lights still on and heard the television's low mutter.

Chino jumped off the couch and ran over, shaking her head sleepily, clearly startled to see Dar, but glad. Dar rubbed the dog's ears, but kept her eyes on the dozing form curled up in the corner of the couch.

Quietly, Dar walked over and knelt beside where Kerry was sleeping, allowing herself a long moment to just study her lover.

Okay. She smiled silently. *So this is why you came home.* Asleep, Kerry's face held a relaxed innocence that always touched Dar's heart, and she found herself looking forward to the surprised delight she knew would be there when she woke the blond woman up.

"Ker." Dar stroked Kerry's cheek gently, and after a second, the pale lashes stirred and lifted, revealing slightly dazed green eyes that fastened on her face, then brightened in welcome as a smile appeared at the same time. "Sorry I didn't call."

"No problem," Kerry replied, her voice slightly husky from sleep. "I like this mode of contact much better anyway." Her smile widened. "I guess the road opened, huh?"

Dar nodded. "Yeah. I had dinner with the guys, and when I got back, they said it had; so I decided to come on home instead of staying down there."

"Good." Kerry caught Dar's hand and pressed it against her cheek, then kissed it. "Crudpuppies. I had so much I wanted to do tonight. I fell asleep figuring your call would wake me up." Her fingers felt something odd, and she turned Dar's hand over. "Holy crap. What did you do to your hands?"

Dar cleared her throat gently. "Ah...well..." She laughed with a touch of embarrassment. "You're not going to believe this, but I um..."

Kerry hitched herself up on an elbow and examined Dar's palm. The surface was scuffed and bruised, and several long cuts were visible. "Is that a splinter? What happened?"

"Probably." Dar sighed. "It involved a bet, some obstacles, and a lot of ego."

"With your ego coming out on top, right?" Kerry guessed, giving her a tolerant grin, seeing the half-hidden look of smirking triumph cross Dar's face. "I thought so. Let me go get the tweezers." She planted a kiss on the base of Dar's thumb, then stretched out, pulling her T-shirt tight against her body and squeaking a little as Dar took that opportunity to lean over and nibble her in a very sensitive spot. "Ooh...Hold that thought."

She squirmed up off of the couch and stood, facing Dar as she straightened. "Dar, you do realize you're covered in mud, right?" Kerry inquired, plucking at her lover's shirt. "Did you spend the whole night like this?"

Dar looked down. "Uh." She blinked at the gray stains, which covered her liberally. "Well, we all did. It was raining...and I was wet...I don't think I—"

"Noticed." Kerry nodded. "No, I guess you wouldn't, if the fabric was wet. C'mon." She inserted her fingers into Dar's waistband and tugged. "Into the shower with you, my little mudpuppy."

"You just want me to get naked and wet with you," Dar observed as she obediently allowed herself to be hauled along. Now that Kerry mentioned it, though, the jeans she was wearing were getting kind of itchy.

"And you have an issue with this?" Kerry stopped and faced her, lifting a brow.

"No." Dar stepped closer. "It sounds better and better every second."

Kerry smiled and resumed her tugging.

They left their clothes in one corner of the bathroom and went under the warm water, with Kerry making little tsking noises as she took their scrub sponge and attempted to clean the mud off Dar's skin. "Do I dare ask what you were doing?"

Dar had been standing with her eyes closed, thoroughly enjoying the attention. The slightly rough texture of the sponge was leaving a nice tingle behind it, and now she lifted one eyelid to see Kerry looking up at her through wisps of steam and water. "Huh? Oh. We had a bet on between me and Chuck: which one of us could make it through the torture pit first."

"Ah." Kerry scrubbed a stubborn spot, keeping her head down and swallowing a jolt of irrational jealousy. "You won, I take it?" she asked. "It's going to be interesting meeting him on Friday...unless you've changed your mind and would rather I didn't go." She forced herself to look up. "I know these are old friends of yours, Dar, and they probably don't know you're gay, do they?"

Dar's eyes widened a little in visible surprise. "No, they don't," she answered honestly. "In fact, Chuckie asked if I was available tonight." A smile tugged at her lips. "I told him I was very taken." She thought a moment, feeling the water beat down on her back. "It's a hard question, Kerry. I'm not going to say I haven't been thinking about it."

Kerry kept still, watching Dar's face, seeing only intent thought behind her expression. "I know. It's hard," she agreed softly. "Telling my family was hard. I've never felt embarrassed by it, but I knew they'd be."

"Mm."

"I think it will make them uncomfortable."

Dar nodded. "I think you're right."

Kerry inhaled, surprised at how difficult it was to get the words out. "So, I think it's better if you go without me, this time."

"It'd make them more comfortable if that's what I did," Dar agreed softly. "They're a very traditional family."

A breath. "So that's what you'll do, right?"

"No." Dar's voice was quite calm, and almost amused. "If I was in the business of making people comfortable, I'd be an airline flight attendant. I'm not. I'm an individualistic nonconformist with a lot more attitude than sense, so if they can't accept the fact that I'm gay and I'm married to you, they can just kiss my ass." She leaned over and brushed Kerry's lips with her own, feeling the small gust of surprise as her lover reacted and exhaled. "But thanks for offering. And by the way, I think you missed a spot."

Hmm. Kerry resumed scrubbing, a dumb grin on her face. "Did I?" She worked her way up Dar's belly to her breasts, making very sure there were no lurking patches of mud. "I'll just have to go over everything twice." Her hands slid over Dar's collarbone and across her shoulders as she licked the warm droplets of water off the skin in front of her nose. "Mm."

A light touch behind her neck moved her hair back, then Dar's teeth were taking tiny nibbles out of her throat as their bodies slid together and she felt Dar's thigh between her own. She forgot the sponge, letting it drop.

Dar felt like her body was on fire, not from the water coursing over both of them but from Kerry's touch, dancing over her skin in gentle motions that teased her senses, running down her sides.

She had a feeling that getting up in the morning was going to be a problem.

Of course, they could just solve that by not going to sleep.

Kerry let out a sigh and burrowed into her fluffy robe as they watched dawn start to color the sky across the water. "We're going to be so toasted by tonight, you do realize that, right?"

Dar sipped slowly on a cup of fresh coffee, closing her eyes as a gust of cool salt air brushed across her face. "Oh yeah. I'm glad I decided to go into the office today. I'd have probably driven off Card Sound road into the Florida straits on the way back from the base, otherwise." She offered the cup to Kerry, who took it. "Besides, I've got a pile of stuff to take care of here."

"Me, too."

They swung quietly in the rope chair for a few minutes. "Guess we'd better get started, huh?" Kerry finally sighed. "I know I need a run to wake me up." She turned her head to look up at Dar. "Unless you want to maybe go over to the gym this morning. I could do circuit, too."

Dar nodded. "Yeah." She winced a little and exhaled. "I think I pulled a little bit of something in my back doing that crazy stunt last night. Running isn't the best idea. I think stretching everything out makes more sense."

Kerry squirmed around and slid a hand behind Dar's back, probing gently. "Where you got hurt?" She saw Dar nod a tiny bit. "Goofball," she scolded. "I've been telling you to have Dr. Steve check that out, Dar, you never did go back for another scan."

Dar scowled. "It hasn't bothered me in weeks," she protested. "Must have been crawling through that tunnel that did it."

"Tunnel?" Kerry queried. "Oh, Jesus. That explains why you had bruises on your knees." She sighed. "Well, come on, let's go get dressed, and see if we can work your kinks out." Neither of them moved, however, and Dar managed to get a snuggly hold on her that turned into cuddle, which turned into some kissing, which...

"This is not getting us anywhere," Kerry murmured.

"Sure it is," Dar replied. "It's just not getting us dressed and headed to the gym." She resumed suckling on Kerry's earlobe, earning a soft grunt of pleasure from her lover. Her hands were already inside the loosened wrap of Kerry's bathrobe, and she ran a light, tickling touch over the ribs she could feel as Kerry inhaled.

"Hey," Kerry laughed softly.

Dar kissed her, then relented, and backed off to rub noses. "Tell you what. I'm going to invent an afternoon meeting we both have to attend, and we're gonna leave early."

"Yes, ma'am," Kerry agreed. "So let's get moving. The sooner this day starts, the sooner it ends."

Chapter
Eight

"Mamá." Mayte slipped inside the outer office of Señora Dar, where her mother was sorting mail. "I just heard something very bad."

"*Sí?*" María looked up. "What is it now? Is José flirting with the new *señorita* in Accounting once again?"

"No." The slim girl looked upset. She walked over and sat down next to her mother's desk. "It's about Ms. Kerry."

María was very surprised. Rumors about her boss, yes, that she was used to; and just after Kerrisita had joined them, she had heard the things they had said about the two of them when they were together.

They had made such a cute couple; it was true. "What have you heard?" she asked her daughter, realizing that Mayte looked very anxious.

Mayte fiddled with her hands. "They are saying that Ms. Kerry, she was with a man here, at night last night, after we all left."

María's jaw dropped. "*Comemierda,*" she snorted.

Mayte's eyes opened wide. "Mamá!" She was shocked. "Someone was here, and they said they heard them, that she was with her hands all over this man and everything!"

"Who is saying that?" the older woman asked agitatedly. "Who is passing these lies? I want to know this, Mayte, right now!"

"B...b..." Mayte stammered. "Mamá, I heard it in the break room. Everyone is saying it."

María drummed her perfectly painted nails on her desk. "Why would they say this? Why would anyone want to hurt Kerrisita?" She thought a minute, then dialed a number on her phone.

"*Sí*, Ricardo? Can you check for me the log, please? Was there someone to visit Ms. Stuart last night?"

There was the sound of ruffling papers. "Looks like..." Ricardo paused, then ruffled some more. "Oh yeah, here it is. Yeah...She had a guy come up last night. 'Round six-thirty, I guess."

Mayte and María looked at each other in stunned shock. "May I have his name, *por favor?*" María asked quietly. "I need to send him something."

"Sure. Roberts," Ricardo answered genially. "Andrew Roberts."

María covered her eyes with one hand. "*Gracias*, Ricardo. I will speak with you later." She released the phone. "Jesús."

Mayte blinked. "Who is that, Mamá? Do you know him?"

"*Sí*." María looked troubled. "He is Dar's papá. He is a very nice, a very sweet man. He is very much accepting of Kerrisita; she is like another daughter to him."

"Ay." The younger woman exhaled. "I have heard her speak of him. There is a picture in the office, I think."

"*Sí*. That is Dar's mamá and papá. It was very hard, I have told you, when Kerrisita had such troubles with her family." María was thinking hard as she spoke. "Mayte, we must fix this problem," she told her daughter firmly. "I cannot let this be said about Kerrisita. Dar will be so upset."

Mayte blinked. "Oh."

"We must find who is saying this." María got up. "Come. We will go to someplace where I know that all the talk gets to be heard." She led the way out of the office and down the hall. As they passed the break room she could hear the chatter, and Kerry's name, and she grew very angry. "Do they not have better things to be doing?" She stopped and peered inside. "Go to work!" she told the startled occupants. "*Vámonos!*"

Mayte just looked at her as the assorted administrative assistants and junior clerks bolted from the room, streaming down the hallway like an assortment of colorful birds.

"I am getting very bold, no?" María asked. "I am learning from Dar."

"Yes, Mamá," Mayte murmured as they continued off down the hall.

At the end of the long walk, María lifted a hand and knocked on the thick metal door before them, waiting a few seconds, then knocking again.

"Hang on; hold your chupacabras." The door swung open. "Oh..." Josh, one of Mark's assistants, blinked. "Hi, María.

What's up?"

"Shoo shoo." María waved him backward. "I am here to speak with Mark. He is here?"

"Uh...uh...sure...um...he's in his office...but I—"

"Tch tch." María brushed by him and circled the equipment-packed console, where three techs were busy monitoring different screens. Mark's office was in the back and she made for it, reaching out to tap on the half-closed door.

"Look," Mark's voice floated out, "I don't give a crap what you think. If you can't deal with other people having private lives that are not your business, find another place to work, dude."

María hesitated, listening.

"From what I hear, it ain't that private," a softer, less distinct voice answered.

"Don't start that shit," Mark warned. "I'm telling you right now, Brent. Don't talk about them, don't repeat bullshit you hear at the urinal, and keep your redneck attitudes out of the office or I'll bounce you right on out of here."

"For what?" The response was outraged. "For having an opinion?"

"For insubordination and fucking with the antidiscrimination regs," Mark stated.

"What about everyone else? They're—"

"Everyone else ain't in Dar's chain of command," the MIS chief interrupted. "You are."

There was a moment of silence. "Fine," Brent finally said. "Can I go now? I got stuff to do."

"Sure," Mark replied. "Take off."

The door swung open a moment later and Brent emerged, his face crimson. He almost crashed headlong into María and Mayte, and he paused to stare at them for a few seconds before he brushed by and left. María eyed him, then she shook her head and walked into Mark's office.

"Hey." Mark looked up, pausing in the act of listening to his voice mail. "Guess you heard." He chewed his lower lip. "About last night, I mean."

"Of course," María agreed. "And we are going to fix it."

"Fix it?"

"*Sí.* You have the little program there, that goes to all the PCs?" María folded her hands. "That makes the funny noise, no?"

"Our messenger service, yeah," Mark replied, puzzled. "What about it?"

"I want you to send a message, please, from me, to all the people, yes?"

"Okaaay..." Mark sat down slowly. "What kind of message?"

"I will write it." María took a piece of paper and one of Mark's cushion grip roller balls and got to work. Mark watched her, twisting his head to one side to read the upside-down letters.

His eyes widened. "Oh boy."

Dar had taken a breath to say good morning to María when she opened the outer door and realized the office was empty. She closed her mouth with a faint click of teeth meeting and entered, shouldering her laptop as she made her way across the quiet space and into her inner office.

The sun was pouring across the floor and she stepped into it, feeling the faint warmth through the fabric of her skirt as she circled her desk and put her briefcase down, pulled the leather chair out, and settled into it with a tiny sigh.

"Morning, guys." She greeted her Siamese fighting fish, removing their jar of food from her desk drawer and sprinkling a little bit into the small tank. Her chin resting on one fist, she watched the fish gobble their breakfasts before she sighed again and turned her attention to her monitor.

"Wonder what disasters we have to deal with this morning?" Dar asked the empty office, spinning her trackball to douse her screensaver and reveal her running programs. Her eyebrows contracted slightly when she saw the blinking Dogbert head in the lower corner, and she clicked on it to bring up the corporate messaging alert the symbol represented.

Slowly, Dar's head tilted to one side, then the other, then she leaned forward and blinked as she read the message. "What in the hell?"

"To All Corporate HQ Miami Employees—you are please to read your handbooks in the section twelve, page 23. This page is saying that you may not say to everyone bad things about the officers of the company that are not true, or we can make you the termination. There is someone who is doing this, and when this is found out, this person I will myself see the termination if these bad things do not stop. *Gracias.* María."

Dar's intercom buzzed and she slapped at it absently. "Yeah?"

"Did you see that message?" Kerry's voice floated into the office. "What the heck is she talking about?"

"I haven't a quarter clue," Dar murmured, shaking her head. "Whatever it is, sure pissed her off though. I'd better find her and figure out what's going on." She shook her head. "I'll call you back."

"Okay." Kerry released the intercom button and opened her mail. "Weird...very weird way to start the day, that's for sure." There was a knock on her door, and she realized Mayte must have stepped away from her desk. "C'mon in."

Clarice entered, giving Kerry a very sweet smile before she closed the door behind her and crossed the floor to settle in one of Kerry's visitor chairs. "Good morning."

"Good morning." Kerry folded her hands on her desk. "What can I do for you?"

Mark leaned back in his chair, unconsciously putting distance between himself and the dangerously glaring ice blue eyes boring into his. "Hey, boss...um..."

Dar rested her hands on Mark's desk and leaned forward, lowering her voice to a mere raspy growl. "I want to know who it was that started that story."

Mark took a breath. "Dar, you know how hard it is to track shit like that down." He tried to keep his tone even and calm, his mind casting for the last time he'd seen Dar this mad. *Ah. That would be never.* "I bet María's message stopped it."

Dar could feel her body shaking with rage. She knew that lack of sleep was making her hold on her temper very tenuous and that she should go back to her office and calm down before she did something extremely stupid. "I want to know who it was," she repeated softly. "Don't you tell me you can't track it down, Mark. There was X number of people in this building, X number of people on this floor, and X number of people in the operations suite between the hours of X and X, which you know from the security log."

Mark took his courage in both hands and leaned toward his boss, reaching out one hand and covering the fist Dar had planted on his desk. "Okay, boss. I'll find that out for you, if you sit down and take it easy for a minute." There was no response in the stern mask looking at him.

He tried again, lowering his voice. "Dar, please, go get a drink of water, huh? You're scaring the shit out of me, and I just dry-cleaned these pants."

Nothing for a few seconds, then Dar's eyelashes fluttered closed briefly and her body relinquished some of its tension. "Sorry," she murmured. "But God damn it, Mark, of all the people in the company to be targeted by that crap, why her?"

Mark winced at the pain in his boss's voice.

"Me, I'm used to it," Dar went on softly. "I've given so many people so many reasons to hate me, I don't even think about it anymore." She took a breath. "But what has Kerry done to deserve that?"

Picked you? Mark wisely decided to not voice the obvious response. "You know how people are, boss. They get jealous and all that crap. And you've got to admit, there's a hell of a lot for people to be jealous of Kerry for."

Dar sighed. "Find out who it was," she replied. "I'll be in my office."

Mark watched her leave, the heavy door swinging shut behind her tall form. "Sonofabitch." He cradled his head in his hands. "Why the fuck do I always get this shit to deal with?"

"'Cause you, like, can?" his assistant Shaun ventured. "You gonna tell her who it was?"

Good question. Mark leaned back and considered. "I'm gonna let her chill for a little while first," he decided. "Because otherwise she's gonna haul back and take the jerk's head off."

"Excuse me?" Kerry felt her voice sharpen.

"I said," Clarice drawled, "you lasted longer than any of the rest of them, honey. Was it a getting bored thing?"

Kerry wondered if she looked as bewildered as she felt. "Clarice, I have no idea what you're talking about. Maybe you should just cut to the chase and be specific."

Clarice leaned closer. "Look, in this place, you can't keep anything secret."

"Right." Kerry nodded faintly. "And?"

"And everyone's talking about last night."

She felt like she was in a dinghy, floating further and further away from the shore. "Last night?" Her mind went to her unexpected waking up, and she felt a blush color her skin. "What about last night?"

Clarice chuckled. "You obviously know. Look, they saw you meet that guy here in the office."

The shoreline receded further. "Yeah, so?" Kerry's brow knit in perplexity. "What about it?"

"What about it?" Clarice repeated. "Honey, do you two have, like, an open relationship? I had no idea."

"Huh?" Kerry felt like grabbing her own head and shaking it. "Excuse me, what in the hell does me getting picked up here last night have to do with my relationship? Which, by the way, is personal and my business, and not any of yours."

Now it was Clarice's turn to look a little uncertain. "Are you saying that wasn't your lover?"

"What wasn't?" Kerry asked.

"The man who picked you up here last night, who you had your hands all over, who you told Dar abandoned you?" Clarice almost shouted. "What the hell did you think we were talking about here?"

It was like being trapped inside a cartoon. Kerry fully expected a clown to pop out of her desk and start laughing at the absurdity of it all. "My lover?" She enunciated the word carefully. "That guy who picked me up here last night?"

"Yes." Clarice nodded, relieved they were finally communicating. "Then he was."

"No." Kerry covered her eyes with one hand. "He was not." She got up and went to the small bookshelf in her office, selecting a framed photo and bringing it back with her. "I think this is who you mean."

Clarice took the picture and studied it. Kerry was standing near a wooden pylon, apparently at some dock, dressed in a pair of water shorts and a bathing suit. She had one arm wrapped around a very tall, powerfully built man, who had an arm draped over her shoulders, and she was pointing to a dangerous-looking lobster clutched in the man's other hand.

"That's my father-in-law," Kerry supplied. "Andrew Roberts."

Clarice peered at the picture, then up at her. "Honey, that's kinky."

Oh no... She was at sea again. "What's kinky? The lobster? We ate it," she told Clarice in exasperation. "He's not my lover, okay? Would you get that idea out of your head? Yes, he picked me up, yes, I hugged him, like I usually do...And why the hell am I standing here explaining this to you?" Kerry's voice rose. "As a matter of fact, get the hell out of my office before I throw your ass out!"

Clarice jumped up and laid the picture on the desk before ducking behind the chair. "Hey, look, I was just trying to warn you—"

"Out!" Kerry yelled at the top of her voice. "Tell all the jerks who want to know that we pay you people to provide information services, not come up with internal freaking company SOAP OPERAS!"

Clarice fled. She turned and scuttled across the floor as fast as her heels would allow, getting around the door and shutting it securely behind her before Kerry could find something else to verbally pound her with.

For a second, all Kerry could hear was her own labored

breathing. Then she sat down in her chair with a thump. "JESUS." She expelled her breath explosively. "What in the hell is wrong with these people?"

A soft creak alerted her, and she swiveled in her chair to face her inside door as it opened and a disheveled, aggravated, stormy head poked itself inside her office. "Have you heard the total idiocy going around here?"

Dar slid inside and walked over, taking a seat on Kerry's desk. "Yes."

"Is that not the stupidest thing you've ever heard?" Kerry went on. "What a bunch of total bonehead losers we have around here sometimes." She stood up and started ordering Dar's unruly locks with her fingers. "Honey, what did you do here, stick your head out your window or something?"

"I was outside on the balcony down the hall," Dar admitted. "Drinking half a gallon of milk and trying to calm down enough not to fire the entire fourteenth floor just to get rid of the jackass who started the whole thing."

Kerry rubbed a bit of white off her partner's lip. "Ah, so that's what that is." She let her hands rest on Dar's shoulders. "Are you okay?"

"Am I okay?" Dar managed a smile. "I think so. I was more worried about you."

"Me?" Kerry chuckled. "Dar, you forget I grew up in a very public household. I've had stories told about me since I was seven and got bitten by a duck while I tried to steal her chicks." She patted her lover's side. "Your poor father...That's twice in one night. The lady at the car dealership mistook us for husband and wife when he dropped me by there."

Dar blinked. "So you're okay with this?"

"Well, I don't like it, but I'll live. Why, you weren't really going to fire the entire floor, were you?" Kerry asked. "Dar?" She traced the flutter of nervous motion under the skin of her lover's cheek. "Hey?"

A sigh. "No, I wasn't."

"You okay?"

Dar gave her an unhappy look. "I have a stomachache from drinking too much cold milk, I'm tired, and I'm cranky, and I want to take a baseball bat to the person who thought you were making out with my dad."

"Oh."

"Other than that, Mrs. Lincoln, I enjoyed the play."

Kerry touched her forehead to Dar's. "With a start like this, the day can only get better."

As if on some evil signal, both of their pagers went off and Kerry's main line lit up.

The phone beeped twice, softly, before Dar lifted her head from her hands and touched the response key. "Yes?"

"Dar, it is Mark here to see you," María stated quietly. "Do you have a minute for him?"

"Sure." Dar returned her chin to its resting spot on her fists and exhaled. "Send him in." She'd given up trying to focus her overtired vision on her monitor a short time before and had merely been sitting there, waiting for time to pass and bring her to the end of a very long day.

The door opened and Mark entered, moving quickly across the floor and taking a seat across from her.

For a moment they studied each other, then Mark shifted. "You look like shit, boss."

For some reason, that brought a smile to Dar's face. "Thanks. It's been a suck-filled day."

"Yeah." Mark nodded. "I know. Listen, that T1 you ordered for the base is in. I had them terminate it and did a loopback to make sure it's solid. The telco tech confirmed your hub's onsite, and everything looks okay."

"Good." One thing off her mind, at least. "I'll connect everything tomorrow morning, then I'll need you to give me space on the big boxes to suck everything up."

"No problem," Mark assured her. "We've got the slots already allocated for you. Just let me know when you're ready, and we'll open the pipe."

Dar nodded. "I will. Did Houston get their data center back up? If the payroll computer doesn't come back online before tonight, we're all in deep shit; you know that, right?"

Mark felt a prickle of surprise at the unusual use of an expletive, which Dar tended to avoid in her normal workplace speech. "I can't believe the power block blew up in there," he said. "American UPS sent a team in and they're working on it, but so far it looks like they're going to have to run an emergency three phase panel in just to fire the main CPUs up. ETA is midnight, but I've got my fingers crossed for sooner."

"Will going there and yelling help?" Dar asked.

"No," Mark answered, not even caring if it was the right answer for the company or not. "They're doing their stuff, Dar. It's all moving; it just takes time to split the power off the main transformer and run the big cables."

"Okay." Dar accepted that with a feeling of relief. Flying to Houston was something she so didn't want to do at the moment. "Can we find out the liability limits of AUPS, and what's going to happen if they can't get the power restored?"

"Kerry took care of that already," the MIS director reassured her. "She's been on it since this afternoon. I think we're covered."

"All right."

Mark cleared his throat slightly and crossed his fingers, held below the level of the desk where Dar couldn't see them. "I also gave Kerry the information on who it was that was hanging around here last night and peeking into offices."

One dark eyebrow lifted sharply. "I thought I told you to bring that here."

"You did," Mark said. "But Kerry asked me to let her handle it, and since she's my direct report, I respected her directive."

Dar observed him for a few seconds. "I don't think I like having my direct orders countermanded," she stated flatly. "Especially by my subordinates."

"I know you don't," Mark responded bravely. "But Kerry said she'd take the responsibility for the decision." It felt cowardly to hide behind Kerry's skirt like that, but one look at the expression on Dar's face made him grateful for the shield. He only hoped it would be a big enough shield to keep him from getting his butt burnt off.

Dar remained silent, watching him from under half-lowered eyelids until Mark started to fidget nervously. Then she drew in a breath. "Fair enough," she remarked. "I'll take it up with her."

Looking profoundly relieved, Mark stood up and circled his chair, resting his hands on the back of it. "Hope you have a better day tomorrow, Dar."

That got a faint grin back. "Me, too." Dar watched Mark leave, then sat back and pondered. Was she mad at Mark?

No. He just did what he was told. Was she mad at Kerry? Dar regarded the wood panel walls. She was too damn tired to be mad at Kerry, and besides, she didn't want to be mad at her. But should she be?

Dar considered the question seriously. Kerry had been the person involved, had been the one with rumors spread about her and was, in fact, Mark's direct supervisor. On the other hand, Dar had given a direct order, which had been ignored and countermanded, something she couldn't recall ever happening before.

No one else would have dared, she decided. Was Kerry using their relationship to take an unfair advantage of her? Dar scowled. Or was Kerry simply making a good business decision, using her admittedly unfair knowledge of Dar to realize having the CIO beat an employee over the head with a paper shredder was not only bad employee relations, it was also just plain stupid? Especially since the CIO in question would be doing it because the employee in question had insulted her strictly-against-company-rules lover and partner?

Hmm. Dar idly watched her fish swim around. She looked up as the inner door opened and watched as Kerry visibly squared her shoulders before she entered and proceeded across the room, arriving at Dar's side with a look of sober determination.

"Listen." Kerry's hands flexed slightly, the fingers curling into a partial fist in unconscious reaction to confrontation. "I just talked to Mark. I want you to back off and let me handle this situation, because it's my department, my issue, and my staff."

"Mm," Dar responded.

One of Kerry's pale eyebrows rose. "What does that mean?"

"That color looks really cute on you." Dar evaluated the coral silk blouse Kerry was wearing. "Very tropical."

The blond woman put her hands on her hips. "Dar, I was being serious."

"I know. You're right. Go ahead and handle it." Dar nodded in agreement. "I'll be down at the base all day tomorrow anyway, so have at it."

Kerry sighed. "Do you know how long I've been standing in the corridor, screwing up my guts and trying to figure out exactly what approach to use with you on this?"

Dar allowed her face to relax into a smile for the first time that day. "Sorry about that. I was just thinking it over when you came in. I know my first reaction was to appease my ego and yell, but you know what? I'm just too tired to." She shrugged. "Besides, you **are** right, it's your issue to handle; and the only reason I wanted to do it is because I go into a crazed overprotective mode when it comes to you."

Kerry's lips twitched, then eased into grin. "Yes, you do." She relaxed and moved a little closer, perching on the edge of Dar's desk. "Very self-aware of you to notice."

Dar smiled and propped her head up against one hand. "They finally got the T1 in place. Now I can get that entire data set transferred, and we can really take a look at it."

"Think you'll find anything?"

"Maybe." Dar shook her head. "There's something there; it's just really hard to pinpoint. Little discrepancies in the programs, things that just don't feel right...I can't really be specific. Just that I know there's something not one hundred percent clicking."

"I've got an idea." Kerry reached out and pushed a few strands of dark hair off Dar's forehead. "I just finished my last conference call for the day, want to take off? Are you covered here, or do you have something else you need to handle?"

"Nothing I can't handle with my cell phone," Dar said. "Pushing to get the payroll systems back online. I don't need to be here to do that." She straightened. "Sounds like a plan. Go get your stuff, and I'll meet you at the elevator."

Kerry got up and twitched her skirt straight. "You're on." She turned and made her way back to the inner door, pausing with her hand on the sill before she exited. "Dar?"

The pale blue eyes flickered as Dar's eyelashes fluttered. "Hmm?"

"It was Brent." Kerry's expression was regretful. "Mark feels pretty scummy about that." She ducked through the doorway and closed the door behind her, traveling quickly down the back corridor and past the cleaning closets to her own office.

Chapter
Nine

The dream was warm and sunny, and Dar stretched into it, reveling in the feel of the sun against her skin as the boat rocked beneath her. Her eyes were closed, but she could hear the strains of a popular tune from behind her and smell the tang of the salt air as it brushed over her.

Her body was pleasantly tired, and she was content to rest in the sun, turning her head slightly as she heard a gull land on the boat. Its claws made soft, ticking sounds as it moved closer, and she kept very still to see how close it would dare to come.

She could almost feel the warmth of its body as it pattered nearer and nearer, and she resisted the urge to open her eyes and look.

Then it blew in her ear.

Dar's eyes popped wide open as her dream world rapidly merged into her waking one, and the gentle waves and warm sun became the rocking of the waterbed under Kerry's laughing form and the startling reality of true sunlight gilding both of them.

"Holy shit." Dar's eyes found the clock, which was displaying a cheerful 7:40. "Jesus. Did we forget to set the alarm?"

"I think so." Kerry propped her head up on one hand and let her chuckles wind down.

"Damn." Dar sighed, her brain still a little fuzzy from sleep. "How could I have done that? I haven't forgotten to set that damn alarm in...in..."

"Honey," Kerry leaned over and rubbed Dar's bare belly, "you forgot because you fell asleep with your clothes half on. I had to pull them off. I was the one who forgot to check the clock, okay?"

"I did?" Dar tried to remember the previous night in the fog of exhaustion she'd been walking through. "Um...I think I remember a strawberry...and you kissing me."

Kerry smiled, her fingers tracing a light pattern over Dar's skin. They'd both been far too tired to eat when they'd gotten home, and had settled for a shared bowl of freshly washed strawberries and two large glasses of milk. She'd put her things upstairs and come down to find Dar sprawled over the bed, already well on her way to sleep.

"I remember that, too." She looked up and almost laughed when she saw Dar's expression relaxed back into slumber. "Hey...Paladar." She gave her lover a tiny poke.

"Eh?" Dar's eyes opened again. "Oh. Damn," she complained, rolling over and capturing Kerry in a tangle of warm arms and smooth skin. "Why can't it be Saturday? I don't wanna get up."

That was okay. Kerry didn't want to either. She tried an experiment, making her little patterns again, and was rewarded by hearing Dar's breathing even out almost immediately and feeling her body go limp and relaxed. She closed her own eyes and reviewed her schedule, thinking about what her morning was like.

Hmm. It was Thursday. That meant her staff meeting at ten, nothing after that until lunch, then network strategy sessions from two to five. She liked those, actually, when her operations team would test different scenarios to see how they could reshape the network to better suit their customers' needs.

So. She didn't need to be in until ten. Dar wasn't supposed to be in the office at all, since she was heading back down to the base. They could actually sleep in a little, if they skipped their morning run. Could they afford it?

One green eye appeared and regarded their intertwined bodies critically, then closed in contentment. Yep, they could afford it, Kerry decided, squirming a little closer and settling down with a silent sigh. She let herself relax into a light doze for another half-hour, then nudged herself awake again.

For a few minutes, all she did was just look at Dar. The sun was spilling in the window through the blinds and painting gold stripes across the bed, and one stripe had captured most of Dar's face. Kerry could see the tiny motes of dust in it and watched the faint flickers as some dream stirred her lover's eyelids.

She is so beautiful. Kerry let out a breath, resisting the impulse to run a finger down one of Dar's planed cheekbones. She did move a lock of dark hair back, though, biting her lip when even this slight motion brought a flutter of eyelids and a pair of sleepy blue eyes into view. "Oops. Sorry."

Dar blinked. "Did you let me go back to sleep?" she asked incredulously. "Ker, we're going to be late as hell."

"Yes, I did," Kerry replied in an unperturbed tone. "My first thing's at ten, and you're OCB today, so take a chill gelcap and relax, okay?" She slid a hand over Dar's hip and lightly scratched her back. "How's this doing?"

The smooth surface under her hand tensed, then moved as Dar stretched, the muscles under her skin shifting under Kerry's fingers.

"A little stiff, but not bad," Dar admitted. "Maybe we can do some swimming this weekend. That should fix it up."

Kerry wriggled over and pinned her lover down, receiving a startled, widened-eyed look in return. "Maybe we can take you over to Dr. Steve's, and have him look at it."

"Aw...Kerrryyy..." Dar whined.

"Pick one: Dr. Steve, or the ophthalmologist," Kerry replied kindly, ignoring the endearing pout that faced her. "Sweetheart, I'm not going to sit by and watch you either hurting or hurting yourself, so you'd better just get used to it, okay?"

"I hate doctors," Dar said. "You know I hate doctors."

Kerry sighed. "Yes, I know you do; but I have to take very good care of you, Dar." She put a fingertip on Dar's nose. "Humor me. Please?"

Dar thought about it, her eyes moving slightly, regarding the eggshell-colored ceiling. Then they focused on Kerry's face and softened. "All right," she agreed quietly. "But you have to go with me."

"Of course I will." Kerry smiled in relief. "In fact, I'm embarrassed to admit it, but I haven't had my eyes checked in a few years, either. We'll both go, okay?"

Dar nodded. "Okay." She rubbed a thumb over Kerry's rib cage, which expanded under her touch. "I think it's time we got our lazy butts out of bed, don't you?"

"Do you really want to?" Kerry laid an arm down on Dar's chest and rested her chin on it. "You know what I'd like?" she added suddenly.

"What?"

"Someday, I'd like us to just..." Kerry nibbled her lower lip, "get a camper, or something, and travel all over the place, just seeing new things." A half smile appeared. "Does that sound strange to you? There are so many places I haven't seen, and I'd like to—together."

Dar cocked her head slightly to one side. She took a breath to

answer, then released it when her cell phone, dropped haphaz-
ardly on the bedside table, buzzed. "Hold that thought," she told
Kerry as she fumbled one-handedly with the instrument. "Because
I really like it."

Kerry grinned wholeheartedly and gave Dar a pat on the side.
"I'll get coffee started." She lowered her voice as Dar answered
the phone, then took the opportunity to suckle Dar's navel gently,
chuckling as she heard her lover's voice break slightly. "Tell Mark
I said hi." She gave Dar a nip, then rolled out of bed and made her
way out into the living room, where Chino was already waiting
impatiently to be let out.

She opened the back door for the Lab, then clicked the coffee
on before she trotted upstairs and into her own bedroom. "Two
bathrooms, no waiting," she told her reflection as she entered
hers, splashing water on her face, more to wake her up than anything else, and scrubbing her teeth industriously.

One of the nicer things about the condo was the amount of
space they both had, she reflected. She'd grown up in such a big
house, with a lot of people around, and Dar had grown up just the
opposite, but they both needed and appreciated the room to get
away a little and be alone sometimes.

Which made her comment to Dar seem really odd, if she
thought about it. But Dar had liked the idea of traveling around
together, so maybe it wasn't so weird after all.

*Of course, showers, now...*Kerry grinned at the rumpled, rak-
ish-looking figure gazing back at her. Showers they liked to take
together. "Hey, scruffy, time for a haircut." She pointed at her
reflection, before she turned and went to her closet, bound on
selecting her clothing for the day.

Dar settled her sunglasses more firmly as she headed from the
parking lot into the staff building. She was dressed in her favorite
pair of worn jeans and a Navy sweatshirt, in deference to the
cooler weather that had rolled in overnight.

The Marine at the door gave her a friendly nod and opened
the portal for her. "Good morning, ma'am."

"Morning," Dar replied politely. She took the stairs two at a
time and ducked around the upper hall doors, glancing around for
any sign of her glowering nemesis. "Eh...maybe I'll get lucky for a
change."

She made it into the network hardware room and put her case
down, then glanced around at the walls full of telecommunications punch downs. With a sigh, she pulled out her Palm Pilot and

opened it, checking the circuit ID Mark had given her and comparing it to the rows of tags hanging from the blocks.

"Ah. There you are." Dar pulled a tool from her briefcase and
studied the network bridges, consulting her Pilot for the network
node the base had assigned her to. Her brow creased, and she ran
a finger lightly down the massive hub, curious about the design.
For no reason she could readily identify, an entire segment was
bridged off to a completely different hub.

One dark eyebrow lifted. "Hmm." Dar followed the cables to
the other hub and peeked in back of it. "Ethernet...Ethernet...Fast
Ethernet...T3?" Dar looked closer. "Twelve network nodes sharing a T3? What the hell is running on them?"

Really curious now, Dar pulled the network schematic she'd
been given out of her briefcase and spread it out, running an experienced eye over the layout. After a few minutes, she folded up the
paper and tucked it away, letting out a careful breath as she considered her options.

Then she walked over and copied down the circuit ID on the
mysterious hub and pulled out her cell phone.

Kerry took her seat in the operations meeting, setting down
her cup of tea and glancing around the table. No one met her eyes,
and she let a wry grin touch her lips as she settled back in the
leather conference chair, extending her legs and crossing them
while she rested her folded hands on the table surface.

Mark was the last to arrive, and he closed the door behind
him before he took his own seat, the one directly across from hers.
There was none of the usual bantering; everyone just sat quietly,
eyes on their agendas, and waited.

"So." Kerry broke the silence. "Heard any good rumors
lately?" She waited for the embarrassed shuffling to quiet down.
"That was pretty counterproductive, wasn't it? I'm used to people
having nothing better to do than speculate about my private life,
but tying up the resources of the entire department for an entire
morning was going a little overboard, don't you think?"

Nobody knew what to say. They all just stared miserably at
the table.

"I'm not sure what's more disappointing," Kerry went on quietly. "The fact that people who know me personally participated
in it and thought so little of my integrity that they'd think I'd do
something like that to Dar in front of the entire company..." She
paused. "Or the fact that in a department full of intelligent people,
only Dar's admin had the sense to check the visitors log."

Mark finally looked up, his jaw muscles visibly clenching as he met her gaze squarely. "I didn't bother checking," he stated. "I knew it was bullshit. The only thing I wanted to do was find out where it started and stop it," he reflected. "I did. But the word flew out so fast, it went through my fingers."

Kerry nodded. "I know. Thank you, Mark." She saw some of the rigid tension in his shoulders relax a little. "Dar and I make a point of keeping our personal lives out of this building. I'd appreciate it if you all would do the same. Find something else to speculate about."

Nods and murmurs of agreement went around the table.

"Okay." Kerry was satisfied that she'd scared, embarrassed, and intimidated the entire room to the best of her capability. Dar, of course, would have done a much scarier job of it, but she felt she'd gotten her point across, and predicted her people would be having little meetings of their own in their areas as soon as the current session was over. "Next item on the agenda. Enid, what's the status on the new accounts in the Northwest?"

Never had there been so many people in one room so glad of a subject change. Enid eagerly sifted through her papers and started into her report.

The small office was very quiet. Only the faint sound of the laptop's hard drive and the occasional soft click broke the silence. Dar had her head propped up on one fist as she reviewed the data flicking across the display.

"What in the hell are they doing?" the CIO asked her computer, which morosely refused to answer. She scanned the data stream for the nth time, trying to figure out the pattern in the weird anomalies she'd been seeing for the last couple of hours.

The cell phone resting on the desk buzzed, and Dar answered it. "Yeah?"

"Hey, Dar." Mark's voice sounded unusually quiet. "I tracked down that T3 ID for you. It's a private subscriber circuit. Not Bell-South."

"Huh." Dar's brow creased. "That's even stranger. I could understand having a—" A thought occurred to her. "Hang on...I'll call you back." She hung up and retrieved a number from the cell phone memory, then dialed it.

It rang twice, then was answered. "Gerry?"

"Ah, Dar!" Gerald Easton's voice sounded cheerful. "I was just thinking of you."

"Someone send you a memo?" Dar hazarded a guess.

The military man chuckled. "Eh...heard from old Jeff, as a matter of fact. He's thrilled to have you down there, Dar."

Dar felt a half grin forming. "He's the only one, Gerry. I'm not a popular person down here. Listen, is there anything black here?"

There was a momentary silence. "Eh," Easton grunted. "Odd question."

"Odd because it's yes, or because it's no?" Dar was conscious of the cellular connection, which could be monitored. "I don't want details, Gerry, just if there is or isn't."

"Hold on a minute." Easton's voice had become crisp. It was replaced with hold music, which Dar suffered through, having an innate dislike for the song *Sleigh Ride.* It cut off thankfully on the third go-round, replaced by a rustle and a clearing of Gerry's throat. "Ah, Dar?"

"Mm...still here." Dar sketched a squirrel on her pad.

"I just checked, and no, we've got nothing dark there." Gerry paused. "Nothing even remotely gray, as a matter of fact."

Dar scowled, and put fangs on the squirrel. "Damn." She exhaled. "Okay, thanks, Gerry. I've got to hunt somewhere else for answers."

"Problems?" The cautious question came back.

"Things that aren't making sense," Dar replied. "I hate that."

A chuckle came through the line. "As well I remember. If you need any more information, Dar, get in touch, eh?"

"I will." Dar hung up the cell phone and reviewed the data she had on her screen. "Okay." She called up a new e-mail, clipped and pasted from the analyzer program into it, added notes, and sent it on its way. "Let's see what Mark can dig up about who bought that nice big hub that mysteriously connects to someone else's network from inside a supposedly secure building."

Then she set up her transfer program and tapped into the base's network, parsing all of its traffic and sending a running dump to her ops center in Miami. The big boxes there would digest the information and run her custom-designed systems analysis programs on it. That code would tell her if her gut instinct was right and there was something weird going on, or if she was just seeing spiders in the shadows.

Dar leaned back in her wooden chair and folded her arms as the data transfer kicked in. She looked up as a light knock sounded at the door. "Yes?"

Chuckie stuck his head inside the room. "Hey there, old buddy. Can I interest you in some lunch?"

Dar smiled easily. "Sure." She set her passwords and locked the laptop down, then stood up and joined Chuckie at the door. "You want to go downstairs or off base?" she asked. "I kind of have an itch for conch fritters."

"You're on," Chuckie agreed happily. "I've been buried up to my butt in status reports all day. I've got ten new recruits coming from this class, and boy howdy, I hope those little suckers don't sink the boat before we clear international waters." He put a hand on Dar's back and guided her down the hall. "Dad says you plan on doing a checkout on the training process here, that right?"

"Right," Dar answered. "That's what Gerry was griping about from here mostly—results on the folks they kick out of here being substandard." She dropped down the stairs with Chuckie at her side. "He wants to know why, and frankly, so do I."

"For real?" Chuckie held the door at the bottom of the hall open for her, then followed her out and into the cool, somewhat damp air.

"Yeah." Dar pulled her keys out of her pocket and headed for the Lexus. "From a management perspective, bad performance usually only has one of a couple sources." She opened the doors and they got in, then she continued her lecture, to which Chuckie listened with interest. "Either your talent pool is empty, your processes are defective, or there's a motivation structure in place that doesn't match what your performance objectives are."

Chuckie folded his arms over his chest and eyed her. "Can we talk about football or something? I didn't get three words out of five in that last paragraph."

Dar chuckled as she pulled out of the base parking lot and sent the Lexus in search of a scrungy crab shack. "Sorry." She recomposed her thoughts. "Your recruits suck, the instructors don't know what the hell they're doing, or someone's being paid to just churn out bodies regardless of whether they know what end of a broom to grab hold of."

"Ah." Chuckie considered this thoughtfully. "How are you going to figure out which one it is?"

How indeed? Dar pulled into an unpaved parking lot and stopped the Lexus. "I'm not sure yet," she admitted. "I've got a program sucking everything down into one of our big processors, and it's going to sort the data out for me. I'll review it and make a plan based on what I find."

"Okay." Chuckie opened the door to the crab shack and they entered, going from the bright light outside into a somewhat dim, weathered wooden interior graced with trestle tables, benches, and several neon bar signs on the wall. "Howdy, Red."

The burly, bearded man with more tattoos than seemed safe waved at him. "Hey, Chuck. Whoa, you moved up in the world, didn'cha?" His eyes flicked over Dar with genial approval. "C'mon in, sweet thing."

Chuckie, to give him credit, winced.

Dar dropped her jacket onto the nearest trestle table and sauntered over to the man, leaning on the counter across from him and tipping her sunglasses down to give him a better look. After a moment, she sighed. "You are still as butt ugly as you were in high school, you know that, August?"

The man's eyes widened. "Whothefuckareyou?"

"Someone you ain't seen in fifteen years," Dar drawled back. "You want to put us up two baskets of fritters and burgers, so at least we'll get something out of this conversation?"

The man scratched his jaw and tilted his head, then reach over and pulled Dar's sunglasses all the way off. He leaned closer. "Oh shit." He started laughing. "It's Dar." He let the glasses drop to the counter. "I'll be a son of a bitch."

Dar scooped up her shades. "You're damn lucky I'm not nearly as much of a hardass as I used to be, Augie. That crack would have gotten you a broken nose once upon a time." She relaxed into a smile as Chuckie decided it was safe to approach and came up next to her.

"Yeah, you're so mellow now," Chuckie commented. "Remind me of that again when I bitch about how sore I am from that little stunt we pulled the other night."

"Irene!" August hollered behind him. "Two burgers, two fritters, okay?" He faced forward again. "Dar, man, it's such a trip to see you. It has been forever and gone, ain't it?" He pointed to the table. "Siddown. I was just gonna have some lunch myself. We were busier than all get-out before, but it slowed down some."

Dar took a seat on the worn wooden bench as her two friends did the same. She rested her elbows on the surface and exhaled, allowing a bittersweet sense of familiarity to wash over her. August's father had owned the shack during her younger years, and she'd spent many hours hunched over the uneven tables, talking crap and swallowing enough fried fish and greasy burgers to have easily killed off anyone with a more sensitive digestive system.

Her nose twitched as she detected the scent of the spicy fritter batter cooking, and she smiled, glad—for the moment—to know that not everything had changed.

"Still workin' with that computer shit, huh, Dar?" Augie asked.

Oh yeah. "Yep," Dar admitted. "Same shit."

"Ms. Kerry?" Mayte's voice crackled through the intercom. "*Señor* Mark is here."

Kerry finished typing her last sentence and flexed her hands, making the joints crack slightly. "Great. Send him this way, Mayte." She sat back and waited as her door opened and Mark entered. "Hi."

"Hi." Mark closed the door and crossed the carpeted floor, taking a seat in one of Kerry's visitor's chairs. "Listen, I...um—"

"Mark, it's okay," Kerry interrupted him gently. "I'm over it."

The MIS chief blinked. "Oh." He sat back and let his hands rest on his thighs. "You know the whole staff's been walking around in a blue funk since the meeting, right?"

"I heard." Kerry ran her fingers through her hair and riffled it, stifling a yawn as she did so. "Jesus, it's not like I was that wacko, was I? I've heard Dar go off. I know I'm not in her league."

"Nah," Mark agreed. "It's worse with you, though, because you're always so nice. When you get postal, it makes everyone's hair stand on end." He gave Kerry an apologetic look. "No offense."

"None taken." Kerry smiled. "I talked to Mariana." She shifted the topic neatly. "She's agreed to let me handle whatever we decide to do with Brent."

"Urm." Mark rubbed his jaw, darkened with stubble now that the day was almost ended. "I talked to him a little. He's way out there, Kerry." He shook his head. "I can't figure out if it's just that he had a...uh, I mean, if..."

Kerry leaned forward. "I didn't think he was serious until after I met you both in the ops center that time and Dar told me that he'd just finished asking her if I was seeing anyone." She propped her head up on one fist. "I thought that was pretty darn oblivious of him, you know?"

Mark waggled his hand. "He's pretty focused."

"So is his problem that I'm not interested, or is his problem why I'm not interested?"

"Why," Mark said bluntly. "His dad's a Southern Baptist minister who was tossed out of the local group for advocating the castration of gay guys and the incarceration of anyone who didn't think we should swap the Bill of Rights for the Bible."

Kerry sighed.

"It sucks, you know? He's a good tech, and not a half-bad guy if you don't mind the freaking nerdiness." Mark shook his head. "I talked to him just before I came in here, and he just can't see why everyone doesn't feel the same way he does."

"Okay." Kerry scrubbed her face. "I'd like to talk to him," she said. "Can you set up a time tomorrow morning? Make it early, preferably before I have to sit in on the marketing projection session."

"Sure you want to do that?" Mark queried.

"Yes."

"Okay." Mark stood up. "Did you hear from the boss? Her data dump finally finished. The processors are chewing on it."

Kerry leaned back. "Yep. She's home, actually." She propped a knee up against the desk and folded her hands around it. Hearing from Dar had been a surprise, especially when her lover had told her she was comfortably seated on their leather couch watching a special on China. "She's...um...cooking dinner."

Mark stopped in mid-motion and stared at her, his jaw dropping in mild shock. "Uh?"

"Yeah." Kerry scratched her nose. "My curiosity is starting to give me wedgies," she admitted with a grin. "I mean, it could be that we'll end up eating ice cream sundaes for dinner—those are well inside Dar's ability; or maybe she'll do eggs, which I know are safe."

"Now you've got me curious." Mark chuckled. "She once told me flipping the power switch on the coffee machine was the limit of her cooking skills." He folded his arms. "You gotta let me know what happens."

Kerry stood up and stretched, wincing as her back popped from the long hours she'd been seated at her desk trying to clear her inbox. She'd even had Mayte bring her up lunch so she could spend the extra time catching up. "Okay." She viewed the outbox with a sense of satisfaction. "I think I'm going to pack it in."

"Walk you downstairs?" Mark offered. "I was just on my way out myself."

They joined a group of fellow employees who were also leaving, including José and Eleanor, and the elevator was fairly crowded. Kerry pressed back against the mirrored wall, not really uncomfortable, but conscious of the air's stuffiness and the clashing scents of Eleanor's aggressive rose perfume and José's vaguely coconutty-smelling after-shave.

Ick. Kerry eyed the ceiling; it was also unfortunate that some people seemed to have a curious absentmindedness when it came to things like deodorant and reasonably frequent showering. She considered holding her breath, wondering if the elevator was being perversely slow just to piss her off.

Oh. Kerry almost hopped up and down to force the car to move faster. *What if it gets stuck?* Her eyes widened a little. How would it look for the VP Ops to upchuck all over half the executive staff in an elevator?

"Kerry!"

She jerked and sucked in a breath, then glanced at Mark. "What?"

Mark leaned closer. "You looked like you were freaking out."

She sighed and leaned back. "Overactive imagination." The car reached the bottom and bounced a little, then, finally, blissfully, the doors slid open and allowed the people to exit and the cold air to enter. "Jesus." She pushed off from the mirrored wall and left the elevator, glancing up into the vast vault of the atrium lobby.

A faint smile crossed her face as she remembered the first time she'd seen this place—a very late, rainy night that had started in despair and ended up being a crossroads in her life she wasn't even aware of until long after she'd passed through it.

She followed Mark out the front doors into the daylight and headed for her car, her mind making the mental jog when it first tried to find her Mustang, then shifted and searched for the new profile.

"Hey, did you get a new set of wheels?" Mark asked as he ambled alongside her. "Ain't that cute...a baby Darcar."

"A who—oh," Kerry laughed. "Yeah, I guess you could call it that." She patted her new blue Lexus on the side. "I like it. I can actually see things now. See you tomorrow, Mark."

"Yeah." Mark put his briefcase in the saddlebag of the big Harley and unstrapped his motorcycle helmet. "Drop me a mail when you figure out what Big D is feeding you, huh? I'm dying to know."

"Hmm." Kerry got into the SUV and rolled the window down. "Dying...not a good word there, Mark." She gave him a wave and started the car, then pulled out of the parking lot and headed home.

It was relatively quiet outside the condo when she pulled into her spot and got out, cautiously examining the front door before she approached it. "Well." She leaned back against the car and crossed her arms. "No smoke, no fire engines outside the place, and it looks like the electricity is still on, so she didn't blow a circuit."

She nodded. "Looking good so far. Now, Kerrison," she addressed herself seriously, "whatever this turns out to be, Dar will have spent a lot of time and a lot of effort on it, so no matter what, you're going to like it. Got me?" She squared her shoulders and took a deep breath. "Besides, you've eaten at the Republican National Convention. Nothing should scare you after that."

She trotted up the stairs and paused, cocking her head and listening before she keyed in her lock code. Nothing but soft music came faintly to her ears, certainly not the strident cursing she'd have expected from Dar if things weren't going well. *Another good sign.* Kerry unlocked the door and opened it, slipping inside and closing it behind her.

And then she just stood there, only her eyes moving as she absorbed the scene in front of her. The lights were dimmed in both the living room and dining room, and there were candles on the table. Really tall, pretty candles, set in holders that complemented the china and crystal place settings patiently awaiting use.

She also realized two other things: there was no sign of Dar, and something smelled great. "Heh," Kerry chortled softly to herself. "I'm liking this already."

"Good," Dar's voice purred from nearby.

Kerry almost jumped, and then she turned to see Dar leaning against the doorjamb of her bedroom, her hair pulled loosely back and her body covered in something very silky and brief. The pale blue eyes held a lazily sensual note as they traveled over Kerry's form, eliciting a small, almost subvocal noise from Kerry's throat. "Hi there," she managed to get out.

"Hi there," Dar replied. "Wanna come in and make yourself comfortable?" She eased away from the door and moved toward Kerry, bare feet soundless against the tile. "Hello? Earth to Kerry." Dar waved a hand in front of her lover's eyes, which seemed to be firmly focused on her.

Kerry let her laptop case slide to the floor and found better uses for her hands, letting them slide over the soft, cool fabric covering Dar's body to feel the warm flesh beneath. She stepped closer and took a deep breath, then tilted her head back to look up at her lover. "So, what did I do to rate this?"

Dar smiled. "Nothing." She brushed a wisp of pale hair out of Kerry's eyes. "I just felt like trying out this romantic thing. Complaining?"

"Nuh-uh." Kerry shook her head firmly. "Where'd you get this? It's gorgeous." She fingered the crimson silk. It barely covered Dar's body, and Kerry found herself losing interest in dinner, or asking questions, or... "Damn, you smell good."

"Glad you think so." Dar nuzzled her hair, then slipped her arms around Kerry and gave her a big hug. "Mom and Dad took Chino for a while."

Kerry gave her a weird look. "Why? She never bothers us."

"No, but she kept jumping up and stealing my mixing thing, and it was driving me nuts," Dar admitted with a faint chuckle. "They'll bring her back and drop her off later in the evening. C'mon, let's get you undressed so you can properly appreciate my creation."

Kerry stepped back and grinned frankly at her. "Sweetie, I don't need to be undressed to appreciate that. I think your creation is spectacular."

Dar put her hands on her hips, hiking up the fabric and only enhancing Kerry's visceral experience. "I meant dinner."

"That too." Kerry's smile grew wider. "Oh." The words finally penetrated, and she laughed helplessly. "Sorry...sorry...you mean the food."

Dar snorted softly, but looked pleased with the appraisal nonetheless. "G'wan." She nudged Kerry toward the stairs. "I'll put the salad on the table."

Kerry had turned and had one foot on the steps. Now she stopped dead and swiveled her head to face Dar. "You," she pointed, "made salad?"

Dar nodded.

"Ah...hah." Kerry slowly turned back around and started up the steps, sneaking disbelieving peeks at Dar as she did, until she disappeared onto the second floor. "Salad." She shook her head as she entered her bedroom and kicked her shoes off. "I feel like I'm in a dream world."

Her closet beckoned and she went inside, shucking out of her jacket and hanging it neatly on a hanger. She unbuttoned and slid out of her skirt and hung that up as well. Then she stopped and considered as she removed her shirt. Normally, she'd just slip into an old T-shirt, but since Dar had made an effort...Her eyes roved speculatively over her wardrobe. "Hmm. It's all business or dressy. I don't have any causally sexy numbers, Dar."

She flipped through the hangers until she finally stopped at one, removing it. "Hmm." It was a sleeveless satin sheath, designed to go under a lacy dress she had. "That'll work." She slipped it over her head and settled the edges, which just barely came to her upper thighs. "Yeah..." She consulted the mirror, which reflected back to her a surprisingly racy-looking image. Thoughts of Dar in her silk strapless number came to mind, and Kerry found herself wondering just how relevant dinner was going to be.

A shiver of anticipation made her grin.

Dar studied the plate, then nodded in satisfaction, cocking her head as she heard Kerry's footsteps coming down the stairs. She put both hands on the back of the dining room chair and smiled in welcome as Kerry appeared, the smile broadening as the warm candlelight exposed the brief clothing and knowing look. "Nice." Dar drew the chair back, and Kerry seated herself with a faint chuckle.

"Thank you." Kerry waited for Dar to take the seat right next to her and moved the chair slightly so their bare legs touched. "Are you actually going to eat some of this here salad, Dardar?"

White teeth reflected the candlelight as Dar smiled. "Only if you feed it to me."

So she did. They exchanged forkfuls, and Kerry found herself enjoying the freshly cut greens very much. Of course, there was enough dressing on them that Dar probably couldn't tell a lettuce leaf from a carrot, but that was okay. That's how she liked her salad. They finished, and she carefully removed some extra dressing off Dar's lips before she let her lover stand and remove the plates. "That was great."

Dar paused at the entrance to the kitchen. "Just you wait."

"Mm." Kerry sat back and folded her hands over her stomach, craning her neck to watch Dar busy at work by the stove. With serious precision, her lover was arranging something on plates and adding scoops of something else from a dish on the warmer. When she was satisfied that both plates had equal amounts and were symmetrical, Dar picked them up and walked back into the dining room.

"Here you go." Dar set the plates down and seated herself, then eyed Kerry for a reaction.

Kerry's eyebrows lifted. "That's a lobster tail," she commented.

"Yep."

Kerry poked the top. "It's stuffed."

"Sure is."

"Those are au gratin potatoes."

"With cheese," Dar agreed.

"And peas."

"LeSeur Very Early Baby Peas."

Kerry nibbled a bit of stuffing. "Dar, this is fantastic."

A very satisfied Dar settled back in her chair. "Thanks."

They ate in silence for a moment. Unable to keep her curiosity under wraps, Kerry finally asked, "When did you learn to cook?"

Dar looked up, and bit the end of her fork in thought. "Four—no, four-thirty today." She reached over and poured chilled white wine into their glasses, then lifted one and toasted her lover. "Incredible what you can find out on the Internet, isn't it?"

With a helpless laugh, Kerry lifted her glass and clinked it, then took a sip of the sweet wine. "So, what's for dessert?"

For an answer, Dar looked her up and down and raised an eyebrow, her lips twitching into a rakish grin.

"Ah." Kerry wrinkled her nose into an appreciative grin. "Got any fudge with that?"

Dar merely chuckled.

"Mm." Kerry stretched her legs out in the Jacuzzi and leaned her head back, regarding the stars happily. "What a great night."

Dar stepped into the tub and sat down, setting two glasses down on the rim and stretching an arm out to encircle Kerry's shoulders. "Glad you liked it." She wiggled her toes in contentment. "I sure did, except that fudge got damn messy."

One green eye rotated in her direction. "Which is why we're here in the hot tub," Kerry reminded her wryly. "Or we would have ended up stuck together, which could have made work a little interesting tomorrow." She reached over and scratched the back of Dar's neck. "How'd it go down by the base today?"

Dar handed her a glass of cold sweet peach tea. "Relatively pointless. I got the circuit hooked up and got the download started, then..." Dar paused. "There was one weird thing. They've got a private T3 dropped in there that's on an isolated segment."

Kerry tipped her head to one side. "Really?" she mused. "That is weird."

"Yeah." Dar nibbled her inner lip. "I've got Mark tracking down the private line, but...I don't know, Ker. It's really odd." She leaned back and sighed. "I wish I knew what was going on."

Kerry caught the mood change, and she slid closer. "Maybe it's nothing."

Dar regarded the stars. "Maybe." She set her glass down and slid her arms around Kerry instead, kissing her lips and removing a trace of fudge from them. "But right now, I don't think I want to care one way or the other."

"Mm." Kerry slid around to face her, going belly to belly with

Dar as she leaned forward.

Dar pulled her closer, circling her arms around the small of Kerry's back. As she looked up, the stars overhead formed an almost halo around her partner's form, and their twinkle was echoed in the mist green eyes gazing back at her. "Know what I think?"

"No, what?" Kerry murmured, gently exploring the curve of Dar's neck with her lips.

"I think I like cooking."

Kerry stopped and went nose to nose with her, her eyes almost crossing as she tried to keep Dar's face in focus. "I think you got into some bad MREs down on that base, Ms. Paladar."

The taller woman chuckled. "Well, okay. I don't like cooking, but I like surprising you." She tilted Kerry's chin upward and kissed her on the lips. "I thought about what I was going to do all the way home on that damn boring road."

Kerry responded, letting her hand submerge to stroke Dar's side, rubbing her thumb along the curve of her breast. "Well, it was a trip to come home to, that's for sure. I don't think I ever had anyone do that for me before," she admitted. "And boy, was it nice after being at work all day. I think I get a clue as to why guys wanted to keep their wives home in the kitchen all those years."

Dar snickered, nuzzling her neck and giving her a nip. "Antifeminism explained. There's a master's thesis in there if you want it, Ker."

"No thanks." Kerry rubbed her body against Dar's, reveling in the feel of their skin-on-skin contact. "Four years was more than enough for me. I'm no scholar."

"Me either." Dar ran her hands up Kerry's thighs, leaning back a little as her partner pressed against her. The frothy water tickled her now sensitized skin, and they spent a leisurely few minutes exchanging kisses.

Kerry unexpectedly giggled. "Um...Dar?"

"Yeees?"

"Look over your right shoulder."

Dar reluctantly left off from a very interesting exploration of Kerry's chest and turned her head, coming face to face, or rather nose to nose, with a curious Labrador Retriever. "Yah!"

"Gruff!" Chino gave her a lick.

Kerry burst into laughter, collapsing against Dar in a delightful swirl of bubbles and warm skin. "We forgot to close the sliding door all the way."

"So I see." Dar splashed the dog with a handful of water. "Least it's her, and not my folks." She caught her breath, her temporarily thwarted libido kicking her in the butt but not having anywhere to go past those cute Labrador ears now cocking her way. "C'mon. It's getting a little chilly out here anyway."

Kerry flexed her shoulders, which had been fully exposed to the wind. "Mm." She got out and wrapped one of their fluffy blue towels around her, reaching over and handing Dar the other as her partner climbed out of the tub. Even after all this time, Kerry glanced around as the moonlight outlined Dar's muscular body, half expecting to see interested spectators on decks nearby.

There weren't. At least none that she saw. She chuckled at herself and followed Dar inside, finding her hand taken and clasped as they closed the sliding door and traded the balmy air for the crisp chill of the condo. They walked together in silence across the living room, jostling each other as they entered the large blue-tinted bedroom.

"Now..." Dar turned and faced her, removing her towel and tossing it into the corner. "Where were we?"

Kerry stepped forward into her embrace, ducking her head slightly to give Dar's nipple a playful lick. "Here?"

"Hmm..." Dar half chuckled deep in her throat. She wrapped her arms around Kerry and picked her up, turning and taking both of them to the waterbed. She rolled over onto her back as Kerry stretched and spread her body out. The heat of their combined skin was shiver inducing, an exquisite counterpoint to the conditioned air.

Kerry slid her thigh between Dar's and traced a teasing path from her groin to her breasts, leaning forward to coax a soft groan from her partner with a pair of skillful lips. Learning what worked with Dar was a never-ending fascination of hers, and she took an unsteady breath as she felt Dar's touch high up on the inside of her leg.

Her body growled sensually, and she craved more as they traded nips, Dar's teeth closing gently over her breast as the warmth of her breath warmed the skin around her nipple. Kerry felt her heart rate pick up and she started to work her way down Dar's body, nibbling the subtle ripples under her skin as she tasted the skin around her navel. The muscles under her lips tensed, and she moved lower, feeling Dar shift under her as she curled her upper body around and took a taste of Kerry's hip.

"Mm." Kerry breathed in, sucking in a lungful of Dar's distinctive scent, just lightly touched with chlorine from the tub. "I want you."

"Heh." Dar chuckled. "Think you got me, cute stuff."

Kerry could feel the pressure building in her guts as Dar's

light touch moved intimately over her in tweaks and gentle
strokes, a rhythm she matched with her own attentions to her partner's tanned body. As the tension wound up, she gasped for air,
arching her back as Dar's attentions brought her to the breaking
point and over it.

Her body contracted, shivers moving up and down her spine
as she felt Dar grip her fiercely. Their limbs coiled together as Dar
let out a heartfelt groan and slid belly to belly again. They rocked
together, stroking each other gently as the contractions eased,
exchanging the light coating of sweat they'd worked up.

Kerry closed her eyes, enjoying the comfortable lassitude. For
all the stress of the day, ending it like this made her look back on
her problems and just laugh at them.

Made it all worth it, really—this being in love thing.

Dar slid her arms around Kerry and pulled her closer, fitting
their bodies together like a living puzzle. They fell asleep like that
as the moonlight painted stripes across their bodies, making them
seem more one creature than two.

Chapter
Ten

Dar leaned back in the leather seat and rested her knee against the wheel as the Lexus made its way down the long stretch of road. She had a soothing New Age CD playing, a new one Kerry had bought her on a recent trip to the mall. Dar pulled out the cover and glanced at it. "Huh." It was an all-instrumental healing CD, with natural background noises worked into it, and she liked it very much.

It was soothing, and Dar felt very calm. She took a sip of the milk she'd put in her travel mug and felt its cool thickness slide down her throat. *Funny.* Her eyes dropped briefly to the cup, then lifted. She'd been staying away from coffee lately, and she was starting to notice a real difference. Instead of her usual five or six cups, she'd been having maybe two, and even her breathing seemed to have slowed down a little.

On the seat next to her rested the laptop, full of data and reports she'd downloaded from Mark's mainframe just before she'd left. Time enough when she got there, Dar reasoned, to take a quick look at them, before she headed off to see the new recruits.

Part of her was looking forward to that, in an odd way. "There but for having a brain cell, go I," she murmured to herself with a smile. "Seaman Roberts, the second." She sighed. "Oh, Dar. Was that ever so not for you."

But then, it had hurt. That one last day, when she'd waited in the driveway for her father to come home; waited, and known, the moment she saw his face, what the answer was.

No.

Andrew had indulged in a rare bit of physical affection, putting his arms around her and hugging her. "Sweetheart, you ain't got to do this. There's lots of damn things you can do in there."

Dar had leaned against him, utterly miserable. "Why couldn't I have been a boy?" she'd whispered. A hand had come and gripped her chin, lifting her head up.

"'Cause God didn't want you that way," her father had told her. "You ain't gonna argue with God, Paladar. What he made you is what he made you."

Dar smiled faintly. *Yeah, I guess he did.* She took another long swallow of milk, then set the cup down as she prepared to turn into the base. The guard opened the gate without her even pausing and she entered, finding a spot under a large tree to park under.

Shouldering her laptop, she got out and walked across the lot, pausing as a group of children dashed in front of her, heading for the bus stop. A harried-looking woman chased after them, dressed in a pair of cotton pants and a haphazardly buttoned shirt.

"Nora! Wait! Slow down!" the woman yelled.

One of the smaller girls, a cute tyke with soft, dark brown hair and a mischievous grin, turned and made a face at her. "Go now, Mom!" she scolded, then turned and dashed after her friends.

"Oh, my God," the woman sighed, pushing her hair back as she ran past Dar. "Kids. Nora!"

Dar chuckled softly and continued on her way, trying to recall ever being that small. Could she? Being here helped, she acknowledged, as she walked through the lower corridor and up the curved stairway. As her hand touched the banister, she had a sudden flash of memory that almost made her stop short.

She did remember, just a little. It had been a very rainy day, so bad that they'd gotten all the kids and the parents from the housing area and put them up in the admin building. Here, in fact. Dar stopped at the landing and turned to look down. Yes. She remembered the blankets spread out.

Maybe it had even been a hurricane. Her dad had been gone, away at sea, and she and Ceci had joined about ten other kids and fifteen or so adults in taking shelter here in the hall. She remembered sliding down the banister, thrilled at the access to the normally closed and guarded building.

"Paladar!" Her mother had looked up to see a small form hurtling toward her at frightening speed.

"Whee!" Dar had leaped off the end of the wood and crashed into her mother, knocking the diminutive Ceci right down on her behind. "Wow! I liked that!" She'd gotten up, intending to race back up the stairs.

But her mother had grabbed her and spanked her, right there in the middle of the hall, and all the other kids had laughed.

Dar hadn't laughed. She didn't now, as she felt again that hot sting of shame.

"Hey, Roberts."

Dar turned at the voice and gave Chief Daniel a cool look. "Yes?"

The stocky chief came down the rest of the stairs, but stayed one up from the landing, to bring her eyes level with Dar's. "Got something you might want to see."

"Like what?"

A faint smile edged the chief's lips. "C'mon. I'll show you." She turned and walked back up the stairs. After a moment of watching her, Dar followed.

"Morning, everyone." Kerry put her PDA down on the conference room table. The extended operations group looked back at her, waiting for her to sit down. Familiar faces all, including the newest, Clarice. Kerry opened her notes and cleared her throat, lacing her fingers together as she reviewed the page. "Okay, Mark, you start. Tell me about those router projections?"

"Well," the MIS chief twirled his pad around the pencil he had stuck in one of its holes, "I don't know, Kerry. I extended out the contracts we have pending to the end of the year, and we ain't got enough hardware for them." He lifted one shoulder slightly. "Not sure what happened."

Everyone shifted uneasily.

"Okay." Kerry tapped her thumbs together. "Either sales oversold, or we underbought. It's not like it's rocket science, Mark. Which was it?"

Clarice spoke up. "I'm sure you could probably tell us right off, right?"

Kerry's hackles invisibly rose. However, she didn't answer; instead, she eyed Mark. "Well?"

"Um..."

"Mark, just spill it." Kerry said. "Someone counted wrong, it's not a crime." She rested her chin against her fist.

"Well, that's the problem." Mark said. "If I use our invoices, and use our contracts, we're not short."

Kerry cocked her head at him. "What are you saying?" she asked. "Are you saying we lost a bunch of routers?"

"That's pretty funny, for the operations machine," Clarice chuckled, getting a few people to chuckle with her. "I guess humans work here, too."

"Considering it means either someone's been incompetent, or someone's been thieving, I wouldn't really call it funny," Kerry stated, overriding the noise.

"Oh, c'mon, Kerry," Clarice said. "They're probably in a closet somewhere, or under a cabinet." She smiled. "It happens."

Kerry waited for the murmuring to stop, which it did when she remained silent. "No, it doesn't, not with our inventory system," she said quietly. "Mark, open an investigation. Track every asset we have by bar code. I want to know the last known location of anything we can't find."

"Well, in my experience, even computers can make mistakes," Clarice said, undaunted.

"Not these computers," Kerry stated with finality. "Not this program. The coder made sure of that." She looked at Mark. "By tonight?"

Mark nodded.

"Thanks." Kerry dismissed the subject. "Carol, give me the rundown on the new VOIP system for the central help desk?"

She was beginning to regret, she realized, a thoughtless moment of kindness.

Dar stared at the empty space. "What happened?"

Daniel shrugged. "Beats the heck out of me. Came in here to adjust some packet sizing, and found the damn thing gone. I called Security, but I got told to keep my mouth shut and take off." She rocked on her heels. "Y'know? I don't like your ass, Roberts, but I don't like being told to shut up worse."

Dar felt a grin tugging at her lips. "Yeah." She put her hands on her hips and took a breath, eyeing the area that had held the mysterious T3 and its router. "I know the feeling." One finger rubbed the strap on her laptop idly, then she pulled out her cell phone and dialed. "Mark?"

"Uh?" The MIS chief's voice sounded distant. "Hang on...I'm under my desk."

Dar's eyebrows rose. "We having bad weather again?"

The voice came much closer. "No." Mark exhaled audibly. "My goddamned friggin' NIC cable came loose again. I gotta replace it. What's up, boss?"

"Remember that T3 I was having you chase down?"

Mark paused for an instant. "Yeah. I was getting install data for you. It's almost all here."

"Good. Now get the disco order for it, because someone

pulled it out of here yesterday," Dar told him. "Did we get anything back on the serial number of that router?"

A long, long beat. "Not that we wanna talk about over the cell," Mark stated firmly. "Can I e-mail the info to you?"

A soft warning bell rang in Dar's head. "Sure," she murmured. "Send me what you have. I'll go pull it down." She closed the phone and looked at the chief. "Something doesn't smell right."

Daniel sniffed. "Must be that weird-ass soap you civvies are always using." She shook her head and turned toward the door to the small telecommunications closet. "But, yeah, I figured. I don't like my stuff going AWOL, then being told it ain't my business."

They walked down the hall to the small office that had been assigned to Dar. It was empty, as always, since Dar brought everything with her she needed and took it home with her at the end of the day. A pencil, left behind on her prior visit, rolled idly in the breeze from the open windows.

Dar put her briefcase down on the desk and unzipped it. "Let me get that mail, and maybe it'll make some sense." She glanced out the window. "Too early for the recruits?"

Daniel snorted. "Bus broke down up near the split to Card Sound." She perched on a corner of the worn wooden desk and watched Dar unpack her laptop. "Nice box."

Dar flashed a quick grin. "Thanks. It's a new generation chip we're testing for Intel." She flipped the screen open and pressed the rapid on, watching the fifteen-inch display light crisply.

"Yeah?" Daniel sounded interested. She edged closer. "Shit, that's fast."

"Mm." Dar reached down, picked up the Ethernet cable lying limply on the floor, and started to plug it into the jack on the computer. An odd sensation under her thumb made her stop, however, and bring the end of the cable up for a better look.

No, it seemed fine. Dar rubbed her thumb over the plastic again while the chief watched her in fascination. *Hmm.* Unable to figure out why she didn't like the damn thing, she shrugged and put the cable down, unzipping the top part of her laptop case and retrieving a second cable, with which she replaced the first. "Here." She tossed the discarded coil to the chief. "I don't like that one."

"Picky." Daniel caught the cable and examined it. "Looks fine to me."

Dar sat down and watched her desktop come up, her mind mulling over the last few minutes. Then she suddenly hit the pause key and stopped the machine's progress. She pulled out her cell phone and dialed Mark's number again. "Hey."

"Yeah? Didn't come through?" Mark asked.

"Put a filter on that T1 from here." Dar's voice became clipped. "One way. Everything. Fast."

"What are you doing?" Chief Daniel eased around the desk and peered at the computer.

"Wh—okay." Mark's keyboard rattled hard for a long moment. "Okay, got it. What's up?"

Dar released the pause button and watched the computer continue to boot. "Read me the talk back."

There was a pause. "Nego," Mark said.

"Go on."

"Protocol's up."

"Okay."

"IP request to the DHCP. You were issued 194.156.168.131."

"Got it."

"RAS coming up...You should get your validation in a second."

The computer beeped softly, requesting input. Dar typed her network login and password and hit enter. "Okay, it's got it."

"You're validated. Services starting." Long pause. "Looks okay, boss wh—holy shit!"

Dar smiled grimly. "Invasion barrage?"

"Son of a bitch! Jesus, what the hell is in that hub?" Mark squeaked. "Shit, let me get a more macho filter on that before it sends my security program running for the hills. Brent! Get me box ten online, wouldja!"

Long fingers drummed on the wood surface. "Let me know when you get something in place to trap it. Then disable it so I can get my goddamn mail." Dar gave Chief Daniel a look. "I don't mind the bullshit, but if this was you trying to bust into my network, I'm gonna hang you out that damn window."

Chief Daniel was staring at the laptop. She looked at Dar with an astonished expression. "Me? Shit, if I could do that, you think I'd be working in a half-assed, sun-baked sand pit down at the ass end of the Navy?"

No. Dar's eyes narrowed. But someone else here was.

Kerry stiffarmed her way into Operations, tossing her folder down on the console as she circled the big desk. "Okay. Let me see the inventory screens."

Mark had walked in behind her, and he paused, leaning against the other side of the desk as he watched her scroll through the program. "Probably ended up being coded to some other account, Kerry. I'm sure they weren't scarfed."

An annoyed wrinkle appeared across Kerry's brow. "That's not the point," she told him. "If they had been scanned right, we wouldn't be having this conversation."

The MIS manager exchanged rueful looks with the tech behind the desk, who had slid his chair back to make room for Kerry to get at the machine. Their blond VP took up less space than her tall boss did, but Mark noticed they both had the same exact habit of restlessly moving their mice around while waiting for the program to give them what they wanted.

He wondered if Kerry had picked that up by watching Dar, or if it was just a coincidence.

"C'mon, c'mon," Kerry grumbled. "This damn thing's slower than my grandmother's cat." Her eyes flicked across the screen, then paused, and she leaned a little closer. "Ah."

Curious, Mark put his briefcase down and circled the console, peering over her shoulder at the results. "Uh-oh," he muttered. "I forgot about that."

Kerry turned and looked at him, putting them almost nose to nose. One of her blond eyebrows hiked up sharply.

Mark backed up hastily. "Okay, so it was my fault. I forgot to recap those routers we sent you in NC, boss," he admitted. "We haven't processed the recovered ones from the old center yet back into inventory."

"And we're just now realizing this?" Kerry's voice rose in disbelief.

The MIS manager half shrugged apologetically. "When Dar calls, we jump...You know how it is, Kerry. My foul-up—I'll make sure it gets fixed and call the warehouse to put those returns back into circulation."

"Grr." Kerry mock-growled at him, relaxing a little now that she'd solved the mystery. Losing that many routers wasn't funny, but finding them in a paperwork snafu was a lot better than having to call Security over it.

Mark's phone rang and he scuttled backward, waving at it. "Duty calls...I'll take care of that in a jiff, Kerry. Promise." He opened the phone and answered it, glancing up at Kerry after he heard the voice on the other end. "Hey...you just got me in big trouble!"

Dar, Kerry guessed, shaking a finger at him before she collected her folders and headed back to her office. She pushed the door open and emerged into the hallway, coming close to colliding with Clarice as the black woman walked in the opposite direction.

"Whoops...sorry."

"No problem, Kerry." Clarice paused, regarding her. "Find that missing stuff yet?"

Kerry had to concentrate on her voice to keep the edge out, which surprised her a little. "Found them, yes. Just an inventory mix-up."

"See?" Clarice laughed. "I told you it was something like that. You shouldn't take things so seriously, Kerry." She gave the smaller woman a nudge on the arm. "Lighten up!"

Kerry's eyes narrowed slightly against her will. "Well, you know how it is," she responded politely. "When I'm responsible for something, I take it very seriously." She paused. "Old-fashioned attitude, I guess."

Clarice ignored the barb behind the words and shook her head in mock dismay. "Well, I can understand that—you working...so closely...with Paladar and all," she said. "If I were in your shoes, I'd have lost my sense of humor, too." She patted Kerry on the shoulder and walked on past. "Later!"

Kerry took a breath, then headed for the stairwell, passing Clarice up as she opened the door. "Lucky me," she commented, making sure she caught the black woman's eyes. "I'm the only one who fits in my shoes." With a pleasant smile, she let the door close in Clarice's face with a satisfying snick.

"Yeesh." Kerry scrubbed her hand across her face, exhaling a little of the frustration out. "Dar, we need to talk." She turned and started up the steps to the fourteenth floor, shaking her head the entire way.

"Did you get that last packet?" Mark's voice emerged tinnily from the cell phone. "I think that's it." There was a pause. "Dar?"

Pale blue eyes were fastened intently on the laptop's screen, flicking over the data it displayed. "What?"

"Did you hear what I just said?"

"No." Dar looked up and glared at the phone. "What was it?"

Mark sighed. "I'm done here."

Yeah, yeah. Dar braced her chin on her fists. "All right." Her eyes didn't stop scanning the lines of code, though, as she attempted to find the pattern that was just—barely—eluding her. "Did you suck out the attack program?"

"Sure."

"Decompile it and dump it down to me, willya?"

Mark was silent for a little bit. "Wouldn't it be easier if you just did the analysis back here?" His voice sounded a touch odd.

"No." Dar's brow creased. "Why would it?"

"We've got more cycles here."

"Bullshit, Mark. Just send it down." Dar called up another file and split the screen, displaying both files and scrolling them at the same time. After a moment, she stopped scrolling and put her chin back onto her fists, studying the results. *What the hell is going on?*

The door to the office opened, and Chief Daniel entered. "Figures. The damn bastard's on some lame-ass trip up to Baltimore."

"Mm." Dar traced a single line with one long finger. "What about Ms. Pit Bull?"

"Says she doesn't know anything about it." The chief perched on the edge of the desk. "Nobody knows anything, nobody saw anything, no vendor was cleared on base, no guards saw anyone carrying a thirty-five-pound hub out of the building."

Dar looked up. "Either someone's covering up, or you've got the worst security outside of the White House." She rubbed her eyes. "Damn it, Mark, facilities don't materialize out of nowhere. Don't tell me you can't locate who installed that pipe."

Mark sighed audibly. "Am I in trouble **again**?"

"Where the hell is Kerry?" Dar was aware she sounded like a cranky child, but she didn't care. "Have her start calling up the chain at BellSouth, it's their POP."

"Um."

"Well?" the CIO snapped. "Get on it, Mark!"

"Hey, honey." A warm voice suddenly emerged, an octave higher than the MIS chief's.

An awkward silence ensued, then Dar cleared her throat. "Hi," she said. "You're on speakerphone."

"Uh-oh." Kerry replied. "Don't tell me you're in a room full of macho sailors, are you?"

"Two hundred of them." Dar felt her annoyance fading. "They all want your phone number." She exhaled. "Listen, I need you to—"

"Shake BellSouth's cage, I heard." Kerry's tone turned crisper. "What's going on down there?"

Dar wished she knew. She was aware of the chief's now somewhat chilly demeanor and guessed the prickly woman was smart enough to figure out that subordinates didn't usually greet their bosses in quite that manner at ILS. "Something," she admitted. "I just can't figure out if it's someone who's just curious as to what we've found, or someone..." Dar stopped speaking as her eyes finally found something in the pattern of code on her screen. Her brow contracted and she leaned closer, blinking as her vision blurred slightly, then cleared.

"Dar?" Mark asked, hesitantly.

"Hang on." Dar typed in a command, then studied the result. "They're using a stepped algorithm."

"Huh?"

"What?" Chief Daniel walked around behind Dar, but conspicuously not too close.

"Right there." Dar pointed. "It's a programming trick you can use to shift data from one field to another in database design." She folded her hands together. "Question is, why?"

Everyone held their tongues. "You still want that dump?" Mark finally asked.

Dar rested her lips against her clasped hands and allowed her eyes to close. The nagging headache she'd picked up after the attack on the network was making her a little sick to her stomach, and she just spent a moment breathing to settle it. "No," she said at last. "Put it on my drive at home, Mark. I'll look at it this weekend."

"Do you want me to get after BellSouth?" Kerry murmured. "I've got some contacts that will probably open up for me."

"Yeah."

Kerry's voice strengthened. "Okay."

"Eh." Dar kept reviewing the damning bit of data. She carefully saved the data and leaned back as the chief scurried out of range. "Mark, take that entire database and run it through the C1F program."

"For real?" Mark sounded a touch puzzled. "I didn't think—"

"Just do it," Dar ordered crisply. "If Duks is in there, tell him I need the CPU cycles."

"All right," the MIS chief agreed. "I'll do it. You coming back here?"

Should she go? Dar considered the question. There was something very wrong, that much her experience was telling her. But what if it was just something like what she knew went on during her adolescent years? When the petty officers and lower-ranking crew found ways in and out of the system to hide a few barrels of this here, and a box of that there, just to make life a little easier.

For her, it'd been peanut butter. She'd traded blocks of her nascent programming talents for Number 10 cans of the stuff in the informal black market that had also produced her Navy shirts and boots.

She'd never seen anything wrong in that, really. Even her father had taken advantage of it, getting little luxuries for her mother and using the trading system to save up a few bucks for a toy for her birthday.

No way was she going to blow the whistle on that.

Was she?

Dar sighed. "Kerry, let me know if you get any answers from BellSouth. I'm going to put this to bed for a while and go review the recruit program."

"Will do," Kerry replied. "Talk to you later."

Dar folded her cell phone up and slid it into its clip at her belt. Then she sat back and turned her head, regarding Chief Daniel in silence.

The naval officer's lip was curled into an almost unconscious snarl of distaste. "I knew there was something wrong with you," Daniel said. "No wonder you didn't make it into the Navy."

Asshole. Dar felt her temper stir. She hitched a knee up and circled it with both arms. "The Navy?" she laughed. "You've gotta be kidding. I'm married to a gorgeous woman, I live in a five-million-dollar condo, I make a seven-figure salary, and I don't have to wear ugly clothing that doesn't fit right. Why the hell would I want to be in the Navy?"

Chief Daniel stepped back. "You're sick."

Dar got up and closed the laptop, after setting its security. "Save your ignorance for someone who gives a crap about what you think." She turned her back on the chief and walked out of the office.

Her phone rang. Kerry hit the button. "Operations, Kerry Stuart."

"Howdy there, Kerry!" Bob Terisanch's booming voice entered the room, making her desk ornament rattle. "Sorry it took so long, but hot damn, lady, that circuit was buried so deep under a pile of rat poop, it took me the whole day and a jackhammer to pull it on out."

Colorful, Dar had often called Bob. "Great, Bob. Thanks for the effort. What do you have?" Kerry pulled her pad over and poised her pencil over the white ruled paper.

There was a rustle of shuffled paper. "Well, ma'am, the private company that installed that sucker's called Fibertalk Associates, and they're based right down by you in Miami, matter of fact."

"Great. Do you have a billing address for them?"

"Sure do. 1723 NW 72nd Avenue," Bob provided cheerfully. "They've done a bunch of little high-priced jobs round town, mostly fiber optics, a little sat."

"Thanks, Bob. I owe you one," Kerry told him. "Lunch, next week?"

"Heh. I'll never say no to lunch with such a pretty lady. You're on, Kerry. See ya!" Bob hung up, leaving Kerry to nibble thoughtfully at her pencil. The office was one of those little mini-warehouses out behind the airport. Odd. Curiously, she brought up her database search and entered the company name in it. Then she sent the little bot on its way and set her pencil down. "Well, that's that. Let's get outta here, okay?"

What in the hell are they recruiting these days? Dar rested her arms on the railing and studied the group of new sailors. *Kids out of grade school?* The twenty new swabs were clustered around the admitting petty officer, looking hapless and mostly bewildered. Watching their painfully earnest faces made Dar suddenly feel older than her years. She put her chin down on her crossed wrists and sighed, wondering if she'd ever really been that young and feckless.

"Can you people not stand up straight? What the hell are your spines made of, Jellah?" the petty officer barked loudly. "Pick up them damn bags and get in line!"

The new sailors looked at each other. "Which you want us to do first, Sarge?" the tall, crew-cut boy closest to Dar drawled. "Gotta get out the line to get them bags."

Dar's lips quirked faintly, as the petty officer's neck veins started to bulge. The kid sounded a lot like her father, and she imagined briefly what she'd have been like in just this sort of lineup, smartass that she'd been.

"Are you finding this funny, ma'am?" The petty officer's attention had been drawn suddenly to his unwanted observer. "I'm not sure what the joke is."

Your toupee? Dar had to clamp her jaw shut to keep the words from emerging. The smart-assed kid she'd been snickered at her. *Been?* "If I were you, I'd just take care of the problems you have right there, not look for more with me," she warned the man. "Those problems you've got a chance to do something about."

The petty officer glared at her, then decided the tall, dark-haired woman he'd been told to be cursorily polite to wasn't going to go away. "All right, you lot of useless baggage. Go to that pile of bags, pick up the bag that has your goddamned name on it, then walk back to where you started and get in line. Is that clear enough, or d'you want me to stamp it in Braille letters on your goddamned useless foreheads?"

Dar resumed her position leaning against the railing as the swabs picked up their gear and shuffled into place. Six of the new sailors were women, and she found herself studying them, making mental guesses as to their backgrounds and reasons for joining.

The two nearest her, she considered, were probably from poor families in tough neighborhoods. They were almost twins: medium height, Latin complexion, dark curly hair, and a permanent suspicious look in their eyes.

The redhead in the front of the line with the pugnacious chin and smattering of freckles looked like an only girl raised with a pile of brothers, some of whom were probably already in service.

One of the remaining three was, Dar suspected, a cheerleader. She had the wholesome good looks and feathered blond hair of one, along with a perky snub noise and a perfect smile.

Dar wondered what wrong turn she'd taken, and when she'd realize she'd taken it. Next to her was a short, heavyset girl with a bulldog attitude, who reminded Dar strongly of Chief Daniel.

Great. Dar exhaled and turned her head slightly, startled to find the eyes of the last female swab fastened firmly on her. For an instant, clear, pale gray eyes met Dar's with startling clarity, and then they dropped as the petty officer started to yell more orders.

Dar blinked. The girl was facing forward now, her blond head cocked to one side as she listened. She was fairly short, shorter than Kerry by an inch or so, and she had a wiry, but very slender build. She held herself with a sense of secure confidence, despite the intimidating petty officer, and Dar felt an unusual curiosity prick her.

But not for that long, as the petty officer shoved them out the door and toward the processing center. Dar pushed off the railing and ambled after them, pushing the hinged doors open and moving to one side of the room as the new sailors picked up their new uniforms.

A computer terminal was on a table to her right, and Dar went directly to it, bringing up a login screen and entering a collection of letters and numbers in a rattle of keystrokes.

"Hey." The petty officer was at her shoulder. "Are you supposed to be in there?"

"I have a password," Dar replied. She scanned the information she was looking for and keyed in a further request. "Your swabs are unraveling." She waited for the man to leave, then examined the record.

Chapter
Eleven

The boat's bow bobbed up and down gently in the surf, a soothing motion that made the woman painting on its fiberglass surface smile. Ceci Roberts dipped her brush into a swirl of acrylic color, studied the canvas for a moment, and then continued her work. The underwater seascape had a wash of blue in a dozen shades and the floor of the sea with its coating of coral, and now she was going back in and putting in the vibrant colors of fish and leafy ocean foliage.

Nearby rested a small tray with a pitcher of iced tea and a bowl of fresh fruit. The slim silver-blond woman paused again and selected a bit of melon, sucking on it as she considered her next stroke.

The sun splashed over her tanned skin and she idly watched the golden light, taking a moment to simply live, adoring the present and giving a silent thanks to the goddess for perhaps the thousandth time.

The boat rocked a little harder, and she looked up to see a pair of large hands clasping the lower railing, long fingers tightening on the metal then straining as the hands were followed by a large, wet, partially neoprene-covered body. Ceci smiled. "Hey there, sailor boy. Find the problem?"

"I surely did." Andrew pulled himself up and over the railing, then removed a bag slung at his waist and dumped its contents onto the white deck. "That there fish got stuck in the intake valve."

"Ew." Ceci grimaced. "Andy, if I wanted sushi on the boat, I'd have ordered out. Can you toss it overboard?"

The big ex-SEAL snorted, but scooped the messy item up and

neatly chucked it over the railing. Then he squished over to where his wife was seated and peered at the painting, careful to avoid dripping murky salt water on Ceci's palette. "I do like that."

Ceci tickled his exposed kneecap, then leaned over and kissed the spot, tasting the tang of the sea. "I do love you," she told him. "I still think this has to be a dream."

Andrew seated himself on the deck. "Seems that way sometimes, don't it?" his deep voice rumbled quietly. "Been through a lot, you and I have. Maybe it's just the good Lord's way of saying we done all right."

Ceci studied the scarred, weathered face next to her, its piercing blue eyes standing out with startling clarity. She traced a grizzled eyebrow gently. "Maybe."

The cell phone resting on the deck next to her warbled. They both glanced at it, then Ceci sighed and picked it up. "Yes?"

"Ceci."

And then again, Ceci gazed plaintively up at the sky, *the goddess has ways of reminding you just how easily karma can change.* "Hello, Charles," she replied. "To what do I owe the honor of this call?"

Charles Bannersley was her older brother, the head of their family, and one of the largest ambulatory anal orifices Ceci knew. She was pissed at him, though she didn't think he really understood why, and wanted to hear his voice about as much as she wanted a salt-water enema.

Andrew merely narrowed his eyes as he recognized the tinny voice coming from the phone Ceci was holding between them.

"I'd like to see you," Charles answered. "Candy and I are here, in Miami."

"Sorry," Ceci replied crisply. "I've got plans tonight."

"Fine. Have a drink with us first," her brother came right back. "Can't you spare ten minutes for your family?"

Andrew rolled his eyes. "Lord."

"My family?" Ceci decided to allow her spleen its moment. "My family's sitting right here next to me. Of course I can spare any amount of time for Andrew." She paused. "And Dar and Kerrison, of course. Why do you ask?"

A sigh traveled through the cell phone's speaker. "Cecilia, please."

Andrew and Ceci exchanged looks. Andrew's eyebrows lifted in amused surprise, giving him an expression very much like Dar's would have been in the same situation.

Ceci considered, then shrugged. "Fine. There's a tiki bar just off the marina here. Meet me in a half-hour. I can only stay a few

minutes, though, Kerry's picking us up for dinner after that."
Poke, poke. Ceci enjoyed the jab at her family's straightlaced sen-
sibilities.

"All right." Charles hesitated. "Alone, Ceci."

Andrew straightened in outrage and almost grabbed for the
phone. Ceci put a finger against his lips and held it out of range.
"You're joking, right?" she told her brother. "Did you really think
I'd subject Andy to you two? Get real." Her hand folded the phone
shut, and she dropped it on the towel next to her. "Into every life,
a little bird crap must fall, hmm?"

Andrew scowled. "Ah could go with you."

"Nah." Ceci ruffled his drying close-cropped hair affection-
ately. "I'll be safe. Charles is an idiot, but the last I checked, he
wasn't suicidal." She tilted his chin up and kissed him. "Let me go
toss on some scandalous clothing and find out what his problem
is."

Andrew watched her leave. He collected the tubes and other
painting gear and tucked them away in the plastic bucket Ceci
used and tidied the area, then stood and made his way aft to rid
himself of his scuba equipment.

"A tiki bar." Charles loosened his collar and glanced around.
"Figures." He gave his twin sister a disgusted look. "I hate this
place. Always have."

Candice fiddled with the table tent before her. She was of
medium height, with reddish bronze hair and green eyes, like her
brother, though his hair was thinning almost to invisibility. "Yes,
well, what the hell did you expect, Charles? You knew what it
would be like."

He snorted and took a sip of his whiskey, his eyes wandering
over the scantily clad bodies and diverse ethnicity of the bar. Candice poked him. "What?"

"Here she comes," Candice told him. They both turned to
watch as their younger sister made her way up the wooden board-
walk toward them. "Well, she looks healthy."

Charles didn't answer. His eyes studied the relaxed, self-
assured person approaching, unable to refute the positive changes
since the last time he'd seen Ceci. She'd let her hair grow out a little, and it was bleached even lighter from the sun, contrasting with
the sun-darkened shade of her previously very pale skin.

She was no longer a ghost, eyes tensed in a remembered pain
that never left her.

No longer lost.

She'd come home, and even Charles, who hated this place—and hated her choice—had to admit the truth of that. "Ceci." He stood and greeted her as she joined their table. "Thanks for coming over."

"Charles." Ceci greeted him with wary cordiality. "Hello, Candy."

Her sister smiled. "Hi, Cec. You look great." She leaned forward. "Did you color your hair, or is that a new lipstick or..?"

"No." Ceci took a seat next to her older sister. "I've just been outside more than inside and put on ten pounds since you last saw me. But thanks for noticing." She caught the eye of the waiter. "Kahlua milkshake, please."

"That's different for you," Candy commented.

"I picked up some new bad habits from Dar." Ceci assumed a pleasant smile. "What do you two want?"

Her siblings exchanged glances. "Can't we just want to see you?" Charles asked.

"No." Ceci looked directly at him. "Andrew told me what you did, Charles." She referred to her brother's refusal to pass on the Navy's notification of Andrew's rescue to her. "It's a good thing you waited this long to contact me, because otherwise I'd have killed you for that."

"Cecilia."

"How dare you." Ceci slapped the table with her hand, making the silverware jump. Her brother and sister jerked in startled surprise. "You pretentious little son of a bitch."

Charles took a breath, clearly caught off guard. "I did what I thought was best for you," he finally answered stiffly.

"Bullshit," Ceci snapped, looking up as the waiter brought her milkshake and hurriedly left, seeing the angry faces. "Do you have any idea how badly I was hurting, Charles? How many days of pain you could have taken away from me with that damn piece of paper?" She slapped the table again. "Do you know just how ironic it is that my estranged daughter had to come back into my life to bring me back my Andy?"

Candy leaned forward and took her hand. "Cec, what Charles did was wrong. But he didn't do it to hurt you." She searched her sister's angry eyes.

"There is no way you can convince me of that," Ceci said, after a moment. "As much as you both hate Andrew, you knew how I felt about him."

A silence fell. Charles looked down at his hands, his fingers twisted together. Candice took several slow, even breaths. "Yes, we knew," she finally said. "We never understood why, but we..."

She glanced at her twin. "I knew." Another breath. "I'm sorry, Ceci."

Charles refused to look up.

"I don't want it to be like it was," Candice continued, filling the awkward silence. "I don't want to lose my sister and not have you be part of my life."

"This is ridiculous." Charles suddenly looked up. "We shouldn't have to sit here and beg."

"Charles!" Candice cut him off.

"No, I'm not going to shut up." He stood angrily, then paused as someone gently cleared their throat next to him.

"Hi." Kerry folded her hands in front of her. "Thought I recognized you. Mr. Bannersley, wasn't it?"

Ceci let her chin rest on her fist, watching her daughter-in-law in action. Kerry had a sweet, engaging smile that totally didn't match the fiery sparks visible in her pale green eyes. Her sense of presence was almost as significant as Dar's, and it was obvious the blond woman had been taking lessons from Ceci's tempestuous and intimidating offspring.

Charles gave her a cursory stare. "What?"

"Kerrison Stuart." Kerry stuck her hand out. "Dar's partner? We met at the funeral."

Charles gave her hand a perfunctory press. "Yes, well, you'll excuse us, please. I'm having a discussion with my sister, and I suggest you leave us alone."

Candice opened her mouth in outrage.

"You're yelling at my mother-in-law, and I suggest you sit down and lower your voice before I shove you into Biscayne Bay," Kerry told him in a mild, kind tone. She folded her arms, and in her snug tank top, her toned muscles looked healthily imposing. "Mind if I sit down?"

Dar cornered the petty officer after he'd taken the new recruits to their barracks and gotten them assigned to bunks. "Do you assess them?"

"What?" The officer stared at her. "Not my job, lady. They do that at intake."

"So where are their scores?"

"Scores? Who the hell cares?"

Dar felt like she was swimming through peanut butter. "How do you figure out where to place them if you don't have scores?" She forced patience into her voice. "Or skill assessments?"

"Are you some kinda idiot?" the man spluttered. "These

dorks don't have skills, you moron. They're nothing but bodies with empty heads. They'll do whatever we train them to do. No one cares what their scores are."

The sheet of white-hot rage hit her before she could defend against it. One moment she was standing with her Palm Pilot out, the next she'd grabbed the petty officer and slammed him against the wall, her hands reaching for automatic holds and a growl of pure animal emotion erupting from her throat. For a split second, she teetered on the edge of madness, and then her rational mind savagely ripped back control and forced her to merely push the man back against the wall.

Damn.

Dar waited for her throat to unclench, and then she took a breath. "I don't appreciate being called a moron." Even she heard the rough touch to her tone. "Especially by someone whose mental power rates lower than a watch battery's."

The petty officer was breathing hard, his hands clenching and unclenching, barely in control. "Who in the hell do you think you are?" he spat out.

For some reason, the question calmed Dar. She got herself under control, feeling the rage subside, leaving her knees trembling. *What in the hell's wrong with me?* she wondered uneasily. A pounding headache followed her return to sanity, and she had to swallow before she answered. "I think I'm the person your bosses hired to find out why this place isn't working." She leaned forward. "Maybe I just have."

Now it was the petty officer's turn to swallow. "Now hold on."

They were alone in the room, and the man looked around quickly before he returned his attention to Dar. "I didn't do a damn thing. Just what I was told."

Dar stepped back and let her hands drop, feeling exhausted. "I've heard that before." She found the stool near the computer console and sat down on it. "Something's going on here, and I'm gonna find it."

The man hesitated, then walked over and leaned on the computer console table. "Hey, look, you really from Washington?" His voice had lowered considerably.

Dar lifted one shoulder in a shrug. "I was hired by the Joint Chiefs, yes."

"All right, look..." The man shifted, and straightened suddenly, cutting off his speech as the door opened. "Sir."

Dar lifted her eyes to see the base commander enter. "Morning."

"Howdy, tadpole." Jeff Ainsbright gave her a big smile. "We all set for dinner tonight?"

The petty officer edged away from her, his eyes taking on a wary look.

"I think so, yes," Dar agreed. "Seven, you said? You want to meet at the steakhouse?"

The older man nodded briskly. "Right you are, tadpole. Chuckie tells me you're sweet on someone—you made the invite to him, too, right? Love to meet 'im."

The complication of the situation almost made Dar wince. "They'll be here," she quietly affirmed. "Mom and Dad, too."

"Great." The commander slapped her on the back. "Carry on, didn't want to interrupt anything. You find any holes yet I need to be plugging?"

Dar looked up at his weathered face, open and interested as it was. His smile indicated he expected no startling revelations from her, and at the moment, she wasn't sure if she had any.

Right? "Nothing concrete yet, Uncle Jeff," she said. "I'm still working through the data."

Maybe it was the way she'd said it. The base commander straightened a little, then glanced at the petty officer who was pressed against the wall doing his best imitation of a strip of wall weave. "Dismissed." He waited for the man to leave and the door to close, then he turned back to Dar, his face now mildly concerned. "What's the poop, tadpole? You really find something?"

Dar's lips tensed as she found herself caught between conflicting loyalties. She felt a mild sense of confusion for the first time in her life, and she had to stop and collect her thoughts for a moment before she could answer. "I don't know yet," she finally answered honestly. "I might have...there's something I don't like in the numbers, but I haven't fully analyzed it."

The CO put a large hand on her shoulder. "Tadpole, whatever you find, you bring it to me, hear? I don't care what it is, I wanna know."

Dar searched his face, seeing nothing but rock-solid resolve in his eyes. "All right," she agreed quietly. "When I have something for sure, you'll know it."

He patted her cheek. "Atta girl. You doing okay, tadpole? You look a little pale t'day."

Dar winced, lifting a hand to rub the back of her neck. "Headache," she explained with a light shrug. "Think I'll go take a walk outside for a few minutes."

"Right you are, my friend." Commander Ainsbright slung an arm over her shoulders and tugged her toward the door. "Fresh air's just the ticket. I'd send you out on a boat if I had one leaving; get you some salt in those lungs." He opened the door and they walked outside into the sunlight. "How 'bout a cup of java? That usually puts a patch on my noggin bangers."

Dar thought back to the petty officer, then realized the man was probably long gone, chasing after the new recruits. "Sure," she agreed. "Then I'll go catch up with the swabs."

"Quite the little Lone Ranger, aren't you?" Ceci commented as she and Kerry watched her siblings retreat into the golden rays of sun. They'd lasted through all of ten minutes of Kerry's pointedly polite chatter, then decided to give up and leave them alone. Ceci hadn't minded, but she suspected her sister, at least, wasn't giving up and would be back in touch.

That was all right. She'd never really minded Candice, who generally just went along with Charles in some kind of twin-like Zen mode. This time, however, Candy had spoken for herself, using the unusual "I" instead of "we," and Ceci had almost warmed back up to her.

A little.

Very little. But if Candy was, at this late stage in her life, attempting to develop a mind of her own, who was she to get in the way? "I feel well and thoroughly rescued."

Kerry leaned back and propped her feet up on the chair Charles had hastily vacated. "Who, me?" She smiled a trifle sheepishly. "Dar's rubbing off on me a little, maybe."

Ceci chuckled and nudged her glass over. "Want some?"

Kerry's brow contracted a bit. "No...my stomach's acting up." She exhaled, putting a hand over the afflicted area. "Or maybe it was just too many stressful meetings...It's been in a...knot all day." She finished the sentence softly.

Ceci watched her face, seeing the expression change as Kerry's focus turned inward. "Kerry?"

After a moment, the green eyes flicked up to meet hers. "Yeah, sorry. I was just thinking about something." Her fingers twitched as she resisted the urge to pull out her cell phone and call Dar. *She's not a baby, and you're not her sitter, Kerry. You can't call her to find out if she's okay every time you get a cramp.*

Ceci hazarded a guess. "About my daughter?"

Kerry's eyebrows hiked up. "Um..."

"She gets the same expression on her face when she's wondering about you," Ceci remarked mildly. "I think it's an indication of her fondness for you."

A faint blush darkened Kerry's already tanned skin. "It's mutual." She played with the napkin from Ceci's drink. She recalled Dar's half-forgotten "fit" before Thanksgiving and decided here, at least, was a person she could broach the subject with who wouldn't think she was weird.

Well, not too weird, anyway. "Can I ask a question?"

Ceci looked around, then pointed at her own chest. "Of me?"

Kerry nodded.

"Sure," the older woman agreed, more than a little apprehensive. "It's not about motherhood, is it?"

Kerry's eyebrows went straight up. "Um...no." She put a hand on her stomach. "Why, do I look pregnant or something? I know I put on some more weight lately, but..."

Ceci chuckled and relaxed. "Not at all...I just used to have nightmares about having 'that talk' with Dar." She cocked her head. "What's on your mind, Kerry?"

What was on her mind. Interesting way of putting it. "It's kind of a weird question," she replied slowly. "But...did you ever..." Kerry paused, frowning. "This sounds so crazy," she apologized.

"Not yet, it doesn't, except you don't usually beat around in the bushes," her mother-in-law remarked mildly.

"No, I know." Kerry circled her knee with both hands. "Okay, well...before Thanksgiving, when Dar and I were both traveling?"

"Hmm."

"My plane had some real problems during the flight, and I have to tell you, I was scared senseless," Kerry said.

"Perfectly reasonable," the older woman stated. "Nothing crazy about that, Kerry."

"Dar felt it," Kerry admitted. "She knew something was wrong." She stopped speaking and watched her mother-in-law's face for a reaction.

It wasn't the one she expected. Ceci cocked her head to one side and then smiled. "And?" she asked with a curious grin. "You want to know if that's normal?"

Kerry nodded slightly.

"Of course not," Ceci informed her.

"Oh."

"But I've felt it. I know Andrew has," the older woman went on. "When you're very close to someone, I think it just works that way. You just...know."

Kerry thought about that for a few minutes in silence while Ceci sucked on her milkshake. "It's weird," she finally said. "It's like...I haven't felt right all day, and if I call Dar, I bet something is making her upset."

"Really?"

"Yeah," Kerry answered. "I think about that and I feel like I'm reading a copy of the *National Enquirer,*" she admitted, plucking lightly at the seam on her denims. "But I know what I feel, so..."

Ceci chuckled softly. "Must have freaked my daughter out."

"Uh-huh." Kerry looked up and smiled. "She thought she was going nuts. I can't blame her, though. If she felt half as scared as I did, I would have thought I was going nuts too," she added. "But it's also sort of nice."

"That you care enough about someone to feel that?" Ceci asked.

A light blush appeared on Kerry's face, making her pale brows stand out suddenly. "Well, it's mutual, I think."

"No, really?" Ceci chuckled. "I'd never have guessed. You two keep it hidden so well."

Kerry's blush deepened. "That brings me to another problem, if you don't mind. I need to get your advice on something."

Uh-oh. Ceci straightened, feeling a mild sense of alarm. During her years on the base, speeches like that usually presaged breakups and divorces, and she wasn't ready to hear that coming from Kerry. "What's wrong?"

Kerry caught the tension in her voice and looked up, her brows contracting a little. "Wrong? No, I don't think it's wrong...it's just something I'm worried about."

Little alarm bells, the really annoying ones like the ones the Salvation Army collectors used at Christmas time, started going off. "Now, Kerry, listen." Ceci leaned forward. "I've known Dar a long time."

"Um...I know that."

"She has her moments, and I've seen most of them, but deep down, I think she's a good person."

Kerry's forehead rumpled. "I think so, too. Listen, Mom—"

"So whatever it is you're having problems with, think hard, and don't give up on that kid too easily, okay? I did, and look where it got me," Ceci told her very seriously.

Kerry's eyes closed, then reopened, and she reached over to take Ceci's hands in hers. "Mom." She drew a breath. "The only thing that's going to ever make me leave Dar is one or the other of us dying." She paused. "And even then, I'm not so sure."

Ceci blinked, now confused. "Oh. Well, that's fine then," she murmured. "Sorry, I thought—"

"I should have just talked faster." Kerry smiled. "No, what

I'm worried about is our relationship being front and center at dinner tonight."

Ceci thought about that. "Oh." She freed one hand and muffled a laugh. "I hadn't even...Oh, boy. Yeah..." Now the laugh escaped. "Oh, my goddess, those stuffed-up military—" She stopped and cleared her throat. "Ahmm...I mean, well, yes, Kerry, you do have a point there." Her face struggled to remain serious. "But don't worry about it—if they say anything, Andy will pick them up and toss them out the window, and they know it. If there's one thing everyone at that table already knows, it's don't mess with my kid in front of her daddy."

Kerry nodded in relief. "Okay. I was just worried about it. I know Dar has strong feelings about how she grew up, and I didn't want to cause her any pain."

Ceci sighed. "Kerry, you're so nice you should be regulated by the EPA." She reached over and patted the younger woman's cheek. "Did you ask Dar if she wanted you to give this a miss?"

Kerry nodded.

"And she said no, right?"

Kerry nodded again.

"So don't worry about it. C'mon, let's go see if Andy's gotten the seaweed out of his ears and gotten dressed. Then we can take off."

They stood, and Kerry suddenly took a step around the table and pulled Ceci into a hug. "Thanks."

Oh, good goddess. Ceci returned the hug and patted Kerry on the back. *I'm becoming a mother...Eeeeeekkkk!*

The coffee helped. Dar had also detoured to her car and tossed back a half handful of Advil, and now she was prowling around the barracks looking for her friend the petty officer.

The base was quiet, otherwise; most of the active groups were out on some kind of maneuvers, and only the new recruits and the usual business units at the base were out and about and doing their daily tasks.

Dar entered the long wooden barracks structure at one end and looked around the empty interior for a moment before she walked down the large central aisle. To either side were partitions with bunks in them, each bunk with its footlocker and open set of shelves made from what looked to her like old orange crates. Now that the new recruits had settled in, shirts were folded and in place, and the beds had obviously just been made.

Dar smiled. Probably remade a half-dozen times before the

petty officer had been happy with them, the dark blankets tucked with meticulous neatness around the thin mattresses. She remembered watching the new groups come in and peeking through the window as they'd been badgered and badgered by the admitting officers.

Not her, she'd decided once. She'd have done it exactly right the first time out. After all, hadn't her daddy taught her to make a regulation bunk and fold pants and shirts when she was only six years old?

With a smile, Dar continued through the room and out the other side, exiting onto a long, wooden porch with shallow steps that led down to the muddy ground. She looked to one side and spotted her little targets, now dressed in their new clothes, struggling to follow the orders of a new, different petty officer.

Dar wandered over and watched for a few minutes, until the new officer noticed her and walked over. This one was a woman, with short, crisply curled dark hair and an efficient attitude. "Ma'am? Something we can help you with?"

With a better attitude, at any rate. "No, just observing," Dar replied. "Where's the guy you relieved?"

The woman cocked her head in question. "Petty Officer Williams?" She waited for Dar's nod. "Off duty, ma'am."

Uh-huh. Dar looked over her shoulder at the recruits, surprised to find her slim blond friend looking back at her. The gray eyes met hers and sparkled, then the girl looked straight ahead, her body stiffening into an efficient attention. "Good group?"

The new officer, whose name was apparently Plodget, looked behind her, evaluating the question seriously. "A few of them, ma'am. It's always the same. Most aren't much use, but we always do find a few that'll make it."

"What's your dropout rate?"

A guarded look fell over the woman's face. "I wouldn't know, ma'am."

"Ballpark," Dar pressed. "I'm sure you've got a feeling as to how many of these poor saps you lose."

"No, ma'am, I don't," Plodget assured her. "We only get them for the first two weeks, then someone else takes over."

"Why?"

"That's just how it's done, ma'am."

Dar nodded slowly. "Where are their admitting records?"

"Haven't gotten here yet."

"Why not? You guys use a computer system to recruit. What's the holdup?"

Unemotional dark brown eyes met hers squarely. "That's just

how it's done, ma'am."

"All right." Dar straightened. "I'll just go see if I can't change that for you."

Dar turned and walked away, feeling the eyes on her back as she headed for the Admittance Center. She ducked inside with a feeling of relief and went to the computer console, seating herself in front of it and cracking her knuckles slightly. "Okay. Answer time." She logged in, and this time, instead of going through the regular channels, she keyed in a master code. "Idiots." The code still worked, and dropped her to a command line. "Where do you want to go today, hmm?"

Master database was where Dar wanted to go, and a string of commands got her there. She accessed the file structure and entered it through a back door, watching as the screen filled with line upon line of file records. Dar watched it for a few minutes, her eyes flicking back and forth searching for a certain pattern.

Ah. One long finger stopped the display. "Gotcha." She keyed in another command string and accessed the recruits' records, bringing them up and comparing them.

Her brow creased. "What in the hell?" Of the twenty, ten were, as the petty officer said, fairly standard, pretty much ordinary kids from lower-class backgrounds, with bad grades and poor ASVAB test results—destined, if they did make it, to be shipped out as seamen or women in whatever grunt job the Navy needed when they spit them out of training. Dar had known hundreds like them. Some might, she admitted, if they worked very hard, break through the ranks and ascend higher, but most would happily fill a berth and take three squares a day for as long as the US was willing to give it to them.

"What in the hell?" she repeated, then shook her head and captured the data, opening a second command page with a flick of her fingers. She snagged the files she'd been studying and zipped them, then sent them up the network path into her own, now specially protected file space.

Dar drummed her fingertips on the keyboard for a moment, then searched another file, working from instinct and an innate knowledge of these systems, the core of which she'd helped design all those years ago.

There. She stared at the results. *I thought I saw something wrong. I thought those accounts didn't match.* One column of the screen showed a normal series of general ledger listings, the other a list of twenty accounts that weren't linked anywhere she could find. She called one up, looking at the account balance, which was well into seven figures. The entries were regular, and substantial, and manually keyed, because there was no equivalent ledger account to charge them off against.

A bucket. A bucket full of money, which nothing in this system could account for.

Dar sat back, her heartbeat picking up. *What in the hell have I found?*

"Hey, Dar!"

She almost jumped at Chuckie's cheerful greeting. Her eyes lifted to see him approaching, and she quickly closed the file and sent it to her file space, then closed out of the command windows she was using just as he rounded the console and peered over her shoulder. "Hey."

"Whatcha doing?" He looked curiously at the innocuous admitting records. "New spuds?"

"Yeah." Dar licked her lips, then signed out of the system. "Just checking them out. Interesting group." Her peripheral vision focused on his face, but saw nothing but benign interest. "You ever see what they're bringing in these days?"

"Nah." Chuckie slung a long, powerful arm over her shoulders. "Hey, we were figuring to go over to the Longhorn steakhouse tonight, that okay by you? Your daddy's a steak man, if I remember right."

Dar took a breath, and released it. "Yep, he sure is. My mother's going to pitch a fit, but I guess she can get a potato or something." She managed a smile. "She's a vegetarian... unless they've got fish there."

"Fish?" Chuckie snorted. "You must be kidding. But, yeah, they've got potatoes, and I think they've got some kinda green beans or something. How 'bout your main squeeze, he a veggie lover, too?"

Something twitched in Dar's brain. "She." The word came out in a calm voice, unexpectedly. "And no, Kerry's as carnivorous as I am."

Chuckie went very still, his eyes fastened on Dar's face for a long, long moment. Then he slowly removed his arm and stepped back. "What?"

Dar allowed a hint of amusement to reach her lips, and she turned on the stool, leaning against the console with one elbow. "You heard me." She watched his face, watched the expression go from consternation to uncertainty to a detectable disgust, then back to a stillness. *So.* Dar felt vaguely disappointed.

"You're gay?" Chuckie asked stiffly.

"That's right," Dar confirmed. "Don't worry, you didn't cause that," she added with a faint smile. "C'mon, Chuck. Rise above your redneck roots."

He looked at his shoes, shock evident in his posture. Then he lifted his gaze and met her eyes, briefly, before he shook his head. "That's fucked up," he said, then turned and walked out, not looking back even once.

Dar sat back and folded her arms over her suddenly aching chest, surprised at just how much that had hurt.

Kerry pulled up to the gate of the base, rolling her window down and preparing her argument for the stolid-looking guard who approached.

"Hey, No Neck, open the damn gate," Andrew rasped from beside her, poking his head truculently out at the hapless man. "'Fore I get out of this here car and break it."

The guard stopped, stared, then his eyes lit up with unmistakable joy. "Commander Andy!" He almost tripped over himself trying to get the barrier open. "Wow, I didn't know you were comin' down here! Wait 'til I tell the guys!"

Hmm. Kerry watched amusedly as the man waved like a child at her passenger. *Guess it does depend on who you know around this place.* "He wasn't nearly that nice to Dar," she commented. "She had to get rough with him."

Andrew leaned over her and pinned the guard with a pair of ice blue eyes. "That right, No Neck? You give mah kid a hard time?"

The guard looked terminally wounded. "Not after she said who she was, sir! If she'd have just said right off, we'd have let her right in!"

"Uh-huh." Andrew sat back. "G'wan, Kerry. Let's get this land boat parked so I can see what a mess they made of this here joint."

"You got it, Dad." Kerry drove on, finding Dar's Lexus in the lot and selecting a spot right next to it. She was glad she was here. Her stomach upset had been getting worse for the last while, and she was seriously looking forward to seeing her partner and satisfying her curiosity as to whether she was the cause. She got out, waited for her passengers to do the same, then locked the doors. "Dar has a little office upstairs in the big building. I'll go find her if you guys want to check this place out."

"She take you over to our old place?" Andrew asked.

"Sort of." Kerry grinned. "I'll explain later. Be right back." She trotted off toward the headquarters building, leaving her in-laws behind to revisit old memories. The guard respected the ID she'd clipped to her collar and opened the door, and she made her way up the stairs and down the hall. The door to Dar's temporary office was closed, and she paused, then knocked lightly on it.

For a moment, there was no answer, then Dar's voice responded. "Yeah?"

I knew it. Kerry pushed the door open and stuck her head inside. One look at Dar's face and she quickly stepped past the portal and closed it behind her, crossing the floor and circling the desk to kneel at her lover's side. "Hey."

Dar had her head propped up on one hand. "Hey," she answered softly. "Hope your day was better than mine."

Kerry put a gentle hand on Dar's knee and rubbed it. "What's wrong?" She could see the tension and unhappiness written all over her partner's face, and she stood and perched on the desk edge to get closer. "Sweetheart?"

Dar exhaled and put her head down on Kerry's thigh, wordlessly seeking comfort. She closed her eyes as the blond woman responded, threading fingers through her hair and rubbing the back of her neck. "Sorry," she mumbled. "I told Chuck about us."

"Oh." Kerry's own eyes closed in sympathy. "Not a good reaction, huh?"

"No."

Kerry leaned over and kissed the top of Dar's head, giving her as much of a hug as she could in their somewhat awkward position. "I'm sorry."

Dar exhaled. "I don't even know why I should care, Kerry. I haven't talked to him in what...ten years? It's not like he's a close friend, even." She put a hand on Kerry's knee and rubbed her thumb against the denim covering it. "Damn, it stung, though."

"I know." Kerry kept up her light massage on Dar's neck, moving lower as she felt the tension knotting her shoulders. "I wish you'd have just let them..."

Dar shook her head. "No." She lifted her head up off Kerry's lap and met her eyes. "You are my partner, and God damn it, if they can't deal with that, to hell with them all." Her blue eyes glinted fiercely. "I am **not** ashamed of this."

Kerry stroked her cheek gently. "I know you aren't. I'm not either. It's just hard, Dar. We both know that. We've both been so lucky there have been people in our lives who do accept us, who accept this without question, to balance the idiots who don't."

Dar sighed and put her head back down for more soothing. "Yeah, I realize that." She closed her eyes. "My folks here?"

"Mm-hmm." Kerry paid particular attention to a knot she could feel in Dar's neck and saw the wince as she pressed on it.

"You need a chiropractor, love."

"Hot tub," Dar countered. "With you in it."

Kerry rolled her eyes at the ceiling. "You are so stubborn."

"Family trait."

"You're lucky I love your family." Kerry leaned over and kissed the spot on Dar's neck, then nibbled her earlobe, getting a soft grunt of surprise in return. "Come on, let's get this dinner over with. I missed my snuggle this morning, and I've been cranky all day."

Finally, Dar smiled, turning her head and peering up at Kerry's face. "Me, too." She sat up and gave Kerry's knee a squeeze, then stood. "You're right. Let's get this over with." Her voice paused as she shut her computer down. "Because tomorrow, we're going to find out just exactly why this place stinks to high heaven."

It was obvious that Chuckie had told his father. Even at a distance, Dar could see the discomfort in the three people waiting for them. She took a breath and tugged on her father's sleeve. "Dad?"

"Yep?" Andrew finished closing the door and peered at her. "What's up, Dardar?"

"I think we're going to have a problem." She lowered her voice, glancing across the car where Kerry and Ceci were getting out on the other side. "I...don't think Jeff and his family appreciate my lifestyle."

Andrew looked over at the waiting group, then at her. "'Cause you drive a fancy car?"

Dar rubbed her nose. "Not that lifestyle," she amended. "I meant Kerry and me."

Her father considered that. "Huh. That might be true," he admitted. "Jeff never did take to anyone who didn't fit his idea of what was right and natural." They walked slowly around the front of the car, joining Kerry and Ceci. "C'mere, kumquat." Andrew put a genial arm across Kerry's shoulders and the other over Dar's. "Let's go."

Ceci gave him a curious look, then caught on and slipped to the other side of Kerry, tucking an arm around her waist. "All righty, then," she agreed. "Ah. A steakhouse. How Republican."

"Hey," Kerry objected jokingly. "I'm the one who eats vegetables." She poked a finger at Dar. "Unlike her."

They chuckled and walked toward the restaurant. Dar felt a little silly, but she could see the exchange of glances as Jeff took in their posture, the look on her father's face, and the very obvious acceptance of both her and Kerry inherent in their body language. *Sometimes,* she mused, *I underestimate my parents.* The thought made her smile, and she slid an arm around her father's waist and gave him a squeeze.

"'Lo there, Jeff," Andrew drawled as they arrived in front of the door. "Been a while."

"Andy," the officer acknowledged quietly, shifting his eyes slightly. "Cecilia, good to see you."

Ceci looked him right in the eye and smiled. "Same here. Nice to have these little family get-togethers, isn't it?" She nodded at Jeff's wife. "Hello, Sue. Have you met Kerrison? No? Why don't we go inside and catch up."

It would, Kerry sighed inwardly, *be almost comical if it were happening to someone else.* They all walked stiffly inside and were taken to a waiting table, where Kerry found herself seated between Ceci and Andrew and across from the dour-looking Chuck. For a moment she felt very sad, because she knew this should have been a happy occasion. Then her common sense kicked in and she straightened, cupping her hands around her water glass. Her eyes met the commander's calmly. "As a matter of fact..." she answered Ceci's question, "the commander and I have met. In fact, we had lunch together."

Unable to avoid conversation, Jeff Ainsbright cleared his throat. "Yes, we did." He managed to get out, ignoring the quick, almost startled look from his wife. "Yes, we did."

"That must have been fun," Ceci remarked. "Let me guess, on base?" She gave Kerry an amused look. "Was it meatloaf or open-faced turkey sandwiches?"

Andrew snorted softly.

"Meatloaf," Dar acknowledged quietly. "Still tastes the same."

"Oh. Yum." Her mother made a face. The table fell silent. Ceci drummed fingers on the table and tried again. "Okay, folks, listen up." She put her hands flat on the wood surface. "Either we agree to have a nice time here, or I'm going to have to start talking about Greenpeace. Which is it going to be?"

The Ainsbrights stared at her. Finally, Sue Ainsbright sighed and pushed a curl of gray hair out of one eye. "Ceci, you always did have the tact of a dead swordfish, didn't you?"

"I'm sorry, get over it," the smaller woman shot back. "Broaden your horizons, adjust your thinking, swallow an Ex-Lax, whatever it takes, but drag yourselves into the twenty-first century and get over the fact that my kid's gay, okay?"

Kerry bit the inside of her lip so hard it almost bled. The

looks on the Ainsbrights' faces were so priceless, she wished she had a camera, though one look at Dar's wide eyes told her that her beloved partner wasn't sharing the mirth.

"Well," Andrew drawled, "guess I can show 'em my rainbow keychain now, huh?"

Jeff Ainsbright took a breath, released it, then just lifted a hand and let it fall. "Haven't changed a lick, have you, Ceci?" He managed a faint smile. "You always took the gut punch if you could."

Ceci shrugged.

Andrew took her hand in his. "Straight talk never killed no one, Jeff," he advised his old friend. "I've been in places that coulda used more of that." Their eyes met, and something passed between them.

The commander nodded. "You're right, Andrew. Dar, I apologize. I...it was just a shock, that's all." He cleared his throat. "Ms. Stuart, my apologies as well."

"For what?" Kerry asked mildly. "Dar and I are used to getting mixed reactions to our being partners. Some people just can't handle it."

"It's not that," Sue Ainsbright interjected. "We're very progressive people. It's just that we've known—or, well, we thought we knew Dar, and it's just...strange, that's all." She reddened. "That you're so...um..."

"Out?" Dar remarked conversationally.

The commander shot her a look, then glanced away.

"It's not contagious," Dar said.

"It's disgusting," Chuckie interrupted.

His mother looked horrified. "Charles!"

"You can sit here and pretend, but I won't," Chuck said. "It's disgusting, and you're perverts." He got up and slammed his chair back, then stalked out of the restaurant as startled patrons watched him go.

The commander and his wife had the grace to look intensely embarrassed. "He doesn't mean that," Jeff finally said quietly. "He's just..." His eyes lifted and finally met Dar's. "He never really did let go of you, and he was hoping..."

Dar let out a long breath. "I know," she said. "He's a good man, Uncle Jeff." She felt the awkwardness in the name. "I'm sorry." She felt a little guilty that she'd never thought of Chuckie, not for the longest time since she'd left the base. Not until he'd popped back up into her life as part of this damned investigation.

Now he was lost to her again. She didn't know whether to feel sorry or relieved. *At least he won't be bugging me to go out any-*

more. Dar looked up to find Kerry gazing across the table at her with a look of quiet compassion, and she managed a smile in return. Suddenly, she wished they were done with this. Wished they were away from this unneeded stress, homeward bound and headed for a quiet night and a warm hot tub together.

Getting cowardly in your old age, Paladar? she mocked herself. "Let me go talk to him." Dar stood and pushed her chair in before they could protest, then turned and walked away from the table, toward the outside door through which Chuckie had left.

The commander and Andrew exchanged glances. "Sorry, Andy," Jeff Ainsbright muttered. "Hell of a reunion."

"Could have been worse." Ceci motioned over the hovering waiter. "I could have invited my brother and sister." She held up a finger. "Do you have beer?"

"Of course, ma'am," the waiter spluttered.

"Bring the largest container of it you have, and seven glasses," Ceci told him. "And what are those, peanuts? Put them down." She handed a peanut to Kerry. "I could have been a social director, don't you think?"

Weak chuckles responded to her valiant attempt.

The air outside the restaurant was cool, and a little damp, and Dar paused to take a steadying breath of it before she let her eyes search the parking lot. Her mother had surprised her, she admitted privately. But then, her parents had been surprising her for a while now, hadn't they?

Dar spotted Chuck standing by a beige Ford Explorer, and she headed in that direction, passing through bars of twilight mixed with the lurid ochre of the security lamps.

He looked up as he heard her footsteps, and his lip curled reflexively. "Get out of here."

Dar paused several body lengths away. "Listen."

"Get the fuck out of here, you freak," Chuck spat back. "Just get away from me."

"Charles." Dar put her hands on her hips. "Get a grip. I'm not touching you." Her stomach twisted in a knot. "Calm down."

He stared at her. "You make me sick."

Dar rolled her eyes. "What in the hell do you think you are, a bad commercial for Jesse Helms? Get off the milk crate, Chuck. I'm not the first gay person you've ever known." She took a step closer. "What's the big deal?"

Chuck's eyes narrowed. "What's the big deal?" he asked softly, balling his fists and coming a little closer. "What's the big deal? You fucking little lying perverted slut."

"Charles." Dar's voice dropped in pitch. "Slow down. I never lied to you."

"Yeah?" Chuckie exhaled. "I knew you'd follow me out here." He turned and grabbed something leaning against the Ford and lunged at her. "I knew I'd have a chance to do this!"

Dar barely reacted in time. She saw the bat headed toward her and half turned, taking the crunching blow on her shoulder. "Chuck!" She dodged the return blow and backed off. "Stop it!"

He was beyond reasoning. "Fuck you. Making a fool out of me. Bet the guys all knew, didn't they? Didn't they, Dar?"

The bat came back at her, catching her on the hip before she could evade it, but Chuck overbalanced and smashed full into her, and they both went to the ground in a tangle of limbs.

Shit. Dar's defensive reactions kicked into gear, and she swung an elbow up into his chin, feeling the shock of the impact as his head rocked back. She got a knee between them and pushed up, then to one side, throwing Chuck off her. "Stupid bastard."

Dar grabbed the bat, which had rolled free from his hands, and flung it from her, hearing it clatter and roll down past the next row of parked cars. She got to her feet just as he did, and her body moved, balancing as she whipped out a roundhouse kick that caught him flat-footed, striking the side of his head with a crunch Dar could feel all the way down her leg.

His body slammed against the car next to where they were fighting, setting off its alarm with a loud, strident sound. They both froze, then stared at each other. "Now what?" Dar asked. "You going to find another bat, or are you going to just get the gun out of the trunk and shoot me, Chuck?"

Very slowly, he lifted a hand to the side of his face and touched it, then looked at his palm. It was stained with the blood still dripping from his ear.

"What the hell is wrong with you?" Dar asked in a hoarse voice. "We haven't seen each other for ten fucking years, Chuck. Why the hell do you care what my preferences turned out to be?"

He had to swallow a few times before he spoke. "Never could figure out why you just walked out on us."

Dar sighed inwardly, lifting a shaking hand to rub her temples. "You know as well as I d—"

"You were just playing with me."

The throbbing in her head increased. "Chuck, we were kids then. We went different ways, that's all."

"Bullshit." He started toward her again.

"Stop!" Dar heard the sharp edge of anger in her own voice.

"It's not bullshit. I had no fucking clue what the hell I wanted then." She held out both hands to ward him off. "Chuck, don't make me fight you. Please."

"No wonder you were always trying to beat the guys, you thought you were one," Chuck sneered. "Why didn't you get your daddy to buy you a prick? You'd have fit right in."

Dar winced inwardly. "I never wanted one."

"Yeah? Bet you use a fake one now with that little slut whore in there, don'cha?" Chuck replied. "I should—"

"You should shut yer mouth 'fore I insert yer leg inside it." The low, raspy voice coming from the darkness behind Chuck made them both go still.

Dar blinked. "Dad, I can handle this."

Andrew Roberts eased out into the orange light soundlessly, sliding between Dar and her adversary in a flickering motion. "Ah do suspect you can, Dardar," he agreed softly. "'Cept one of the privileges of being a daddy is that ah get to take out the trash, and ah do believe there is some trash here that needs to be taken," he paused significantly, "out."

There was no humor in his voice.

There was no humor in the ice blue eyes that pinned the now silent Chuck with deadly intent. "Seems you're pretty good at taking shots at women. You ready to give an old retired sailor a try?"

Chuck's gaze held for an instant, then dropped to the ground. "No, sir."

"G'wan inside," Andrew said flatly. "Get yer ass cleaned up, and act like a man."

"Yes, sir," Chuck muttered. He turned, letting his eyes flick to Dar for a single, long second before he retreated toward the restaurant.

Andrew exhaled. "Suck yer brains out your head when they put the stripes on, I swear t'God." He turned and studied his daughter anxiously. "You all right?"

Dar sat down on the low wall that separated the parking lot and let her head drop into her hands.

Kerry ducked past an exiting station wagon and broke into a run that brought her up to Dar's side moments after she sat down. "Jesus. What the hell is going on?" She hopped over the wall and settled next to her lover, putting an arm around her waist and resting a hand on Dar's knee. Only an awkward tangle with the waiter had delayed her leaving the table after a stunned moment when she was absolutely sure Dar was in trouble.

Dar rubbed her face. "Shit." She straightened and took a deep breath. "I didn't expect that."

"Expect what?" Kerry looked around Dar at Andrew. "Dad, what happened?"

The ex-SEAL scowled. "Big bagload of no sense hurting."

Kerry glanced at Dar's face, searching it anxiously. "Did he hurt you? I'll get that brand new SUV and run him over, I swear it," she announced seriously. "You'd hardly feel it with those tires."

Dar's lips involuntarily twitched into a half smile. "I think I did more damage than he did," she admitted softly. "Physically, at least. I don't know, Kerry; I wasn't expecting a reaction like that. It's like he's taking it all personally." She glanced over at her father. "Guess we'd better go back inside."

"You can't be serious," Kerry snorted. "And have dinner with that little—"

"Ker," Dar interrupted her quietly. ""I am not going to let him think he scared me off."

Kerry stared at her. "Dar, this isn't a ego contest."

"It's not," Dar replied, just as seriously. "But if we leave now, he wins. You can't let people like that win and get comfortable, Kerry."

Andrew patted her on the back. "Want to skip the hot plate and go right for the good stuff? I saw them ice cream plates on that tray back there," he remarked practically. "Dar's right, kumquat. Get that boy worse if we stick it out."

Kerry watched a quiet, sad knowledge settle into Dar's eyes. She folded her fingers around her partner's hand and squeezed gently. "Go ahead, Dad. We'll meet you in there." Her gaze lifted to meet Andrew's, very briefly, and they exchanged a look, then the ex-SEAL stood to go.

"Sorry 'bout that, Dardar." Andrew leaned over, surprisingly, and kissed his daughter on the head. Then he turned and slipped away into the shadows, leaving the two women alone in the cool night air.

Kerry waited a little while, just flexing her fingers around Dar's as they sat in silence. "Did he hurt you?" she finally asked, seeing the muddy scuffs on Dar's skin. "You look a little pale."

Dar drew in a breath, held it momentarily, and then released it in a sigh. "I'm trying to reconcile the friend I used to have with that person who just spewed a gutload of hate at me," she said. "I don't understand it, Kerry. I just don't."

The blond woman gazed out at the parking lot unseeingly. "Yeah. I know. It's how I felt when my father hit me that night, and then again when I woke up in that hospital," she said. "I didn't understand it. I hadn't changed at all, so why did they?"

"Mm." Dar nodded. "That's it exactly. I'm the same person he knew yesterday. Hell, the same one he knew this morning. Why should this matter?" Her voice trailed off. "I just don't get it." She looked down at her hands, then flexed the one Kerry was holding. The motion caused a jolt of pain to course up her arm. "Ow."

Kerry turned a very concerned look on her. "What? Did he hit you? Where are you hurting, Dar?"

"My shoulder." Dar winced, easing the sleeve up over her left arm and peering at it.

"Oh." Kerry sucked in a breath, seeing the mottled red and purple area. "Jesus Christ."

"Hmm." Dar moved her arm a little, then realized that wasn't a good idea. "Hell of a bruise."

"You need to get that X-rayed," Kerry decided. She put a hand over Dar's mouth. "Don't even bother. No arguments, Paladar." Slowly, she removed her hand. "Okay?"

Dar studied her. "So does that mean I get out of the optometrist's appointment tomorrow, then?" she asked, with a tiny, mischievous sparkle in her eye.

Kerry put her hands on her hips and gave her lover a dour look. "I should take you to the hospital tonight." She lifted Dar's sleeve again and looked at the injury. "Dar, that looks awful."

"No way." Dar shook her head and stood up, stretching her body out carefully. *Oh boy.* She made a face, not sure what hurt more, her shoulder or her side. "I'll make it through dinner just fine, then we can go home. It's not going to kill me, and spending the night at Sinai just might."

Kerry scowled but joined her as they started to walk slowly toward the restaurant. "Okay. Which one of us is going to let Dad drive their car home? 'Cause you are not driving, let me tell you that right now."

Dar sighed. "I will." She gave Kerry a wry look. "Yours is newer."

"Hmm." Kerry squared her shoulders before she opened the door. She didn't like the idea of waiting, since it was obvious to her that Dar was in considerable pain, but maybe... A small smile touched Kerry's lips. Maybe when they got home, Dar would have a different perspective.

From across the room, she saw eyes look up and find them, and noted the guilt in the base commander's expression as he fiddled with his napkin. Chuckie was seated next to him in silence, and Ceci was carrying on most of the conversation with the commander's wife. She felt Dar straighten next to her and saw her lover's chin lift and her posture stiffen as they approached the table, taking her seat with easy grace and dignity.

Like nothing was wrong.

"Everything okay?" Ceci asked as Kerry took her seat.

She spared a quick glance at Dar's face. "Just great," Kerry assured her. "Got any beer left?"

Chapter
Twelve

"You know," Kerry carefully buttoned a pair of Andrew's old pajamas around her fidgeting lover, "you could just go get this taken care of."

"Kerry," Dar sighed, trying not to let the pain get to her. Too much. "Sorry. I'm tired, and very cranky, and I just want to go to bed." Her shoulder had stiffened up, and despite a handful of painkillers, she could hardly move her arm. It was making her a little nervous, and she really wanted nothing more than to lie down and not stir for a while.

"Dar..." Kerry took a breath to continue their argument.

"Please?" Dar heard the break in her voice and winced. It had its effect, though, because Kerry paused, exhaled, then put a gentle hand against her chest. "First thing tomorrow, I promise. We'll go right over to Dr. Steve's and let him take a look." She gazed hopefully at Kerry. "Okay?"

Kerry gazed unhappily at her. "No." Her lips tensed. "Not okay, because I hate seeing you in pain." Her shoulders dropped. "But I guess it'll have to do. C'mon, let me help you get into bed." She glanced through the open bedroom door. "You want a heating pad or an ice pack?"

Chino was already in her basket, her soft brown eyes watching Dar with a worried expression. Andrew and Ceci had followed them almost home, then had driven on toward the marina, accepting Kerry's assurance that there was no problem, Dar was just tired.

Now Kerry was beginning to doubt that reassurance. She'd tried a dozen ways to convince her stubborn lover to let her drive her over to the nearby hospital, but Dar steadfastly refused, preferring to suffer from the noticeably swelling injury rather than submit to the emergency room's tender care.

On the other hand, she had to admit, as she helped Dar lay down in the waterbed, her lover looked completely exhausted; and with their luck, they'd end up sitting in the waiting room for three hours. Kerry pushed Dar's disheveled bangs out of her eyes. So maybe she had a point. "Ice pack?"

Dar closed her eyes and luxuriated in the simple pleasure of lying down. Her body relaxed, and that helped with some of the pain. She was very glad to be home, and still, and away from the uneasy company they'd spent the evening with. Though the atmosphere had relaxed a little as dinner progressed, the pain and the sullen looks from Chuckie were enough to want to make her stand up and just chuck something.

Like her beer glass. "Ice pack." Dar opened one eye and considered the concept. "Yeah." She gave Kerry an apologetic look, very much aware of just how unhappy her partner was. "Thank you." Her uninjured hand reached out and slid up Kerry's bare thigh. "I know you think I'm being an idiot."

Kerry sighed. "No, I don't, but I won't lie and say I really understand it," she said. "It's what hospitals and doctors are for, Dar. That's why they get the big bucks, remember? I wish you'd let me take you over; they'd have given you some painkillers, at least."

Dar stroked her leg. "I'll be fine," she said. "It feels better already, just being still," she objected stubbornly.

Her lover folded her arms. "What am I going to do with you?"

"Anything you like." The unrepentant blue eyes studied her. "Except take me to Sinai at midnight."

"You could have let me tell your folks." Kerry frowned. "What was the point in keeping this from them?"

Dar chewed her lower lip. "They worry." She shrugged her uninjured shoulder, then averted her eyes from Kerry's intent ones. "And, um...my dad tends to be a little overprotective."

"Really," Kerry murmured. "Imagine that."

Dar gave her a quick look. "I never told him when I got into fights if I could help it. He..." She paused. "He'd sometimes go a little nuts, if you know what I mean."

Kerry considered that. "You mean he'd have gone after the little wiener?"

Dar nodded.

"Where's my cell phone?" Kerry started to get up. "I've got their number on speed dial—"

"Kerry!" Dar grabbed for her leg. "C'mon now." She was surprised at her lover's aggressive reaction. "It wasn't that bad."

"Wasn't that bad?" Kerry sat down and gave her a severe look. "Don't give me that patootie, Dar. I saw that arm. That jackass deserved to have his damned bat shoved so far up his..." She left the sentiment unfinished and sighed loudly. "It pisses me off!" Her voice rose into an aggravated shout.

Chino whined. Dar caught Kerry's hand and held it. "I know," she replied seriously. "But I want to handle this, Kerry. Okay?"

"Mm." Kerry looked unconvinced. "All right." She patted Dar's leg. "Well, let me go get that ice pack. Don't go away."

Dar watched her leave, then exhaled and let her eyes close again. *What a completely jackass day.* She mentally reviewed the compound disasters of the last twenty-four hours. *Damn.* Her shoulder was throbbing. She could feel the swollen pressure that occasionally shot prickles of pain all the way up her neck and down to her fingers, and she shifted, trying to find a more comfortable spot for herself.

Was she being idiotic? Dar reviewed her reasoning again. Should she have just let Kerry take her to the damn hospital? Kerry was upset, and Dar hated when Kerry got mad at her, especially if it was for a good reason. Glumly, she opened her eyes and reviewed the off-white popcorn ceiling. *She has a good reason. No, she has several good reasons to be pissed off, because I am acting like a stupid adolescent again, aren't I?*

"Damn, damn, damn," Kerry muttered to herself as she walked through the living room and entered the kitchen. "What in the heck's wrong with her, Chino?" she asked the Labrador, who had followed her. "I swear, she's got a streak up her back this wide..." Her hands spread apart, and she let out an exasperated gust of air. "Jesus!"

Chino sat down in front of her cookie jar and looked up expectantly. "Gruff."

Kerry allowed herself to be distracted for a moment. "Oh, you think I came out here for you?"

"Gruff."

"Hang on." Kerry went to the refrigerator and took out one of the frozen gel packs they kept ready for overly rambunctious gym sessions. She set it on the counter, then retrieved a cookie from its jar and held it. "What do you say?"

Chino obediently sat up, lifting one paw and placing it neatly on Kerry's knee. "Aorgh."

"Good girl." Kerry gave her pet 'the treat and watched her crunch it contentedly. "Why can't you teach Dar to do that, huh? She never listens."

Her conscience nudged her as soon as the words slipped out. *That's not true, Kerry, and you know it.* She sighed and went to the pantry, retrieving a soft, fluffy maroon towel from the laundry area. Dar did listen to her. "I got her to try green beans the other week, right?" she commented to Chino. "Maybe it's because she usually does listen to me that this is driving me so nuts."

Kerry leaned against the counter. "Or maybe it's because it just doesn't make any sense to me."

Chino nuzzled her knee and gave it a lick.

"But you know what, Chino, me yelling at her isn't helping," Kerry admitted quietly. "It's just making her tense and giving me a stomachache." She squared her shoulders and folded the towel around the ice pack. "Time to go make nice and have a snuggle. You with me?"

"Gruff." Chino wagged her tail.

"Good girl. C'mon." Kerry released a deep breath and let the irritation wash out of her. A smile returned to her face as she started back toward the bedroom.

Dar raised her head as footsteps approached, and girded her loins. Metaphorically. "Kerry, listen..."

"Here you go." Kerry reentered the room and sat down on the waterbed railing, carefully leaning over and placing the wrapped ice pack against Dar's shoulder.

"And here." She set a glass down by the table. It had a straw sticking out of it, the kind that bent. "In case you get thirsty." Kerry brushed her fingertips over Dar's lips. "You know something, I forgot it was Friday night."

Dar's fine, dark eyebrows knit together over the bridge of her nose. "Huh?"

"It's Friday night," Kerry repeated. "We're not a drug overdose, a multi-car accident, or an attempted homicide. We'd have been sitting in that waiting room until well after dawn." She put the tip of her finger on Dar's nose. "So I think it's for the best we did this."

Slowly, a faint grin spread over Dar's face. "And here I was about to give in and meekly let you drag me off there," she admitted, a huge wave of relief almost making her shiver.

"You? Meek?" Kerry leaned over and replaced her finger with her lips, kissing Dar gently. "Never." She pulled back and went nose to nose with her lover. "Besides, I'm really tired."

"You look it," Dar replied. "C'mon into bed." She reached out and doused the bedside lamp.

Kerry nodded in agreement, then stood and walked around to the other side of the waterbed, getting in carefully and squirming under the freshly laundered sheets until she felt the warmth of Dar's body very close by. She put her head down on the pillow and folded her hand over Dar's as it lay on the taller woman's stomach.

Their fingers twined.

Kerry could see Dar's profile in the dim starlight from the window, and the faint curve of her ear close by. "Dar?"

There was a soft crackle of movement as Dar turned her head, and the light now reflected faintly off her open eyes. "Hmm?"

"I love you."

The face opposite Kerry dissolved into a grin. "You even love me when I'm being a stubborn cranky bitch?" Dar asked in a low drawl. "What's up with that, Kerrison?"

"I'm a sucker for a cute face," Kerry smiled, "and a bad attitude. What can I tell you?"

Dar kissed her soundly. "Thanks," she murmured into Kerry's half-open lips. "I love you, too." She felt Kerry smile before her kiss was returned in equal measure.

"Hold still."

"I am holding still," Dar answered through gritted teeth.

"Dar, you are not." Dr. Steve circled the X-ray machine and nudged her over a little. "Now, will you stop wriggling?"

Dar's lip twitched into an almost snarl. She'd been under the device for hours, at least, and the hard table was stressing her to her limits. "Wasn't three hundred pictures enough? You going for a record?"

"Dar." Dr. Steve leaned over and put a hand on her forehead with surprising gentleness. "It's only been five minutes. Give me another five minutes, and it'll be over, okay?" The doctor gave her a pat, then went back to adjusting the X-ray machine's aperture. "Kerry, keep her busy while I do this, willya?"

"I'll try." Kerry walked to the end of the table and pressed her body up against Dar's socked feet, which only just rested on its padded surface. Toes flexed against her belly, and she rubbed them through the cotton, smiling down the length of the long denim-covered legs stretching before her. "Hey."

Grumpy blue eyes peered back at her. "It felt better this

morning," Dar griped.

Kerry laughed softly. "Dar, you are something else," she said. "I swear, if someone poked you through the belly with a spear, you'd call it a flesh wound and stick a Band-Aid on it."

"Oh, she told you that story, huh?" Dr. Steve looked up from his settings. Usually a trained tech would perform the procedure, but the doctor knew his unruly patient better than to subject one of his innocent staff to her. "It's hereditary. Her daddy's the same damn way, and believe you me, Kerry, it used to about drive me insane to take care of these two."

"Hey," Dar objected. "We weren't that bad."

"Yes, you were," her family physician corrected her. "Be still, Paladar Katherine, or I'll tell Kerry about you and that tailpipe."

Kerry watched her lover's eyes widen in alarm, and she stifled a giggle. "You know," she cleared her throat. "I only **wish** I'd had a doctor like you when I was growing up. The practice that my family used was about as patient friendly as those open-back hospital gowns."

The doctor looked up at her and grinned. "That right? Bet they made a hell of a lot more than I do, then." He adjusted one last dial. "Okay, behind the shield, Kerry."

Kerry gave Dar's toes one last squeeze, then joined Dr. Steve behind the lead shield. "Remember to get her neck while you're in there," she whispered to the gray-haired man. "She's been having backaches."

"Got it already," Dr. Steve whispered back.

"What the hell are you two whispering about?" Dar growled.

Kerry and the doctor exchanged amused glances. "How cute you look in your sports bra, hon," Kerry piped. "Didn't want to embarrass you."

"Got it," Dr. Steve managed to say around a snicker. "Okay, Dar. You're finished." He removed his apron and pulled the machine arm back, freeing his very reluctant and now noticeably blushing patient to sit up. "Hmm. Guess I don't have to check your cardiovascular system; seems to be pumping just fine." He pulled the X-ray plates out and winked at them. "Lemme go get these processed."

Kerry waited for him to leave before she circled the table and faced her lover, who was now sitting up with her legs dangling off the table, cradling her injured arm with her good one. "See? Not so bad." She deliberately sidled between Dar's knees and gazed into the stormy blue eyes facing her. "C'mon, Dar, don't you want to feel better? I know you can't be comfortable with that." She touched Dar's elbow, where the lurid bruise had extended to during the night.

Dar sighed. "I know," she muttered. "I just—"

"Hate doctors," Kerry finished for her. "Honey, it's almost over." She stroked Dar's cheek gently. "Just relax."

"Easy for you to say," Dar grumbled. "You're not sitting here half-naked, having people whisper about your sports bra." She slid off the table and stretched, sidling away from the X-ray machine toward the large louvered window in the examination room.

Kerry took the opportunity to admire the body under the garment being discussed, and smiled. She walked up behind Dar and slipped her arms around her, hugging her and planting a kiss right between Dar's shoulder blades. "Mm." She breathed out softly, watching goose bumps travel over the skin her cheek was pressed against. "I'm glad you decided to get checked, Dar."

Dar peered over her shoulder at her engaging blond limpet. "Yeah, well, maybe he'll give me a pat on the head and a bottle of Percodan. You going to help me analyze that base data when we get home? Typing's going to be hell."

"Of course." Kerry released her and stepped back as they heard Dr. Steve coming down the hall. "You really think there's something there?"

Dar's face grew quiet and rather grim. "Yes." She looked up as Dr. Steve entered. "If you're back for more pictures, forget it."

Her old friend whipped his hand up and focused. He snapped a picture of the surprised and very off-guard Dar, then grinned at her. "Gotcha. Okay, kiddo. C'mon down the hall, and I'll tell you the bad news."

"What was that for?" Dar objected, pointing at the camera.

"Family scrapbook." Dr. Steve picked up her shirt and tossed it to her. "Here, don't scandalize the nurses. They've got delicate egos."

Dar allowed Kerry to help her ease her shirt on, and then they followed Dr. Steve down the hall to his office. This was a fairly large room, lined with book-covered shelves and an impressive set of diplomas scattered over the wall. On the opposite wall, pictures took pride of place—of Dr. Steve and his family, and some of him at a much younger age in uniform.

He also had nice, comfortable leather chairs. Dar sat down in one and leaned back. Kerry studied the pictures, reacting a little when she found one with a familiar, if younger Andrew Roberts in it. "Hey. It's Dad." She half turned. "Ooh...he was a cutie."

"Kerry, if you'd just consent to repeat that if I dragged that old sea dog in here, I'd pay you, big time." Dr. Steve laughed, then put his hands on his desk. "Now, young lady," he fixed his eyes on

Dar, "you have a nasty bone bruise."

Dar eyed him warily. "Yeah?"

"Yeah," the doctor replied. "You're a very lucky little munch-kin, my friend. If it wasn't for the fact that you have an nice, big, juicy deltoid muscle there, you'd be looking at a fracture, and put-ting a cast there ain't fun." He stood and walked over to the X-ray box, pointing at a dark spot in the long bone of Dar's arm. "Right there."

Kerry and Dar peered at it. "And?" Dar finally asked. "What's the treatment?"

"Amputation." Dr. Steve turned and gave her a deadpan look, getting a halfway hysterical giggle from Kerry. "You get a sling which you will keep on, young lady, a bottle of blood thinner in case anything in there is considering doing something icky like clotting, and some painkillers." He pointed at Dar. "I want you off your feet and doing nothing stressful for at least the rest of the weekend."

"Okay," Dar agreed readily, having planned to spend the day on the couch with her laptop anyway. So far, it didn't sound too bad, and as long as the process did not involve plaster or fiberglass in any incarnation, she was happy. "That it?"

Dr. Steve sat on the edge of his desk and leaned forward. "Sweetheart, I mean it." He reached out and traced a line from the injury up Dar's neck. "Do you see how close this is to your noggin? I don't want any clots getting any ideas and sending you into the hospital with a stroke."

Dar blinked. "A stroke?"

"You heard me," Steve stated. "So I want you to make like a vegetable for the next few days, and take those damn pills. I wish you'd called me yesterday."

Dar drew breath to answer him, but Kerry got a word in first. "It was late," the blond woman told him, leaning over Dar's chair. "We got home near midnight." She tousled Dar's hair. "We thought about going over to Sinai, but—"

"But you'd still be sitting there, with a sore butt and the same problem," Dr. Steve finished. "Yeah, well, next time, forget the hospital, just give me a call, hmm?"

"We will," Kerry stated, then glanced down. "Won't we?"

Dar smiled wanly. *A stroke?* Her mind jerked in horror at a threat she'd never even considered. Getting injured was nothing new to her, but this was different. She could imagine living with losing a limb, but strokes were a crapshoot. She could end up half-paralyzed, which was bad enough, but worse—she could lose part of who she was if it hit the wrong spot at the wrong time. "Yeah, we will," she muttered hoarsely.

"Good girl." Dr. Steve patted her knee. "Let me get you set up with that sling. I already called in your prescription to that high-society mambo pusher they call a pharmacist on your Fantasy Island."

Kerry reached over and picked up her mug, taking a sip of the strawberry tea as she reviewed the data on the laptop screen for the nth time. She was curled up on the soft, comfortable leather chair in the living room, one leg slung lazily over the chair arm. Her eyes lifted over the mug's rim and eyed the nearby couch, and then she put the cup down and went back to her statistics.

She could, she knew, have gone into either of their offices and used the large monitors to make viewing the data easier, but she preferred to stay where she was and suffer the eye strain so she could keep an eye on Dar.

The drive home had been very quiet, and her usually unruly lover had meekly taken the medicine the island pharmacy delivered, then settled down on the couch. She'd even let Kerry fuss and put a pillow behind her head and tuck a soft fleece blanket around her.

Waiting for me to say I told you so, Kerry mused. The blood thinner and vasodilator Dr. Steve had prescribed, along with the painkiller, knocked Dar out in no time flat, and her lover had been sleeping for the past few hours. Which was good, Kerry thought, because if Dar was sleeping, it meant she wasn't awake and worrying, having had the living daylights scared out of her by Dr. Steve's warning.

Poor Dar. Kerry leaned toward the couch and gently pushed a bit of Dar's hair back away from her closed eyes. She had a white cotton sling fastened around her neck, holding her injured arm close to her body, and even in sleep a tiny crease was present across her forehead. As much as Kerry appreciated Dr. Steve's forcing Dar to take her injury seriously, it hurt her to see her lover so subdued, obviously scared and keeping silent about it.

Kerry riffled her fingers through the dark hair spilling over the pillow, straightening its silky strands as she watched Dar sleep. Then she sighed and returned her attention to the damn laptop.

So, what was all this, Dar? She scrolled through files, seeing Dar's notations but not seeing the patterns her lover had painstakingly constructed or the significance of them in the data stream. It wasn't that she was oblivious to the method; she just didn't understand where Dar got the little hooks she was using to connect all the pieces together.

Maybe that was because Dar had worked on the original system software? Kerry pushed her hair back behind one ear and leaned closer to the screen. Sure, that must be it. She knew how this whole thing worked, so naturally she could...

Kerry let the thought trail off as her eyes found something. Curiously, she left the bowels of Dar's program and called up the associated data files, studying the personnel assignments and the ship schedules coming in and out of the base. Slowly, her forefinger lifted and touched the screen, making a little scratching noise against the LCD.

*Why...*she wondered. *Why would one ship get all the new recruits?* Operationally, it made no sense, especially to someone steeped in day-to-day operations, as she was. *You don't put all your newbies in the same bucket, because then you have a useless bucket of confusion. You spread them out among other, more experienced workers, so they can learn from them.*

Kerry looked up the operational record of the craft in question, a supply ship that apparently worked with larger groups of vessels but was small enough to dock in small ports. Slowly, she picked up her cup and took another sip, not taking her eyes from the screen.

Dar became vaguely aware of her surroundings, the medicated sleep still having a fairly firm hold on her. There was a slightly tinny quality to the sounds she was hearing, and she had no inclination to open her eyes.

Her shoulder ached, but it was a far-off kind of ache, and it took several minutes for her to sort through a very foggy mind and remember what had happened. *Oh yeah.* Dar wondered if the medication was supposed to make her feel so completely washed out.

A soft clicking was coming from nearby, and she heard a faint sound of ceramic on wood, then a sigh and the shift of a body against a leather surface. Dar spent a moment drawing a mental picture, imagining Kerry in the chair with the laptop. Very slowly, she opened one eye, then turned her head and blinked, the image in her mind resolving into reality.

Kerry was intent on the screen, her brow furrowed and the end of a pencil being gnawed on between her teeth.

For some reason, that made Dar smile.

After a second, Kerry looked up and their eyes met. "Oh."

She put the machine down and leaned on the chair arm. "Was I making too much noise?"

"No." Dar cleared her throat. "Wow. I feel like I'm swimming in clam chowder."

A blond brow arched. "Clam chowder? Ew."

"What time is it?"

Kerry checked the laptop's system tray. "Two." She studied her injured partner. "Here, take a sip of this; you look dry." She handed over her tea, then paused and changed her mind, getting up out of the chair to hold the cup for Dar to sip from. "I forgot how awkward it is when you're wearing one of these." Her free hand plucked the sling.

Dar sucked thirstily at the tea, enjoying the sweet taste. "Glad you put some tea leaves in this sugar water," she teased.

Kerry stuck out her tongue. "It's your fault," she accused Dar. "I didn't used to." She leaned over and kissed her partner on the lips. "Want some of your own? I was going to put some soup up."

"Soup?" Dar felt a little more alert. "Was that inspired by my chowder, or do you think a bone bruise requires that for healing?" Firmly, she pushed aside thoughts of clots, halfway convinced she'd have been better off just letting the damn thing heal on its own, with her in blissful ignorance of her risk.

"Hon, I'll order in baby back ribs if you want them." Kerry laughed. "I'm hungry, and I've got a container of that spicy Thai soup in the fridge, so..."

Dar's eyes lit up. "With the coconut milk?"

"Uh-huh." Kerry had to muffle a smile. "That changes things, hmm?" She ruffled Dar's hair. "I need a break anyway. I found something I think you need to look at when you're a little more awake." She made her way past the coffee table toward the kitchen.

Dar knew she should get up and look at the computer, but the drugs still had a tight hold on her, and her body was more than content to remain where it was. *Probably so fuzzy I wouldn't know what the hell I was looking at anyway,* she mocked herself. But the thought started her mind churning, over the problems she'd seen the day before.

As if on signal, her cell phone rang. However, since Dar was dressed in a pair of soft gym shorts and not much else, she didn't have the phone near her. "Hey, Ker?"

"I hear it." Kerry came trotting out of the kitchen sucking on a wooden spoon. "Ooh...you're gonna like this. There's more chicken than vegetables in it." She picked up the buzzing phone and opened it. "Hello?"

"Is that Roberts?" a female voice asked crisply.

"No." Kerry glanced at her lover. "Can I ask who's calling?"

There was a brief silence. "Chief Daniel."

*Ooh...*Kerry narrowed her eyes. *The bulldog.* "She's—"

The chief interrupted Kerry. "Look. I need to talk to her. Just tell her who it is. Believe me, lady, I wouldn't be on this phone if I didn't need to be."

Hmm. Fair enough. "It's that petty person," she told Dar, after muting the phone.

Dar's brows lifted. "Chief Daniel?" she asked in surprise. "Damn. Give me the phone."

Kerry walked over and handed it to her, then knelt and helped Dar to sit up a little. "Easy," she murmured.

Dar's head spun for a minute, and she waited for the buzz to fade, then held the phone to her ear. "Hello, Chief."

"Roberts."

"Yep, that's me," Dar agreed. "Did you miss me so much you had to call on a Saturday?"

"Roberts, just shut up a minute." The chief lowered her voice. "All crap aside, there's something here you need to see."

A prickle went up Dar's back. "Like what?" she said.

A distinct hesitation made itself felt. "I can't explain it," the chief said. "Bad enough I'm dealing with the devil, as it is. Just get down here."

Dar met Kerry's gaze. The blond woman was shaking her head no, in a very serious way. "I can't," she finally replied. "If you want me to know about it, you've got to come up here."

"What?" the chief hissed. "Don't be a—Jesus, I can't believe I'm doing this. I'm trying to help you out here, damn it."

"I know." Dar decided to try honesty. "I had an accident last night, Chief. I'm not driving to the base, so if you've got something that big, get moving."

The chief was quiet for a long time, and then she sighed. "Son of a bitch," she finally said. "What the hell, I'm in this so deep now, it won't matter. Where the heck are you?"

Dar told her. "Chief?"

"What?" the woman snapped back.

"What made you change your mind?" Dar asked. "About me, I mean."

Chief Daniel snorted, clearly audible even to Kerry. "Change my mind? Like hell, I did." She paused. "You ever hear the term 'least evil choice'?"

Dar allowed a dry chuckle to escape. "Oh yeah. I've heard that before."

"I bet." The chief hung up.

Dar folded the phone closed and relaxed back onto her pillow. "That was a surprise." She glanced up at Kerry. "Last time I saw her, she was cursing me for a pervert."

Kerry gazed soberly back. "I can't believe she'd just turn around and help you, Dar."

A faint shrug. "She's not a..." Dar lifted her uninjured hand and rubbed her eyes. "She's a good officer, Ker. She knows her stuff, and she's just protecting her people. She views me as a threat." Dar considered her words. "Question is, what's she found that's more of a threat to her than I am?"

"Hmm." Kerry tapped the end of the spoon against her chin. "Well, it'll take her a while to head up here. Let me get this soup done." She pointed the wooden utensil at the couch-bound woman. "Then you're going to sit there and let me feed it to you." She turned and headed back to the kitchen, leaving an amused Dar behind.

"I don't suppose I can get away with staying dressed like this?" Dar asked, as she used a washcloth and cold water to bring a little more life into her face. "Can I?"

Kerry leaned against the doorsill and regarded her. "If it were up to me..." she ran a fingertip under the elastic waistband of Dar's soft gym shorts, "sure." She traced a rib. "But I think your petty person is going to pop a solenoid."

"I'm not in the mood to coddle her solenoids," Dar responded, awkwardly trying to manage her toothbrush one-handedly. "Ker, could you..."

Kerry reached across her and picked up the toothpaste, spreading it neatly on the brush for her. "There you go." She put the cap back on and watched as Dar brushed her teeth. "Well, all you need is a T-shirt or something." Her eyes dropped to the very short shorts, which exposed almost all of the length of Dar's very long legs. "On second thought, c'mon into the bedroom and let me see what I can do for you."

Dar turned, a very rakish grin on her face. "Now that's my kind of offer."

"Tch." Kerry moved forward and her hands found their way around the sling. "Do you remember how we...Ah." Kerry found Dar's arms wrapping around her, and the sling settled around her own shoulder, attaching them together body to body. "That's right."

Dar ducked her head and they kissed. She felt Kerry's body

press against hers, and the sensual rush erased the lingering aches like magic. "Much better than drugs," she murmured.

"Oh yeah?" Kerry slid her hands across Dar's skin. "How about this?"

Dar growled softly in response and nudged Kerry backward a step. She held her lover's body close with the sling and unhooked Kerry's bra, feeling her gasp a little in surprise as the snug cotton came free. "Not bad for one hand, huh?" she whispered in the pink ear near her lips, which then was delicately nibbled.

"Uh." Kerry's fingers roamed restlessly over Dar's half-clad body. "This could get complicated."

"Oh." A soft, breathy purr. "I hope so." Another nudge toward the bed. "Simple's no fun." Dar rubbed lightly against Kerry's skin and smiled as the blond woman melted into her, a jolt of warmth flaring as their bodies joined. She could feel Kerry breathing, her chest moving against Dar's, and as she took another step toward the bed, she felt that breathing quicken in time with her touch circling Kerry's breasts.

They stopped and rid themselves of extraneous clothing, still linked together by the sling. Dar slid her other arm under Kerry's and half-turned, easing down onto the bed, pulling Kerry down with her. Amidst a tiny giggle, Kerry ended up sprawling over her, their legs tangling together.

"Y'know..." Kerry licked Dar's neck, then bit down lightly around her collarbone. "With our luck, she drives fast."

"I haven't cleared her on the ferry yet," Dar replied blithely. "She'll wait."

Kerry's chuckle turned into a soft moan, and she forgot about visitors.

Or ferries.

Chief Daniel drove along the causeway, looking nervously right and left when she wasn't glancing at the piece of paper on which she'd written the directions. "What the hell is that nutball talking about? She sent me to the goddamned Coast Guard terminal. Damn her...Thinks I'm joking."

Abruptly, she spotted a right hand turn and took it, almost causing a two-car collision behind her. The car she cut off honked furiously, and she stuck her hand out the window, giving him a rude gesture as she made the tight turn into the small, not-well-marked ferry base. "Son of a bitch." She shook her head. "Should have figured."

The chief maneuvered her pickup truck through the roped-off

lanes and arrived at the edge of the dock. A uniformed guard greeted her courteously. She rolled her window down. "This how you get on?"

"The island? Yes, ma'am." The security officer nodded, obviously used to the question. "Are you visiting one of our residents, or are you interested in purchasing a home?"

Momentarily distracted, the chief leaned on her window frame and pulled her sunglasses down to get a better look at the neat, almost military clean Latino man. "How much do they cost?"

The guard blinked. "Um...w..."

"Round numbers." The chief smiled. "Leave off the pennies."

He cleared his throat. "I think the little ones start at a million..."

"Ah. Is that all?" The chief fixed a smile on her face. "Tell you what, there's someone called Roberts who lives out there. Dar Roberts. I'm supposed to go see her."

The guard flipped through his clipboard, then read a page intently. "Ms. Daniel?" He looked up. "Is that you?"

The chief's nostrils flared. Ms? She'd get the little catfish bait for that. "Almost."

The guard directed her onto the patiently waiting ferry and they chocked her wheels, then after a few minutes and a few more cars, they got under way.

Out of long habit, the chief reviewed the boat, noting the properly secured lifesaving equipment and the stock of life preservers. The ferry itself was flat, with room for perhaps twenty cars, and had a small cabin where people who were just riding over could stay in comfort. It was neat and clean and well ordered, and the chief found herself approving of it despite her inclination otherwise.

In short order, they docked at the islandside dock, and she watched as the ramp to offload the cars was lowered. The island was plush and had lots of fancy-looking landscaping. She bet the hedges she was driving past cost more than a month of her salary.

The sudden impact of water on her windshield made her jump and grab for the window controls. "Hey!" She glared at the dockhand, who was washing off the front of her car. "What th—oh." *Salt spray. Sure. Seventy-two Mercedes per square foot; can't have them rusting, now, can we?* She drove on and glanced at her directions again.

One road, clockwise. Simple enough. She turned left and followed the road around to the second drive, then slowed her pace until she found the parking she'd been told about. She slid the pickup into a visitor's spot and got out, holding a briefcase close to her.

She looked around, curiously. "Damn place shits money." She shook her head and then made her way up the short path to the steps that led up to the door that matched the address she'd been given. It was a short flight that led up to a buff-colored door with a discreet doorbell. Chief Daniel paused and twitched at her uniform, dusting off her sleeve before she squared her shoulders and rang the bell.

Barking answered her, which was a surprise. She hadn't figured Roberts for a dog. After a moment, and a quick command from inside, the door was opened. Chief Daniel found herself facing the intense gaze from a pair of steady green eyes almost on a level with her own. She spoke crisply. "I'm here to see Dar Roberts."

"I know," Kerry replied. "I don't think we've met. I'm Kerry Stuart, Dar's partner." She held out a hand.

Chief Daniel almost backed up a step in pure reflex. Her distaste for queers had almost overridden her wanting to find out what the hell was going on, and this was pushing her buttons way too hard, way too fast. But she realized she wasn't getting past the blond door guard, so she gritted her teeth and took the proffered fingers. "A pleasure," she enunciated precisely, hoping it was clear how untrue that was.

Disgusting. She had to steel herself not to wipe her hand off when Kerry released her.

"Come on in." Kerry stepped back and held the door open. "Don't mind Chino, she's harmless." Standing behind Kerry was a large cream-colored Labrador retriever, who was watching her alertly. "Mostly."

The chief edged around the big dog and stopped, while Kerry closed the door behind her. The first thing she noticed was the smell. Equal parts leather and polish, with a touch of spice in the air. She looked around, taking in the huge living room with its comfortable leather furniture and expensive entertainment center. A door led off to one side, and through its half-open panel, she could see it was a bedroom. Behind the living room was a formal dining room, then the arch that led, she speculated, to the kitchen.

Nice place. The art on the wall was interesting, and the stereo was clearly top of the line. As a techno buff herself, the chief was impressed.

Kerry walked past her. "Dar's just getting something to drink." She gestured to the furniture. "Would you like to sit down?" The Labrador trotted past her and jumped onto the couch, curling up and putting her head down, but keeping an eye on the intruder.

"No thanks," the chief said, her eyes shifting as she caught a flash of motion.

Dar appeared from the kitchen, holding a glass in one hand. She was dressed in shorts and a T-shirt, but one arm was in a white cotton sling. "Afternoon."

"What'd you do, finally piss someone off who could do something about it?" Chief Daniel asked bluntly.

"Sit down." Dar ignored the snarky comment and took a seat on the couch. She noticed the chief hadn't moved. "Either sit down, or get the hell out of here." Her voice lifted and gained an edge. "You were all hot to show me something, so show me or get lost."

Kerry opened her mouth, then closed it and simply sat down, pulling her laptop over and starting to review its screen. She didn't look up as Chief Daniel took a reluctant seat as far away from them as she could.

"Fine." The chief put her briefcase down on the coffee table and unzipped it. "See what you think of this, hotshot." She pulled something out and threw it on the table. It slid across the glass surface and stopped right before Dar. "Looks like I didn't need any outside help to find it, did I?"

Dar put her cup down and pulled the packet over, investigating it curiously. "What the hell is it?" she asked, glancing at the chief.

"Open it. I don't have X-ray vision," Daniel sniped back.

Dar unfolded the wrapping one-handed and finally got through the plastic wrap that covered the parcel. She pulled back the last fold and stared at the results. Her brow crinkled, and she exchanged a look with Kerry, who appeared equally puzzled. "You found a gift-wrapped brick?"

The chief laughed shortly. "And here I thought you had some brain cells. Maybe your perverted lifestyle made them leak out. That's not a brick, Roberts. It's cocaine."

It came out of left field and almost smacked Dar upside the head. She stared at the object. "Cocaine?" Her voice rose. "You've got to be joking." Kerry edged over and examined it in fascination. Dar rubbed her temples with one hand. "Must be the drugs I'm taking. I'm hallucinating that I'm in a bad episode of *Miami Vice*."

Kerry bit her lip. "Is this where they break down the door and start yelling?"

Dar stared at the brick, then up at the smug Chief Daniel.

"They're smuggling drugs?"

A shrug. "Found that in a storage locker that's supposed to have remaindered ammo in it." She smirked at Dar. "You didn't have a clue, did you?"

Dar sat back and exhaled. "No." She stared over the chief's head bleakly. "Not about this," she admitted. "But that might explain something else."

And it probably did explain the journal entries. Dar tried to grasp the enormity of the situation. But how far did it go? How many people knew?

How high? Dar slowly let a breath out. All the way?

Chapter
Thirteen

Ceci looked up from her brush as she heard a throat being cleared. She shaded her eyes, then felt her eyebrows lift. Sue Ainsbright was standing at the edge of their gangplank, looking warm and very uncomfortable. "Hello, Sue."

"Ceci." The older woman took a breath. "May I come aboard?"

It was so very naval. Ceci almost gave in to the temptation to refuse the boarding request, which, along with yelling "avast, ye maties," was something she'd always wanted to do. "Sure." She put away her brush, unsullied as yet by paint, and stood up as Sue crossed over onto the boat. "You look thirsty; c'mon down."

"Thanks."

Her guest followed Ceci down the steps into the cabin. Ceci walked over to the compact galley, gesturing toward the chairs as she did so. "Sit down. Andy's taken a walk over to the store." She walked over and handed Sue a glass of iced tea, then seated herself across the table from her. "This is a surprise."

The gray-haired woman stared at her glass, turning it slightly between her fingers in silence for a few seconds. "I know." Sue looked up finally. "I just wanted to come and talk to you." She hesitated. "To apologize for last night."

Ceci laced her fingers together and rested her chin on them. "To me? For what?"

Sue just looked at her.

"I mean it," Ceci said. "If anyone's got an apology coming, it's Dar and Kerry, not me." She got up and got her own glass of tea, more just to do something than anything else. "Poor Kerry. You know, what happened last night was exactly what she was afraid of."

"She seems like a nice girl," Sue replied softly.

"For a dyke, you mean?" Ceci shot back.

"Ceci." Her old friend gave her a wounded look. "I'm trying here, give me a touch of slack, will you?"

Ceci took a sip of her tea, feeling very unsettled. "Sorry," she said. "That automatic dismissal and exclusion of anything you don't understand has always been a peeve of mine." A breath. "I've been on the wrong side of that line all my life."

Sue remained silent for a bit, then she, too, sighed. "You know, I'd forgotten all about that." Her eyes lifted. "Did that make it easier for you to accept her being...ah..."

"Gay?" Ceci supplied the word. "No, it didn't." She crossed back over and sat down. "By the time Dar told us that, nothing would have surprised me. Hell, Andy and I talked it over that night and I think... Yeah, you know, we were mostly just relieved."

Sue's eyes opened wider. "Relieved?"

A dry chuckle issued from Ceci's throat. "We knew she'd been working up to tell us something. Andy was just glad it was that, and not that she was running off somewhere, or pregnant, or on drugs. A thousand things went through our minds before we found out."

"Oh," Sue murmured. "She was a...she was pretty headstrong, I remember."

"Yes, she was," Ceci agreed. "And is." She paused reflectively. "Andy says she gets that from me." A curious expression centered itself on the slim woman's face for a moment, and then she shook her head. "Accepting Dar was never an issue for us," she stated crisply. "Welcoming Kerry into our family was never an issue either. Andrew and I made a decision early on in our lives that one of the things we'd never teach our children is how to hate." Her eyes pinned Sue. "Unlike you, apparently."

Sue stood up. "Cecilia, that's not fair," she snapped. "We most certainly did not teach Charles to hate anyone. We're good, God-fearing people. I resent that."

Ceci also stood. "Do you? Let me tell you what I resent." She put her cup down and circled the table. "I resent my child being called a pervert. I resent your half-assed, no brain, boot-licking son thinking he can judge her, and I really..." she came closer, poking a slim finger at the startled woman, "I really, really resent the fact that you didn't even have the grace to teach him to hide his sick bigotry in polite company."

Sue stared at her. "You didn't have to smear our faces in it,

Ceci. To be out in a restaurant like that—"

"Like what?" Ceci's voice rose. "We were eating dinner, Sue. If you hadn't been acting like we were lepers, no one in the place would have looked twice. They don't wear fucking brands on their foreheads."

"Ceci!" Sue was breathing hard. "I think I'd better leave."

"Truth sucks, doesn't it?" Ceci stood her ground.

They stared at each other for a long, silent moment. Then Ceci exhaled and folded her arms across her chest. She eyed the carpet pensively. "Sue, you were the first wife on the base who came to knock on our door." Her voice was quiet now. "The first one to brave the pagan unknown and reach your hand out." She looked up. "What happened to that person?"

Slowly, Sue sat back down and laid her hands on the table. They were weathered, and she looked at them as though they were a stranger's. "Time." She exhaled. "Berkeley was a lot fresher in my mind then."

"I remember being so impressed by that." Ceci managed a faint smile. "Wow, she went to Berkeley."

"I remember," Sue admitted. "Big shot that I was...I felt sorry for you. So young, so..."

"Feckless." Ceci nodded.

"Different," her old friend disagreed. "So out of place there." She hesitated. "But Dar wasn't."

"No," Ceci said softly. "And she cherishes her childhood, Sue. Despite everything we went through, she really does; so when something like last night happens, it's like having to give part of that up."

Sue nodded and finally took a sip of her tea. She took a deep breath before she went on. "Ceci, there's no excuse for what my son did." She pronounced the words carefully. "Jeff and I talked it over last night, and if you—" She stopped and rubbed her temples. "I'm sorry. I sound like such a parent. If Dar wants to press charges, she should."

Ceci felt like the world had just shifted slightly to the left. "Charges?" she asked. "For what, Sue? Verbal abuse?"

Her friend's dark blue eyes blinked twice. "Didn't—" She stopped, then took a breath. "Ceci, Chuck went after her with a baseball bat."

"What?"

"I thought surely she'd..." Sue's voice trailed off again. "Jeff was so angry last night. He...he and Chuck had it out in the living room. It was...very ugly," she said. "I don't know what happened, but Chuck just...he broke down and said it was driving him crazy, and how he'd taken the bat and..."

Ceci concentrated on breathing. In, out; in, out. "Oh, dear goddess," she whispered. "Dar said she twisted her shoulder. We had to drive her car home."

"She didn't tell you?" Sue seemed dazed. "I don't understand."

Ceci got up and walked across the cabin, coming to the window and looking out at the peaceful, sunlit water. "I do." She heard steps on the rampway up above. "Dar knows her father too well." She turned toward Sue. "Don't say anything to him."

"But Ceci—"

"I'll tell him," Ceci replied. "I don't keep anything from him, never have, but let me do it my way."

Sue nodded faintly as the cabin door opened and Andrew entered.

"'Lo." His eyes raked over her in wary surprise. "Didn't figure t'see you here."

"Sue came to apologize for last night." Ceci walked over and took the grocery bags from her husband. "We've been talking."

Pale blue eyes flicked to Ceci's face and studied it, then went to their visitor's. Then they narrowed slightly. "Have you now," Andrew drawled softly. "Ain't that special."

It had started to rain again. Dar stood by the sliding glass doors and watched it fall in sheets that almost obscured her view of the ocean. A low rumble of thunder sounded overhead, and she could feel the vibration through the hand she had resting on the wall.

She hadn't expected this.

Petty theft, yeah. Some finagling with the bills, yeah. Fudging on the recruits' scores, yeah. Maybe even so far as someone falsifying fitness records, to hide old friends they didn't want to have to make hard decisions on.

But smuggling?

Dar was no fool, and she wasn't naive. Florida was a prime choice for smuggling because of its relative closeness to South America and because of its multinational population base. It would take a lot to stand out in this city, so hiding in plain sight was something easy a smuggler's operation wouldn't have to worry about.

In addition, it was a peninsula. Surrounded on three sides by water, with ample opportunity for someone to slip in to the thousands of small bays and islands unseen and undetected. The largest stretch of continuous coastline in the US, in fact.

So the fact that drugs or anything else was being brought in didn't surprise her.

That the Navy was involved...

No. Dar cut that off angrily. Not the Navy. Some pig scum who were using the Navy to break the law and line their own pockets. Who were using a place she considered more than any other to be home, and hurting the people who were a part of that who were not involved.

Maybe even, since they were bringing in recruits who didn't belong there, endangering the innocent sailors who would be depending on those people to do their jobs. Sailors like her father was, once. Like she might have been.

Bastards. Dar felt her anger rising. Despite everything, and especially despite last night, she still considered the service part of her family. It had given her a place to belong for many years, had accepted her, given their family a home and put bread on the table, and she was damned if she was going to let a bunch of criminals hurt that.

"So." Chief Daniel's grating voice made her wince. "You got a plan, or are you just gonna stare outside for a few hours?"

"Do you have a plan?" Kerry's voice answered instantly, a distinct challenge in its tone. "If you came here for help, your best bet is to just sit down and shut up and wait for Dar to think."

Dar watched her reflection smile in reflex.

"If you're her secretary, then you'd better get your steno pad, kid," the chief answered.

Dar held her breath, wondering what her lover was going to hit back with.

Kerry simply laughed. "Boy, do you have your stereotypes crossed."

Dar turned and faced them, leaning back against the cool glass and feeling the pressure of the rain outside against her shoulder blades. "The problem is this. I want to locate and pin down every son of a bitch who's involved in this. If the Navy sends police in there, they won't catch one in twenty."

"They'll run." Kerry nodded. "And they'll dump the systems. We've only got a soft data capture, Dar. We don't have the file structure or the algorithms you found. I'm surprised they haven't started doing that already."

"They went for what they knew I was looking at." Dar shook her head. "Must have known I found that data hub." She looked directly at the chief. "Who'd you ask about it?"

Chief Daniel was momentarily taken aback. "It's my right to

ask!"

"That's not in question." Kerry took a dried cherry from the bowl on the table and nibbled it. "Point is, someone was nervous enough about it to get it removed, and that says a lot in itself. Dar, I did a trace on the company that installed it. They're a private fiber house who do a lot of work for the city."

Dar lifted an eyebrow.

"The last big thing they did was wire the mayor's place for teleconferencing," Kerry added, as they both exchanged looks.

"Shit." Dar closed her eyes and rubbed her temples. "This is getting too big for us. Let me go call Alastair and find out what the hell he wants me to do. We stepped into a cesspool here." She walked past them and into the study, shutting the door behind her.

Kerry released a held breath. "Shit," she echoed Dar. "She's right. This is way outside our contract."

Chief Daniel snorted. "Sure. Stir up everything, then run, and let us all sink."

"It's not that," Kerry snapped. "Do you understand what we're talking about here? These are federal crimes."

"No kidding."

Kerry turned her back and walked into the kitchen, grabbing a glass from the cabinet and going into the refrigerator. She studied her options, then gave in and took two squirts of chocolate syrup and filled the glass with milk.

Troubled, she leaned back against the counter and swirled her milk to mix it. So many complications crowded into her mind. First, the problem of the drugs. It was far beyond anything Dar had expected to find, and she knew it had thrown Dar for a loop. That was hard enough, without the possibility of someone Dar knew being involved.

What if it was Jeff Ainsbright? Kerry took a long swallow of her chocolate milk. She'd liked the big commander and had found him open and straightforward, even in the uncomfortable situation they'd found themselves in last night. What about little Chuckie? Kerry's lip curled up into an almost unconscious snarl. *Dear God*, she realized uneasily, *I'm hoping he is. I'm hoping they take his obnoxious ass and thrown him in the federal jail for twenty years.* A very unchristian thought stared her in the face. *Maybe he'll develop a taste for a different lifestyle.*

Jesus. Kerry put the glass down and covered her face. *Do I really feel that way?* She folded her arms unhappily. *Damn it, yes I do. He hurt her.* Kerry felt a sense of helpless rage. *He hurt her, and all I want is to...*Her muscles tensed, and her shoulders twitched with tension. *I want to beat him senseless.*

She'd never felt like this before. Even in the bad times, even with Kyle, she'd never thought about physically fighting back. A soft snort left her. "Look at me," she whispered. "A year's worth of martial arts and a dark blue belt, and I think I'm the Terminator."

A noise at the door made her look up to see Dar quietly looking back at her. "How'd it go?"

Dar entered and walked over to her, taking up a spot leaning on the counter at her side. "He's as gobsmacked as I am," she admitted. "All I got out of him was, 'Dar, do what you have to do, you know I trust your judgment.'"

"Oh boy. That helps." Kerry picked up her glass and drank from it. "So, what's your best judgment, boss? You know I trust it, too."

Dar took the glass from her. "He's calling Hamilton, though, and briefing him." She took a sip. "I honest to God don't know what to do, Ker. I know we should turn this over to the military, and let them handle it. It's out of our league."

Kerry nodded slowly. "You're right," she agreed. "This is outside our expertise, and it could potentially be very dangerous to be involved in. General Easton should take it from here."

They were both quiet for a few minutes, sharing the glass of milk until it was drained to the last drop. Finally, Kerry put the glass down and turned her head to look at her lover. "You think they'll botch it."

A tiny cocking of Dar's head indicated reluctant agreement. "I want to get all of them," she murmured. "I'm afraid of two things, Ker: one, that they'll take too long; two, that they'll go in there and lose the data that will identify all the people involved."

Kerry folded her arms. "Dar, I understand how you feel, but this is beyond us."

"I know." Dar's voice was unhappy. "Let's go call Gerry. We can't sit on this any longer."

Kerry followed Dar out of the kitchen and across the living room. "Chief, we're going to turn this over to the Joint Chiefs— who contracted us."

A snort. "Figures." Chief Daniel got up. "Do you know what that'll do? They'll take a brush the size of an aircraft carrier and paint us all with it. Some reward for helping you out. Assholes." She went to the door and was through it before Dar or Kerry could respond. The slam reverberated, making Chino bark in surprise, then it was quiet.

"Ugh." Kerry rubbed her forehead. "What a totally unlikable person."

Dar picked up the telephone. "Yeah," she agreed. "She's a nastier son of a bitch than I am. I never thought I'd live to see that." The phone buzzed in her ear, then was picked up. "Gerry? It's Dar."

Andrew walked to the end of the dock and took a seat, extended his long legs out, and squirmed to get more comfortable on the hard wooden bench. He didn't have that long to wait, as footsteps sounded after a few minutes, and he turned his head slightly to see the tall, burly figure making its way toward him.

He waited until the intruder was very close, then he swiveled to meet him. "'Lo."

Jeff Ainsbright slowed and came to a halt a body's length away. "Hey, Andrew." He cleared his throat. "Thanks for saying you'd meet me."

Quiet, patient blue eyes surveyed him. "Sit yerself down." He moved over to let his old friend take a seat, then he waited in silence. The anger inside him would be patient for a while longer.

"Listen, Andy..." Jeff seemed at a loss. "About last night."

"Y'know," Andrew interrupted him, "been a long time since I been to a parent-teacher meeting. Dar's a grown woman, has been for years. If you got something t'say about what happened last night, y'need to be saying it to her."

Jeff exhaled and rested his weight on his elbows. He laced his hands together and studied them. "Andy, you know I always liked Dar."

"I always got that idea, yes," Andrew said. "She always talked well of you."

The commander was silent for a few moments. "I just wasn't ready for last night," he admitted. "Chuck came home and told us, and I just didn't...I didn't have a chance to think about it." He looked up. "D'you understand?"

A shrug was eloquent. "Never mattered to me, so no, I do not understand."

Jeff sighed. "You always had a blind spot with her."

Now, Andrew looked up and met his eyes fully. "She is a gift God gave me." He spoke slowly and with an almost gentle passion. "He made her, and I love all that she is." A breath. "Ah do not know why people do not understand that."

Jeff looked at him, then dropped his eyes. "Because you're a better man than most of us are, Andy."

"That's bullshit," Andrew snapped. "And what the hell's wrong with that kid of yours?"

The commander shifted away a bit. "What do you mean?"

"What the hell you think I mean? Goddamn ship captain goin' off his damn gourd, lashing out at some civ?" Andrew's eyes flashed. "He leave his brains on board, or what?"

Jeff gave him a defensive look. "C'mon, Andrew. He was under a lot of stress. He was really stuck on Dar."

Andrew stood and paced restlessly. "No, no no. Ah don't buy it, Jeff." The ex-SEAL shook his head. "Not after all this damn time. Don't you be telling me he's stuck on her since they was in high school. So stuck he goes nuts when he finds out he ain't got no chance, fer the **second** time." Andrew turned and put his hands on his hips. "Don't sound like somebody I want running mah boat, let me tell you that."

Ainsbright looked at him warily. "He's a good ship captain."

Pale, ice blue eyes regarded him. "Seems to me, I'm remembering they washed his ass out of command school."

"He tried again. Had to grow up some. You know how it is."

Andrew's jaw worked. "From what I seen outside that steakhouse, he ain't growed up near enough to be in charge of himself, much less a boat full of other folks."

Frustrated, Jeff threw up his hands. "C'mon, Andrew, he lost his temper. Don't tell me you never did. I know better."

"I never ran me no boat," Andrew replied softly. "But I never picked me up no baseball bat and went after no civ woman, either," he added. "I'm thinking that should be enough to take back them stripes."

Jeff went very still. The two men stared at each other for a long moment, then Ainsbright sat down again and rested his head in his hands. "Yeah, he fucked up." His voice echoed off the pavement. "Damn stupid kid."

Andrew leaned back against a wooden pylon and gazed up at the clouds. Thunder rumbled overhead, but it had not, as of yet, started raining. The headache that had started when Ceci had told him, in her own way, about the bat now worsened. "Damn lucky kid."

Jeff jerked his head up. "Lucky?"

The chill in Andrew's eyes was unmistakable. His nostrils flared. "Lucky ah did not come out that door thirty seconds earlier than I did."

The commander snorted in weary bemusement. "Shit, Andy. Dar didn't need your help. Chuck's in the base hospital with a ruptured eardrum and partially dislocated jaw." He closed his eyes. "They'll probably discharge him for that. Maybe it's for the best."

Andrew sat down. "You ain't going to report him, then?" he

asked, quietly. "'Cause if you don't, ah will."

Ainsbright looked up at him, taking in the uncompromising stance and the inflexible will showing on his old friend's scarred face. "Andrew..."

"Not fer me, or fer Dar," Andrew said. "You're right. Dar don't need me to take care of her anymore. She's a big girl, and she can handle herself as well as most." He straightened. "But out on that boat, Jeff, there's folks down under decks who don't deserve t'have someone like that taking charge of their lives."

"He has a spotless record!" Jeff protested.

"I used to be one of them folks below decks," Andrew shot right back. "Someone has to watch out for them, if you ain't."

"Andrew, for God's sake!" the commander yelled. "It was a little scuffle, c'mon now!"

"No, sir!" Andrew went nose to nose with him, jabbing a finger into his chest. "It was a Navy captain attacking a civilian and displaying conduct unbecoming to a goddamned officer!" He glared at Ainsbright. "And if it was Dar that done that, I'd report her, too!"

Silence. "Would you?" the commander asked softly.

"I would," Andrew replied.

"Well," Jeff Ainsbright dusted off his uniform, "I'm not you." He turned and walked around the bench, then headed off down the dock without a backward glance.

Andrew let out a sigh, then he sat down on the bench and stretched out his long legs, studying their denim-covered length with a frown. The rising wind blew a tiny bit of sea spray against his face, and he tipped his head back, eyeing the dark clouds pensively.

"No luck, eh, sailor boy?" Ceci stepped lightly over her husband's outstretched legs and settled down on the bench at his side.

"Naw." Andrew shook his head. "Stubborn old fool." He turned his head slightly. "You sure Dardar's okay?"

"Why don't you call her?" Ceci held out the cell phone. "Make you feel better."

Andrew examined the electronic device, then handed it back. "Got me a better idea." He stood, and held a hand out. "Let's go see for ourselves."

Ceci allowed herself to be hauled to her feet, and they started down the dock. They were halfway back when the rain caught them, sweeping across the way with a scent of ozone and damp, warm wood.

"Hey." Kerry sat on the edge of Dar's desk. "Why don't you let me get you another shot of those pills, huh?" She could see the pale tinge to Dar's normally tan skin.

"No." Dar shifted her arm in its sling to try and ease the ache. "They put me out, and I don't want to risk that before Gerry calls us back." The pain had gotten worse as the medication wore off, though, and now she had bursts of sharp agony moving up her shoulder and into her neck.

"Okay." Kerry tried another tack. "I'm going to make some herbal tea, want some?"

Dar thought about that, then nodded. "Yeah. Do we have that peachy kind?"

"It's apricot and honey," Kerry told her. "And yes, we do."

"I'd like that." Dar smiled. "I guess I can go lay down on the couch for a while, huh? I'm sure Gerry's going to be a few minutes."

"Sounds like a great idea to me." Kerry got up, waiting for Dar to join her, then tucked a hand inside her elbow and walked with her to the living room. She got Dar settled back into her comfortable nest of pillows and fleece, and then she headed off toward the kitchen.

"Hey, Chino." She greeted the Labrador, who had followed her. "You want some tea, too?" The blond head cocked curiously at her. "No, probably not, huh?" Kerry put some hot water up, then pulled a bowl from the cabinet and raided the crisper, pulling out some fruit and washing it. Cherries, which were a favorite of Dar's, and grapes, apples and peaches, and the bananas that were her own favorite. Then she removed a thick, sweet banana nutbread from the refrigerator, and sliced off a few slices, spreading a coating of cream cheese on them before setting them on a plate next to the fruit. "There." She pulled a bottle of Advil from the cabinet and set it down, idly spinning it as she waited for the water to heat.

Dar tilted her head back and regarded the popcorn ceiling. Her findings had surprised Gerry; she knew that from the shock in his voice. She also knew he would react quickly, and that troops were probably already heading for the base—military police and Marines, more than likely.

It bothered her, though, to simply release control of the situation.

Kerry was right. She knew they'd botch it. She knew they'd miss out on catching all the bastards who were involved, and maybe only get the obvious ones. And people like Jeff Ainsbright, who, even if he wasn't involved, would be taken down because he

damn well should have known what was going on in his own command.

Dar sighed, remembering the long afternoons she'd spent as a
youngster running wild with Chuckie and the other kids in the
housing area's grassy spaces as their fathers huddled over barbe-
cues in the front yard. If she tried, she could close her eyes and
hear the football games playing in the background.

A warm touch on her arm made her jerk, and she opened her
eyes. "Sorry. I was just thinking." The scent of apricot drifted over
from the tray Kerry was setting on the coffee table.

Kerry took her partner's hand in her own and chafed the fingers. "Dar, if you're tired, go ahead and go to sleep. I'll wake you
up as soon as the phone rings."

"Hmm." Dar shook her head. "I slept half the day, Ker." She
shifted her head on the pillow, then pulled herself up a little. "Did
you wrap that brick up?"

Kerry nodded, then handed Dar her cup. "Wrapped it up,
taped it up, put it in a box, and put it up on top of the cabinet so
Chino can't get at it." The Labrador, hearing her name, came snuf-
fling over looking for goodies. "Stuff gives me the creeps just looking at it."

Dar took a sip of the tea. "You never experimented?"

"No." Kerry shook her head. "I stuck to beer, thanks, and
that got me in more than enough trouble." She paused in the middle of handing over a piece of bread and looked up at Dar. "Did
you?"

A pained sigh gave her the answer. "Once," Dar admitted.
"Not the hard stuff. A bunch of us got hold of some wild weed
growing back south of the base and decided to have a party."

Kerry finished handing over the nutbread. "And?" she asked
curiously.

"I was sick as a dog for three days." Dar nibbled her treat.
"Throwing up, seeing spots, couldn't keep anything down until my
mother finally got me to the doctor's and he got some intravenous
Dramamine into me."

"Oh." Kerry bit her inner lip. "I thought you couldn't take
that."

"That's when we found that out." Dar grimaced. "Next time
someone asked me if I wanted a joint, I slugged them." She took a
bigger bite. "Mm...I really like this."

"I know." Kerry seated herself on the floor, leaning back
against the couch and exhaling. "Me, too." She handed over a
handful of cherries. "I was only really tempted when I was in college," she said. "Everyone did it. All those late nights and

stress...I had a couple of friends who had a source for just about everything. They were always telling me what they had and asking if I wanted any."

Dar watched her profile and the motion of her jaw muscles as she chewed. "We had that a lot in college, too."

"Mm." Kerry exhaled. "I remember one night, I had this paper due in my writing class and a systems design due on the same day. I'd had a full schedule of classes that day, and I was totally wiped out. Just exhausted. Even double espressos weren't doing a thing for me."

"Mm," Dar murmured encouragingly.

"Jane came over and saw how trashed I was. She offered me a handful of amphetamines and a shot of coke and told me it would get me through the two assignments, no problem." Kerry took another bite thoughtfully. "I took the drugs from her."

Dar bit into a cherry and skillfully separated the fruit from its pit. "And?" She echoed Kerry's earlier question.

"I came pretty close to taking them," Kerry admitted honestly. "And would you believe, it was my father that kept me from it?"

Dar's eyes opened very wide. "Your father?"

Kerry laughed softly. "He had this speech he used to do about people needing crutches. You know, Dar, that old thing about liberal programs being a crutch for the poor that kept them from really going out and making a living?"

"That's such a crock of shit," Dar stated.

"Not the point. It reminded me that I'd chosen to take this double major, and if I couldn't handle it, I shouldn't use an illegal substance as a crutch. Either do it, or don't do it, but don't fake it," Kerry replied. "I wanted to do it on my own, so I could look back and say, yeah, I did that. No one helped me."

"Hmm." Dar depitted another cherry and took another bite of her banana nutbread. "Yeah, I see your point," she admitted. "So, what did you do?"

Kerry thought back to that long night, with its aching struggle she'd spent alone. "I worked through it. I wrote the systems design first, because you need brain cells to do that, and the creative writing paper..." Now a smile crossed her face. "Dar, do you know I still don't know what I put in that paper? It got me a B, but I have no idea what I wrote."

Dar chuckled. "Whatever works." She looked hopefully at the plate. "Any more of that bread?"

Kerry turned her head and eyed her. "What's it worth to you?"

Dar poked out her lower lip.

"Ah. So you think that's all it takes to get me to give up this really great tasting nut bread?" Kerry inquired.

Dar gave her a sad look.

"You're such a brat." Kerry handed it over. She peeled a banana and settled back as Chino put her chin down on her thigh hopefully. "Oh no, madam. Last time we gave you fruit, you got sick, remember?"

The phone rang, and Kerry shot a look back at Dar, then she picked up the portable receiver and answered it. "Hello?"

"Ah...yes, is Dar there?"

"Yes, General. Just a minute." Kerry handed the phone back and half turned, resting her chin on the couch as she listened.

Dar took a breath before she pressed the phone to her ear. "Gerry?"

There was a soft knock at the door. Kerry frowned, then scrambled to her feet and trotted over to it, peeking through the eyehole. "Uh-oh." She hesitated, then realized she really had no choice and opened the door. "Hi."

"Howdy there, kumquat," Andrew drawled. "Y'all going to let us inside there?"

Oh boy. Kerry slipped outside instead, closing the door behind her.

Dar gave the condo door a curious look as she listened to the voice on the other end of the line. "Gerry, we're not equipped for that." Dar closed her eyes against the throbbing she could feel growing in her neck. "I have security teams that can protect data, sure, but this is a damn Navy base."

"I'm aware of that, Dar." Gerry's voice was uncharacteristically serious. "The trouble is, we can't shake a team loose to go down there for at least forty-eight hours."

By then, it would be too late. "Damn."

"John Taylor from the JAG office is on a plane headed your way," General Easton stated. "He'll handle the official part, but if there's any way your people could protect the evidence—"

"Gerry, people could get hurt," Dar said. "This isn't the kind of thing we get involved in. Corporate double-dealing, yeah, but smuggling? I'm responsible for these people, and for their safety." She paused. "And I don't know how many bastards are implicated." Injudiciously, she shifted, and stifled a gasp. "Shit."

"Dar?" Gerry spoke quickly. "Are you all right?"

Dar bit her inner lip for a long moment, then exhaled as the sharp pain receded. "Yeah, I'm fine. I just twisted something."

"Well, listen, my friend, I'll find some other way of doing this," General Easton replied. "If nothing else, we'll just round up the lot of them and start shaking."

The unfairness of that, Dar acknowledged, was exactly what she'd been afraid of. "Hang on a minute, Gerry." She put the phone down and let her head drop back on the pillow, thinking hard about her options.

Was it dangerous?

Be honest, Dar. Sure it is. Look what happened to you last night, and Chuck was a friend of yours. Dar rubbed her forehead. This was a military base, full of sailors and Marines, an unknown number of whom could be involved in criminal activity and react with violence.

But...

If she didn't help, innocent people could and probably would get blamed, and the criminals would probably get away. Dar mulled that over. Question was, how could she help Gerry, help the base, protect the innocent, and keep her people safe at the same time? "Jesus, Paladar," she murmured to herself. "What the hell do you think you are?"

Finally, she picked up the phone again. "Gerry?"

"What's that? Oh, still here, Dar."

"Let me see what I can do." Dar heard herself say the words, and wondered how she was going to back them up. "Maybe I can get a small volunteer team inside." Then an idea occurred to her. "With an escort."

There was a momentary pause. "Dar, do me a favor, eh? Don't take chances. I want to see your whole family this Christmas. Been waiting for that for a long while now."

Dar evaded the question. "See if you can contact that JAG staffer, send him over to my office. We'll get things moving here. Talk to you later, Gerry." She disconnected and put the phone down on her belly, considering what to do next.

It was a crowded doorstep. Kerry stood effectively blocking the entrance, despite her relatively small size. "Dar's on the phone," she explained. "It's business."

"Uh-huh." Andrew crossed his arms. "Not like we'd know one word in six she was using." He eyed Kerry curiously. "Something bothering you, kumquat?"

"Me?" Kerry exhaled. "Uh, no, no. I'm fine."

"How's Dar?" Ceci asked casually.

Ah. "She's... Why are you asking me that?" Kerry temporized.

Dar's parents exchanged knowing looks. "All right, kumquat. What's going on?" Andrew asked. "I knew something wasn't right."

Oh boy. "It's—"

"She get hurt last night?" The question snapped at her.

"Well—"

"That little half-assed bastard hurt my kid?"

"W...y..." Kerry sucked in a breath. "Yes, that's what happened, but—"

"Son of a biscuit." Andrew was visibly angry.

Kerry put both hands out in a calming gesture. "It's not that bad. We've already been to the doctor's and had tests done. It's more painful than anything else."

"You got her to go to the doc's?" Andrew had both fists planted on his hips. "I am going to whip her behind for not tellin' us."

"Dad." Kerry gave him a pleading look.

Ceci ruffled her silvered blond hair. "Some things just never do change, do they?" she murmured. "Keep your BVDs on, Andy. I can remember many a time I had to drag you kicking and yelling to the base hospital."

Her husband gave her a look. "That is not the point," he replied with a scowl. "We are not talking about me."

"No, no." Ceci patted his arm. "We're talking about your daughter. Remember her? The tall, blue-eyed, dark-haired girl with an attitude and more guts than sense?"

"Hey. She's got a lot of sense," Kerry objected.

"Exactly," Ceci remarked.

Andrew scowled harder. "If I'd a known that little—"

"Yes, which is why Dar didn't tell you." Ceci circled his arm with both hands. "Now, come on, let's go in and see the poor kid. See if you can make her feel better instead of yelling at her, hmm?"

"Ah do not like Dar thinking she can't tell us something like this," Andrew replied. "I do not like it one bit." He nudged past Kerry and opened the door. "Son of a biscuit," he muttered, leaving Kerry and Ceci behind to gaze at each other in amused sympathy.

"He'll be nice," Ceci told her. "He talks a good game, but the minute she looks up at him, he's going to cave in like one of those marshmallows you toast over a Bunsen burner."

"I know." Kerry smiled. "I've been on the receiving end of

those baby blues." She sighed and opened the door. "But we've got a big problem. I'm sort of glad you're here." She followed Ceci inside. "Dar went looking for trouble down at that Navy base."

Ceci stopped, watching Andrew kneel at Dar's side. "And?"

"And she found it," Kerry replied grimly.

Dar sat on the couch, watching her father pace. The brick of cocaine was on the coffee table, and her mother was sitting across from her, staring at it in bemused fascination.

Kerry entered and sat down next to her lover, absently slipping an arm around her back and gently rubbing it. "I know it seems bizarre," she stated. "We certainly never expected this."

Andrew halted, and shook his grizzled head. "Ain't that saying something." He walked over and crouched down in front of Dar, putting a hand on her knee. "You know who done all this?"

Dar met his eyes, so very much like her own, and shook her head. "I haven't had time to analyze all the data we copied, and a lot of the structure is in the programming."

"You think Jeff knows?"

Dar shook her head again. "I don't know. I'd have to check the physical documentation, see what had his signature on it or what passed through his personal authorization."

"What's yer gut telling you?" Andrew persisted quietly.

That took some thought. Dar focused her mind inward, reviewing the facts she did know and the assumptions she'd made. She was vaguely aware of Kerry's arm, warm against her back, and she could feel the slim fingers tracing a soft, irregular pattern against her skin.

It felt really good. She leaned against Kerry a little, and the blond woman's embrace tightened as Kerry rested her cheek against Dar's shoulder.

Dar set the puzzle pieces out and examined them carefully. One, she had a situation that was obviously a long-term plan in progress—the evidence she'd seen indicated it had been going on for quite some time. Jeff Ainsbright had only been in charge at the base for three months. Not enough time. Dar put a tick in that mental column.

Two, whoever was organizing the situation had technical skills beyond Jeff's, and the general sense she got of the meticulous arrangements didn't fit the commander's personality. Dar put another tick in the column.

Three, with the number of people apparently involved, it would be damn near impossible for the base commander to be blind to the fact that something was going on. Dar put a tick in the opposing column.

Was it possible Jeff Ainsbright thought, as Dar had, that whatever irregularities he noticed in the books and procedures were evidence of some harmless, petty larceny to which he could safely turn a blind eye? Three months wasn't a long time to get a handle on a place as big as that was, after all.

Be honest, Dar, her conscience quietly spoke. *If this were just another target acquisition of Alastair's, would you even be considering the question? Or would you assume the worst?*

Dar's eyes narrowed.

Ceci sat back in her chair and tucked a leg up under herself, watching the silent tableau with fascinated eyes. Her daughter was obviously deep in thought, the blue eyes unfocused and remote, their lids flickering lightly as the mind behind them worked. Ceci had always had respect for the intellect she'd watched Dar develop, despite its edgy restlessness that often made her daughter hard to deal with.

She'd had her child tested, without Andrew's knowledge, when Dar had come home from grade school one day with a note from her fourth grade teacher informing Ceci that he was giving up on trying to retain Dar's attention in class. Even then, she'd tested years older than her age, and Ceci had been shocked to find out just how high octane her little fourth-grader's mind was.

Genius, the doctor had told her, was a two-edged sword. On one hand, Dar's potential was unlimited. On the other hand, the very fact of that intelligence put Dar on a plateau that separated her at a time in her life when being different was tantamount to a prison sentence.

And there she'd been—someone who'd had a high school education, and had grown up in a family who valued the price of a person's car more than the depth of their thoughts—trying to deal with decisions on what to do about the whole thing. Ceci had felt so out of her depth raising her child.

Now, watching that same intellect, grown and matured and shaped by Dar's intense personality into the sharp, incisive force that it was, she wondered if she'd ever have been able to deal with Dar, even if she hadn't had her so young and been so isolated.

Dar's head lifted, and the introspective look vanished as she drew in a breath and returned to the here and now. A cool expression settled over her face as she met her father's patiently waiting gaze. "No." Dar's voice was calm. "I don't think he was involved."

Andrew's eyebrows lifted a trifle.

"But I do think he was aware," Dar went on. "The question is, to what degree."

Kerry nodded slightly, as though confirming thoughts of her own. "We won't know that unless we get all the data."

"Exactly," Dar replied. "Call Mark. Have him call in a security team. Make it five or six people, but tell him volunteers only." She turned and regarded Kerry. "I want them to know where they're going, and that there's a possibility of getting hurt. No pressure." She watched Kerry nod. "We'll meet at the office."

"All right." Kerry stood up and headed for the phone.

Dar looked at her father. "You want to help?"

"Hell, yes," Andrew responded immediately. "Tell you what. You stay up in that penthouse of yours and rest yer arm, and I'll take them kiddies down to the base and shake their shorts out clean." He patted Dar's knee. "All right?"

Dar's lips edged up into a tense smile. "I don't think so. But thanks for the offer, Dad."

"Dar, I'd be the last one to encourage your father to get into trouble, but it makes sense," Ceci offered, a trifle hesitantly. She felt a faint flush as a pair of sharp blue eyes pinned her, and reminded herself again of just how little right she had to give her daughter advice. "Doesn't it?"

"No." Dar got up from the couch, moving fluidly around Andrew's still crouching form and stalking toward the study. "There's too many ways for someone who knows what they're doing to stop even one of our best techs from getting what I want." She paused in the doorway, the restlessness evident in her flexing hand. "But they won't stop me."

Dar disappeared into her office, leaving the rest of them to exchange looks.

"Nice try," Kerry offered, holding her hand over the receiver. "I could have told you she wouldn't go for it, though." She returned her attention to the phone. "That's right, Mark. It's the base...No, I can't even start to go into it." A pause. "Dar wants volunteers. Can we get a few?" Another pause. "No, that'll be up to Dar...Okay, we'll meet you there." Kerry put the phone down. "Okay, that's that." She glanced at the study through the half-open door, seeing Dar's tense form crouched over her PC. "Be right back."

Ceci exhaled as Kerry, too, disappeared. She watched Andrew as he got up and crossed to her, then sat down on the tile floor with a sigh. "What do you think, sailor boy?"

Andrew shook his head. "Ah think this is the goddamndest piece of horse's butt end I ever did see."

"Mm." Ceci could only agree.

Kerry paused in the doorway, then entered the study and pushed the wooden surface closed behind her. Dar was studying something on her screen, but after a moment she stopped pointing and clicking and looked up.

Blue eyes gave her a direct stare. "Coming to tell me how stupid I am?"

Kerry felt her heartbeat pick up as she heard the tension in Dar's voice. "Have I ever said that?" she asked quietly, meeting Dar's gaze with patient honesty. "I don't think you're capable of being stupid."

Dar glanced at the screen, moving her hand restlessly.

Kerry sat down on the couch and rested her forearms on her knees. "I could question your faith in my abilities, of course."

"Don't," Dar snapped. "This has nothing to do with you."

"Excuse me." Kerry gave her a direct look. "You are sending my people into that place; it most certainly does have everything to do with me." She pushed herself to her feet and advanced on the desk. "I know how to supervise a security sweep, Dar. I've been doing it for months."

Dar avoided her gaze. "This is different."

Kerry studied her. "Your father was right. You should stay here." Her voice gentled to remove any sting. "You're too close to this, Dar."

Her lover drew a forceful breath and stiffened. "That's bullshit." She tipped her head back as Kerry rounded the desk and confronted her. "I'm perfectly capable of doing my job, thanks."

"No one's debating that." Kerry sat on the edge of the desk, realizing by the defensive tensing of Dar's muscles that looming over her wasn't a good idea. "But this is different, Dar. Think about it. You grew up at this place. These people are your friends." She put out a tentative hand and covered the larger one resting on the desktop. "I don't know if I could handle it if it were me."

Dar's face kept its set expression for a moment, then the jaw muscles relaxed slightly, and she blinked. "Because I did grow up there is why I have to do this," she answered softly. "It's not that I don't trust you." Her eyes flicked up to meet Kerry's. "But I can't give you what I know, how I know the way things work there."

Kerry studied her lover's face, seeing the pain etched into the tense lines around her eyes. "I've seen the layout, honey. It's just a big complex system," she protested. "I know how to get it locked down."

"It's not that," Dar answered. "I just don't want to take a chance. Too many people can get hurt."

"What about you taking a chance with yourself?" Kerry countered. "I don't want to see you get hurt, Dar." Slowly, she slid off the desk and knelt, looking up now into Dar's face. "Nothing is more important to me than that. Not this job, not that base. It's not worth the risk."

A faint smile finally tugged at Dar's lips. "Don't worry."

"Dar—"

"You'll be right there next to me." Dar touched Kerry's cheek with her fingertips. "The only muscle I'm going to be using is this one." She lifted a hand and tapped her forehead. "I promise."

She wasn't going to win this one, Kerry knew. She was also smart enough to realize that what Dar was saying was completely true—they'd have a much better chance of not missing anything with her there. "Okay," she agreed. "You should take the rest of your drugs though, even if you don't want the painkillers."

Dar's face took on a wry smile. "I do want them." She sighed and leaned back, relaxing a little now that the fight was over. "I want to take them, and lie down, and just go out for the rest of the day." Her body felt stiff and achy, and the tension had given her a headache again. "But yeah, I'll take everything but those, if you wouldn't mind bringing the others over, and some Advil."

Kerry nodded. "Sure." She leaned forward and kissed Dar's knee. "Mark and the rest of the team are going to meet us at the office in an hour."

"Mark?"

"Of course." The blond woman smiled. "You said you wanted volunteers."

Dar sighed. "Figures he would. I wonder if anyone else will."

Wonder if anyone else won't, Kerry amended silently.

Chapter
Fourteen

Ceci carefully put her hands precisely behind her back and clasped them. *So, this is where Dar and Kerry work.* Her eyes traveled up and up and up to see the top of the atrium skylight, then back down across the marble and steel walls to the pretentious fountain in the very center of the space.

Somehow, she resisted the urge to yodel. The temptation to hear the echoes was almost overwhelming.

A security guard ambled over and handed her a piece of plastic. "There you go, ma'am. That's your badge."

Ceci accepted it and clipped the item to her shirt. "Outstanding," she complimented the guard. "Does it check for radiation hazards as well?"

The guard cocked his head in puzzlement. "Ma'am?"

"Let's go." Dar had come up next to her. "Thanks, Devon."

"Any time, Ms. Roberts." The guard ducked his head politely at Dar. "Haven't seen you here on the weekend in a long time." He managed not to look too curiously at her beslinged arm. "Have a good day."

"Thanks." Dar led the way across the huge lobby toward the elevator, Kerry a pace behind her and followed by her parents. She felt a little unfocused from the drugs, but still fairly alert. "Did we tell Devon to be on the lookout for the JAG rep?"

"Yes," Kerry replied. "Twice." She swiped her keycard into the elevator receptacle and held the doors when they opened. "All aboard."

"Tell me, Dar," Ceci commented as they rode up. "Do you rent out mausoleum space in this place to South Miami Cemetery?"

Dar was leaning against the mirrored wall, staring at her reflection. An extremely grumpy-looking, slightly scruffy figure with a scowl was looking back at her. With an effort, she wrestled a little of her normal work attitude into place. "No." She eyed her mother. "We charge too much," she replied. "The American Cryogenic Society has the top floor, though."

Kerry chuckled. "That explains why it's so cold upstairs all the time," she remarked. "I had to wear a parka the first few months I worked here."

The doors slid open and they left the elevator, moving along the very quiet hallway, past closed or darkened doorways. No one on fourteen worked on the weekends, save the operations group on occasion, and it was pleasantly unchaotic for a change. "Wish it was like this all the time," Kerry muttered. "It's usually Circus City at this time of day." She swiped her card at the front door to Dar's outer office and heard the lock click.

Andrew reached around her and worked the handle, pushing the door open and allowing them into the darkened interior. "Cec, this ain't half nothing. That there place in Houston's got this beat hands down."

Ceci strolled in and looked around curiously. It was a good-sized space, with seating on one side and a neatly appointed desk on the other. Across from the main entry was a set of inner doors, and one had a plaque on it. She looked at it as Andrew flipped the lights on.

Dar's name and title.

With a sense of surreality, she followed as Dar opened the door to her office and went inside. It was light, Ceci noticed, and as she cleared the door she saw why.

Good Goddess. She stopped and stared. The place was huge: floor-to-ceiling teak paneling framed two walls; the other two were floor-to-ceiling plate glass, giving a breathtaking view of the sea all the way to the horizon. The room was filled with light from outside, which fell on the fine wood furnishings and the curved expanse of Dar's desk. Against one wall was a comfortable-looking leather couch, and against the other, a credenza with a neatly put up silver tray holding a now empty pitcher and glasses.

Ceci noted a few other things. That the desk was absolutely spotless and contained exactly zero clutter, something she'd noticed about Dar's study in the condo. Remembering what a wreck her daughter habitually kept her adolescent room in, this seemed almost funny. The only things on the desk were the computer screen and keyboard, Dar's trackball, her in and out box, and a...Ceci walked closer and squinted...and a pair of Siamese fighting fish in a small, interlocked Lucite tank.

Interesting choice. Ceci eyed her husband, who was rocking slightly on his heels, his brow tensed in thought.

"I'm going to start pulling up their network schematics and printing them off," Kerry said as she headed toward the small door in the rear of the office. "Hope someone left the plotter up and linked."

"I'll check it." Dar went to her desk and sat down. "G'wan and take a seat," she told her parents as she kick-started her PC. The phone rang, and she hit the speakerphone button. "Yes?"

"Hey, boss." Mark's voice echoed slightly. "Saw your IP come active."

"Don't you have anything better to do than watch, snoopy?" Dar asked, testily. "Is the plotter active?"

"Hang on." The sound of a keyboard cut clearly through the connection. "It is now. Let me boot the print server if you're gonna be sending anything big to it."

"Diagrams. Kerry's sending," Dar replied. "You get some people to come in?"

"Yeah." Mark sounded preoccupied. "I had to rig a lottery though."

Dar braced a knee up against the edge of her desk. "What?" Her brow contracted. "Mark, damn it, I told you I wanted volunteers. What part of that didn't you understand?"

There was a momentary silence. "Um...you said you only wanted six people, boss. I had to do a lottery to get it down to that," Mark replied carefully. "I had twenty-five of those suckers show up here." He paused. "Did I do something to piss you off today?"

Dar regarded her hiking boot in mild embarrassment. *Get your head out of your ass, Dar.* "No, sorry, Mark," she replied. "I just want to get this started. Give Kerry twenty minutes to get those diagrams done, then c'mon up here."

"Will do," Mark replied, then hung up.

"Ahm going to get me some coffee," Andrew said. "You want some, Dardar?"

"No." Dar shook her head. "Dr. Steve said to stay away from that for a couple of days." Awareness of her injury nibbled uncomfortably at her. "Thanks for the offer."

Her father left, and Dar became aware of her mother's pale eyes glancing her way curiously. She lifted a hand and indicated the room with wry irony. "What do you think?"

Thus invited, Ceci obligingly got up and toured the room, ending up next to Dar's desk. "It's...um..."

"Pretentious?" Dar dryly supplied.

"No, actually it has very pleasant proportions," Ceci disagreed gravely. "Nice view, lot of open space, clean..." Her eyes and Dar's met, and she hesitated, a teasing remark on her tongue she wasn't sure she should utter.

Dar's cool gaze gentled slightly. "What am I doing in here, right?" A hint of a smile warmed her features.

Ceci returned the smile. "Nah. I think you fit right in here," she disagreed. "I especially like the blue jeans; they go well with the teak paneling."

That got an actual chuckle out of Dar, who plucked at the denim fabric covering her knee. "It's not how I usually dress here," she admitted. "Wish it was. Those damn business suits drive me nuts."

Her mother studied the faded jeans and untucked cotton shirt Dar was wearing, the easiest things she could manage with her arm in a sling. "That strap's twisted," she gestured. "Want it fixed?"

For a moment, there was a flash of wary uncertainty in Dar's eyes. Ceci merely waited, wishing for the thousandth time she'd made some different choices years back. She was almost sure Dar would politely decline the offer, when her daughter shifted and leaned forward slightly.

"Sure," Dar said. "Felt a little weird."

Ceci unbuckled the strap and straightened it, tucking the cotton fabric under Dar's collar and refastening the buckle. She had to move a bit of thick, dark hair out of the way to do so. "I always wondered what Andy would have looked like with long hair."

Dar slowly turned her head and both eyebrows arched almost to her hairline. "Dad?"

"Mm." Ceci nodded, giving Dar's shoulder a light pat. "There you go."

"I don't think he's ever had it even covering his ears, much less his neck." Dar relaxed a little, settling back in her chair as Ceci stepped away.

"Nope, he sure hasn't." Ceci shook her head. "But when he was your current age, his hair was just like yours, same texture and everything. I remember he let it grow...oh, all of two inches over one summer before he had it buzzed again." She studied Dar's angular face and smiled. "I can almost imagine it, now." It was nice, a wistful thought intruded, to be able to see her husband so clearly in their child, and have it not hurt.

She wondered if Dar realized that. They'd both changed so much, it was hard to say what went on behind those very familiar eyes anymore. *Ah well.* "How's your shoulder doing?" Ceci changed the subject.

"Lousy," Dar answered, with surprising honesty. "Sorry I didn't mention it the other day."

"I'm not," Ceci replied, with equal honesty, seeing the quickly shuttered wariness in Dar's eyes. "Don't get me wrong, Dar. What happens to you matters to me, and I'm sorry you got hurt by that a—" She paused. "By Chuck, but we both know it was better for him and Andy for your father not to know."

"Mm." The door opened and Andrew reentered the room, carrying two cups. Dar and her mother exchanged glances, then Dar smiled. "Thanks, Mom. Glad I made the right choice."

Well. Ceci accepted the cup of coffee, feeling pleased, if a touch bemused, by the reaction. *I think that was almost a Kodak moment.*

She liked it. Ceci moved off toward the window and studied the view, half listening to her husband and Dar in the background talking about the base.

Dar had moved the strategy meeting into the big conference room down the hall from her office. Kerry had gotten in ahead of her and clipped the network diagrams to the big presentation board, and now she watched as the operations team filed in and took seats.

Mark, of course, was in the lead, carrying the backpack Kerry knew held the big network analyzer and its cables. He set it down on the floor and took a seat as the rest of the group settled around him. Kerry's eyebrows rose as she recognized Brent among the group, but she refrained from commenting as Dar entered from the back door.

The JAG officer and Andrew were with her, and they took chairs near the other end of the conference table as Dar circled it and headed toward the podium. Ceci had seated herself near the window and was watching quietly, her eyes flicking between the charts and her daughter, and occasionally crossing gazes with Kerry herself.

"All right." Dar's low, vibrant voice cut through the quiet. She put a sheaf of papers on the podium and drew in a breath, letting her eyes run over her audience. Kerry could almost see the subtle shift as her lover assumed her professional demeanor, and she sharpened her own attention as she listened.

Even in casual clothing, and with her arm in its white cotton sling, Dar still managed to capture the room, the normal intensity of her attitude only slightly blunted by all the medication she was on. Kerry could tell it was an effort, though. There was a persistent crease in Dar's forehead, she was blinking more than usual, and there was an uncharacteristic slump to her posture that was easily visible to her watching partner.

"We've gotten an unusual request from the government." Dar started her speech. "As most of you know, we were contracted to perform detailed structure and performance analysis on a number of military bases."

The techs were glued to her every word. They nodded almost in concert, which almost made Dar laugh. "As part of that investigation, information was obtained detailing irregularities in their data, which could extend from minor theft to felonious activities."

Mark shook his head and let out a sigh. "I was thinking that, boss. That stuff you sent down stank to hell."

Dar nodded. "With good reason." She turned to the whiteboard. "Normally, I'd have just turned this over to the government at this point." She spared a glance for the JAG man. "In fact, that's what was originally intended. However, due to logistics, they can't get a security team here for at least twenty-four hours, and we have reason to think data destruction would occur before that time.

"Mark, we're going to need to put the scope in here." Dar ran a hand over the diagram. "The three critical mainframes are here, here, and here, and we'll need to pull the drive arrays from all three."

Mark was scribbling. "We just going to walk in there, DR?"

This was the tricky part. "No." Dar folded her hands on the podium. "Kerry and I are going in first." All heads jerked her way. "The guards are used to seeing me, and they won't react." *At least, I hope they won't.* "Two of you are going to ride with us and duck down in the back seat as we go through the gates."

"Check." Mark made a note. "How 'bout the rest of them?"

Dar felt a smile twitching at her lips at Mark's claiming of his spot. "A volunteer who's familiar with the base is going to pay a visit. Everyone else will go with him."

"Them," Ceci muttered, just loud enough for Dar to hear her.

The techs all looked around and finally spotted the two guests at the end of the table. Mark waved at Andrew. "Oh, hey."

"'Lo," Andrew drawled.

Kerry watched Brent's face as he focused on the tall ex-SEAL, then returned his gaze straight ahead. She wondered what he was thinking.

"This is Captain Taylor from the military justice department and my father, Andrew Roberts," Dar introduced them succinctly. "My father's the volunteer who'll get the rest of you into the camp. He's very familiar with it." She let her eyes rove over the watching faces. "If either of them instruct any of you to do something, do it." She paused. "Understand?"

"Gotcha, DR," Mark replied. "You guys all clear on that?"

The techs nodded.

"Good." Dar paused, then nodded. "Get moving. Don't do anything stupid when you're out there. I don't want to be spending half the week doing paperwork on anyone. Got me?"

Another round of nodding.

"All right. That's all." Dar stepped back from the podium. Everyone stood and a low murmur of discussion started. Dar exhaled and ran her fingers through her hair as Kerry crossed the room and came to her side. "Ready?"

"I've got all the equipment downstairs, ready to go," Kerry told her. "I brought the portable hundred-gig array along, in case we need to transfer something we can't just take." She leaned forward. "And I picked up the black box, so you can run your code on it if you need to."

Dar considered that. "Good work," she said. "Thanks, Ker."

They followed the crowd out of the room and toward the elevator. Dar found herself between her father and Kerry as they entered the open car, and she leaned back against the mirrored wall, aware of the warmth as they joined her. Slowly, she turned her head and regarded Kerry, who had folded her arms and was gazing ahead of her. Then she turned and glanced at her father, who had adopted the same pose. The rest of the occupants of the elevator were studying the tiled floor with great interest.

Dar's brow creased. They were all acting a little weird, she thought, then realized it was probably due to the very odd circumstances. With a sigh, she let her head rest against the cool surface and waited for the drop to end. The JAG captain had been quiet and reserved and pretty much unhelpful, even after Dar had given him the cocaine brick.

He needed concrete proof, he'd said seriously. That brick could have come from anywhere, and the chief could have just been looking to get someone in trouble. Which was true, Dar acknowledged, and the exact reason she was dragging her butt down to the Upper Keys on a Saturday afternoon when she felt like crawling into bed and passing out.

A hand on her elbow almost made her jump, and she glanced up to see the doors open, and everyone else exiting. "Whoops...sorry." She gave Kerry a smile. "I was just thinking."

Kerry glanced up at her and returned the smile. "I could tell."
She linked her arm inside Dar's, and they continued across the
lobby toward the front door. "How are you feeling?"

A little annoyed to be asked again, Dar almost retorted. "I'm
fine," she replied. "Damn drugs are making me a little light-
headed, that's all." Deliberately putting more energy into her
steps, she pulled free of Kerry's grip and stalked toward the
entrance.

Kerry sighed. "Shit."

Andrew glanced at her. "Stubborn cuss, ain't she," he com-
miserated wryly.

Kerry looked at him. "Wonder where she gets it from," she
answered with equal wryness.

"Ah have no idea," Andrew said. "You better git moving 'fore
she decides on driving."

Kerry sighed and broke into a jog, ducking past the straggling
techs as she tried to catch up with her partner.

Kerry waited until they were almost at the base before she
slowed the pace of the Lexus and glanced into the rearview mirror. She spotted Andrew a bit back, in Dar's car, and also caught
the half-asleep faces of Mark and Brent in the back seat.

It was very quiet in the car. She'd deliberately turned the stereo down to allow her passengers to relax and doze off if they
wanted to. In fact, she encouraged them to do just that, knowing
Dar would remain awake and alert if everyone else was, just out of
sheer cussedness.

But Mark had taken her hint and loudly announced his intention to nap, poking Brent in the leg until the slightly slow-on-the-
uptake tech realized what he wanted and huddled down in his seat
with a glum expression.

Then, of course, and only then had Dar allowed herself to
relax and slump against the doorframe, using a folded sweatshirt
of Kerry's as an impromptu pillow as she closed her eyes and sur-
rendered to a light doze.

Now Kerry wished the trip was longer, but she reached over
and gently touched Dar's thigh, squeezing it twice before she got a
reaction. Dar's eyelids fluttered open and she blinked, turning her
head to peer at Kerry in confusion for a moment before her
expression cleared and she straightened in her seat.

"Okay, duck down, guys," Kerry said. "Just pull those com-
forters over you while I go through the gates." She turned into the
base and eased slowly down the approach road, pulling up next to

the guard shack and leaning back a little so Dar could see the guard.

"Afternoon," Dar greeted the man. "Looks quiet."

The man came closer, then smiled. "Ms. Roberts...hey." He glanced around. "Didn't expect you here on the weekend."

Dar smiled back. "Got some little things to clear up," she said. "And my parents are coming down, just for old time's sake, to look around in the daytime."

The Marine's eyes lit up. "Big Andy's coming in today? All right. Man, wait 'til the guys hear. You know they got a big old UD get-together going on today, right?"

"No, I didn't," Dar replied. "That'll be a damn nice surprise for him, though. Thanks for the word." She waved casually. "Gotta get to work."

The guard raised the gate and waved back. "Take it easy, Ms. Roberts."

Kerry drove into the parking lot. "Will that be a problem?" she asked. "That meeting or whatever?"

Dar was rubbing her eyes, and now she looked up. "Problem?" Her lips quirked. "I doubt it. This place'll be crawling with SEALs. This could be easier than we thought."

"Crawling with SEALs." Kerry parked and set the brake. "Interesting visual, Dar, but how does it help us?"

Dar opened the door and got out, stretching out her body as Mark joined her on the passenger side and Kerry, with Brent, walked around the front of the Lexus. "It means we have friends here, Kerry." She felt better already. "The kind of friends you like to have when you're in a potentially dangerous situation."

Kerry considered that, as Mark removed the analyzer from the back of the car. "Unless some of them are involved," she commented, looking up to see ice-cold blue eyes looking back at her. "Um. I mean—"

"Never." Dar said, low and forcefully. "Not these guys."

Kerry and Mark exchanged glances. "Okay," Kerry agreed softly. "You're the expert." She patted Dar's back. "Glad to hear that. If they're all like Dad, this'll be a piece of cake." Her eyes slid past Dar to meet Brent's, which darted off in another direction. "I feel better already."

"Brent, gimme a hand with this." Mark was kneeling next to the analyzer. "I need to fit the wiring harness."

Brent walked over and they fussed over the equipment, leaving Dar and Kerry standing a little apart as they waited. Dar glanced around, then exhaled and ducked her head a bit. "I know I'm being a bitch. Sorry."

"Were you?" Kerry asked mildly. "I hadn't noticed."

Their eyes met. Dar managed a smile. "Liar."

Kerry shrugged slightly. "It's all right." She forced herself not to think about the churning in her guts. Suddenly, she found her shoulders circled by Dar's arm, and her senses were barraged by the abrupt closeness and warmth as Dar pulled her close in a hug. A voice whispered into her ear, and it took her long seconds to acknowledge the words.

"If I get too obnoxious, slap me."

Kerry felt some of the tension seep out of her as she circled Dar's waist with an arm and squeezed. "All right, I will," she promised, releasing her and swatting her lightly on the butt. "Right there. Deal?"

"Deal." Dar let go of her as Mark and Brent came around the side of the car again, carrying the equipment. "Soon as the others get here, we move."

A fusillade of gunshots made them all jump. "Holy shit." Mark backed against the car. "Is that for us?"

"War games." Dar peered over the hood of the Lexus. "We got lucky again."

"Lucky?" Kerry winced as she heard an echoing boom. She edged a little closer to Dar and peered behind her to where Andrew was just haphazardly parking her car's larger cousin. It was still overcast, and the air was thick with moisture. She sniffed at the wind. And thick with what smelled like gunpowder. "Those aren't real bullets, are they?"

"Sure," Dar replied. "But don't worry. Everyone will be participating, or watching, or keeping the hell out of the way. We can get in and get out and not attract attention." Unanticipated, but Dar wasn't a person who argued with good luck when it happened to thump down on top of her head. Things had been strained enough lately; a little smooth sailing was definitely called for.

"Ah." Kerry frowned. "Well, as long as we stay inside. I'm allergic to bullets." A group chorus of deep, male chanting carried over. "Mm...way too mucho macho for *moi.*"

The rest of the group came over and gathered around them. "All right," Dar spoke. "We're heading for the administration building, over there. It should be pretty much empty." She glanced around, seeing that most of the area was, in fact, pretty much empty.

Kerry shouldered one of the portable scopes. "I'll take Mark to the telecom center," she offered. "I remember where it is, and

I've got my badge, still." She displayed it. "He can hook up there and control the network."

Mark looked up. "Brent, you and Josh come with us. Bring that cable kit, willya?"

Dar nodded. "Okay, the rest of you come with me to the computer center. Bring that array and the black box," she said. "Dad, go along with Kerry. She's headed toward the ops center, and there might be people around."

Andrew regarded her thoughtfully. "All right," he drawled after a moment.

"If anyone questions you," Dar told them seriously, "just tell them you're doing your job, and refer them to me, understand?" She made eye contact with the techs. "Don't act like you're not supposed to be here, got it?"

"Got it," Mark assured her.

"Captain, you come with me." Dar squared her shoulders and started to lead them toward the building.

The group sorted themselves out and followed her. Dar took the few moments of peace to run her plan through her mind again, checking the details and making sure she knew what she was going to do once they got to the computer center. After a few strides, she realized she had a diminutive shadow. "Thought you'd go with Dad."

Ceci rubbed the side of her nose. She and Andrew really hadn't talked about what they were going to do once they got to the base, but after Dar had told him to go with Kerry, it had seemed only natural that she— *What in the hell are you talking about, Cecilia? This isn't natural for you in any way!* "Well," Ceci glanced around, "I figured that if you ran into any trouble, I'd just tell them that I'm your mother, and I said it was all right."

Dar's eyes perceptibly widened and went round. She gave the two techs a startled look, grateful they hadn't heard.

Or, at least, they were pretending very hard not to have heard. She lowered her voice. "W...what?"

Ceci smothered a grin, and shrugged. "It always worked when you were a kid," she explained soberly. "Those Marines usually recognized my authority a lot faster than their CO's."

Dar felt a blush coming on, and she hoped her employees wouldn't notice. Having her mother along wasn't something she'd figured into her battle plans. She sighed. Not that Ceci wasn't right, she grudgingly admitted, remembering many a time when only her mother's intervention had saved her from fates worse than death. Like cleaning the recruits' latrine.

Dar felt her nose wrinkle in remembered disgust. "Good

point," she finally said aloud. "Maybe you better write me up an admin pass while you're at it."

They climbed the stairs, and one of the techs scurried forward and opened the door, holding it courteously as the rest of them approached. Resting a hand on the doorsill, Dar paused and looked around.

No Marine. She wondered about that. Hadn't there always been a guard at this door? It seemed very quiet, though, and after a moment she shook her head and continued inside the building. *It's been years, Dar. They could have changed a procedure or two.*

The door closed behind them, its metal lock clicking home with an exaggerated sound that echoed slightly in the empty hall.

Kerry walked next to Andrew, one hand nervously running up and down on the strap of the scope she carried. So far, they hadn't seen anyone on their walk to the telecom center, and she was trying to decide if that was good or if would be better for them to meet the first potential objector instead of anticipating it.

Not that she was all that worried, not with Andrew strolling beside her, his long and somewhat rolling stride making her lengthen her own steps a little to keep up. She had no doubt her father-in-law could handle whatever uniformed minion got in their path, but still...

She looked around. It was creepy. "Is it usually this quiet?" She finally voiced her worry aloud, seeing from Mark's quick look he'd been thinking the same thing. "I remember it being a lot busier the last time I was here."

Andrew regarded the hallway, then turned and walked backward for a few steps, his pale eyes flicking over every inch of the painted wooden walls and the studiously polished tile floors. He reversed himself again and continued forward. "Well," he paused, "Admin's usually emptier than a sack of sand with a wet bottom on the weekend."

"Kinda like our office," Mark supplied.

"Yep," the ex-SEAL agreed. "Usually a body or two more 'round hereabouts, though." He glanced down an offshoot corridor. "Figure everyone's out watching the pups."

"Pups?" Mark asked.

Brent, walking beside him, was listening intently but pretending not to. He hadn't said a word since they'd left the office, and Kerry found herself wondering again why he was there. She glanced at the shorter man's face, and just then he looked up, and their eyes met. It only lasted an instant, then Brent jerked his head forward.

Kerry had felt the icy coldness behind his eyes, though, and she drew in a faintly unsteady breath.

"Got a couple of new SEAL teams goin' through some situations," Andrew said. "That's what's all going on outside."

The door to the telecom room loomed up, and Kerry tried the latch. She was surprised to find it open, and she looked over her shoulder at Andrew in question. "That's pretty careless."

Andrew grunted and held the door open as the techs passed inside. "Y'all g'wan in there. I'll be right back." He let the door close, then turned and just stood for a moment in the hallway.

Listening.

They found their first two Navy personnel inside the computer center. Dar pushed the door open and stuck her head inside, giving the two console operators a nod as they looked up in surprise. "Afternoon."

One had been on duty the day she and the chief had tangled, and that one stood up as Dar entered. "Ms. Roberts—"

Dar held a hand up. "We're just collecting some data." She waved the woman back to her seat. "Relax."

"B—" the woman protested.

"You're not going to ask me for authorization, are you?" Dar swiveled and gave her a patented glare.

"No, ma'am, I'm not, but—"

"Great." Dar continued toward the console and sat down in front of it, eyeing her arm in irritation.

The console operator opened her mouth, then closed it and gave her companion a little shrug. The male sailor also shrugged and shook his head.

Dar leaned on the console and scanned the screen. "Hook that up to the aux port," she absently directed the shorter tech, a young man with curly red hair and russet freckles sprinkled over half his face. "I want it direct."

"Yes, ma'am," the tech replied quietly. "We do have the net direct card in it."

"I know." Dar hunted and pecked, scowling. "I don't want it addressable," she answered, cursing silently at the length of time it was taking her to set up the program she wanted. After a moment more, she gave up and unhooked the sling holding her arm close to her body and removed it, laying it over her thigh.

Ow. Whether from lack of use or her injury, it was hard to tell, but her muscles were screaming as she flexed her injured arm.

Dar grimaced but kept up the motion, finally laying her forearm down on the console and using both hands to type. *Ow, ow ow. Son of a—* A glance up at her reflection in the screen showed a tense, drawn face looking back, and she paused, taking a deep breath and releasing it, trying to will the pain away.

Stupid damn arm, her mind muttered in disgust. *Stupid damn Chuck and his stupid damn bat and his stupid parochial macho ego.* The jolts of pain went down her shoulder and all the way into her fingers, so intense it almost made her sneeze.

It was hard to keep her mind focused with all that. She had to retype the same line twice and then reenter a parameter before she finally had things set up the way she wanted them. It was a simple program, really—just a looping bit of code that would transfer the contents of the base's main system to her storage box, sector by sector—at a machine level that would not allow for any interference in the copying from any high level security that might be running. Sort of like copying the encoded digital signal from a CD, rather than recording the sound as it was produced. She hoped that would protect the integrity of the data. Any attempt at a simple copy could trigger God only knew what, if someone really knew what they were doing and had protection in place. Dar was surprised, actually, that her previous intrusions hadn't been detected and objected to. She'd figured that either meant whoever was doing this wasn't as good as she was—or the person was a lot better.

Dar sighed and hit enter. She wished she knew which it was, remembering a time when considering anyone to be "better" was an alien thought to her. Another sigh. God, she'd been such a cocky son of a bitch.

She moved slightly, and a shot of pain made her suck in her breath and hold it, her eyes blinking away the sudden tears. Dar realized the painkillers she'd taken before they'd left were wearing off. *Shit.*

C'mon, Dar. You used to just work past this, remember? For a moment, she just closed her eyes and concentrated, allowing the ache to become something she could handle and put into the background of her conscious mind. It took a little longer than it used to, but after a bit she was able to start breathing normally, and let her eyes open, focusing on the screen and the task before her.

Okay. I can do this. Her mind cleared, and she started typing again. Logic strings emerged grumpily from long unused memory cells, but it only took two or three tries before she had a relatively working loop going. "Okay." She glanced at the tech kneeling nearby. "Ready?"

The redhead looked up at her confidently. "Ready, ma'am."

Dar hit the enter button. For a moment, she thought she'd screwed up the program, then the screen flickered and started scrolling a hexadecimal display with commendable obedience. *Whew.*

"Wow." The tech watched, evidently impressed. "You did that on the fly?"

Dar shrugged modestly. She was aware of the Navy console operators watching over her shoulder with interest. One whistled under their breath. Dar rested her chin on her hand and wished herself elsewhere.

"'Scuse me." Ceci's voice came closer. "Here." The older woman put something down on the console, then rested a hesitant hand on Dar's shoulder. "They were out of Evian."

Dar eyed the cute container of MacArthur Dairy chocolate milk and found herself smiling. God, her mother had always hated her constant consumption of this stuff. "Guess I didn't turn into a chocolate cow after all, huh?"

"No," Ceci said. "All those sleepless nights worrying about you keeling over from scurvy, wasted."

Dar half turned and glanced up. "Did you? Really worry about that?"

Ceci studied her daughter's tense face. "Yeah," she admitted quietly. "I worried about you all the time, for a lot of reasons." She paused. "I guess I shouldn't have."

Dar thought about that, then she shrugged a little. "Maybe it's a mother thing."

One pale eyebrow lifted. "It sort of grows on you after a while," Ceci said. "Surprises the hell out of me sometimes."

Dar grinned slightly. "I bet."

Her mother chuckled with a hint of wry humor. "I've got some ibuprofen. Interested?"

Dar nodded in thinly disguised relief. "Thanks." She accepted the handful of small pills and opened her milk, washing down the painkillers and drinking the cold, sweet liquid with a feeling of pure relief. The program was running, transferring the information to her secured storage at a very good rate, she had ibuprofenn, she had chocolate milk—things were looking up.

The only thing she was missing at the moment was...

"Dar." Kerry's voice made her look up and spot her lover coming in the door. "Mark's having trouble syncing the circuit. He wants to know if you know anything odd about the data rate."

Ah. Dar leaned on the console and regarded the blond woman. Kerry's brows were creased and her pale hair was messed, apparently from her running her hands through it. Definitely a sign of her lover being a little distraught. "Nothing concrete. He want me to go take a look?"

Kerry came up to her and leaned on the console, peeking at the screen before answering. "He didn't say that, just wanted to know if you had any hints."

One of Dar's eyebrows lifted. "He couldn't just call and ask?"

"Um." Kerry fiddled with a button on her shirt, then peeked up from under pale lashes. "He didn't want to chance the cell?"

"Uh-huh. And he had to send you to ask?"

Kerry's lips tensed, masking a smile. "I volunteered."

Ah. Dar felt an absurd contentedness. Kerry had come to check up on her. Mom was bringing her milk. Next thing she knew, she'd be in a rocker with someone putting a shawl over her shoulders. "Tell him to try an extended packet size on TCP/IP—look for an added four-byte segment."

"Oh." Kerry got up. "Okay, I'll go tell him. Thanks, Dar." She started for the door, but paused as she heard Dar get up to follow her. They walked together past the consoles and edged out into the hallway.

"Everything else going all right?" Dar asked in a low voice. "We've got the transfer going here, Ker. I estimate another twenty minutes, and we'll be done."

Kerry looked up and down the hallway. "I don't know. This place is giving me the creeps today, Dar. Dad went off a little while ago, and he hasn't come back yet. It's just too quiet."

"Yeah." Dar exhaled. *Okay, so maybe she didn't come to check on me.* "Maybe he's just scoping the place out. He knows his way around, and he can take care of himself, so there's no point in worrying about that."

"Hmm." Kerry folded her arms. "Any sign of that petty person?"

"No," Dar stated. "No sign of just about anyone, except for the two console ops in there. Everyone else must be watching the war games."

"Mm." Kerry murmured again under her breath. "You okay?" she finally asked. "You took your sling off."

"Had to type," Dar explained. "I'm all right. It's just sore."

Kerry once again looked up and down the hallway, then she leaned foreword and very gently kissed Dar's injured shoulder. "Be careful." One hand lifted and rubbed Dar's belly. "I worry about you."

And then she turned and strode back down the hallway, the twitch of her shoulders indicating her awareness of Dar's watching eyes.

Which weren't precisely on her shoulders, despite the situation and the ache in her arm, and the worries that were now running through her mind. *Boy.* Dar couldn't help the observation: *she's got a sexy walk.* It had a little swagger to it, a gentle roll to her hips and a muscular strength that Dar found very, very attractive. She watched her lover until she turned a corner at the far end of the corridor, then she sighed and returned to the ops center.

"Ms. Roberts?" The console operator stepped into her path. "Are you part of this exercise, ma'am? I was just wondering…We weren't told to expect you, and Dave and I figured you got stuck in just for a challenge. Are we right?"

Exercise? Dar stopped and eyed her warily. "Are you talking about the war games?"

The Navy tech exchanged glances with her partner. "It's not a war game, really. It's a security drill," she replied. "You mean you didn't know?"

"Security drill? At the gate they told us it was a SEAL exercise," Dar stated. "Graduation for some new teams."

The sailor named Dave got up and trotted over. "Well, yeah, but they're graduating from the Urban Warfare School," he explained eagerly. "They've got to counteract a terrorist infiltration of a critical operations center."

"Crit—" Dar glanced around. "You mean here? This is the target?"

The woman tech nodded. "Yeah, we were expecting the terrorists. We thought you were them when you came in, but then we fi—"

The door slammed open with a loud bang, and the room suddenly filled with grungy-looking men in green-and-brown fatigues. "Don't move! Don't move!" the one in the lead screamed, brandishing an M16. "Get back against the wall, you pigs!"

Dar felt the situation explode out of control with frightening speed. Two of them men rushed at her and grabbed her arms, causing her to let out a startled yell of anger and pain. "Cut that out!"

The man on her left slammed her against the wall and leaned against her. "Shut up! Shut up, or we'll kill you!"

Dar struggled out of pure panicked instinct, wrenching her body around and shoving off from the wall, throwing her surprised attackers back as she twisted, ignoring the pain. One grabbed for her again and she swiveled, lashing out with a kick that caught him in the gut as she tried to move away from the second one.

Something exploded against her head, and she was barely aware of slamming against the wall as her knees buckled and darkness quickly overcame the stars in her vision. She was unconscious before she hit the ground.

Chapter
Fifteen

Kerry was aware of every creak of wood and every scuff of her boots against the tiled floor as she walked down the hallway. The atmosphere was getting creepier and creepier every second, and she had to keep herself from looking around nervously as she walked.

C'mon, Kerry, she finally told herself in irritation. *Stop acting like a terrorist is going to jump out of every doorway.*

As she passed the next one, a shadow shifted and suddenly engulfed her. Kerry reacted by letting out a yell, which was half muffled as a hand clapped itself over her mouth and strong hands grabbed her.

"Hey...hey...kumquat...relax." Andrew's voice almost made her go completely limp. "Stop that hollerin', willya?" Cautiously, the ex-SEAL released his hold and looked anxiously at her. "You ain't hurt, are you?"

"No." Kerry leaned against him in relief. "Sorry, this place is just making me nuts. Where've you been?"

Andrew awkwardly patted her back. "Just checking things. Somethin' ain't right here. Saturday's quiet, but not like this is."

"So I'm not just imagining things?" Kerry said. "Okay, let me go tell Mark what Dar said to do, then we can come back here and see if we don't want to just cut this all short." Kerry started down the hall with Andrew ambling along beside her with his loose, powerful stride. "What do you think is going on?"

"Ah do not know." Andrew's head was swiveling back and forth, watching everything. "Haven't found anybody t'ask." He glanced at her. "Dardar all right?"

Kerry looked behind her. "I think so," she answered. "She

seems okay. Tired, though. I think her arm's hurting."

"Aw." Andrew patted her shoulder. "She's a tough kid. Don't you worry."

"That's true." Kerry sighed. "I just wish this was over—Hey!" She found herself suddenly grabbed and yanked back into a doorway, with a large, warm hand covering her mouth.

"Hush," Andrew barely whispered. "Don't you move none."

Kerry nodded in understanding and stayed perfectly still. The doorway in which they were standing was dark, and she could almost feel the shadows reaching around her, but she couldn't hear anything, and she wondered what, exactly, they were hiding from.

Then she saw the soft, gray, almost indistinguishable reflection on the tile floor, inching toward the gap where the door met the hallway. She strained her ears, but she still couldn't hear anything, though she could see that tiny shadow moving closer and closer. Puzzled, she looked up at Andrew's face, able to see only the utter stillness there, save for the faint flaring of his nostrils.

The shadow slipped closer and closer, and Kerry felt her breathing increase. She glued her eyes to the edge of the doorway and almost jumped when the edge of a rifle barrel cut the straight line. *Oh, my God.* Kerry clamped her jaw shut so her teeth wouldn't chatter. She felt Andrew's body shift behind her and sensed the tension that came into the arms he had wrapped loosely about her.

The barrel moved forward, further away from the door than she'd first thought, and now the hands and body of its wielder came into view. It was a young man of medium height, dressed in fatigues, his eyes flicking nervously up and down the hallway.

Surely, Kerry's mind screamed, surely he'd look right at her.

But he didn't. He kept going, and before she could relax, another man edged into view, moving with careful silence. This man was taller and thinner and had a scruffy beard. Then more of them moved past—six or seven in all, Kerry had lost count—before the last one, a huge bear of a man, crept past. They were wearing backpacks, and their clothes had a well-used air about them. Kerry's nose twitched as the scent of gun oil came to her.

Andrew waited almost an entire minute before he eased past Kerry and very slowly edged his head around the doorway. Then he relaxed and scowled. "What in hell's that all about?"

"I don't know, but it was seriously creepy," Kerry told him, peering down the now empty hallway. "Hey, maybe they're Cuban terrorists!"

Andrew allowed a tiny snort of laughter to emerge. "Not

hardly," he said. "C'mon, kumquat, let's get us back to that there closet. I figger we'll find out what's up soon enough."

Ain't that the truth. Kerry shook her head, and they started down the hallway. She'd taken maybe ten paces before she stopped dead, a fist clenching her heart. "Oh." A sense of panic filled her and she turned, evading Andrew's outstretched hand as she launched into a headlong run.

There was a moment's frozen silence. Then the lead terrorist pulled the wool mask off his face. "Shit," he panted hoarsely. "It's a civ!"

Ceci, frozen in shock for several long heartbeats, now surged into motion. She ducked between two of the men and shoved a third out of the way. "You stupid pigheaded son of a bitch clueless useless excuse for jarhead buttholes." She dropped to her knees beside Dar's very still, slumped figure. "I should pull your damn privates off." Anxiously, she touched her daughter's face, which was pale and relaxed.

"Shit," the lead terrorist said. "What do we do, Sarge?"

The second man who had come in fingered his rifle. "Just stay where you are. We've got our orders."

"What?" the man who'd taken his mask off objected. "Are you crazy? This ain't part of the orders. This is a fucking civ!"

"You don't know that," the sergeant snapped back. "What if they are? They could be part of the gig, you know that. They said there'd be something unexpected. This is it. So shut up and just go over there." He turned and looked at the rest of the room. "You all just sit your asses still and keep your mouths shut."

"Dar?" Ceci patted Dar's cheek gently. "Hey, Dardar?" The pet name felt strange on her lips, but she ignored that. "C'mon, kid, open your eyes, hmm?"

For a far too long instant there was no response. Ceci patted Dar's cheek again, and this time her daughter's eyelids fluttered in reaction, sliding half-open to expose dazed, pale blue orbs. Much to her consternation, Ceci found herself babbling in near panic. "Hey, munchkin, c'mon...you okay?" The eyes tracked to her and fastened on her face, then blinked and opened a little further. "Dar?"

"Urmf." It felt like a building had fallen in on top of her. She just wanted to let her eyes close and go back to sleep. It was quieter there, and it hurt a hell of a lot less. But someone was shaking her, and she had a sneaking suspicion it was her mother, who would just keep on shaking.

Always had.

"Okay." Dar fended off the prodding. "Okay...okay...I'm awake...Jesus..." She squeezed her eyes shut, then opened them fully, blinking until her mother came fuzzily into focus. Her face was suddenly cupped between Ceci's hands, and she could feel the tremor in them. A faint, but distinct feeling of surprise filtered through her admittedly half-conscious mind.

"Here, see if you can sit up," Ceci urged. "I think the brainless wood chip back there just clipped you."

The terrorists were nervously deploying around the room and had herded the two console operators over in the corner where Dar and Ceci were. They hadn't yet seen Dar's two techs, who were prudently hiding behind the large twin drive arrays from which Dar had been transferring data.

Okay. Dar managed to get upright and took stock of herself and the situation. Her head hurt like hell. Her arm hurt worse. Her dignity was screaming in mortal agony. Her mother, for God's sake, was petting her like a kitten.

Jesus! What the hell could happen next?

A wild yell punctured the room, and the door was flung open. The terrorists whirled and brought their guns up, screaming warnings as a disheveled blond figure stumbled into the room, looking around frantically. The man closest to the door leaped at her only to be intercepted by a tall, menacing shadow that grabbed him, disarmed him, and tossed him against the wall in one long, sweeping motion.

"Awright," Andrew's voice boomed out. "Y'all stay still, or figgure yourself Swiss cheese." With a solid, scary sound, he cocked the big black shotgun the man had been carrying, then lifted it and aimed it at the biggest guy there, a man half again his weight but about the same height as he was.

"Dar!" Kerry bolted for her.

Oh. Dar's tired mind sighed. *That's what could happen next. Do yourself a favor, Dar. Don't imagine anything else.*

"Tell me again what this all is?" Andrew stood, with his hands on his hips, glaring at the hapless leader of the "terrorists." "Them people out there sent you all in here?"

"Look, sir." The bear-like soldier had both hands empty and held out in abject defense. "It's the training exercise. They told us to come in here and take hostages." He looked around. "We came in here and took hostages. They weren't supposed to fight back."

Andrew's eyes narrowed. His voice lowered in pitch. "You

saying it was my kid's fault she got hurt?"

"N...no, sir." The soldier shook his head. "I'm saying we got surprised, and Niles over there got kicked in a place that really needs ice, if you know what I mean."

Andrew threw a glance at the tallest soldier, who grimaced and crossed his legs gingerly. "What comes next?" he asked, though he had a pretty good idea. "Them youngsters outside come git you?"

The man nodded. "We're assigned to hold them off. I've got explosives and extra ammo in those packs. We're supposed to blockade the room and maintain a defensive perimeter." He hesitated. "Sir, they told us they were going to throw in some unexpected things. I thought..." He glanced over to where the rest of the "hostages" were seated. "I thought they were part of it."

"Uh-huh." Andrew gave him a very disapproving glare. "Well, I'm fixing to end this here exercise right quick. Don't you go nowhere." He shouldered the shotgun and turned toward the door, only pausing when he heard Dar's cell phone ring. "Now what?"

"I'll get that." Kerry slid the phone out of the holder clipped at Dar's waist and opened it. "Yes?"

I can answer my own phone. Dar protested, but the words never emerged, and she was content merely to listen. It was easier to think that way.

"Mark...Mark...wait...slow down." Kerry's voice sharpened and took on urgency. "Hold on...ho—What?"

"Give me that." Dar took the phone from her and listened to the chaotic sounds from the other side. She let out a yell. "MARK!" The chaos continued, then subsided.

"Boss...boss...this place is going nuts. We gotta get outta here," Mark yammered. "Some half-ass wackos came into that com center and trashed it! We hid in the punch down closet." His voice went muffled. "Get down, Brent. You fucking jerk, get your fucking head down before I kick it off!"

Ah. Dar took a breath. *He's learning my management style.* "Mark, calm down. Were these military guys? They've got some war game crap going on in here."

"I don't know what the fuck they were." Mark sounded unusually panicked. "They had guns, Dar. They fucking shot the Ethernet hub."

Dar frowned and glanced up at Andrew, who had crossed over to kneel at her side. "Are they supposed to be firing live rounds?"

"Hell, no." Andrew removed a shotgun shell from the gun he was carrying and showed it to her. "Dummies."

"Can dummies blow holes in electronic equipment?"

"No way." The terrorist leader had also come over. "We're not supposed to break anything—in fact, my CO told me if I dented any of these machines, he'd take 'em out of my paycheck for the next twenty years."

What the hell was going on? "Mark, stay right where you are," Dar ordered into the phone. "Don't take any chances. If those idiots are shooting real bullets, you three stay put until we figure out what the deal is."

Andrew nodded. "Good idea."

"Yeah." The terrorist scratched his jaw and agreed.

There was a scuffle, then the sound of a slamming door, and it got more or less quiet. "Okay," Mark panted. "We're in here, but let me tell you, boss, I'm bucking for a bonus after this."

Dar let her breath out with a soft grunt. "You'll get it." She folded the phone and let it drop onto her thigh as her eyes lifted to Andrew's. "Dad, what the hell is this?"

"Maybe it's a mistake," the terrorist leader offered. "I don't think they really shot anything up, ma'am."

Kerry shook her head. "No. The man on the other end of that phone isn't someone who makes things up or panics for no reason," she disagreed, putting a hand on Dar's forearm. "If he says they were shooting, they were."

Ceci cleared her throat. "Does that mean they're coming here next?"

Everyone exchanged glances. "Well..." The burly terrorist hesitated. "We're their target, so yeah, I guess."

"If they're shooting real bullets, that could be a problem."

Andrew scrubbed a hand across his face. "Lord," he sighed. "Ain't this a mess. I think we'd better all just get on out of here, Dardar. Pick up your gear, and let's move." He touched Dar's lower leg. "Need to get you back to where Dr. Steve can take a peek at that skull."

Dar had to admit that was probably a good idea. The spot where she'd been hit felt hot and swollen, and it ached. Kerry had found a large bruise spreading down her neck, and with everything else that had happened, even Dar couldn't argue with being on the safe side. "Okay." She glanced at her redheaded tech. "Is that download done?" Doug, his name was, if she recalled.

"Almost," Doug replied.

"Dar, forget it," Kerry urged gently. "Let's just get out of here. It's not worth risking you." She could see the unevenly dilating pupils in Dar's eyes and guessed she had a concussion. It was all too much, and she found their jobs counting for less and less as each minute went on. "C'mon."

For a moment, she thought Dar was going to refuse. The blue eyes studied her face quietly, searching it intently before Kerry saw the surrender, then the faint nod of agreement. Dar handed her the cell phone. "I'll tell Mark to sneak out and meet us in the parking lot."

Ceci stood up and let Andrew get around next to Dar, gently helping her up. She had put the sling back on her daughter's arm with surprisingly little resistance, and now Dar accepted Andrew's assistance with the same silent gratitude.

Frankly, that scared the poo out of Ceci. The only time she'd ever seen Dar meekly submitting to this kind of babying was when she'd been really, really hurt. That broken leg, she recalled, was the last time, when the sixteen year-old Dar had huddled in Andrew's arms, trying very hard not to cry as he carried her into the hospital.

Leaving, she decided, was a very good idea. "All right, let's go." She started to lead the way toward the door when it was abruptly thrust inward and Chief Daniel entered, slamming it behind her. "Ah."

"I knew I shouldn't have trusted you." Daniel pointed at Dar, so angry she was almost spitting. "Went right to your buddy and told him, didn't you?"

Dar stared at her. "No. We didn't tell anyone here." She glanced over to where the JAG officer had been crouched, then realized he was gone. "Wh—"

"Someone did," the chief spat. "'Cause they're coming through this place and wrecking everything they can get their hands on." She turned and looked at the terrorists. "You better get your asses out of here, because they're on the way. Unless you want to end up looking like hamburger, get lost."

They heard a crunching sound, from not far away.

"Too late fer that," Andrew stated quietly. "Looks like we got us a problem."

Ceci watched the men in fatigues move cabinets in front of the door. "Should we call the cops? Andy, this is getting out of hand." She was standing behind Dar, who was seated again at the console, laboriously pecking at the keyboard with a single index finger.

"Don't got time," her husband replied as he hopped up onto a desk and peered out through the glass panels that topped the wall separating them from the hallway. "Cops gotta come down from

Largo, anyhow. They get a lick of traffic, might as well ferget it."

"So what are we doing?" Ceci knew she sounded nervous, but the loud noises of destruction were coming closer, and she had a lot of things to worry about in the room. Andrew, for one, who tended to believe in his own indestructibility.

"'Specting us to hold em off, so that's what we're gonna do," Andrew replied. "Give 'em 'nough trouble to make 'em run off somewheres else."

Chief Daniel snorted. "This is where they want to be." She pointed at the mainframes. "They won't leave those standing."

The leader of the terrorist SEALs glanced between Andrew and the chief, obviously confused. "Ma'am, just what the hell's going on here?"

"You don't want to know," the chief told him point blank. "Because if you did, you'd have to spend the next ten years in some admin's office doing paperwork on it, got me?" She looked around the room and shook her head. "We can't hold this place."

"Sure we can," Andrew disagreed. "Just need us some unconventional ammo, that's all." He looked over to see Kerry crouched next to Dar, ostensibly watching the screen, but with her attention obviously focused on her injured friend. "What you got in them guns, paint?"

The lead terrorist nodded, then jumped as they heard the distinct sound of bodies thumping against the wall in the hallway. "Here they come."

"All right." Andrew pointed. "Ceci, get down behind that there cabinet. Take the kids with you."

Dar and Kerry exchanged glances, then looked at Ceci. "Kids?" Kerry objected, but got up to move anyway. "Come on, Dar."

"In a minute," Dar replied absently, typing in a final command. "This is almost done."

"Dar." Kerry heard the crackle of a megaphone outside. "Now, please?" She tugged very gently on her lover's uninjured arm.

"You there inside," a voice boomed out. "We know you've got hostages. If you know what's good for you, let them go."

Dar reluctantly got up and joined Kerry and her mother behind the big computer consoles, where Doug and his co-worker were also crouched. She took out her cell phone and opened it, redialing Mark's number.

"You stay where you are, or these guys get it," the terrorist leader recited dutifully. "I got women in here, and I'll waste 'em."

Andrew gave him a look.

"That's what they told us to say, sir," the man rumbled apologetically. He deployed his men to either side of the doorway and told them to keep down. "They're going by the plan, too. You sure this isn't just part of the exercise?"

At that instant, the lights went off. A thick, dark silence fell over the room as the air conditioning stopped and the computers shut down in a sad, dying whirr of fans.

"Note to self." Dar's voice cut through the gloom. "Recommend independent UPS systems."

"Jesus," Kerry whispered.

"Doug, disconnect the box, and pull it over toward me," Dar said quietly.

"Yes, ma'am."

Andrew blinked, then blinked again to see if that would help him see anything in the darkened room. No such luck. His mind ran through the possibilities and didn't much like any of them. "Figure they're gonna toss something through them there winders next," he muttered.

"Gas? Yeah," the terrorist leader agreed softly. "We got masks."

"Not enough of 'em." Andrew let his eyes close as he stood up. "Stay here. You hear something, get down."

"Yes, sir."

Doug crept across the tile floor dragging the big box. "Okay, here it is, ma'am."

Dar felt the equipment, making sure the cover was tightly on and the back ports were secured. She thought a minute, then felt around her until her hand touched a box of fanfold paper intended for the big line printer nearby.

As is always the case with computer paper, it was nearly empty. Dar inverted it and slid it down over her black box. Then she sat down comfortably on top of it and exhaled. "Okay. Whatever happens, keep your heads down and don't move."

In the darkness, she felt Kerry nestle closer to her, pressing their bodies together and sliding a hand to curl around Dar's thigh.

"You've got one chance to come out," the voice boomed.

Dar heard a slithering sound nearby, and something that sounded like dead fish being slapped on a dock. "Dad?"

"Hush." Andrew's voice echoed softly. "Just you stay down."

"We are," Kerry whispered back. "What are you doing?"

"Never you mind, kumquat. Just stay put, and keep yer head low."

"I'm warning you!" their terrorist called. "You do anything, I start shooting in here, and I won't care what I hit!" A few whispered orders followed, and the shuffling, very faint, of booted feet. "We got gas masks, so don't bother trying anything, not unless you want these hostages gassed!"

"Didn't know they were selecting them for intelligence this year," Ceci muttered under her breath. "Nice."

"Mom." Dar bit back a smile, invisible as it was.

"Yeah, yeah, I know, they only pick SEALs who are smart enough to save the teams' asses."

"Don't none of you be standing 'fore that door there," Andrew rumbled softly.

The SEAL team leader stepped a pace closer. "You sure this isn't just reg stuff, sir? They're going right by the plan so far."

"Ah don't know," Andrew replied. "But I am not taking chances with mah wife and my kids in here. Them folks had best hope they come in with them little paint balls and a lot of hollerin', and not with anything worse, or it's gonna get messy."

A loud thump was heard. Then there was silence. Everyone waited, sweating in the motionless air.

Then everything happened at once. The top windows blew in, and hard, round things entered, bouncing off surfaces with wild abandon. That was followed by a very strange noise, like an overshaken soda can being popped.

An acrid smell began to fill the room, then stopped as an indescribable noise started and the stink was replaced with a second overwhelming scent, this one chemical.

Dar wrapped her good arm around Kerry and ducked her head as popping noises started and a crash came from the front door. She could sense things happening around her, but the sounds didn't evoke any logic, and the smell of smoke and sweat and chemical made her queasy.

Now men were yelling. The attacking SEALs poured in the door, and the explosive sound of guns firing filled the room. Tiny red tracers raced everywhere, dotting the walls and floor; then the yells turned to hollering as the odd noise returned, along with a loud whoop Dar recognized as her father.

"What in the hell is he doing?" Dar hissed to Ceci.

"You're asking me?" her mother hissed back. "You're the one who checked out the entire *Jane's* weapons series from the library, remember?"

"Son of a bitch!" A yell rose up. "What the fuck!"

Now the noise sounded more like cattle being herded into a pen, one filled with Jell-O. Dar could hear bodies colliding, and the chemical smell became almost overwhelming. Then she heard something behind them.

Boots. Shuffling. The cocking of a shotgun.

Instinctively, Dar grabbed hold of Ceci and Kerry and pulled them all down to the floor, ignoring the pain in her arm as the world exploded behind her. She felt the shudder in the equipment they were leaning against, then heard a grunt, another cocking, and pressed her body against the floor.

Another shot. Pieces of plastic showered over them. The shouting continued on the other side of the room.

A red tracer danced lazily through the blackness.

Dar watched in stunned disbelief as it traveled over her chest and stopped. For a second, all she could hear was her own heartbeat turned into a thunder as her mind realized what was happening.

The shotgun cocked.

"Dad!" Dar let out a yell, knowing if she moved, she'd expose Kerry and her mother.

She closed her eyes.

Then there was a thud, and a curse, and the sound of something ripping.

Metal hitting flesh. Flesh hitting flesh.

An animal growl.

"All right." A commanding voice rose over the chaos. "Hold it! Everybody stand down!"

And then the lights came on.

"What in hell is going on in here?" A tall, burly man strode into the room and put his hands on his hips. "I thought I—Andy?"

Andrew dropped the arm he was holding and straightened from a crouch, turning to face the newcomer. "'Lo, Steve." His eyes anxiously checked the sprawl of bodies between the ruined computer consoles. "You all okay?"

Ceci squirmed out from under Dar's outstretched leg. "Fine."

Kerry didn't move an inch, preferring to remain where she was with both arms wrapped around her lover. "Yeah."

Dar grimaced, shifting her weight off her bad arm as she met her father's eyes. "Thanks."

Andrew nodded, then returned his attention to the newcomers. The SEALs, both protectors and attackers, were sprawled everywhere, fatigues in jungle pattern and black smeared with paint and a thick, glutinous coating that also covered the floor and was spattered on walls, consoles, equipment, and every other surface within the room.

Andrew let the end of the fire hose he'd been wielding drop off his shoulder, then he glanced down at his feet with a sense of tired disappointment. He reached out a sneakered foot, rolled over the slumped form dressed in similar black fatigues, and gently booted the rifle he'd taken from the attacker far out of range. "Damn."

"Holy shit." Steve Drake had picked his way over to where Andrew was standing. "What the hell's the CO doing here? Did you hit him? Why? What the hell are you doing here? Who—Hey, ain't that your little girl and the missus?"

"Steve," Andrew exhaled.

"What happened to these damn machines?" The SEAL commander turned and glared at the slowly disentangling team members. "I thought I told you people not to touch any of this—" Steve stopped talking as a large hand fit itself over his mouth.

"Hush," Andrew exhaled. "We got a lot to talk through. Get some medics in here first."

"But—"

Andrew's voice took on a crisp, stern quality. "Just do it."

Dar managed to push herself upright, hampered by both her arm and Kerry's tenacious hold on her. She let her head rest against the wreckage of the console and blinked. "Doug?"

"Just fine, ma'am." Doug and his companion crawled out from between the computer and the nearby wall. They were both covered in dust, but unharmed. "That other lady officer took off in the dark, though. I don't know what happened to her."

Several possibilities occurred to Dar and caused her to smile unpleasantly. She hurt too much to enjoy them, however. "Take the box and get outside. Mark's waiting for you. Get it into my car, and just get off base." She kept her voice low. "Move it."

Doug hesitated, then his freckled face scrunched into a grimace, and he nodded. "Yes, ma'am. Be careful." He and the other tech carefully uncovered the disk assembly and lifted it between them, then started to make their way quietly toward the door, dodging the cursing, slipping SEALs.

Kerry's eyes were on the still form at Andrew's feet. "You were wrong," she murmured.

"Yeah," Dar agreed sadly. "I guess I was. I was hoping I wasn't." She closed her eyes. "He was trying to use the exercise to cover wiping his tracks, I guess."

Kerry shook her head. "I don't get any of this. What about that petty person? Was she part of it, too? Is everyone in this place messed up, Dar?"

"I don't know," Dar answered. "I don't want to think about it right now." She let her eyes open and examine the hole in the console just opposite her. "I hate this."

"Well, hon, I don't think anyone would like being in a half-shot-up room full of fire retardant foam and cursing sailors," Kerry joked weakly. "I know I don't."

It was more like a bad dream. Dar felt a hurt beyond the physical as she considered the consequences of the day. *Never had to nail a friend, have you?* She accepted the self-acknowledgment with a bitter taste in her mouth. *It was sure easy enough for you to do this to some damn strangers, wasn't it, Dar? You used to laugh about it, remember?* It was true, she knew. She remembered exchanging bets with Duks on how many people she could nail at companies they consolidated. What was her record? Fifteen, wasn't it?

Her eyes went to the ceiling. Well, she had a job to do; after this, chips were going to fall where they fell, that's all. After all, there had been that laser scope on her chest, and now Dar had to face the possibility that given another few seconds, her family's "old friend" might have chosen to pull that trigger.

That close, with a shotgun. There was no doubt she would have died. It would have been a "mistake" during an exercise; that was all. Friendly fire. And civilians who had no authority to be where they'd been, anyway.

Dar's lips twitched. *Damn, life just really sucks sometimes.* She inhaled, then rolled her head to one side to meet Kerry's eyes. Had Kerry seen the scope? Did she know what almost happened? "You okay?"

"Me?" Kerry almost spluttered. "I'm perfectly fine, Dar. Can you stand up? I'd like to get the hell out of this room. The smell of that foam is making me sick."

No, Dar realized. She didn't know. After a moment's hesitation, she decided to save the news for later, when they were alone. "Sure. That's a good idea." She got her feet under her and slowly stood up. Kerry held onto her, for which she was glad, as a wave of dizziness nearly sent her right back down to the ground again. "Whoa."

"Easy." Kerry wrapped an arm firmly around her. "I got you."

Dar waited a moment for the buzzing to fade, then laid her arm across Kerry's shoulders and took a look around the room for the first time. "Holy shit," she blurted, shocked at the compound disaster the area had become.

"Leave it to your father." Ceci had come up on the other side. "He could do that to a perfectly clean carport, too." She looked up at Dar. "You doing all right?" There was a faint hesitance in her voice. "Or is the smell in here killing you as much as it is me?"

Dar felt sick to her stomach, and the pain in both her shoulder and head seemed to be getting worse. Or maybe it was just a combination of things. "It's pretty bad," she agreed. "We're going to get out of here."

"Good idea," Ceci remarked, noting but not commenting on the stark paleness of her daughter's face. "I'll walk out with you." She exchanged glances with Andrew, who nodded, a sober, very serious look on his face. After a moment's pause, she drew in a breath, then settled a hand firmly on Dar's back as they made their way slowly to the door.

Dar glanced to one side, then to the other, a dozen words of protest rising to her lips about this overly solicitous behavior. Then her stomach almost rebelled, making her glad of Kerry's grip, and she decided to make an exception.

Just this once.

Andrew watched his family leave, then turned back to his old friend, Steve Drake.

"So what's the deal, Big A?" Steve asked, folding his arms across his chest. "Better come up with something good 'fore Ainsbright wakes up and throws you in the brig." He glanced down. "Gonna be some pissed."

"Can't," Andrew replied. "I mustered out." His eyes fell on the still-unconscious form of the base commander. "You got medics coming? Ah think I might have busted something in there."

"Yep. On the way," Steve agreed. "You really retired? No shit?"

Andrew nodded. "Got me a nice, peaceful job watching out for mah damn kid." He shook his head. "This ain't a good day, Steve. We got some bad stuff going on here."

The big SEAL snorted. "Here? Nah. Nothin' ever goes on here, Andy. You know that better than most. It's so quiet, they picked this place to let us do our urban playpen weekend here."

Andrew shook his head, remembering those weekends.

"So, what are you gonna tell the heat when they get here? You gonna explain why a retired frogman's holed up inside an official Navy action area, spraying some poor kids with foam and whacking the hell all out of the base commander?"

"No," Andrew replied. "Ah am not going to explain it."

Steve cocked his head in a puzzled fashion.

There was a rifle lying near the wall. Andrew walked over and crouched next to it, examining the weapon with knowledgeable eyes. "C'mere." He waited for Steve to come over and kneel down. "This what you're arming with?"

A blink. "Hell, no," the SEAL commander said. "You know better."

Andrew nodded. "Yep." The rifle was a standard issue, old style M16 rifle, with a night scope attached. "Trouble is, what made them holes in them there pieces of machinery sure wasn't this here rifle." He turned and looked. "12 gauge Remington, I'm thinking."

Steve walked over and examined the holes. "Damn." He straightened. "None of my people were carrying those." He came back over. "Andrew, what is going on here?"

Andrew looked from the holes, to his old friend—now starting to groan—then to the rifle he'd taken from Jeff's hands and slammed against the wall. "Ah wish to hell I knew."

Kerry adjusted the passenger's seat back a little, watching Dar's eyes blink slowly in the midday sun. "You okay here, honey? Would the back seat be better?"

"No, this is fine," Dar murmured. "Feels better to be half sitting. I think if I laid flat, I'd end up chucking my guts all over your pretty new car."

"It's leather. It cleans." Kerry let her hand rest on Dar's thigh as she glanced around. Ceci had gone to get some water, and Mark had already left in Dar's car with the drive array box. It was sunny now, and peaceful out here in the parking lot, with a nice breeze blowing. Kerry felt a lot better, and she hoped that Dar did as well. "How are you doing?"

Dar tilted her head to one side and regarded her wryly. "I must be doing horrible."

Anxiously, Kerry clasped her fingers in her own. "Why? Does it hurt that bad?"

"No." The blue eyes twinkled, just a little. "It's the seventh time you've asked me in ten minutes," Dar said. "Am I turning green or something?"

"Psshst." Kerry had to laugh. "Sorry." She lifted Dar's hand and kissed it. "This was just a little too much, I think. My mind's going in a thousand different directions."

"Yeah." Dar pulled her closer into a hug and laid her cheek against Kerry's soft hair. She could feel warm breath through the fabric of her shirt as the smaller woman sighed. "You know what?"

"What?"

"I love you." Dar was mildly surprised at how easily that came to her lips now. She felt Kerry smile, and one of her arms snaked around Dar's waist, giving her a hug.

"I love you, too," Kerry murmured.

They stayed that way, even though Dar could see her mother's approach through the windshield. "Sorry I was such a raging bitch today," she said. "This didn't really go like I planned it."

"Oh." Kerry didn't budge. "You mean you didn't expect someone to suspect what we were up to and use a SEAL exercise to cover the destruction of all the evidence?"

"No."

"Tch. Bad Dar. No biscuit." Kerry squirmed a little closer. "You must be slipping." She felt the motion under her as Dar chuckled just a bit. "Your tummy's rumbling."

"Not from hunger," Dar sighed, as her mother rounded the door and paused, watching them bemusedly. "Hi."

"Is it ticking?" Ceci hazarded. "Here, drink some of this. I think it's safe. There's enough chlorine in it to kill anything nasty." She handed Dar a bottle she'd filled from the tap.

"Thanks." Dar accepted it and took a sip, licking her lips thoughtfully. "Mm. Tastes like home." She rolled a mouthful around and swallowed it, perversely enjoying the sharp tang of the minerals and chemicals infusing the tap water. "Nothing else tastes like it."

Kerry lifted her head and straightened, pulling the bottle over curiously and taking a sip.

She blinked, then spat it out immediately. "Yahh!"

Ceci and Dar both chuckled.

"Boy, is that ever an acquired taste." Kerry looked like she desperately needed something. *Like a drink of water.* "Good grief, Dar! How on earth could you drink that?"

Dar winced as a wave of nausea hit her. "I'm wondering that myself at the moment," she said. "Better step back, in case I lose what I just swallowed."

Kerry didn't move an inch. She took the bottle from Dar's hands and gently rubbed her forearm, caressing the warm, bare skin as she watched Dar close her eyes and lean back. "I think we'd better get going," she told Ceci. "Go on and get in. I'll drive over there, then run in and get Dad."

Ceci nodded. "Good idea." She opened the back door and climbed inside. "But you drive, I'll go fetch him." She watched Kerry carefully close the passenger side door, then jog around the front of the Lexus. Awkwardly, she patted Dar's arm very lightly.

"Hang in there, kiddo."

Hang in there. Dar swallowed, uncomfortably aware of the pain in her head and shoulder getting worse. "Do my best." Even the sound of Kerry's closing the door hurt. "Did Mark get that box?"

"He got it, honey." Kerry backed the car, then put it in gear and headed for the building. "Don't worry about that."

Okay. Dar closed her eyes and concentrated on taking shallow breaths. She didn't want to throw up. That would hurt. That would make her head hurt a lot worse than it did. It would also, the more ingenious part of her argued, ruin the new-car smell of Kerry's little blue buggy.

That would be bad.

She wouldn't get a biscuit.

Dar winced. Right now, the last thing on earth she wanted was a biscuit.

Chapter
Sixteen

Kerry rubbed her hands and settled back against the wall, crossing her arms as she watched Dr. Steve fussing over Dar. It was cold in the emergency room, and she found herself wishing she had a sweatshirt.

Actually, she wished she wasn't here at all, having to watch all the activity around Dar with a heavy, nervous knot in her stomach. Dr. Steve had taken one look at her lover and sent them both straight to the hospital, with him driving right behind them.

What was worse was that Dar hadn't protested. Even now, she was resting quietly on the padded rolling bed, with her eyes mostly closed as both doctor and nurses poked at her. That made Kerry realize whatever was wrong was serious, because otherwise she knew Dar would be pitching God's own fit.

She wondered how Andrew and Ceci were coping out in the waiting room, where they'd reluctantly retired to wait after Andrew had carried Dar inside, an image that had imprinted itself on Kerry's heart.

"Kerry?"

Kerry jumped, then focused on Dr. Steve's kindly face. "Oh, God. Sorry." She searched his eyes anxiously. "How's she doing?"

"I'm guessing she feels like the turd end of a pig in a bog right about now," the doctor told her. "She got herself real concussed there, and looks like she did more damage to her shoulder."

"Oh." Kerry's brow knit. "Is she going to be okay?"

Dr. Steve patted her cheek. "Eventually, sweetheart," he told her. "I need to get a CAT scan of that head, though. Would you mind going on in with her, just in case she realizes I've gone and stuck her inside a blinking white tube?"

"Sure." Kerry felt a little better. "Anything I can do to help."

The CAT scan room was a short elevator trip away, and Kerry spent the moments gently rubbing her lover's fingers as the blue eyes peered muzzily at her. "Hey, sweetie."

"Ow," Dar replied.

"I know." Kerry walked alongside the gurney as they exited the elevator and moved down the hallway. "Dar, honey, they need to take pictures of your head, okay?"

A groan.

"Yeah, I know, you hate that, but Dr. Steve really needs to see what's going on in there," Kerry told her. "So you just keep your eyes closed, and it won't be that long, I promise."

"Promise?" Dar mumbled.

"I promise," Kerry repeated, as they rolled over to the big machine. "Just keep your eyes closed, okay?"

"Okay," Dar agreed. "Just stay here with me."

Ooh. Kerry eyed the plethora of machinery, then her lover's pale face. "Don't worry, I will. I promise." She took hold of Dar's hand and squeezed into a corner, as much out of the way as she could manage.

The technician came over and glanced at her. "Ma'am, you can wait over there." He pointed toward a low bench, giving her a friendly smile.

Dar's fingers tightened on hers, and Kerry met the tech's eyes squarely. "No, I can't," she said. "My friend here is extremely claustrophobic and has a concussion. You don't want her freaking out."

The man glanced at Dar, then at Kerry. "Okay," he agreed cheerfully. "I can buy that. Just try to stay as clear of the machine as you can."

Kerry was pleasantly surprised by the easy capitulation. "Thanks." She relaxed. "I will."

The tech, a young blond-haired man about Kerry's age, expertly arranged Dar on the table and moved the machine to cover her. "Was she in a car accident?"

"Ah, no," Kerry replied. "She...um..." *Got hit in the head with a rifle? No, you can't say that.* "It's complicated."

"Okay." The tech signaled to his partner, who was behind a console. "Whatever you say. I never argue with a lady wearing two cell phones and three pagers."

Kerry glanced down at her belt, then felt herself blushing. "Ah, yeah." She heard the machine start humming and felt Dar's grip tighten painfully. "I'm carrying for both of us right now." She chafed Dar's fingers. "Easy, Dar, I'm here."

The grip lessened, just a trifle. "I'll always be here," Kerry whispered.

"Okay." Dr. Steve entered the emergency room alcove they'd been assigned. Andrew and Ceci were standing on one side of Dar's rolling bed, and Kerry was on the other, all of them attempting to comfort her. "Sweetie pie, you did quite a job on yourself."

Dar had her eyes open a little more now, having been pumped full of several syringes of things. "Yeah?"

"Yeah." Dr. Steve walked over and rested his hands on the bed. "I'm admitting you."

Dar grimaced.

"Ah, ah, ah." The doctor shook his finger at her. "It's all your own fault, young lady. If you'd have stayed at home and rested like I told you do, you'd still be there, and not here."

Dar's lips twitched into a scowl. "I had something I had to do," she protested tiredly.

"Uh-huh, and now what you have to do is spend some time in here, letting me fix you," Dr. Steve replied. "You have a concussion, honey, and there's some swelling in there because of that. You're not going anywhere until I'm sure that's gone." He touched the side of her head, which was dark with bruising. "And I'm calling in an orthopedic surgeon to look at your shoulder."

Dar's blue eyes popped wide open, but then, so did Kerry's, Ceci's and Andrew's. "What?"

Dr. Steve put a finger on Dar's nose. "What part of that wasn't in American English? Now you relax, and let them take you upstairs and get you comfortable." He patted his profoundly unhappy-looking patient's arm. "Don't give the nurses a hard time. I like the ones here, and you'll give me a bad name if you do." With that, he left, after giving Andrew a reassuring pat on the back.

"Shit," Dar exhaled.

"Now, Dardar." Andrew put a hand on her shoulder. "Just you relax, like Steve said, and get you some rest."

"In here?" Dar eyed the white ceiling. "Not likely."

Kerry actually smiled. "I never thought I'd be glad to hear you griping," she admitted. "But I know it means you feel better, so I am glad."

Dar eyed her. "Easy for you to say. You get to go home," she grumbled. "I have to stay here and be poked, prodded, messed with, and put up with God knows what."

Kerry exchanged glances with her in-laws. "Honey, I'm going to go give them your insurance card, okay?" she said diplomatically. "I'll be right back." She tweaked Dar's toe, then left, passing through the divider curtains and letting them fall closed behind her.

Dar closed her eyes and counted to twenty. Then she counted to twenty again. Then she opened her eyes and found she was still in the hallway, waiting to be shoved into the elevator. She closed her eyes again.

Dar didn't like frustration. She usually dealt with it in one of two ways: she got rid of it by getting rid of its source, or she went out and did something physical until the feeling of rage faded. At the moment, neither of those two options was available to her.

If she was being very honest with herself, it wasn't the hospital she hated. The gurney started into motion with a jerk, and she opened her eyes to see the walls moving past. It was the lack of personal control over what was going on, and the fact that she was forced to allow strangers to invade her personal space and strip away her dignity.

Not to mention the damn gowns. Dar had let them put one on her, but she'd refused to remove her jeans, even after Dr. Steve had threatened her with a pair of surgical scissors. She still had them on now, providing extra warmth beneath the thin hospital sheet that covered her, smelling of bleach and antiseptic.

The elevator doors closed, and she listened to the nurse's tuneless whistling as the car lurched into motion. That made her still-aching head hurt more, and she sighed, biting her tongue to keep from snapping at the man. The nausea had faded, and Dr. Steve had firmly strapped down her arm again, making the pain bearable; but the various aches and the aggravation were wearing very hard on her temper.

And Kerry had disappeared. Dar spent a moment glumly wondering if her cranky ill temper had finally pushed one button too many, even with her lover's usual patience. The thought brought an irrational jolt to her chest as the fatigue wore down her defenses and let her darker insecurities surface.

Fortunately, she didn't really have time to dwell on it, as the elevator doors opened and her porter pushed her out onto a relatively quiet hospital floor, with shoe-squeakingly clean floors and weave walls the color of road kill. Dar hated it immediately, especially when she was guided into a half-darkened room midway down the corridor.

"Here we are," the man pushing her announced cheerfully. "Let me just swing you over here, and we'll get you settled into this nice bed."

Dar realized she was too tired to even be disgusted. She eyed the bed, then glanced around the room, realizing it was the only bed in it. Could she have gotten that lucky? She'd been hoping, at the best, for either no room neighbor or a sleeping one. It was a fairly sizable room, too, with a wide bay window and a sort of padded daybed lounger near that, presumably for the patient to relax in.

Hmm. Maybe they were out of double rooms. Well, Dar wasn't going to argue with that. Sharing the space was one thing she'd been truly dreading. She waited until the rolling bed was even with the stationary one and the nurse had lowered the rails, then before he could grab hold of her, she moved herself from one to the other in a single, fluid motion.

"Hey," the nurse blurted. "Honey, I was going to help you."

"I know," Dar exhaled. "It's okay." The effort had exhausted her, and she lay back against the pillows and allowed the nurse to fuss with the blankets.

"Are you one of those really independent people?" The man's voice was sympathetic. "I'm like that, too."

Dar glanced at him. "Yeah, I guess I am," she admitted.

"Well, you just take it easy, okay? They'll take good care of you up here, even if you don't want them to," the nurse chuckled. "The floor nurse will be in soon to take your vitals and get your chart started, and then they'll bring you up some dinner." He checked a tag on Dar's arm. "They'll probably want you to take your jeans off, too."

Dar's eyebrow edged up.

"Don't let them intimidate you," the man whispered, giving her a wink. "Sleep in 'em if you want." He grinned and patted Dar's leg, then made his way out of the room.

Hmm. Dar had to smile, just a little. Then she sighed and let her head fall back, her mind turning over vague worries and more concrete ones, like what the hell they were going to do with her shoulder. Her head turned, and she peered at her own arm in worried annoyance. Then she looked around the room, which was depressing and silent.

Surprising how alone you can feel inside a busy place like a hospital. Dar closed her eyes and allowed herself a moment of shockingly pungent self-pity. She really didn't want to be here.

She just wanted to go home.

Kerry paused in the doorway for a moment, watching the

quiet figure lying on the bed. There was something so vulnerable about Dar, she almost didn't want to walk in, for fear of startling her lover too badly. She took a breath, hesitating before she called out. "Hey."

Dar's head came up and she looked around, their eyes meeting with an almost palpable intensity. "Hey." Dar managed a smile. "Thought you went on home."

Kerry walked over to the bed. "You thought wrong." She eased the bag on her shoulder off and let it drop to the ground. "I'm not going anywhere." She leaned on the railing, absorbing the look on Dar's face. "I'm staying right here with you."

Dar felt a little ashamed. "Hey, you don't have to do that," she replied. "Not that I don't appreciate the thought, but you need to go get some rest yourself."

"No." Kerry spoke the truth she felt in her heart and saw in Dar's eyes. "Mom and Dad are going to stay at our place and keep Chino company." She took Dar's hand. "This is where I want to be, and you're not convincing me otherwise, so just forget it."

Dar's eyes dropped to the blanket, then lifted again, filled with simple, yet poignant gratitude. "Thanks," she said, softly. "I'm feeling pretty ragged right now."

"I know," Kerry replied. "Dr. Steve said some of that is from your concussion, and he knows you must be hurting a lot, but they can't give you much for the pain because of your head."

Dar nodded. "I figured that out." She glanced around the room. "At least it's quiet in here, hmm?"

Kerry also looked around. "Yeah, not bad." She nodded at the window. "Nice view."

Dar studied her profile, seeing the slight tensing of the muscles on either side of Kerry's mouth. "Did you arrange for this?"

Now the green eyes drifted around and met hers, and the hidden smile emerged fully, making those eyes twinkle. "Yes, I did," Kerry replied. "And you're in no condition to argue with me about it."

Despite the aches and the pains and the aggravation, Dar suddenly felt much better. "You know something?"

"Hmm?" A blond eyebrow raised in question.

"You're better than ice cream."

The smile turned into a broad grin, which wrinkled Kerry's nose up and transformed her entire face. "There goes my life's goal...Now what do I do?" she laughed. "C'mon, tiger. Let's get those jeans off. I brought your travel bag in, and it has real pajamas in it."

Dar relaxed and accepted her fate. "Oho," she remarked

wryly. "Now I know why you arranged for a private room."

"Absolutely." Kerry agreed with the banter. "You're helpless and alone in my clutches here, and I can do whatever I want to you." She removed one of Dar's socks and tickled the bottom of her foot. "I am in total control."

Dar snickered. "You know, Ker, that would be more effective if you didn't have that cute little nose."

A sigh. "I'd never be cast as a domineering world conqueror, huh?"

"No." Dar muffled a laugh.

"Guess I'll have to just make the best of it." Kerry leaned over and bit her on the toe.

"Ooh." Dar jumped, allowing herself to be absorbed into the play and forgetting for the time being where she was, and how she felt.

Which is exactly what Kerry intended.

They heard the rumble of the dining cart long before it screeched to a halt somewhere near their door. Kerry glanced up from her laptop—which was open on, of all places, her lap—then set the machine aside and got up from the low couch.

After she'd changed into pajamas, Dar had dozed off, finally succumbing to the events of the day, leaving Kerry to work on sorting and organizing the data from the base. She was glad her lover had gotten some rest; the dark circles apparent under her very blue eyes had started to be worrying, and she debated waking Dar up for the dinner she knew was on the way.

Dar forestalled her decision by stirring, and Kerry quickly crossed over to put a hand on her arm as her eyes blinked open and she looked around disorientedly. "Hey, it's okay," Kerry reassured her. "You just took a nap."

"Ah." Recognition flooded Dar's face, and she flexed her hands. "Yeah, guess I did. What time is it?"

"About six," Kerry told her, looking up as an older woman dressed in Pepto-Bismol pink entered. "Dinnertime."

"Hello." The woman smiled at Dar. "Ready to eat?" She slid a tray onto the rolling bedside table and maneuvered it in front of her noncommittal patient. "Your doctor ordered you a regular diet, so we brought you something pretty standard. Tomorrow you'll get a card, so you can order what you want, okay?" She had a kindly face and beautifully arranged silver gray hair.

"Anything?" Dar drawled, still half-asleep.

"Well," the woman laughed, "anything on the card. My

name's Pam, and I'm here at nights. Give me a call if there's anything you need while I'm up here. No guarantees, but I'll see what
I can do." She waved at them, then left the room.

"Mm." Kerry leaned on the railing. "What a nice lady."

Dar fingered her silverware and studied the plastic tray and
its contents with wary suspicion. "The guy who brought me up
here was nice, too. Did you arrange for that, while you were at
it?" She smiled at Kerry.

Kerry chuckled, but shook her head. "No." She lifted the
cover off the tray and allowed steam to escape. "Ah. Chicken."

"Yes, chicken," Dar agreed, examining it. "But on the bright
side, those are sort of mashed potatoes, aren't they?" She poked at
them.

"So they are," Kerry said. "They even brought peas, your one
concession to vegetables," she noticed. "And Jell-O."

"I like Jell-O," Dar allowed. "You think it's strawberry?"

Kerry selected a jiggling cube and put it into her mouth
experimentally. "Yeth."

"Eh." Dar stabbed the half-chicken with her fork. "Considering the last thing I had to eat in a hospital, this isn't too bad." She
managed to rake a bit of the white meat off and tasted it. It was
fairly bland, but not as dry as she'd expected, and she found it tol-
erably edible. "Mm."

"Here." Kerry held her hand out. "Let me borrow your fork
and knife, and I'll cut that up for you. Must be a pain trying to do
it one-handed."

Dar hesitated, then handed the implements over. "Yeah." She
busied herself with the cup while Kerry leaned over and sawed
industriously at her main course. "On the other hand..." Dar
found a very tasty-looking bare shoulder very near by. She licked
it.

"Yipe!" Kerry jumped. "Oh...Jesus, Dar. I had no idea what
that was."

Dar nibbled the soft skin, breathing in the warm, clean scent
of her lover with a sense of quiet pleasure. "Mm. Much better than
chicken."

Kerry put the knife and fork down and responded, sliding a
hand up to rest against Dar's cheek as she found the exploring
lips, tasting a hint of the chicken on them, and the sweet tang of
the apple juice Dar had taken a sip of.

Boy, that felt good. Kerry lost herself in the moment, tuning
out everything to concentrate on how smooth Dar's skin was, and
just how wonderful it was to kiss her. After a moment they parted
and gazed into each other's eyes. Kerry was very conscious of how

unsteady her breathing was. "Mm."

Dar's eyes reflected a quiet passion of her own. "To hell with dinner," she murmured softly, running her fingers down Kerry's shirt and finding a gap in the buttons.

"Um." Kerry glanced up. "We're in a hospital, honey."

"So?" Dar defeated the button and smiled as she felt Kerry respond to her touch, pressing her body forward against her exploring fingers. "You did ask for a private room." She leaned forward a little and kissed her lover again.

"You're hurt." Kerry's breath whispered against Dar's lips.

"This makes me feel much, much better," the ready argument came back at her.

"The door's open," Kerry feebly parried.

"We're not in the cardiac care unit."

Kerry found herself walking a fine line, her body's overwhelming craving warring with her conscience and the knowledge that a legion of censorious nurses could walk in at any moment. *Well, a few more seconds of this can't hurt.*

And it didn't. She ended up half sitting on the bed, both arms around Dar's neck and Dar's arm around her waist.

Then a loud crash occurred outside, and they stopped, separating a little and looking at each other. "Did we cause that?" Kerry asked nervously.

"Why don't you look?" Dar answered.

Look? Kerry imagined turning her head to see a doorful of people staring back. "Nuh-uh. You look."

"Me?" Dar remained where she was, looking intently into Kerry's eyes. "You sure?"

She was getting lost again, this time in those rich blue pupils, wanting nothing more than to lean forward and take up right where she'd left off. Her body was craving it now, Dar's hand moving slowly, teasingly across the fabric of her jeans, pausing to pluck lightly at the seams.

Footsteps clacked nearby, though. Kerry swallowed and got her breathing under control, then released one arm so that she was merely perched on the bed. Dar's hand captured hers and they twined fingers, letting out twin sighs as the footsteps hurried past, and she caught a glimpse of a white-and-blue uniform go by.

"That was fun." A tiny, mischievous glint danced in Dar's eyes. "Bet it's quieter here later on."

Kerry's nostrils flared. "Oh." She let out a faint laugh. "I hope so."

They both looked at the tray. "Chicken, huh?" Kerry picked up the fork and stabbed a piece, then offered it to Dar. "If you share, I'll go get a pizza later."

Dar munched contentedly. "Deal," she agreed.

"How's it going?" Ceci's voice crackled softly over the phone at Kerry's ear. "Andy's been pacing for hours, so I hope Dar's gotten more rest than he has."

"I think she's okay," Kerry murmured, casting an eye over her sleeping partner. Dar had half curled onto her side and was resting comfortably, the blankets tucked up around her shoulders as the soft night-light threw shadows over her strong, planed features. "She's been sleeping for a little while."

"That's a first," Ceci chuckled. "I'd have thought she'd be climbing the walls by now."

"No." Kerry stretched and leaned back. "We had dinner, then we, ah, talked for a while. The nurses came in and took readings and stuff; then I got her to lay down. She's been fine." The medical attention hadn't gotten Dar too upset, really. Her blood pressure had been low, she'd had no temperature—she'd even smiled at the nurse.

Of course, Kerry had felt pretty relaxed by then, too. A smirk appeared on her face.

"No signs of anything with the concussion?" Ceci asked. "She's alert, and all that?"

The smirk widened. "Oh yeah. She's um...very aware."

"Good." Dar's mother sighed. "Last time she had a concussion, she was in a fog for two whole days, and she scared the—" Ceci abruptly fell silent. "Listen to me. You'd think I was—"

"Her mother or something?" Kerry finished warmly.

Ceci sighed. "I'm glad you're there for her, Kerry."

"Me, too," came the soft reply. "I'm not sure which one of us is benefiting more, though. I know I'd be really unhappy if I wasn't camping out with her." Kerry checked her watch. Eleven-thirty. She wondered if she could get comfortable on the little couch, wishing she'd brought something useful like a sleeping bag to make the furniture more bearable. "How's Chino?"

"Bouncing," Ceci replied. "But now that we know Dar's all right, maybe she'll settle down if Andy does." A low rumble moved closer. "Honey, she's fine. Kerry said she's asleep, and there's no problem." A rustle.

"Kumquat?"

Kerry grinned. "Yes, Dad?"

"Dardar's not giving you any fuss?"

"Nope," Kerry assured him. "She's been a model patient."

"Yeah?"

"Yeah. Better bring her ice cream tomorrow as a reward, don't you think?" Kerry teased. "She's being such a good girl."

Andrew chuckled. "Glad to hear that, Kerry. We'll be there, don't you worry. I got something I need to take care of early, then we'll be down."

Kerry's ears pricked up, but she hesitated, not wanting to ask questions over the hospital's phone lines. Time enough tomorrow to ask him, when they were face to face. "Okay. See you then."

"All right," Andrew said. "Tell Dardar..." He hesitated.

"Tell her you love her? Sure." That was an easy one. Kerry said goodbye and put the phone back in its cradle, then she got up and reviewed her little couch. It wasn't like she was a giant or anything, either, Kerry reasoned. At all of five foot six, surely she had to fall into the wide part of the bell curve.

Yet the padded couch seemed barely large enough to lie down on, much less to accommodate her admittedly restless mode of sleeping. "I'm going to end up on the floor," she murmured. "I just know it." But it was all she had to work with, unless she wanted to cut to the chase and take up residence on the chilly tile. She cast a glance over her shoulder. Or crawl into bed with Dar, and give the nurses a real shocker in the morning.

Mm. Her body liked that idea. Kerry rubbed her temples and firmly turned her thoughts elsewhere. But in a moment, she found herself standing at Dar's bedside, her hands resting lightly on the railing that fenced her partner in. She reached over and gently moved a lock of disheveled black hair, stroking its silky smooth texture and letting it tangle around her fingers.

She felt more peaceful, Kerry realized, just being close to Dar, and she spent a few minutes idly wondering why. Was it just because Dar's sleeping expression was so relaxed? There were none of the usual tensions that characterized her expression—the slight narrowing of her eyes and bunching of her jaw muscles that made Dar appear restlessly alert all the time.

Not now. Kerry could see only the faintest motion of her eyes under their lids and wondered what her lover was dreaming of. She gazed down for another moment, then she walked over to the heavy visitor's chair and picked it up, putting it down right next to the bed. *Okay.* She lowered the guard rails, then sat down and rested her arm on the bed, putting her chin down on it and reaching up to circle Dar's slack fingers with her own.

They were clasped instinctively, a welcome warmth that made her smile. She decided to just rest here a minute, then get up and try to get comfortable on her torture couch. Kerry closed her eyes, smiling a little when she felt Dar's breath warming the skin on her forearm. *Mm. That felt nice.*

Yeah.

Dar was chiefly aware of a lot of things aching as she hauled herself out of a deep sleep and responded to her body's nagging crankiness.

Ow. She had a headache that would have felled a bison in its tracks, and her arm and shoulder felt like they'd been forced into a bad position for several days. Grumpily, she opened one eye, blinking as the fuzzy surroundings very slowly came into focus.

Ah. Dar had to smile despite the discomfort. Kerry was slumped against the bed, holding her hand, fast asleep. In the room, the first pale light of dawn was starting to show through the windows, but otherwise it was dark, save for the dim night-light above them.

But there was enough light for Dar to distinguish the curve of Kerry's cheek, covered in fine, soft down. Light enough for her to see the delicate gold eyelashes. Light enough to catch the faintest hint of a smile tugging at one corner of her mouth.

What an amazing thing love was, Dar thought. It even drove you to do really dumb things like sleep leaning against a set of metal railings. *Oh, she's gonna regret this when she wakes up.* "Ker?" Dar squeezed the fingers clasped in her own. "Hey, chipmunk."

"Uh?" Kerry murmured. "Dar?" She stirred, then shifted. "Ow." Her eyes opened in surprised displeasure. "What in—augh. I can't believe I did that," she hissed. "Jesus!"

"Easy, sweetie," Dar laughed softly. "Stand up slowly." She released Kerry's hand and eased over onto her back, grabbing hold of her lover's shoulder as she tried to straighten up. "Easy."

"Son of a..." Kerry managed to get upright, her legs and back cramping like all get-out. "Oh my God, how stupid was that." She leaned on the bed and groaned. "And wouldn't the nurses have just loved walking in here."

Dar ruffled her hair, then rubbed the parts of her within reach. "Ah, they'd live," she disagreed. "Now, if they found you in bed with me..." She grinned.

Kerry looked up, grinning back rakishly from between very disordered bangs. "Oh, I was tempted," she admitted. "That's how I ended up over here. I just came over to, um..." She met Dar's eyes and felt suddenly shy. "Anyway, I sat down for a minute, and whammo." She fell silent, and her gaze dropped to the mussed sheets.

Dar watched her. "Ker?"

"Mm?"

"Thanks for staying," Dar said. "It would have been such a nightmare for me if you hadn't." She waited for Kerry to look up. "Literally."

Kerry gazed at her. "Why?" she asked. "No one likes being in the hospital, Dar, but they're not that bad, really."

Dar shifted and settled her arm in a less uncomfortable position. She found herself studying the ceiling, its tiled surface bearing tiny pockmarks, barely visible to her. "I fell out of a tree when I was little." Her tone was quiet and casual. "They thought I'd cracked something, so they took me up to Baptist and had my head X-rayed."

Kerry put a hand on Dar's arm in silent comfort.

"They decided to keep me overnight, and they put me in a room with a real nice gal, an older woman," Dar went on. "She was funny. Decided to spend the night telling me stories; had grandkids of her own, I guess." She paused and thought, then went on. "I woke up in the middle of the night, and looked over, and I—" Dar stopped, staring off into the distance.

Kerry waited.

"I knew something was wrong," the quiet voice went on finally. "I got out of bed and went over, and I realized she was dead."

It was like getting hit in the gut, hard. Kerry hadn't expected this, hadn't expected an answer to her question that even remotely resembled this. "Sweetheart." She barely whispered the word.

"I think I started screaming," Dar murmured.

Kerry didn't give a damn about the nurses. She hauled herself up onto the bed and put her arms around Dar, pulling her close and hugging her. "Lord."

Dar let her head lay against Kerry's chest, reliving the moment. Even all these years later, she could still feel the terror, the unreasoning fear that had haunted her dreams for a very long time after.

She remembered the nights she'd been afraid to go to sleep, terrified that she'd wake in the middle of the night and go in search of her parents, only to find them cold and stiff and staring. Dar drew in a shaky breath. It still shook her, even now. "Guess it made an impression."

Kerry stroked her hair gently. "How old were you?"

"Five or six," Dar replied, blinking. She was surprised to feel a tear roll down her face. "Silly, I guess, to even think about it now."

"No." Kerry closed her eyes and held on, kissing Dar's head, then laying her cheek against the spot. "Not silly." She felt her throat closing up, her entire body hurting for the child Dar had been, wanting to go back in time and be in that place, at that time, to hold Dar just as she was now and chase the fear away.

Dar allowed herself to accept the safety of that embrace. The ghost of that night lurking inside her loosened its hold, and as she reached up and clasped Kerry's arm, she felt the terror unwind and drift away into the dawn's breaking.

Silence settled peacefully over them.

They did, in fact, surprise the nurses.

Andrew Roberts walked down the hallway, dodging sleepy interns pushing carts of equipment at a far slower pace than his rolling stride.

It was early, he reckoned, before the visiting hours of the hospital; but if there was one thing Andrew had learned in all his years of service it was that if you acted like you knew what you were doing, folks tended to leave you be.

Since he knew where he was, and knew where he was going, sure 'nough, nobody did ask him what he was doing in the hospital so early. Exchanging gruff nods with a security guard, he went past the nurses' station and down the next corridor toward one specific door set among many up and down the hall.

As to why he was there? Andrew circled around a laundry cart. Well, it wasn't that he didn't trust Kerry to keep an eye on his daughter—he surely did; it was just that he knew how Dar felt about being inside these damn places and it never hurt to make sure.

Did it?

At the doorway he'd identified as Dar's, there were two nurses standing and staring inside the room, and Andrew found his heart starting to go double time as he came up behind them. "Somethin' not right here?"

The women jumped, and one simply turned and left. The other looked up at Andrew's towering height. "Oh, sir, visitors are not allowed now." She started to take his arm to lead him away, glancing over her shoulder into the room. "Excuse me now—"

"Ah, ah." Andrew simply stood still, knowing the petite dark-haired nurse wasn't going to be pulling his six-foot-four-inch bulk anywhere. He glanced into the room anxiously, then let out a chuff of relief when he spotted the two figures snuggled together on the bed. "Would you just lookit that."

"Sir." The nurse pulled on his arm with complete ineffectiveness. "Please."

"Chill yer jets." Andrew turned his head and regarded her. "You got something you need doing, g'wan. I can wake these here kids up."

The woman stopped tugging. "You can?" she asked. "Oh. Would you? This is a situation we're just not willing to get involved in."

One of Andrew's grizzled eyebrows lifted. "Waking folks up?" he queried. "Damndest thing I ever heard. That malpractice stuff must be hitting you all pretty fierce."

"M—ah, no, no." The nurse gave up. "Excuse me." She turned and left, quickly walking away toward a door marked "Nurses Lounge."

Andrew watched her go, then he scratched his jaw thoughtfully before shrugging and returning his attention to the room. He stepped inside with utmost quiet and padded over to the bed, spending several moments just watching his children sleep.

Then, with a rakish grin, he pulled a camera out of the pocket of his pullover and opened it, examining the controls carefully before he put it to his eye and allowed the gizmo to focus. When he had the scene properly adjusted, he released the shutter and heard the click and whirr of the camera operating. After a second, he pulled it down and reviewed the LCD screen on the back, examining the digital image. "Huh."

He shook his head, then closed the camera up and tucked it away before moving closer to the bedside. His daughter was curled half onto her side, with her head pillowed against Kerry's chest, with both of Kerry's arms wrapped around her.

Andrew felt a smile pull at the skin on his face, still stiff after all the scarring and the surgery. Hospitals weren't his favorite place, either, but to be honest, he'd spent more time in them than Dar had. Even now, after all the work they'd done, he knew the scars were still damn ugly to look at, and he was conscious of that even with Ceci.

God bless her, she never so much as flinched, even at the worst of it, but it didn't stop Andrew from remembering the averted eyes or open stares of others.

Like them nurses had been staring, only they'd been looking inside this here room. Andrew laid his big hands on the railing. Looking at something so beautiful made his heart ache, having seen so much hate in his lifetime that love could only be exquisitely beautiful to him.

Very gently, he put a hand on Dar's shoulder. He kept his voice low. "Paladar."

Dar's eyes quivered, then blinked open, the dark brows over them contracting as she tried to place where and when she was. She turned her head and peered up at him, then realized why it was so nice and warm, and promptly turned the heat up by blushing a deep, vivid crimson. "D—"

Andrew had to chuckle. "Dardar, I ain't seen you turn that color since I done caught you skinny-dipping out at that waterhole when you were ten."

"Erk." Dar's throat issued an adolescent squeak.

It was enough to wake Kerry up, though, and she also gazed at Andrew with sleepy eyes for a few seconds before her brain booted and nearly caused her to fall off the bed. "Uh...Hi, Dad," she managed to cough out.

"Hi there, kumquat," Andrew responded amiably. "You look right comfortable."

Kerry looked at Dar, who was still doing her best McIntosh apple imitation. "Sorry, honey," she apologized weakly. "Didn't mean to do that."

Dar sighed and rubbed her heated face with her good hand. "S'all right," she said. "Could have been worse." She glanced at her father. "Morning."

"Morning, Dardar," Andrew said. "I'd ask how y'all were feeling, 'cept I figure you look pretty good to me just now."

A weak laugh forced its way out of Dar's throat as she untangled herself from Kerry's embrace. She rolled over onto her back as her lover slid out of bed and straightened her T-shirt with as much dignity as she could muster.

Which, to be honest, wasn't much.

"What was your question again?" Dar finally asked, running her fingers through her mussed hair. "Oh, right. How do I feel." Slowly, she straightened out her body and flexed her arm. The results mildly surprised her. "Better than yesterday," she said, lifting a hand to touch the lump on the back of her head. It seemed to have gone down some. "Yeah, headache's not so bad, and my arm hurts less."

Andrew gave her an approving look. "Good to hear." Kerry had snuck into the restroom with her overnight bag and was apparently utilizing the sink there with a good amount of vigor. "Had me a little worried yesterday."

Dar tensed her lips, then shrugged. "What a botched event that was," she exhaled. "A total screw-up, and it was my fault."

Andrew rolled his eyes. "Git yer head out of that there bucket of whup, Paladar," he scolded. "You ain't responsible for them folks, and you know it."

Dar shook her head. "I should have found out more about what was going on. One of our people could have really gotten hurt in there." She pulled herself up a little straighter. "I should have checked first."

Andrew looked around, then leaned over and smoothed the dark hair out of his daughter's eyes with a gentle hand. "Don't beat yourself up, Dar. Y'all are gonna make me start beating up my mah own head, 'cause sure as the day is long, I should have figgured what was up when we got there, don't you think?"

Dar looked at him thoughtfully.

"Them people just knew how to use a diversion when they had one, all right?" Andrew went on. "Now we got to get them pieces back together so none of them dirty dogs gets off." He waited for Dar to nod, and she finally did. "Good girl. I'm going to take a ride down there and see what I can figure out."

Dar lodged what she knew was a futile protest. "You don't have to. Let me have Gerry handle it, Dad."

"You saying I ain't up to this?" Andrew asked.

"No." Dar felt very off center. "I'm not saying that."

"Good." Andrew patted her arm. "You take it easy now, Dardar. Keep an eye on that kumquat of yours. Make sure she gets some breakfast, all right?" He waved and started out before Dar could say a word, disappearing around the corner of the door with stealthy speed.

Dar stared at her bare feet, sticking out from under the mussed covers, and wiggled her toes. It was not starting out to be a very organized day.

Chapter
Seventeen

Kerry flexed her hands and peered at her laptop screen. Her report was almost done, the data cataloged neatly into columns that laid out in black and white the discrepancies she'd found. It wasn't a smoking gun, she realized, more a pattern of carelessness and lack of accountability in moving funds from one account to the other, but the pattern was there, and if they got nothing else, would provide the government auditors a place to start.

If nothing else. Kerry rubbed her lower lip. Mark had taken the data storage cube back and secured it at the office, but the information they may or may not have gotten from there would have to wait for Dar's inspection. Only Dar had the algorithms to unlock the tracks they'd copied, and those were tucked inside her head and nowhere else.

Kerry hadn't asked her, yet, if she remembered what they were. It was a scary kind of question, and she knew concussions did strange things sometimes. She didn't think the injury was affecting Dar, but it was hard to say; certainly her lover had been quieter and more withdrawn than usual since she'd been here.

She knew Dar was grateful for her presence. Kerry was equally grateful that she'd followed her instincts and did what she'd done, especially after Dar had told her this morning what had happened to her as a child. "That poor little kid." She shook her head slowly. "I wish I'd been there for you, Dar. I swear I do."

The room, of course, was empty except for her and her laptop. Dar had been taken down for another scan of her head and for a visit to the orthopedic surgeon. Kerry had offered to come with her, but it appeared her lapse into needing to be cuddled was getting to Dar, and her natural pride poked its head up in outrage and reasserted itself.

There were two sides to that, Kerry admitted. One, she was a little disappointed in being gently rejected. But two, it meant Dar was feeling better, and that was a good thing. She put aside the laptop and stood up, stretching out her stiff and somewhat cramped body. Sleeping sitting up hadn't been restful, and the couch was less so. She strolled over to the window and looked out, resting her hands on the sill and leaning on them.

"What I should do is take a break and run the stairs a few times," she decided. "Loosen myself up a little and get some exercise." With a nod, she went back and closed her laptop down, turning it off and slipping it inside its padded backpack. She looked around, then shrugged and shouldered the pack, shifting it until it was comfortably centered on her back. "A little extra effort won't hurt me any, either."

She walked out of the room and straight to the stairwell, opening the door and letting it close behind her. Since they were on the top floor, she really only had one way to go, and so she started down the steps at a rhythmic, even pace. It was quiet in the stairwell, and clean. Kerry decided it probably wasn't used much, since most of the movement between floors involved wheeled equipment or vehicles, which could get a little tricky going up or down stairs.

Halfway down, at the fifth floor, she met her first fellow walker, a young man carrying a thick bag, who smiled at her as he dropped down the steps alongside. "Hi there."

"Hi," Kerry replied, with a friendly smile.

"You new here?" the man asked. "Haven't seen you around."

Hmm. Kerry eyed him. *He's a cutie.* The man had curly reddish hair and a lithe, athletic build. "That's because I don't work here," she informed him. "I'm just visiting."

"Oh yeah?" He looked surprised. "I figured you were an intern or something, with that book bag. Sorry." He flashed her a smile. "Well, that's too bad. My name's Curt." He stuck out a hand.

Kerry took it as they kept walking. "Kerry." She produced her name. "It's a computer backpack, actually. I work with them."

"Yeah?" Curt released her hand. "You don't see many visitors taking the stairs either." He looked down and laughed a bit. "Or staff either, to be honest. I think you're the first person I've seen in here in weeks."

"You take them, though." Kerry turned the corner on the steps and started down the next set. "Good exercise, right?"

"You bet," Curt agreed. "I have to get in all the leg work I can. I'm training for the Olympics." He grinned at her surprised expression. "I'm a gymnast."

"Really?" Kerry turned her head to look at him. "That's wild."

The man nodded. "Yeah. It is. I've been into it since I was a kid, but my folks could never afford me just going to school for that, so I've kept at it on the side. I'm going to the trials next year." He glanced over at Kerry. "You look like you're into sports."

It suddenly occurred to Kerry that she was being flirted with. *Hmm.* And by a really cute guy, too. It felt...kinda cool, actually. "Oh, nothing official," she told Curt. "I just do some diving, swimming...climbing." She caught his very interested eye. "Martial arts, that sort of thing."

"I thought so. You've got great muscle tone." Curt grinned at her. "Ever try gymnastics?"

Kerry suffered a flash of memory of her childhood, the arduous hours spent trying desperately to balance on a four-inch chunk of wood. "When I was younger, yes," she admitted. "My parents thought it would make me graceful." She adroitly dodged a pipe sticking out of one of the stairs.

"They were right," Curt laughed. "Hey, I just have to drop this bag off...you interested in sharing a pop?"

Fortunately, Kerry was from the Midwest and realized he was talking about a soda, not proposing something indecent. "Wish I could." She softened the words with an honest smile. "Thanks for asking."

They'd reached the bottom floor, and he shifted his bag to his other shoulder and held a hand out again. "Maybe next time, okay?"

Kerry took it and returned his firm handshake with one of her own. "Sure."

He turned, pulled the door open, then ducked through and let it close behind him. Kerry regarded the door for a moment, then turned and leaned against the wall, folding her arms over her chest as she rested a moment before starting her climb back up. *That was interesting,* she mused, examining the sensation. It was nice, once in a while, to have someone think you were attractive, wasn't it?

Other than your partner, of course, Kerry amended hastily. She'd never suspected Dar of thinking otherwise, had she? She thought about that, then blushed a vivid crimson, remembering a certain night not that long ago when she'd looked up from working on a report in her home office to find Dar watching her from the doorway, eyes half-closed, her thoughts very evident by her expression. No, she was pretty confident that they were both very much attracted to each other. But it was nice to have a stranger give your ego a pat on the head once in a while.

Kerry pushed off the wall and started up the steps. *Besides,* she grinned, *he sure was a cutie.* In fact, she thought, he reminded her of someone. *Now who...ah.* She nodded. *That's right—Josh.* She'd gotten an e-mail from him that morning, saying he'd accepted her offer and was going to come to Miami.

Sorting through various other issues, Kerry kept jogging upward, catching her wind and falling into an easy rhythm as her body adjusted to the exertion.

The machine buzzed softly. Dar kept her eyes firmly closed and spent the moments roundly cursing herself for being a stubborn jerk for not taking Kerry up on her offer of company. This was the third round of scans, and her nerves were beginning to twitch badly, wanting out of the machine and away from the cold, impersonal hands that invaded her personal space and moved her body.

Hands gripped her chin and she jerked, her eyes snapping open and pinning the doctor standing over her with an angry glare.

"Okay, Ms. Rob—" The tall, willowy woman stopped speaking and removed her hands. "Sorry, did I startle you?"

Dar took a breath and forced her irritation down. "No. I thought this was about done."

The doctor folded her arms. "Just about," she agreed, wrinkling her well-shaped nose in thought. "You don't much like being touched, do you?"

Dar scowled a little at being so easily read. "Not much, no," she admitted. At least this doctor—Alison was her name?—wasn't the usual condescending, iceberg type. "Sorry."

"That's all right, Ms. Roberts," Dr. Alison reassured her. "Some people don't. We're so used to just grabbing what we want and pulling, we forget that sometimes. Could you tilt your head up and to the right?"

Dar complied, watching the woman make adjustments to the machine. The doctor was taller than Kerry but couldn't have weighed more than a hundred pounds, so thin that Dar was sure she'd blow away if the air conditioning cycled too strongly. Her white lab coat hung loosely on her, and the wrists that extended from it seemed barely wider than two of Dar's fingers. The machine whirred again.

"Okay." Dr. Alison looked down at Dar. "We're done." She pushed the machine arm back and leaned against the padded table on which Dar was lying. She had hazel eyes and a high forehead made all the more so by a hairstyle tightly pulled back into a knot. "Why don't you sit up and let me take a look at your shoulder, okay?"

Dar obliged, tensing her abdominal muscles and pulling herself upright, then swinging her legs over the edge of the table. She hopped off and stood upright, startling the doctor, who took a step back.

"Oh." Dr. Alison made a face, then smiled. "Somehow, patients always look shorter lying down. I didn't expect you to be that tall." She gestured toward a side room. "Why don't we go in there so you can sit?"

Dar followed her in silence, taking a seat on a lower, but also padded bench in the examination room. She was still wearing her sling, but they'd allowed her Tylenol for the nagging headache, and she felt pretty good at the moment. "Well?"

Dr. Alison had been reviewing something on a computer terminal, and now she looked up over the screen at Dar. "Well, you want the bad news first or the good news?"

"Bad," Dar replied instantly.

"You know, Ms. Roberts, I thought you were going to say that," the doctor laughed. "Okay, well, the bad news is that you've got a lot of swelling in that shoulder. Aside from the bone bruise, you also strained some of the tendons and muscles around there, and everything's pretty tense."

Dar ran that over in her head and decided it didn't sound life threatening. "Okay."

"You're going to need to do a lot of physical therapy to get the blood moving in there and get the damaged bits out," Dr. Alison told her. "It's going to hurt."

Pain was something Dar could live with. She'd worked through enough injuries in her years of martial arts, after all, and while she never enjoyed the process, she knew ways of getting past it. "And?" She watched as the doctor left her console and came over, carefully unsnapping the sling to release Dar's arm.

"I need to see what kind of range of motion you have, okay?" Dr. Alison waited for Dar to nod, then she took hold of Dar's wrist and slowly lifted her arm. "Let me know when it starts to hurt." She first flexed the arm at the elbow, then gently pulled upward, getting no reaction from her wary patient. "Okay, that's what I thought. Now I'm going to move it out to the side; I think that's where the problem is going to be."

Dar nodded and shifted a little, straightening up as the other woman carefully extended her injured arm out to the side, then started to lift it. About halfway, Dar let out a sound somewhere between a cough and a hiss, and the motion stopped.

"Okay." The doctor examined the angle. "Well, that's not too bad, actually." She sounded surprised. "Given what I saw in the pictures, that's pretty darn good." She put Dar's arm back down and started poking at her shoulder, touching and prodding the skin with absorbed interest. "You have a very well developed deltoid here."

Dar's brow lifted and she eyed the woman warily. "Thanks."

"I don't think I've seen a structure like this on a female in a while," Dr. Alison added. "You're not doing steroids or other anabolics, are you?"

Dar glared at her. "Absolutely not."

"Just asking," the doctor replied mildly. "No offense intended, Ms. Roberts. A lot of people do, you know. In my line of work, I deal with an enormous number of athletes. It's a standard question." She walked over and checked her screen. "You have an incredible bone density, did you know that?"

How was she supposed to know that? "No," Dar replied.

"Well, you do." The doctor typed something. "That's a good thing. It's what kept you from getting hurt worse. You take calcium supplements?"

Dar's brow creased. *Supplements?* "No, I just drink milk."

"Can't stand the stuff myself." Dr. Alison shook her head. "Well, good for you, Ms. Roberts. You weight train, correct?"

"Yes."

The doctor nodded. "Okay, I just need to get some stats on you so I can send them to the therapist. Could you take your shirt off, please?"

It suddenly occurred to Dar why she'd always been more comfortable with male doctors, an interesting moment of self-revelation that almost made her start laughing. "What stats does a therapist need?" she asked, standing up and pulling her T-shirt off over her head one-handedly. It left her in a pair of gym shorts and nothing else.

"Oh, height, weight, limb len—" Dr. Alison stopped speaking for a second as she looked up. "Wow."

Dar's eyebrow went right up.

"You have great body structure," the doctor continued enthusiastically. "You have almost perfect symmetry, did you know that?" She picked up a tape measure and trotted over. "Outstanding."

Dar didn't know whether to feel like a show horse on parade or what. She held her arms out when told and felt the tickle of the tape measure as it was run across her back.

"I thought so. Seventy-four inches." The doctor towed Dar over to a scale. "Let me get your height and weight." She pushed the height bar up and stood on her tiptoes to let the top of it rest on Dar's head. "Seventy-two and three-quarters. Yep, I knew it." Next, she ran the weights across and nudged the smaller one back and forth until the arm balanced in the center. "One fifty-six." She nodded and scribbled. "That about normal for you?"

"Give or take a few, yes," Dar replied. "Why?"

"Just curious." After measuring Dar's upper and lower arms, Dr. Alison finished her writing. "Okay, we're done." She looked up, reviewing Dar with an air of scientific satisfaction. "Very nice bones, Ms. Roberts. Congratulations."

Dar picked up her shirt and slipped it on. "Thanks," she muttered. "But I think it's my father's fault."

"Really?" Dr. Alison smiled. "Are you a daddy's girl? Everyone tells me I am." She straightened her papers and slid them into an envelope. "I hate that. Don't you?"

Dar picked up her sling and looked at it, then glanced up at the doctor. "No," she said. "I've always considered it a compliment."

"Well, you're just a lucky woman, then." The doctor held a hand out and gripped Dar's. "Good luck, Ms. Roberts. Keep up what you're doing, and I guarantee you'll be rock climbing into your seventies." She nodded briskly. "Any questions for me?"

Dar cocked her head. "Yeah, one," she drawled. "If you think what I'm doing is so great, why don't you do it?"

Dr. Alison blinked. She glanced at herself, then at Dar. Then she laughed, a touch sheepishly. "I'm a doctor." She grinned and shrugged. "We never listen to our own advice." With a wave, she left the room.

Dar straightened up and looked around at the now empty room. Okay. She'd gotten her head examined several times, and apparently her arm wasn't going to require amputation. A smile appeared. That meant she could get her ass out of here and go home. She went to the door and peeked out, seeing no sign of her solicitous orderly with his ready wheelchair. "Heh." Dar planned her route and slipped past the nurses' station toward the doors.

"Damn." Kerry felt the strain as she hit the seventh floor, her breath coming short and her legs starting to really burn. "That's what you get for slacking off at the gym for the last month, Kerrison. You're one lazy son of a biscuit when you want to be." She sucked in a deep breath and pushed through the discomfort.

It annoyed her. She'd kept her running up, hadn't she? Every morning, without fail, there she was at Dar's side in the early-morning cool air. So, okay, she'd cut back on the climbing wall to let her shoulder heal, and they were between martial arts classes, but still. Kerry scowled. She'd even kept up with Dar lately...*Hey.* A thought occurred to her. Was Dar slowing down on purpose and letting her do that? Dar wouldn't do that, would she?

Not to make Kerry feel better, right? White teeth chewed on a lower lip. Okay, but maybe she did it just to have company, how about that? Dar would do that, right? Slow down so they could talk to each other, like they'd started to, using that time to go over problems at the office and plan their day.

Hmm. Kerry reached the eighth floor and turned the corner, feeling her heart rate starting to climb. So here she thought she was cruising along, doing so well. "Looks like I'm going to just have to try harder, that's all," she panted, forcing herself to leap up the next set of stairs two at a time. She rounded the corner and swung a little wide, a little out of control toward the door that led to the ninth-floor entrance. She put out a hand to steady herself, then suddenly blinked as the solid surface started to move toward her.

Kerry tried to stop, but her momentum was too great and she ended up crashing into the opening door, knocking herself senseless as she reeled backward dangerously close to the steps behind her. "Oh!" She fought for balance, reaching out for the handrail, but the sweat on her hands betrayed her and she started to fall.

And then, just as suddenly, she wasn't falling. She was caught and held in a powerful grip, and her senses scrambled to reconcile the abrupt presence of Dar's distinctive aura surrounding her. "Ow."

"Hey." Dar's voice confirmed her dizzy revelation. "Kerry? Kerrison!"

Oh boy. Did I do something wrong? Kerry felt her knees buckle, and the next thing she knew, she was on the ground, its cold hardness pressing against her legs, with her upper body cradled in a nice, warm, very Dar-smelling nest. She blinked a few times. "Didn't know seeing stars wasn't just an old saying." She stuttered the words out. "Ow."

"Easy." Dar's voice sounded worried. "Take it easy. Why are you breathing so hard? Honey? Look at me, okay?"

Kerry obeyed, tipping her head back and opening both eyes,

very glad she did so when she was rewarded with Dar's concerned face inches from her. "Wow." She finally felt her heart rate start to calm. "Are you ever a sight for sore eyes." She lifted a hand and gingerly felt her forehead. "Or a sore head."

Dar stroked her face gently. "What in the hell were you doing?" she asked. "You're all wet."

"You have that effect on me," Kerry joked faintly, getting a halfhearted smile from her lover. "I'm all right. It's just sweat. I was running the stairs."

Dar tugged her shirtsleeve over and wiped the droplets of sweat out of Kerry's eyes. It was warm in the stairwell, and the smaller woman was still breathing hard. "Can I ask why?"

Kerry took a long, shaky breath, then released it. "Seemed like a good idea at the time?" She gave Dar a wan smile. "I was just working the kinks out—getting a little exercise." She settled her back against the wall and untangled her feet from Dar's.

"And?" Dar shifted to a more comfortable position. "You decided to make it a decathlon event instead?"

"No." Kerry dredged her self-disgust back up. "I was getting tired after seven measly flights, and it pissed me off," she admitted. "I've been telling myself what good shape I'm in. Hah." She forced a laugh and rolled her head to one side, gazing at Dar. "I'm a wuss."

"Sweetheart," Dar laid her good arm over Kerry's shoulders, "our floors at work are eight feet high," she said. "The ones here are twelve. You just ran up the equivalent of about fourteen flights of steps at full speed."

Kerry gazed at the steps, then tipped her head back and looked up. "Oh." She felt like an idiot. "Really?"

"Mm-hmm." Dar gazed fondly at her. "So you're entitled to be out of breath. I would have been." She leaned forward and stuck two fingers into the collar of Kerry's shirt, pulling it outward and peeking inside. "Besides, I really like the shape you're in."

Kerry looked down, then up at her. "Really?"

"Really." Dar released the fabric, transferring her touch to Kerry's face. She traced the rounded cheekbones and snub nose delicately, examining the crystal clear green depths of her lover's eyes. "You are the most beautiful person I've ever known."

It was amazing. Kerry felt a little fuzzy happy ball settle inside her stomach, its tickling presence causing a smile to spread across her face, achieving an immediate echo on Dar's. How could a sterile-scented stairwell be this romantic? "Thank you for telling me that." Kerry leaned forward slightly and brushed Dar's lips with her own, then made a more solid contact. "Especially since I feel like a slimy, skanky old pair of gym socks right now, so I know you're just saying that to make me feel good." She gave Dar a wry smile.

Dar studied her in silence, a tiny furrow appearing in her brow. "I most certainly wasn't."

"Dar, c'mon." Kerry nudged her. "Don't sit there and pretend I'm attractive sitting here all sweaty and covered in hallway dirt." She held up a hand, which was almost black, then blew her disheveled hair out of her eyes. "I'm a mess."

"I think you missed my point," Dar replied. "Ker, you'll always be beautiful to me, no matter what you look like."

Kerry gazed back at her seriously. "Do you really mean that?" she asked. "No matter what? Even if I shaved my head, put on fifty pounds, and got a tattoo across my neck that said 'Bud-weiser'?" She kept her tone light, but she felt the anxiety as she watched Dar's face, twenty-five years of her mother's voice hammering into her conscience.

"Hmm." Dar cocked her head, giving the vision its due and sober consideration. "Nope. I think I'd have to draw the line at the Bud tattoo," she said gravely. "Maybe 'Corona' I could live with."

Kerry smiled and dropped her gaze, more relieved than she was willing to admit.

"But as for the rest, yes, I do mean that." Dar tipped Kerry's chin up and forced eye contact. "We're not going to look like this forever, Ker. I don't know how you feel about it, but I want you to know I don't give a damn."

It was ridiculous, Kerry decided, that they were having this absurdly critical discussion sitting in a hospital stairwell. But Dar's speech deserved an answer. "All my life I've had it hammered into me that appearance is what matters," she said. "And I'd always hoped that..." a slight shrug, "...being in love would mean more than just being physically attracted to someone." She met Dar's eyes. "For me it is. There's something about you that has captured me completely, and I hope it never lets go."

Dar nodded slightly.

"So, I don't give a damn, either," Kerry went on. "I know I joke about it a lot. Maybe it was just that I bumped into a cute lit-tle gymnastic boy, and he stroked my ego for me."

Dar eyed her. "When was this?"

"On the way down the stairs," the blond woman admitted. "He admired my muscle tone."

"Ah." Dar settled back against the wall. "Well, I just had a good-looking young woman tell me to take all my clothes off."

She eyed Kerry's profile, which went suspiciously, suddenly still, save for the flaring of her nostrils.

"And?" Kerry asked.

"And I spent the next ten minutes being told what a lovely specimen I was."

Kerry's eyebrow lifted.

"Did you know I have dense bones and perfect symmetry?" Dar asked, arching a brow of her own.

Kerry half turned. "Who is this person?"

A puckish grin appeared. "The orthopedic surgeon."

"Tch." Kerry started laughing. "A lovely specimen, huh?"

Dar chuckled. "Nice muscle tone, huh?"

They both simply laughed for a minute. "Oh my God, Dar, I'm sweaty, and I'm tired, and I want to go home. Are they letting you out yet?" Kerry finally said.

"They'd better be," her partner replied. "C'mon. Let's go share a sponge and call Dr. Steve." Dar stood carefully, and held onto Kerry's arm as she joined her. "Thought I saw a tube of that bath soap in your bag."

"The mango one?" Kerry put an arm around Dar's waist as they climbed up the steps toward the tenth floor.

"Mm."

"You thought right, my little subtropical perfect specimen."

Dar snorted, then reached down and pinched Kerry's butt. "Oh yeah, that's nice tone all right."

"Ouch! You wench!" Kerry felt her spirits rise into the bubbly range. "Wait 'til we get to that sponge. You'll be sorry."

"Oh yeah?"

"Yeah."

"Send her in." Commander Ainsbright twitched his jacket sleeves straight and folded his hands on his desk. Aside from the bandage taped over a gash on his left temple and a bruise the size of a mango on his jaw, he appeared the very picture of composed military dignity. He watched as the door opened and Chief Daniel walked in. "Chief."

The chief walked to the edge of the desk and saluted, then stood at ease.

"Report," the commander requested.

"It seems the training exercise caused a great deal of damage in three areas, sir," the chief replied. "Primarily in the computer center, the telecom room, and the programming center."

The commander nodded. "And?"

"I expect the systems will be down until we can replace about twenty percent of the hardware," Chief Daniel said. "Apparently the backup systems were damaged as well, and we lost a good portion of our data storage."

The base commander leaned back and propped a knee up against his desk. "All right," he said. "Write up the damages, and I'll charge the SEAL program for them. They had their instructions. They failed to follow them."

"Yes, sir." Chief Daniel kept her gaze firmly fixed on the desk.

"Anything else you want to report, Chief?"

"No, sir," came the quiet reply.

"Anyone asks you for anything, we don't have it."

"No, sir."

"Dismissed."

The chief turned and left the room, closing the door quietly behind her. Jeff Ainsbright sighed and shook his head. The phone rang, and he picked it up. "Yes?"

"Cleanup's almost done," a terse voice informed him. "We got lucky. Damn lucky."

"Tell me," the base commander snorted. "You get rid of everything? We'll have a security team down on us at 0700 tomorrow morning."

"Everything," the voice answered. "Scrubbed to the bare steel. I brought a dog in just to be sure."

Ainsbright nodded. "Good." His eyes narrowed. "I've got those guards on court-martial for letting that damn bastard Roberts in here during off-hours. You know how close that was? They were in the goddamned computer center. I just hope we got everything."

"We did." The voice held infinite assurance. "She thought she was so smart. That data stream she has won't tell her anything. We made sure of that." A chuckle. "Don't worry, Jeff. All they'll find is some ruined equipment. I already reconstructed the database. It's clean."

"All right." Ainsbright nodded. "It was too damn close, I tell you. We should have shut down the minute that bitch came on the base."

"You were supposed to take care of that," the answer came back sharply. "You and that kid of yours, remember? He was supposed to distract her. Hell, I thought he'd end up screwing her—"

"That's enough," Ainsbright snapped. "Forget about it. We found another solution." He checked his watch. "I've got to go. Chuck's ship's leaving, and I want to make sure he's on it."

"Right. Out of sight—"

"Out of my hair," the commander snorted. "Bye." He hung up the phone and took a deep breath. It had been close. Far too close, and the problems weren't over yet. He wasn't stupid enough to think he was rid of Dar Roberts, for one thing. She'd dug enough into the base to report back to Washington, and now it was up to his team to do damage control.

Negligence? Sure. Someone would be court-martialed for it. Shoddy record-keeping, sloppy processes. Every base had them, and all it would generate was a damn study and recommendations as long as Roberts hadn't found anything worse.

And she hadn't. He was sure of it. All he had to do was get Chuckie out of here, then wait for the rep from DC. Thank God the damn JAG had called to warn him. With a sigh, he put his hands against his desk and pushed himself to his feet, wincing at the ache in his bones.

Too dark, he'd been told, to see who'd hit him. "Sorry, sir. It was just too dark," the SEAL captain had maintained stiffly. *Yeah? Too dark my ass,* Jeff Ainsbright scowled as he circled his desk and headed for the door.

Only to find it blocked.

He stopped in complete shock and stared at the dark blue-clad figure standing silently inside the door. There hadn't been a sound. *How in the hell?* He took a cautious breath. "Andy."

Ice blue eyes watched him steadily. "'Lo, Jeff," Andrew drawled very softly.

Ainsbright took a step back. "Didn't hear you come in."

Frighteningly, that caused a smile to appear on the scarred face. "Folks never do," the ex-SEAL allowed. "That's how come I stuck around this long." Andrew moved forward toward the commander with a curiously smooth amble. It combined an economy of motion with an impression of prowling energy that caused the commander to take another step back, then turn and retreat behind his desk.

"What can I do for you, Andy?" Ainsbright forced a tense smile. "I've got a meeting I'm due at."

"On Sunday? You ain't visiting the preacher now, are you?" Andrew asked.

The commander hesitated. "No, no, just a lunch date with my wife." He was very conscious of the cold menace radiating from his old friend who, though retired and with all that gray in his crew cut, still posed a very potent threat he knew he had no hope of countering.

Andrew had always been like that. A big man, made bigger by

weight training and SEALs fitness regimen, with lightning reflexes and lethal combat skills. Cool in action, levelheaded, steady, reliable—but with a blind spot a mile wide all centered around his family and that damn stubborn pigheaded bitch of a daughter of his.

Dar was dangerous because she was so goddamned smart. Andrew was dangerous just because he was dangerous, and anything that touched or threatened his kid sent him past reason.

"We need to chat," Andrew told him. "So sit yer ass down."

Ainsbright sat down slowly and folded his hands. "Andrew, this ain't a threat, but I can call the guards and have you taken out of here. You're not in the Navy anymore."

"That's all right," Andrew told him. "When I'm done with you, you ain't gonna be either." He sat down on Ainsbright's desk. "So if you have half a brain left, you will sit in that chair and start talking about what you all are doing here."

Ainsbright looked steadily at him. "Andrew, I have no idea what you're talking about. I think you need to leave."

Andrew leaned closer. "Listen, you jackass. How'n the hell you think you got that crack on the side of your haid?"

Unconsciously, Ainsbright lifted a hand and touched it.

"Ah took that damn gun you had out of your hands and smacked you 'cross the face with it," Andrew continued, standing up and circling the desk, his temper rising. "So you will, sir, you will tell me what is goin' on here that makes a career jack like you point a damn gun at mah kid!" The ex-SEAL's voice rose to a low roar. "NOW!"

Ainsbright froze, staring at the dark form looming over him, seeing the fire in those pale blue eyes surging toward the edges, ready to consume him. Andrew's hands were tensed and his body coiled, his center of balance up on the balls of his feet, full of a stillness that bore its own warning.

"Andy, take it easy." Ainsbright kept his voice low. "I'll talk."

"Yes," a low, fierce growl agreed. "You surely will."

"Dr. Steve." Dar inhaled, visibly holding her patience. "They've taken enough pictures to star me in the next Sears, Roebuck catalog. I'm fine. Let me the hell out of here."

Dr. Steve patted her arm as he reviewed a chart. "Just hold on to your britches, rugrat. You've still got a ton of swelling up in that rock head of yours." He made a mark on the chart. "We're not taking any chances with you."

Dar peered over the doctor's arm to where Kerry was curled

up on the daybed, watching. Her brow creased as she scowled. "I'm not spending another night in this place," she decided. "I can sleep just as well at home."

Dr. Steve didn't even look up. "Ain't got nurses there. Though you gave the ones here a story to spread around over the water cooler."

Dar glared at him. "I don't give a damn," she growled. "They can kiss my ass."

Dr. Steve looked up to see a pair of truculent blue eyes looking at him. "Lord, you must be feeling better," he teased her, reaching over and chucking her on the chin. "That's the Dar I know."

Kerry watched in amusement, resting her chin on her forearm. She could see Dar getting more and more annoyed, and wondered briefly if her sometimes mercurial lover wasn't better off going home. "Hey, Dr. Steve?" she called out.

The doctor turned and put the chart down, walking over to her and looking down. "How'd you get that bump, Squeaky?" His fingers touched the side of her head cautiously. "That hurt?"

"A little," Kerry admitted. "I had a close encounter with a door. Nothing major." She took advantage of his proximity. "Dr. Steve?"

"Hmm?" The doctor crouched down and continued to examine her bump. "You feeling all right, Kerrison? You look a little pasty." Behind him, Dar sat up and peered over, her brow creasing.

"I'm fine, really," Kerry assured him. "Just a little headache, and I haven't had my lunch yet."

"Mm-hmm." Dr. Steve turned her face a little toward the light from the window. "Feel a little shaky?"

Kerry sighed. "A little."

"Uh-huh. When was the last time you had your blood sugar levels checked?"

That caught her by surprise. "Um..." She took a breath. "I usually don't have a problem."

"That's not true," Dar spoke up.

Kerry peered around the doctor's arm, annoyed. "Dar."

"It's not." The dark haired woman gave a little shrug of her uninjured shoulder. "You get dizzy when you don't eat, and you know it."

"That true?" Dr. Steve asked.

Kerry sighed again. "Sometimes," she said. "I try to make sure it doesn't." She met his gaze. "I ran out of granola bars today."

Dr. Steve fished in his pocket and came out with a package of cheese and peanut butter crackers. He handed it over to her. "Here."

She accepted them, then changed the subject. "Does she really need to stay here?" Kerry asked quietly. "I think she'd rest better at home."

The doctor rested his hand on her knee and gave her a direct look. "Would you go home if I said no?"

Kerry shook her head, opening her crackers and removing one. She put it between her teeth and bit down, chewing the salty snack slowly. "Where she goes, I go."

Dr. Steve let out a chuckle, then pushed himself to his feet and returned to Dar's bedside. "Found you a good match, Paladar." He shook his head. "Two of a kind, I can see that."

Dar tore her eyes from Kerry's face and looked at him. "What?"

The doctor picked up her chart and made a notation on it. Then he looked up as footsteps sounded outside, and a young man carrying an envelope entered. "Ah, that the last of them?"

"Yes, sir," the man confirmed, handing over the envelope. He gave Dar a professional smile, then turned and left. Dr. Steve removed some papers from the envelope and read them, scanning over the first page and concentrating on the second. Finally, he grunted and folded them over.

"All right, rugrat." He turned and put his hands on the bedrails. "I'll let you go, on one condition."

Dar's eyebrows hiked up in pleased surprise. "What?" She glanced over at the watching Kerry. "Name it." The doctor's attention to her lover had caused a twinge of unease, even though she knew Kerry was conscious of her body chemistry and usually had little problem with it. She had seemed a little wrung out when they'd gotten back, but Dar had put that down to her stair-climbing.

"You," Dr. Steve took hold of her chin and forced her to look at him, "will get your ass in bed and stay there for at least three days."

Dar took a breath to answer.

"Promise me," Dr. Steve stated flatly. "I mean it, Dar. This is no joke. You want to go home? Well, I've known you since you were born, and I know you'll get more rest there than here with all them nurses poking at you. But you must—I'm saying must, Dar—stay in bed and let your body heal." His manner was unusually no-nonsense. "Yes or no?"

The blue eyes flickered, then narrowed slightly. "Just stay in bed?" she countered. "Not asleep?"

Dr. Steve warily eyed her. "Flat on your back," he qualified. "No gymnastics or anything like that."

Well. Dar sighed inwardly. That meant three days of using her laptop, but there was probably enough data and crap she had to sort through to keep her busy for at least that long. "All right." She nodded. "I promise."

Dr. Steve looked relieved. He reached over and ruffled her hair lightly. "Okay. I'll go process your paperwork."

Dar watched him leave, then looked over at Kerry. "Hot damn."

Feeling much better, Kerry finished up her crackers and dusted her fingers off. She got up off the daybed and went over to Dar, curling her fingers around the bedrails and leaning against them. "Three days, huh?"

"Three days," Dar agreed. "You should get plenty done at the office with me stuck at home."

"Mm." Kerry made a noncommittal noise. "Well, let's get you packed up." She slid her hand through the bars and circled Dar's wrist with her fingers, rubbing her thumb against the soft skin. "And get you into that waterbed."

Dar smiled. "Keep me company there?" She waggled an eyebrow.

Kerry grinned back.

Kerry chewed on a carrot as she watched the large pot of soup cook. Discharge had taken less time than she'd thought it would, and they'd gotten home before lunch was served at the hospital.

Which was, she reflected wryly, a good thing, because it was fish. Now, normally Dar liked fish, and so did Kerry, but as Dar put it, she liked her fish to be of some identifiable species and not pasteurized processed cod-like fishcakes.

Ugh. Even the boiled smell coming down the hallway had made Kerry wince. So she'd been glad when the orderly showed up with a wheelchair to take Dar downstairs. Of course, it'd taken her ten minutes of arguing with her lover to get the stubborn woman to **sit** in the wheelchair, but they were out at last, and tucked in the Lexus headed home.

Dar had been quiet. Kerry suspected she was in some pain, but she didn't press her on the subject, theorizing that Dar had been poked and prodded and messed with almost past her tolerance the last twenty-four hours and would only resent the mothering.

She won't resent the soup, though. Kerry poked a wooden spoon in and gave the mixture a stir. The spicy, rich scent of seafood gumbo wafted up, and she felt her mouth water in response. "Mm." She lifted the spoon and took a taste. "Glad I had a container of this in the freezer, Chino."

"Yawp," Chino agreed, peering up at her hopefully.

"No soup for you." Kerry took a biscuit from the dog jar and tossed it to her. "This would make you chuck up your Labrador guts all night."

Chino crunched on her biscuit contentedly. "Growf."

Kerry smiled, then turned and pulled two good-sized bowls down from the cupboard. They were sturdy, a nice shade of bone inside and a pretty cobalt on the outside. She and Dar had purchased them at the Mikasa outlet just a few weeks prior on a rare afternoon's shopping together. That had been fun, Kerry mused, as she ladled portions into each bowl. Just a long Saturday that had started with breakfast at, of all places, McDonalds, and ended with dinner at the Cheesecake Factory.

"And you didn't get any of that doggie bag, didja, Chin?" Kerry put the bowls on a small wicker tray and added silverware, then popped the door on the convection oven and removed a few buttermilk biscuits. "Okay, let's go bring mommy Dar lunch." She picked up the tray and walked into the living room, where Dar had resumed her nest on the couch.

"Hey." Kerry put the tray down on the coffee table. "Hungry?"

Dar lifted her head and sniffed at the bowls. "Is that gumbo?"

"Mm-hmm."

"Mm." Dar smiled and settled back against the soft leather. She was dressed in her pajamas, with a fleece blanket tucked around her and her laptop resting on her knees. Now she watched as Kerry picked up one of the bowls and brought it over, settling it into her lap. "Where did this come from?"

"FedEx delivered it," Kerry answered without a beat. "Didn't you hear them?"

"On Sunday?" Dar asked.

"New service." Kerry offered her a spoonful, pleased when Dar opened her mouth and accepted it. "How's it going?"

"Eh." Dar chewed a bit of conch and swallowed it. "I don't know. It's..." She reached up and rubbed her eyes a little. "Hard to concentrate. My head hurts."

Kerry checked her watch. "You can take a couple more Tylenol," she offered. "Or you could just—oh, I don't know, lie down and get some rest."

Dar considered. "Let me try the pills first," she decided. "I'm really not tired." She accepted the spoon Kerry held out and settled the bowl on her stomach. "Thanks for the soup."

"Any time." Kerry ruffled her hair. "You know, you're not nearly as bad a patient as I thought you'd be."

Dar sucked on the spoon and regarded her lover thoughtfully. "Would you like me to become an unruly curmudgeon?" she asked with a faint smile. "I could. But I figured it made no sense to have both of us be miserable."

"I appreciate that." Kerry reached over and gave Dar's thigh a squeeze. "I just want you to know that I don't mind taking care of you, Dar."

Dark lashes fluttered. "I don't mind letting you," Dar said.

Kerry picked up her bowl and sat down on the couch, picking up Dar's legs and sliding underneath them. She wriggled into a comfortable spot, then crossed her ankles and took a spoonful of soup. "What are we watching?"

"Mpf?" Dar hastily swallowed, then glanced to her left. "Oh. I don't know, I was just browsing and I—"

"Good grief, Dar, that woman is almost naked." Kerry stared at the screen in fascination. "What in the hell is she doing with that stick?"

"Um." Dar bit her lip. "I'm not sure. It's one of those action things. You know I never watch that stuff." She watched anyway. "Hey, she's pretty cute."

Kerry glanced at her. "I guess."

"Looks a little like you," Dar went on.

"No she doesn't," Kerry laughed. "Not unless I spent twenty-four hours a day for six months in a gym, and got a serious haircut." She watched the image on the screen. "Ooh. Nice kick."

"Mm," Dar agreed. "Nice outfit."

Kerry's eyebrows lifted, and she gave her lover a sideways look. "Are you hinting at something?"

"Me?" Blue eyes opened a little wider. "Are you insinuating that I might want to see you in two strips of leather and a pair of floppy boots?"

A grin tugged at Kerry's lips. "Would you?"

"Bet your ass I would," Dar laughed.

Kerry reviewed the screen. "I'd look ridiculous."

"You'd look mouth-watering." Dar bit into a chunk of spicy fish. "Can I have that for a birthday present?"

"Dar!" Kerry blushed, pleased at the compliment but embarrassed at the same time. "You sound so carnal."

Dar chuckled, then jumped a little as her cell phone rang.

"Crap." She balanced her bowl on her lap and put the spoon down, then picked up the buzzing instrument. "Yeah?"

"Dar!" Alastair's voice boomed down the line. "Good gravy! What in the hell happened? Why didn't you call me? Where are you?"

Dar held the phone away from her ear and grimaced. "When you're done yelling, lemme know." She waited, then, when no other sounds issued from it, moved the phone closer. "Good afternoon, Alastair."

"Dar." He sounded exasperated. "For Christ's sake, they said you were in the hospital!"

"I was." Dar stretched a little. "We ran into a little trouble on the base," she said. "I got a knock on the head, they wanted to take some pictures. No big deal, Alastair."

"That's not what I heard," her boss retorted. "I heard you were already hurt when you went down there and got knocked out by some jackass with a gun."

Dar took a breath, then released it. "You told me to find a solution," she said. "I found one."

Alastair let out a gust of air. "What makes you think any solution or any problem is worth risking you? Why didn't you tell me you were hurt, Dar? You think I give two shits about some half-assed piece of crap government contract?"

Dar was quiet for a moment. "Alastair?"

"What?" her boss bellowed.

"Thanks for caring."

There was silence for a few heartbeats, then Alastair sighed. "Well, damn it all to hell, Dar."

Time to take back control of this conversation, Dar's more logical half asserted. "All right. Now that you've called, let me get this over with." She composed her thoughts. "We went down there trying to retain the data evidence. I told you that was the government's concern, right?"

"Right," Alastair exhaled.

"Well, I fucked up." Dar had to pause slightly after saying that, so unusual was it for her to have to pronounce those words in reference to herself. "I didn't find out what was going on first, and we walked right into both a military exercise and a setup."

Alastair didn't even say a word.

"Thank God my father was with us," Dar went on in a quiet, unemotional voice. "They knew we were coming, and they were using the exercise to cover their tracks. With real bullets. If it hadn't been for Dad, things would have been a lot worse."

"So," her boss's voice sounded grim, "what's your analysis?"

Dar watched Kerry's profile as she sat moving her spoon around in her soup with her eyes on the television screen. "I was too close to the problem," she said, watching Kerry's movements still. "I should have backed out of it."

"Ah."

"We should have just dropped the results into the government's lap and submitted our bill," Dar went on. "Now we're going to be involved in lawsuits at the very least."

Alastair's only comment was a sigh. "Anyone else get hurt?"

Dar remembered Jeff Ainsbright's slumped form. "Not any of our people," she replied. "I take full responsibility for this, Alastair."

"Mm," her boss murmured. "You always do, Dar. I've never seen you do less." He considered a moment. "Still and all, we did fulfill the contract, didn't we? As far as that request for service?"

"Yes."

"All right," Alastair said. "Let's keep things in perspective, Dar."

"From a man who was yelling at the top of his lungs when I picked up the phone, that's quite a statement," Dar remarked dryly.

"Well, I was more concerned about you," Alastair admitted. "The fact is, we achieved our goal, and we were just going above and beyond for the customer when things went badly."

"Alastair," Dar sighed.

"I'm not making excuses," her boss snapped. "Easton took advantage of you when he asked you to intervene, and you know it, Dar. He was counting on your being personally involved, and he used that."

Dar opened her mouth to refute the charge, then closed it again as her mind ran over what her boss had said. *Had he?* She looked up to see Kerry regarding her with a sympathetic look on her face.

"I don't blame him for that," Alastair continued hurriedly. "He was in a tight spot and saw a way out of it. I'd have done the same thing."

Dar sighed. "Maybe."

"So, take it easy, all right?"

"Alastair," Dar replied, "you can tell me all day long I was within spec, but we both know I wasn't."

"Eh." A verbal shrug came over the line. "We can talk about it later, Dar. How are you, anyway?"

Dar recognized a deliberate change of subject when she heard one, but didn't have the energy to protest. "I'm all right," she

replied. "I had a concussion, and I messed up my shoulder a couple of days ago. It's really no big deal." Something occurred to
her. "I do have to stay home for a few days, though. I'll call in for
the board meeting on Tuesday."

"Great," Alastair said. "Looks like the budget's right on for
the fourth quarter, and projections are up for next year, thanks to
your network."

Dar smiled. "Trying to cheer me up?"

A chuckle. "Is it working?"

Dar felt better for having told her boss what was going on.
"Yeah."

"Good."

Dar held the phone against her ear and took a spoonful of
soup. "How'd you find out about me in the first place?" she asked,
around a mouthful of shrimp.

"Your mother called me," Alastair told her, a touch of smug-
ness in his tone.

Dar stopped in mid-chew and almost snorted bisque out her
nose. "My mother?"

Kerry snickered. "Uh-oh."

"I had to do it," Jeff Ainsbright stated for the tenth time. He
was seated behind his desk, watching Andrew Roberts's tall, burly
form pace back and forth. "Andy, you don't understand."

"Hell I don't," Andrew snapped, turning to face him. "You
had to sell your damn soul out? That what you're saying?"

Ainsbright sighed and shook his head. "God damn it, Andy,"
he said, "spare me your moralistic hogwash, will you? Maybe you
never wanted to work your way out of that three-bedroom shack
down the row, but I did."

Andrew glowered at him. "Least what I had, I got honestly."

"And what was that?" Jeff replied. "You couldn't even afford
to get your damn wife a new dress most of the time. You never had
nothing, you never left her nothing; you couldn't even send your
kid to college." He stood up and poked a thumb at his own chest.
"I wasn't about to live like that. So yeah, when they offered me
some good money to look the other way, you bet your ass I did."

"Ah would not have, not for all the damn money in the US,"
Andrew stated flatly. "And what'd it get you?"

"A nice house," Ainsbright answered. "A nice car. My wife's a
member of the country club and she loves it. My kid's a ship captain."

"You buy him that, too?" Andrew asked sarcastically.

"What'd you ever give your kid?" Jeff taunted. "A used tennis ball?"

"Care," the ex-SEAL replied. "And knowin' what was right and wrong." He folded his arms. "I didn't have to do nothing else. She made her own future without beggin' me for handouts."

Ainsbright rolled his eyes. "You're a fool, Andrew. You always were." He stood up. "All right, look." A hand lifted. "Yeah, I knew about everything here. I knew about the shipments, and I knew they were covering them. But I never had anything directly to do with any of it, hear?"

Andrew studied him.

"I did what I did for my family," Jeff stated. "To give them a better life."

"Now they ain't gonna have nothing," Andrew said. "With your ass in jail."

Ainsbright snorted. "Not for bad record-keeping, Andy." He managed a thin-lipped smile. "That's all your brilliant little wunderkind is going to find now."

Thoughtful blue eyes regarded him. "Think so?"

"I know it. I made sure of that personally," Ainsbright snapped. "Despite you getting your ass in the way, that is. I wasn't after your damn kid."

"You had a damn M16 with a scope." Andrew closed on him again. "Who were you after?"

"No one," Ainsbright answered coolly. "It was all part of the exercise." He pointed at Andrew. "Which your daughter interrupted with an unauthorized breach of the base. If anything happened to her here, it's her fault, not mine." He paused. "For that matter, you better just hope I don't bring you up on assault charges."

Andrew blinked. "You do that, and ah will make direly sure you'll have been assaulted for it."

"That a threat?" Jeff snorted. "Get out of here, Andy. You're out of your league, and you don't belong here anymore."

Andrew turned and walked to the window, gazing out at the grassy space before the building. "Ain't that the truest thing you done said here today," he rumbled. "If you ain't the one who's running this show, Jeff, who is?" He turned and eyed the CO, who remained silent. "They pay you to take the fall for them?"

The base commander shook his head. "I'm not taking a fall, Andy. I told you that."

"'Cause you think you out-thunk my kid, is that it?" A smile twisted Andrew's face. "Better hope you're right. I sure never could."

Jeff snorted. "I'm smarter than you are, Andy. We both know that."

A slow nod. "That may be true, Jeff. But you ain't smarter than she is. So you better be damn sure you've got all your tracks covered, or it's your ass what's going to be run up that there flag-pole outside." He turned and pointed, then turned back and walked over to the base commander, stopping within a pace of him. "Because she will nail you."

Their eyes locked. "I'm sure," Jeff finally said. "I've got good people who made very, very sure of that." He turned and straight-ened his jacket. "Now, if you'll excuse me, Andrew, I've got a lunch date with my wife." He gestured toward the door. "I'll have you escorted to the gate." He turned back toward his desk, then stopped dead.

The office was empty.

"Son of a bitch." The base commander raced to the window and looked out, leaning out to look up and down. Then he pulled his head back in and searched the room with anxious eyes. "Where in the f—" Cursing, he reached for the phone and lifted it, dialing a number quickly. "Security? This is the base commander. We've got an unauthorized entry. Send a security team to my office and put the base on alert."

Chapter
Eighteen

The alarm went off before dawn, and Kerry reached over quickly to silence it. It stopped its low buzz, and she let her hand drop back down onto the pillow as she glanced over at Dar's sleeping form.

Her lover didn't stir, her body relaxed in slumber and her breathing slow and even. *Good.* Kerry sighed in relief. Obsessively, Dar had worked until after midnight on what data she had in her laptop, only surrendering when Kerry coaxed her off the couch and into the waterbed, where she'd fallen asleep almost in the middle of a protest.

Kerry spent a moment just watching Dar's profile, outlined by the pale blue night-light in the bathroom. Then she rolled over and eased out of bed on the opposite side, twitching the down comforter back into place. She stifled a yawn with one hand as she made her way into the bathroom and closed the door quietly behind her before she flipped the light on.

"Ugh." Kerry winced and closed her eyes, waiting for a moment before she reopened them and blinked at her reflection. A very disheveled, grumpy woman looked back at her, and she stuck her tongue out at the image.

She had such a damn busy day planned at work. First, she'd have to coordinate the recovery of whatever Mark had retained in that black box, assuming Dar remembered how to reassemble the puzzle pieces. Then she'd have to assign a high security team to work with the database, reconstructing it meticulously and recording their steps line by line.

Then, since it was a Monday, she knew there would be at least five or six major disasters for her to handle, along with the usual running operations issues. Thank God, Kerry mused, as she splashed water on her face and lathered up some soap, that Dar's new network had reduced her crisis calls by eighty percent, its flexibility and reliability making her life much more pleasant.

So she'd get some liquid breakfast, throw on her running gear, do her laps, then shower and head for the office. Kerry dried her face and nodded at her still scruffy, but more alert-looking reflection. "Right?" She watched her lower lip poke out as though of its own volition.

Her brow creased. "Okay, what's wrong?" The lip poked out further in a pout. "Kerrison Stuart, you are not going to pout because Dar gets to stay home and you don't, y'hear me?"

"Growf." Chino hopped up and put her paws on the sink, peering up at Kerry as if wondering who her mom was talking to.

"Sure, that's easy for you to say." Kerry turned and tapped the end of her toothbrush on Chino's nose. "You get to stay here with her."

Chino's tail wagged.

"Yeah, yeah. Rufh min fin," Kerry spoke through a mouthful of toothpaste.

It was a beautiful morning. Kerry took a deep breath of the cool, salt-tinged air as she walked down the path to the beach, enjoying the lack of humidity that made their running uncomfortable, bordering on brutal during the summer months. When she reached the winding path that led around the island, she paused to stretch out her muscles, as a few seagulls drifted by to watch.

It was quiet at this hour, the soft clanks from the marina and the birds' curious squawks the only sounds that broke the dawn hush. Kerry finished her warm-up and started down the path at a slow jog, waiting for her body to wake up and get into sync before she picked her pace up and settled into her run.

She'd finally gotten used to this. Kerry watched a small tug move past the south side of the island as she headed around the marina. In fact, she'd come to look forward to the time she and Dar set aside for their joint morning exercise, because it was a great way to start the day with some peace and quiet.

Okay. Kerry smiled as she rounded the island's northern side for the first time. *And some companionable togetherness.* They'd started debating current events the past few weeks, and she found herself missing the company this morning.

How had Dar stood it all those years alone? The thought intruded itself. Then another thought made her almost stop in her tracks. *How did you stand it all those years alone, Kerry?*

Wow. Kerry tried to remember what her life had been like before she'd met Dar. It had been—well, all right, she guessed.

She'd had fun with her friends at work and with Colleen. She hadn't been lonely, had she?

Second lap already? Kerry sighed and nibbled her lower lip. No, she really hadn't been lonely. She'd been more like...waiting. That was it. She nodded to herself. She'd always had the feeling that just around the bend, just around that next corner, she'd find someone special.

Okay, so it wasn't around a corner, and the person had barged into her office intent on firing her, but she'd found it. Kerry smiled and leaned forward a little, picking up her pace. *Faster I go, faster I get back.*

Dar kept her eyes closed, aware of the fact that she was alone in bed. This didn't make her very happy. The waterbed was comfortable, but it was a lot warmer and more comfortable if it was full of a certain blond woman she knew, who tended to drape nice smelling and cutely shaped parts of herself all over Dar.

On the other hand, Dar reasoned, she could also smell cinnamon and the scent of fresh coffee, which meant she was trading off waking up chilly and grumpy for sticky buns and a cup of Santa's White Christmas in her big blue mug.

Hmm.

She heard soft clinks from the kitchen, then the light scuff of bare feet against tile heading in her direction. It was strange, but she could actually feel Kerry's presence as her lover entered the room, bringing the nice smells closer and combining them with apricot skin scrub and the clean cotton T-shirt that covered Kerry's freshly showered body.

Mm. Dar briefly wondered if she could just suck on Kerry and forgo the sticky bun. She opened one eye. "Morning."

"Hi there, cute stuff." Kerry set the small tray down on their bedside table. On it was the anticipated blue mug and a plate with two buns. "How do you feel?"

Dar closed her fingers on the knee conveniently close by and squeezed. "Mm, not bad," she joked wryly. "Like crap, honestly," she then admitted. "I feel like I'll never get rid of this headache, and my arm's killing me. I think I slept wrong."

Kerry rattled the small bottle on the tray. "I came prepared." She removed a small glass from next to the mug. "Here." She handed Dar some juice and three tablets. "You might want to spend some time outside later—it's gorgeous."

Dar finished the juice and handed the glass back. "Thanks. I'll take the laptop out there," she said. "You better get dressed."

"Oh." Kerry plucked at her shirt, which had an almost life-size Dilbert sprawled across its surface. "You mean I can't go to work like this? C'mon, Dar."

Dar cocked her head slightly. "Well, okay, hon, but don't stand with your back to the light, okay? It's a little translucent."

Kerry looked down. "It is?" she asked in surprise. "Where?"

A finger reached out and tickled a very sensitive spot.

"Yeak!" A snorting laugh escaped Kerry. "Okay, okay. I see your point." She gazed fondly at Dar. "Let me go get into my monkey suit."

Dar tangled her fingers in the soft cotton and tugged. "Thanks for breakfast," she said. "And you can go to work dressed casual today if you want. It won't kill anyone."

Kerry considered that, then nodded. "Okay, I will," she decided. "I'm in the mood for jeans." She turned and made her way into the living room, then took the stairs two at a time.

"When're we gonna see what we got?" Brent asked, sticking his hands in his pockets and regarding the locked steel box in the corner of Mark's office.

Mark didn't look up from the folder he was writing on. "When Dar says we do. Go do something, willya, Brent? It's not going to levitate out of that box."

Brent stayed put. "We risked our necks to get that thing."

Now Mark looked up. "You volunteered."

"So?" The tech squared a pugnacious jaw. "We still did."

"And your point is what?" the MIS chief asked. "Look, you wouldn't know what the hell was in there even if I did open and link it. It's not readable."

Brent's brow creased. "Huh? Then what'd we do it for? You mean we can't use it?"

"I didn't say that." Mark took an impatient breath. "I said you can't read it. I can't read it. Yoda the Jedi Master can't read it." He pointed at the box. "But Dar can. She knows what formula she used to structure the sector copy. She's the one who has to reconstruct it, okay?"

Brent looked interested. "Oh."

Mark leaned back. "Hey. Why the fuck did you go with us?" he asked bluntly. "You spent the last two weeks blowing shit all over this office about how you felt about the boss."

Brent studied him sullenly. "It's not right."

"Yeah, yeah, yeah. You, my aunt Matilda, and Dr. Laura with your homophobic bullshit," Mark snapped. "All of you can kiss my ass. So why offer to help out someone you hate so much?"

Brent shrugged. "The Navy sucks," he commented, then turned and walked out, leaving a bewildered Mark to stare after him.

"What the hell was that?" Mark asked the empty air. "Why the fuck do I get all the warped SIMMS in Miami working for me?" He shook his head and glanced at his screen. "Ah." An alert showed him that Kerry had logged into the office systems. He checked a second alarm, scowling a little on seeing it remain dark. "Shit. C'mon, Dar. I want to know if we got those bastards, too."

The boat rocked up and down in the very light chop as Ceci walked along the edge of the deck. *Good thing*, she mused thoughtfully, *that I'm not prone to seasickness. That would have been a hell of a thing to find out after I talked Andy into this thing, wouldn't it?*

She spotted her husband seated on the very front of the bow, resting his arms on the railing as he watched the sun rise over the sea. He was dressed in his shortie wet suit, which glistened with the seawater that also dampened his grizzled hair and scattered sparkles over his tanned skin.

"Hey, sailor boy." Ceci took a seat next to him.

"Y'know, Cec," Andrew turned his head and looked thoughtfully at her, "I do believe I do not consider that a compliment anymore."

Ceci looked at him. "Andy," she put a hand on his leg, "don't say that. A bunch of jackasses shouldn't take a lifetime of pride away from you. C'mon now." She found herself in the weird position of defending a service she'd never really liked or understood. "You know the vast majority aren't like that. They're like you." She gazed into the pale blue eyes. "Well, not just like you."

Andrew sighed. "Ah remember doing bartering myself back on that there base."

"Everyone did," Ceci laughed. "C'mon, Andy. That's how we managed to trade enough for that Christmas party that one year, remember? When you won that stuffed tiger from Brad at the carnival, and gave it to Dar?"

Andrew brooded. "How was that different than what this was? Jeff said he done it for his family. Well, I done that for my family."

"Hon," Ceci managed not to smile, "I don't think even the attorney general, bless her good, cracker heart, would see tins of peanut butter and a case of beer in the same light as selling black-market M16s and cocaine."

"Mph."

"Besides, how could we possibly deny Dar her peanut butter?" Ceci asked. "She ate so much of that, I'm surprised she doesn't carry a cane and wear a top hat and spats."

Andrew laughed wryly in pure reflex. "She surely did like that stuff," he agreed, then sighed. "Maybe that's how it starts, though. Folks think that's all right, then it just goes a little further, and further—"

"No." Ceci shook her head. "There's a line there, Andy. You and I both know that. Someone made the decision to cross that line." She put a hand on his arm "It just so happens that person was a friend of ours."

Andrew scowled. "Jackass."

"Mm."

"Hope Dar nails his ass t'the ground with a sharpened flagpole."

Now it was Ceci's turn to laugh.

Dar lay quietly in bed, soft New Age music providing a background as she drowsed, allowing the painkillers to ebb some of the throbbing from her arm and head. There were a dozen things she could be doing, she admitted, but it was much easier to do what she'd promised she'd do, which was rest and allow her body to heal.

It was hard to remember the last time she'd just slept in all day. She and Kerry kept pretty busy; even on weekends they were out on the boat, or driving down to the Keys, or...Dar smiled sleepily. Or shopping.

She'd discovered she liked shopping with Kerry. Even when they were looking for something totally mundane, like plates, she found herself enjoying the process. Last time they'd gone to the mall, she'd even done a little clothes shopping, both she and Kerry having fun remembering the first time they'd done that, mere weeks after they'd first met.

And this time they shared a dressing room. Dar chuckled softly as she indulged herself in a memory of the two of them buttoning and zipping each other.

And unbuttoning and unzipping.

Dar idly hoped Saks Fifth Avenue didn't videotape their patrons.

The phone rang, causing her to reluctantly open her eyes and peer at the table. With a groan, she rolled over and reached out to slap the speaker button. "Hello?"

"Good morning, Dar."

Dar let her eyes close again. "Morning." She returned her mother's greeting cordially. "What's up?"

"Your father's temper."

That got one eye open. "Don't tell me it's the Priceline.com commercials again," she said.

Ceci chuckled wryly. "Actually, his new pet peeve is the erectile dysfunction minimovies that have been playing recently."

Dar's brow wrinkled. "Ew."

"Mm," her mother agreed. "At any rate, he took a ride down to the base yesterday and didn't come back very happy. Apparently they're covering their tracks pretty thoroughly."

"Um," Dar tried to dredge up some interest. "Figures."

There was a moment's silence. "You doing all right?" Ceci finally asked warily.

"Pretty much," Dar answered. "Been laying in bed most of the morning."

"Ah. I see." Ceci seemed to consider this statement seriously for a little while. "Well, I went to the technological depths of iniquity and managed to produce a pan of something that might, if you don't look too closely, pass as brownies to cheer your father up."

Dar chuckled in pure reflex.

"Mind if I drop some by?"

Dar lifted her head up and peered at the phone in honest surprise. For a second, she almost politely declined, then a sudden impulse took over. "S...sure." She cast a quick look around. "Place is a mess."

Her mother laughed audibly. "See you in a bit."

"Okay," Dar replied, then heard the line drop. She rested her chin on her wrist and stared at the phone, then shook her head. "Look out, Chino. We're getting a visitor."

The Labrador lifted her head up and wagged her tail. She was curled up in her bed next to where Dar was lying.

"My mother's coming over," she informed the dog. "And she's bringing brownies." Dar rolled over cautiously and regarded the ceiling. "Bet if I look outside, it'll be snowing."

"Growf."

"Mm. But if she offers to do the laundry, we're outta here." Dar covered her eyes with one hand. "Scary. Very scary."

Kerry knelt beside the lockbox and lifted the security tag,

reading the number off it and recording it on a large manila file clipped onto the clipboard she was carrying. "Okay." She stood and wrote the cataloging entry on the file folder. "Do we have point-to-point concurrence that this never left anyone's view?"

"Yep," Mark said. "I made sure I kept three guys with me to sign off on it."

"Good." Kerry took a step back and dropped into the chair across from Mark's desk, crossing one denim-covered ankle over her knee. "Now we just have to find out if there's anything useful in there."

"Yeah," Mark sighed. "Boss won't be in 'til Wednesday, huh?"

"Nope," Kerry said. "And I'd feel better if we did all the analysis here, rather than have that brought to the house. It's going to be touchy as it is."

The MIS chief nodded. "I'm with you. They get that team into the base?"

Kerry chewed on the end of her pen. "Yeah. I got a call from that JAG officer. They've been there all day, and so far, it all looks clean."

Mark snorted.

Kerry acknowledged his derision with a twitch of her lips. "Not that we don't already have some data on them. But nothing major. Mostly bad or shady bookkeeping on stuff like supplies."

"So, if there's nothing in this thing," Mark kicked the lockbox, "that's it? They just get off?"

Kerry stood up and exhaled. "If we can't prove anything, then, yes," she agreed. "Or, to be more specific, if we can't provide information to the authorities that will allow them to prove it. We're just the analysts."

"Bet Dar doesn't feel that way," Mark commented. "Man, I can't believe she grew up there. My brain can't process that." He glanced at Kerry. "Weird."

"Why?" Kerry asked, pausing in the doorway on her way out.

Mark shrugged, a little uncomfortably. "I don't know. It was like when she took us out to that little island place, y'know? I just figured she went through the same kind of growing up around here that I did. Malls, football games, whatever."

Kerry studied him. "Didn't figure her for a redneck?"

Mark scowled. "She's not a friggin' redneck. She's just a, a—"

"Cracker," Kerry supplied gently.

"No way."

"Mark." Kerry came back over and sat down, resting her hands on her knees and putting her envelope down. "I love Dar.

You know that, right?"

He blushed.

"She's my best friend, and my partner, and I wouldn't trade her for anyone or anything in the world," Kerry went on. "She's not embarrassed by her origins, so why should you be?"

Another shrug. "It's just weird."

Kerry sighed. "I think it makes her achievements all the more spectacular," she said. "Because she really did start from nothing, and everything she's gained has been on her own terms, and by her own brilliance."

Mark looked up. "Yeah."

After a speculative look, Kerry admitted, "I envy her for that. It must be an amazing feeling to know you've totally controlled your own destiny."

Mark played with the chip puller he used as a paperweight. "She has, hasn't she? I never really thought about that," he told Kerry. "Hey, you had lunch yet?"

Kerry let the subject change pass. "Not yet. Want to go down? They've got lamb shanks today." She stood back up. "I think Mari said she was going down about now, too."

Mark joined her and carefully locked the door to his office behind them. "Not like you could drag that box anywhere, but ya never know."

"Mm," Kerry agreed. "You never do know." She glanced around the office, and gave the staff there a brief smile. Most smiled back.

Brent just looked away from her.

Ceci set a glass on the counter and studiously filled it with milk. The condo was quiet, and despite Dar's disclaimer, seemed no untidier than it usually did. Which was not at all, save a collection of laundry awaiting attention in the utility room.

That didn't really surprise her. Though Dar had maintained a nest of teenage clutter in her younger years, the room had never been dirty, per se, just full of stuff. Things that held Dar's capricious interest, or things that Andrew had given her, all jealously hoarded in neatly labeled boxes stacked everywhere.

She'd had time, when she and Andrew had dog-sat, to wander over the condo, and had found herself smiling at childhood vestiges she'd found tucked away in inconspicuous corners.

Those things had meant something to her daughter. Ceci studied the glass of milk, then picked it up and made her way through the living room and into the bedroom where Dar was resting. She held out the glass. "Figured you'd need this."

Dar got caught in mid-chew. She hastily swallowed a mouth-ful of brownie and accepted the milk, taking a sip of it to wash down the rich treat. "Thanks." She indicated the tray. "Not bad for instant."

"Mm, yes." Ceci sat down in the comfortable chair near the bed. "Shocked the hell out of me, I have to admit."

Dar grinned slightly. "I know the feeling. I made dinner the other week and was totally amazed at it being edible."

One of Ceci's silver blond eyebrows rose. "What was the occasion?"

Dar hesitated, then shrugged. "Nothing special. I just felt like doing it." She was aware of the always perceptible discomfort between them, and suddenly felt very tired of it. Life was, she'd come to realize, just too damn short sometimes. "Hey, Mom?"

Ceci detected the change in Dar's tone, and she leaned forward a little. "Yes?"

Dar took a deep breath. "We've got a pretty lousy past with each other."

Uh-oh. Ceci felt her heart move up into her throat. "Brownies weren't that bad, were they?" she joked faintly.

That made Dar smile, and she realized her mother was a lot more nervous than she was. "No." She glanced down and col-lected her thoughts, then looked up. "Can we just forget it all and start fresh from here?"

It came around a blind corner and smacked Ceci right between the eyes, leaving a sting as though she'd been hit with a mackerel. She found herself gazing right into Dar's intense face, the echo of the question reminding her strongly of the one she'd asked Andrew the night they'd been reunited. "That what you really want?" she asked quietly.

Dar nodded.

Ceci felt absurdly like crying. "I'd really like that, too," she said. "I know it sounds ridiculous, but you don't realize all the good things about being a mother until you aren't one anymore."

Now it was Dar's turn to be caught off guard. She blinked and felt a surge of juvenile memory as she stared at her mother's face. "That's all right," she finally said, a touch of hoarseness in her voice. "When you're a kid, you never appreciate your parents until you don't have them."

Ceci felt the sting of tears, and she reached out instinctively, laying a hand along Dar's cheek. "I'm sorry," she whispered. "I'm sorry I abandoned you."

Dar sucked in a breath that was almost painful, so tight was the pressure against her chest. She was caught by her mother's gaze, unable to look away. "I'm sorry I didn't understand the pain you were in."

The tension lessened. Ceci rubbed a thumb against her daughter's skin. "I'm glad we're getting a second chance at this."

The surface under her fingers moved as Dar smiled. "So am I," she answered softly, glancing away, then returning her eyes to her mother's. "I think I like you."

Ceci bit her lip, a surge of improbable, ridiculous relief almost making her burst out laughing. "Yeah, I think I like you, too."

It was turning out to be an interesting day after all, Dar decided happily.

Kerry sat behind her desk, one hand propping up her head as she scrolled through screens of data. She paused to make another sticky note, punching out the letters with one finger, then continued her task.

"Ms. Kerry?" Mayte's voice broke into her concentration. "I have the Navy officer here to see you."

Ah. Kerry straightened and took a sip of her herbal tea. "Great. Send him in." She leaned back in her chair as the door opened and Captain Taylor came in. He was dressed in his Navy uniform, and he tucked his hat under his arm as he crossed the carpeted floor to her desk. "Afternoon, Captain."

"Ms. Stuart." The officer inclined his head politely. "May I sit down?"

Kerry gestured toward the chair. "Of course. How's it going down there?"

Captain Taylor shook his head gravely. "I'm afraid we're going to come up empty-handed, Ms. Stuart. My team's been in there for hours, and they haven't come up with anything other than the mess that was left of the computer center." He paused. "And we have six people who swear it was just a botched exercise. They even submitted the docs for the setup and showed me the dummy rounds. Apparently some live ones got mixed in."

"Uh-huh." Kerry took another sip of tea. "Do you believe them?"

The captain gave her a direct look. "Ms. Stuart, it doesn't matter a hill of beans what I believe. All that matters is what I can prove. I can't prove anything beyond some colossal screw-ups, and some of them involve your personnel."

Kerry's eyebrows lifted. "My personnel?" she asked sharply.

"We didn't make any mistakes."

The captain shifted uncomfortably. "The fact is, ma'am, you were there without the permission of the base commander."

"Cut the BS." Kerry smiled kindly at him. "We were there because General Easton asked us to go there and cover his butt because you couldn't get a team on the plane fast enough."

Captain Taylor made a face, seemingly unconscious of it. "The general asked that you protect the data. You didn't. In fact, because of your presence, its destruction was pretty much guaranteed."

Kerry pointed a finger at him. "Captain, if you seriously think you're going to shift blame to me or to anyone else at ILS for your inability to maintain military and administrative control of your own base, think again." She stood up behind her desk and fixed him with a resolute stare. "We did the best we could, and you don't know just what that best is yet."

"Ms. Stuart, you don't seem to re—" The naval officer stopped and regarded her warily. "What exactly do you mean by that?"

Kerry opened her mouth to explain, then slowly closed it again. Some instinct was telling her to keep the lock box under wraps, and she'd learned over the last year that this instinct of hers was usually right. "We have a lot of data. We're not finished analyzing it yet," she temporized. "We may not have a smoking gun, but we may have enough to nail the people there most responsible."

The captain relaxed a notch. "It's just administrative stuff, though. The base is clean."

"For now," Kerry agreed quietly. "Doesn't it bother you that stuff was going on?"

Taylor dusted a bit of lint off his shoulder. "Do we know it really was?" he countered. "That informant of yours could have been lying."

Kerry shrugged. "Why?"

"To get someone in trouble. Maybe they're the ones involved in some funny business, and they thought bringing in drugs would shift the attention," the JAG officer replied reasonably. "C'mon, Ms. Stuart—do you honestly think we've got an entire smuggling operation going on at a Navy base? Low-grade black market, yeah, I can buy that. But drugs?"

Well. Kerry thought about it. It was possible, she guessed. They hadn't seen any of the smuggling, just the evidence the chief had brought over. "What about that telecommunications gear that was ripped out?"

The captain chuckled. "You know, I was thinking about that. You know what I bet happened? I bet someone in some office somewhere had a requisition to yank it out, or some wire got crossed, and an order was cut, and that's why no one knew about it. Doesn't that happen in your company sometimes?"

True. "Sometimes," Kerry agreed, "but not often."

"Well," Taylor stood up, "I'm going to file my preliminary report to the general. I think we overreacted a little bit here. Comes from putting civilians into a situation they don't really understand, I think."

Kerry's eyes took on a perceptibly cold glint. "You do that," she told the captain with deceptive pleasantness. "By the way, Captain?"

He had turned to leave, but now he paused and glanced back. "Yes?"

"Where did you go hide Saturday?" Kerry inquired. "I had count of everyone who was with us, and I lost you after we went into the computer center." She held up a clipboard. "I need to know for my...report."

His face became a mask. "You must be mistaken, Ms. Stuart. I was there the whole time." He turned and walked out, settling his hat squarely on the top of his head as he went through the door.

"Ooh." Kerry slowly let out a breath, and crossed her arms. "You little pinheaded starch-butt."

"Ms. Kerry?" Mayte asked uncertainly, as she stuck her head around the corner of the door. "Did you say something?"

"Not to you." Kerry sat down and sucked down a big mouthful of her tea. "Mayte, do you have a number for General Easton? If you don't, I bet María does."

"I will get it," her assistant promised, disappearing quickly.

Kerry chewed her lip, then put her cup down and punched the speakerphone button, hitting the top speed dial on her console. It rang twice, then was answered. "Hey."

"Hey." Dar's voice sounded alert and faintly amused. "I was just thinking of you."

Kerry felt her train of thought gently derail and move off onto a siding somewhere. "Were you? How come?"

"Underwear," Dar replied succinctly.

It wasn't the response Kerry was expecting. "Excuse me?"

"I'm doing laundry."

"Oh." Kerry's brow creased. "You didn't have to, Dar. I'd have done it tonight." She knew her lover hated doing laundry and avoided it whenever possible, sending everything she could get her hands on to the island's cleaners.

Except things like underwear, of course. Kerry smiled to herself as she took a sip of tea.

"Mom thinks yours are cute."

The mouthful of tea was expelled across the desk's surface, narrowly missing her keyboard. "What?" Kerry wiped her forearm across her mouth. "Paladar! Why are you showing your mother my underwear?"

Dar chuckled softly. "You sound so cute when you're flustered."

"I'm not flustered! I'm flabbergasted! Two very different emotions!" Kerry said. "And you didn't answer me!"

"Relax," her lover replied. "She's just helping me do laundry. It's tough with one arm."

Kerry covered her eyes with one hand. "Oh." She exhaled, then paused in thought. "So Mom came by, huh?"

"Mm," Dar answered.

"Everything okay?" Kerry asked guardedly.

"Very much so," the surprising answer came back. "We had a talk." The pleasure was evident in Dar's tone. "It's great."

"Oh yeah?" Kerry felt a smile cross her face. "Wow. That's really good to hear, Dar."

"Yeah." Dar let out a happy little sigh. "So, what's up there?"

Plans suddenly got sidetracked, and Kerry concentrated on the job at hand. "Ah. I had a visit from Captain Butter-wouldn't-melt-between-my-butt-cheeks."

Dar snorted in laughter.

"He's already putting together his version of a story to make everything look like nothing," Kerry said seriously. "If we don't have something in that box, Dar, we really don't have much."

"Mm." Dar sounded serious now, too. "Open it up, then."

Kerry took a deep breath and carefully asked the question she'd been avoiding. "I'll need the algorithm codes. Do you have them?" She crossed her fingers and toes and bit her lower lip as she waited for the answer.

"Sure," Dar replied easily. "My birthday, offset, your birthday." A pause. "In hex."

Kerry's eyes popped open and she stared across her office with a look of chagrin. "Oh, you're kidding."

"No," her lover replied. "Those are a bitch to memorize, Kerry, and it's not like I had a pad and pencil handy. I picked something I knew I'd remember."

Duh. Kerry almost laughed. *I should have known.* She gazed up at her ceiling. "Okay, listen, I think I'd rather wait until you got back here to do it. We can hold them off that long."

"You sure?" Dar asked. "Yeah, on second thought, let's give them a chance to think they're home free. Then they'll relax a little."

"Right," Kerry said. "Is Mom staying for dinner?"

There was a muffled noise, a low buzz of conversation, then Dar's voice came back. "If you pick up Captain Crab's Takeaway Seal."

"You got it," Kerry snickered. "One bucket, coming up." She hung up and leaned back, a dozen thoughts zooming through her head.

One remained. "Oh, crap." Kerry winced. "I hope it wasn't the pink ones."

The boat was rocking gently on the tide as Kerry made her way along the dock. It was very quiet, and she didn't see anyone around, even after she stepped up onto the gangway and crossed onto the boat's white deck. "Hello?" she called out, looking around for Andrew. "Dad?"

Silence. Kerry ducked down and stuck her head inside the cabin. It was quiet down there as well; the worktable, covered in painting supplies, sitting mutely near the windows. "Dad?"

Still nothing. Kerry stood up and walked across the stern deck, which had comfortable looking bench seats on either side and a storage locker in the center that doubled as a table.

"Huh." She walked over and leaned on the railing, peering down into the dark blue-green water. "Maybe he went to the dock shop." She watched a sea grape float by, lulled by its peaceful bobbing.

Then the water heaved and a hand surged up to grab the railing between hers, scaring the living daylights out of her.

"Yah!" Kerry squealed, jerking back and scrambling away from the railing. "Jesus!"

Andrew peered through the metal bars at her and the curious expression on her face. "Hold on t'yer shorts, kumquat. I sure ain't the good Lord."

Kerry sat down on the center console, and put a hand on her chest. "Wow," she laughed weakly. "You got me."

The ex-SEAL pulled himself up and climbed over the railing, the boat's deck rocking a little under his weight. He was dressed in a half wetsuit and his minimal diving rig, which he shed as he ambled over to where Kerry was sitting. "Didn't mean to scare you, Kerry," he apologized. "Just wasn't sure what that shadow was looking over my rail." He knelt beside her and put a damp hand on her knee. "You all right?"

Kerry felt her heart rate start to slow, and she ran a hand through her hair. "Yeah," she said. "Boy, a dolphin's got nothing on you."

Andrew chuckled. "Long as you don't smack me in the snout with no mackerel." He cocked his head at her. "Didn't 'spect visitors t'day."

Kerry abruptly remembered her task. "Ah." She folded her arms, holding her news close and cherishing it. "Do you know where your wife is?"

Andrew's grizzled brows creased in puzzlement, and he glanced around at the empty deck. "Figgered she went down to the shops," he hazarded. "Why? You know different?"

"Mm-hmm," Kerry nodded. "She's at our place."

"Ah see." Andrew seemed to relax as he stood up and walked over to the padded bench, picking up a towel and tousling his short-cropped hair dry. "Dar need something?" He peeked at her from behind a corner of the terrycloth.

"No. They were just spending some time together." A gentle twinkle entered Kerry's eyes.

A big grin spread across the ex-SEAL's face. "For real?"

Kerry nodded.

"Hot damn!" A chortle of joy escaped. "C'mere!"

He held out his arms and Kerry scrambled over and threw herself into them, not minding the wetness one tiny bit. She felt the laughter as they hugged each other. "I couldn't believe it," she said as they released each other. "I called Dar, and she sounded so happy."

Andrew shook his head in amazement. "Damn, that's good to hear," he breathed. "I knew things were getting easier, but I never figured it would go this fast."

"Me, either," Kerry admitted. "They're both pretty stubborn."

"Ain't that the truth," he chuckled. "You just stop by to tell me that? Y'coulda just used the land line, kumquat." He went back to drying himself off.

Kerry shook her head. "No," she said. "They asked me to stop and pick you up for a family dinner."

Andrew stopped in mid-motion and let the towel fall, his eyes fastening on Kerry and his eyebrows lifting up. "'Scuse me, young lady?" he asked in a surprised tone.

Kerry reviewed her statement, then blushed. "Oh crap." She started laughing. "That's not what I meant."

"Uh-huh." Andrew snorted. "Damn straight."

"Speak for yourself." A slim finger pointed at Andrew. "That got me in enough trouble the other week."

Andrew cocked his head at her. "Trouble? I thought them folks were all right with you and mah kid?"

Kerry smiled briefly. "They are, but a couple of nosybodies saw you pick me up the other night and thought I was cheating on Dar." She chuckled, shaking her head. "What a morning."

Her father-in-law's jaw dropped. Then it shut with a click. "That is not funny."

"It wasn't then," Kerry admitted. "But we laughed about it later on that night. Dar's secretary María chewed everyone a new...um..." She paused. "Anyway..."

Andrew frowned. "Ah do not like that," he said. "Them people got no sense at all." He dried one ear. "Ain't they got better things to do than spread all kinds of foolishness?"

Kerry regarded the horizon. "Well," she pursed her lips, "there's a lot of folks there who aren't really comfortable with Dar and me, and..." Her eyes narrowed slightly. "A few with personal agendas, too, I guess."

"Uh-huh."

"The guy who saw us was kind of, um," Kerry blushed slightly. "He liked me."

"Ah." Andrew snorted softly. "Figgers."

"And the other person doing the most talking kind of used to like Dar," she concluded. "But we got it all settled, so..." But she frowned, Clarice's continued aggressiveness coming into memory. "I suppose people will be people."

"Jerks'll be jerks," Andrew amended succinctly. "Ain't no changing 'em. Like a few we bumped heads with down south." He shook his head. "Mah wife ain't doing no cooking for us, is she?"

Kerry found herself glad of the change of subject. "Actually, I was told to pick up a bucket of Captain Crab's Takeaway Seal." She grinned at him.

Andrew put his hands on his hips. "Mah wife say that?" He watched Kerry nod. "Uh-huh. All right then, we'll just go get us exactly that." He draped his towel over the railing and headed for the cabin. "Y'all just stay put, kumquat. We'll give 'em some crabs."

Uh-oh. Kerry sat down on the center console. *Is that good or bad?* She nibbled her lower lip as she thought about her father-in-law's sometimes peculiar sense of humor. "Dad?" she called down the hatch.

"Yep?" Andrew answered.

"You're not talking about live crabs, are you?"

"Nope."

"Or the icky kind, right?"

"'Scuse me?"

"The ones that require medication?"

"What?"

Kerry sighed. "Never mind." She swung her feet back and forth idly. *Guess I'll just have to wait and see for myself.*

Dar stretched her legs out along the couch, the cool leather warming to her bare skin. She settled her arm in its sling and exhaled in satisfaction. It had ended up being a nice day after all. Laundry had gotten done, a set of cookies had been dubiously pre-pared, and she'd even managed to spend a lot of the day lying down as she'd promised she would.

"Don't tell me you watch this," Ceci commented from the loveseat.

Dar glanced at the television. "Sure. All the time," she replied. "We love the croc guy."

"Dar, he's a lunatic," her mother complained. "His brains have all dribbled out, and he uses cat food stuffed through his ears as a replacement." She was curled up in the smaller couch's con-fines, a visible smudge of chocolate present on the knee of her white cotton pants.

Dar had known better. She had put on a pair of ragged denim cutoffs and an old gym shirt, so of course she hadn't gotten a drop of anything on her. "Nah, he's not that bad. I like the way he respects animals."

Ceci's silver-blond eyebrow lifted. "Dar, he doesn't respect animals, he sleeps with them."

Dar pointed. "No, that's his wife," she said mildly. "She's not an animal."

"Dar, that's not his wife. That's a chimpanzee."

Dar looked closer. "Oh. Sorry." She tilted her head. "I saw the hat and thought it was Terry. It's hard to tell up in that tree." She leaned back against the soft cushion and let her eyes close, more tired than she'd expected to be. For a while, she'd tried to do a little work in her office, but after a few minutes her head was pounding, and using only one hand was driving her nuts.

Oh well. Dr. Steve had warned her about that, right? She'd gotten off pretty lucky, he'd told her, showing her the scans of her head. The swelling inside her skull hadn't really put much pres-sure on her brain, but still, it was there.

Expect some blurred vision, he'd said. And the headaches. Maybe a little dizziness. Dar sighed silently. At least he'd promised it would be temporary, which was a damn good thing, because it was going to take a lot of concentration and long hours in front of a keyboard to produce the analysis everyone and their uncle was waiting for.

Dar felt her breathing slow, and the sounds of the condo faded a little. She could feel Chino's warmth pressed against her legs, and if she concentrated, hear the faint sounds of movement from her mother.

Her mother. Dar freed herself for a moment of thought about that. She felt a little off balance, thinking about the talk they'd had and the hours they'd spent together afterward. It had been a curious, almost weird feeling as they'd both let down barriers and simply gotten along as two people who had more in common than either of them had ever realized.

Dar took a deep breath and released it. She frowned as her brain analyzed the intake of air and detected something unusual on it.

Garlic. Lots of it, and spices, too. Dar opened one eye and peered around in surprise, almost jumping when the expected empty air was suddenly filled with a very solid-looking Kerry. "Hey. Where did you come from?"

"Saugatuck," Kerry replied with a grin. "Glad to see you're behaving and taking a nap."

Dar frowned. "I wasn't napping." She glanced over at her mother, who muffled a smile. "Was I?" She didn't wait for an answer. "What the heck is that smell?"

"Ah." Kerry turned and pointed toward the dining room table, which had sprouted some mysterious-looking buckets and assorted bags. "Crabs."

"Crabs?" Dar looked over at them, then up at her father. "Crabs?" Her voice perked up considerably.

"Oh no," Ceci groaned. "Not those damn things."

Andrew chuckled. "Yes, ma'am. You did send this here young lady out for takeaway, and we done did that." He looked quite pleased with himself. "Got us three kinds, too, and them taters you like, Dardar."

"Heh." Dar eased upright. "All right."

Kerry winced. "Honey, you're not going to tell me you actually eat those things, are you?"

Ceci sighed and covered her eyes. "Hope you got some corn. Kerry and I can at least share that." She got up and walked around the couch to the table to investigate the packages. "Oh, goddess, Andrew. Did you have to get the hot pepper ones?"

"Heh." Andrew chuckled, moving across the tile floor to join his wife at the table. "Yep, I surely did."

Dar swung her legs off the couch and sat up. "You have to try them, Ker. They're great."

Her lover crouched down between her knees, resting a hand on either one, and grimaced. "Dar, they look like big old bugs," she whispered. "I can't eat those."

"Sure you can," Dar whispered back, leaning forward. "C'mon, I'll show ya."

"Daaaarrrr..." Kerry bit her lip. "Eeeeewwww."

"Don't be a chicken," Dar chided her. "Trust me."

Easy for her to say. Kerry sighed and gave her partner a hand up, keeping hold of it as she joined Dar and they walked over to where Andrew and Ceci were unpacking the bags and buckets.

"Ooh." Dar pried the cover off one and peered inside. "Yum."

Kerry peeked over her shoulder at the pile of red-hued, spice-speckled marine insects, complete with beady little eyes looking back at her. "Oh," she moaned softly, and leaned against Dar's arm. "I'm going to have nightmares."

Dar picked up a crab and examined it. "Sure you are." She deftly removed a claw, exposing some white flesh. "Here. Suck on this."

Big round pale green eyes looked up past the curve of her breast. A tiny squeak issued from Kerry's throat.

"Go on," Dar laughed.

Kerry glanced over at her in-laws, who were bent almost double with silent laughter. "Dar, I can't suck on that leg. It looks like a grasshopper leg. I'm going to throw up."

Dar sighed, removed a bit of the crabmeat, and held it out. "There. Can you suck on my fingers?"

A sigh. "Oh, God, if you insist." Kerry closed her eyes and leaned forward, opening her mouth and closing her teeth gingerly on the bit of white substance. She closed her lips and carefully tasted it, then opened her eyes. "Hmm." It wasn't at all like lobster or shrimp. It was much more tender, and... Kerry licked her lips. "Mm." The spices stung her tongue pleasantly. "Okay, that's not bad."

"See?" Dar sounded triumphant. "Told you." She sat down and pulled out a chair for Kerry next to her. "Now, c'mon. Grab a hammer."

Her lover, who had been heading for the kitchen for a pitcher of something cold, stopped dead in her tracks. "Hammer?"

Chapter
Nineteen

Andrew relaxed, stretching his long frame as he settled more comfortably in the large leather chair. "So, that's what that old bag of wind told me," he drawled. "All 'bout how he'd been gotten to some years back, and he just didn't want to say no."

The television played softly in the background as the two couples shared coffee and each other's company.

Dar shook her head sadly. She was lying on the couch with Kerry curled up against her, and she had her injured arm draped over her lover's body. "Hard to believe."

Ceci snorted from her perch on the loveseat. "No, it isn't. He always was a pompous asshole." She ignored her husband's round-eyed look. "You know it's true, Andy. He was always wanting to be in charge. Remember that bowling team he hornswoggled you on to? He had to be the captain."

Andrew grunted.

"Bowling?" Kerry opened one eye lazily, so completely stuffed she wouldn't have moved even for a fire drill. "I didn't know you bowled, Dad."

"Ah most certainly do not," Andrew replied. "Damn fool just would not listen."

"Andy is so good at everything, Jeff just assumed he'd be a good bowler," Ceci told, blithely ignoring another outraged look. "Unfortunately, Jeff loved to stand behind his team and make comments."

"Ah," Kerry noted sagely.

"That lasted all of one time." Ceci gave her husband a look. "Until Andy threw the ball backward."

"Heh." Andrew produced a rakish grin, amazingly like his daughter's. "Never did hear a man make a sound like that one before."

"Ow," Kerry winced. "So you guys were rivals?" she asked curiously.

Andrew shrugged. "Naw."

"Yes," Ceci corrected him. "Don't look at me like that, Andrew. You know you were." She picked up her cup of coffee and sipped it. "Jeff always had to be first. His family had to be first. His kid had to be first," she said. "I think that's what busted his chops so bad. He tried so hard, and pushed Chuck so hard, and neither one of you ever had to try hardly at all."

Andrew and Dar exchanged glances. "Now, Cec," Andrew rumbled, "wasn't really like that."

Ceci rolled her eyes. "Yes, it was. The two of you just never noticed," she informed her husband and child. "Andy, you made your grades before he did, got the jobs he wanted, and copped the medals he coveted, and you never gave two whoops about it."

Andrew folded his arms across his chest and gave her a sober look.

"And you," Ceci gazed over at Dar with a half smile. "I'll never forget the night Jeff and Sue were over, talking about how Chuck was going to enlist so he could save some cash for vocational school, remember?"

Dar nodded. "I remember."

Kerry turned her head and looked at her. "What happened?"

Dark lashes fluttered as Dar blinked. "It was just a coincidence," she murmured. "I'd gotten my acceptance letters that day."

Kerry studied her profile. "For college?"

Dar nodded silently.

"How many?"

She shrugged. "A couple."

"Seven," Ceci corrected her.

Dar rolled her eyes.

Kerry returned her attention to Dar's mother. "Seven?"

"Mm-hmm," Ceci agreed. "All full scholarship." She folded her hands across her stomach and gazed at her child.

"That was a damn proud day for me," Andrew said suddenly.

Everyone now looked at Dar, who looked back pensively. "I didn't even think about it," she admitted honestly. "That's why I dropped them on the dinner table while they were there and told you." Her thumb rubbed idly against Kerry's side. "I thought it was pretty cool."

"So did we." Ceci smiled. "But you didn't see Jeff's face," she sighed. "He and Sue were so jealous. I'm not surprised, Andy, if he went along with whatever those crooks wanted, if it finally got him the good life he'd always craved."

Andrew shook his head a little. "Don't make sense. He never did that poorly, Cec," he protested. "Collected him plenty of rank, and pretty good jobs, I figure. He just never wanted to have to work hard for it." It was a long sentence for him. "Dardar, you figure you got something on them people? Jeff thinks there ain't much chance you do."

Dar shifted a little, her eyes unfocused in thought. She felt Kerry twine her fingers around the hand she had draped over her partner's body, and she breathed in Kerry's distinctive scent as the thoughts tumbled over in her head. "I don't know," she replied truthfully. "If we got everything, and I can reconstruct it, yes." Her eyes flicked up and met her father's. "I'll have it."

Ceci leaned forward. "Have what, Dar? What the heck were they doing?"

An almost introspective look crossed Dar's face. "Laundering money," she answered simply. "Millions and millions of dollars, funneled from the sale of contraband and government property."

Jaws dropped.

"You mean to tell me," Kerry finally said, "they used the government's own computer systems to do that?"

Dar nodded. "Feel better about your tax refund?"

Kerry covered her eyes with one hand and groaned.

"Jesus P. Fish," Andrew blurted.

"Well," Ceci murmured. "And here I thought maybe you'd found the truth about Roswell."

Dar shrugged modestly. "Want me to audit there next?"

Kerry put the piece of paper down on her desk and dropped into her chair, leaning forward and resting her head in her hands.

What a day. She scrubbed her face wearily. It was Thursday, Dar's first day back; and her lover had spent the entire time since seven that morning holed up in the MIS command center, sequestered in a quiet, plain office around the corner from Mark's, refusing to take a break even though Kerry could plainly see she badly needed one. She'd taken off her arm sling, and by the very messiness of the dark locks framing her face, it was obvious she'd been running her fingers through her hair.

Always a sign of frustration, Kerry knew.

So here she was, about to order in a pile of Thai food in hopes that, at least, would get her boss to kick back for a few minutes and relax. Kerry reread the order, making sure she'd gotten everything down, and quickly typed it into a fax form, which she sent on its way.

To be fair, Dar had been exceedingly good for three days. She'd kept her promise and remained resting at home, though by halfway through Wednesday, she was already prowling around the island and spending a couple of hours swimming in the heated pool.

Her headaches had disappeared, and she'd started to use her arm, careful not to overstress the shoulder joint. They'd gone out on the boat the night before and had dinner under the stars, and Dar had remained alert the entire time; in fact, she'd ended up driving the boat back after Kerry had fallen asleep on the bow.

The pressure from Washington was getting critical, though. General Easton had called twice, each time reporting the minor issues the security team had found and the fact that he was under a lot of pressure to back off the project entirely.

Someone had gotten annoyed, it seemed, that a private company was prying into military affairs. If they didn't come up with something more significant than fouled-up accounting and some black-market supplies, the entire contract was in jeopardy.

So, despite the fact that Kerry thought the enforced rest was doing her partner a lot of good, she had to admit she'd been glad to have that tall form pacing at her side when she'd entered the building that morning.

When the phone rang, Kerry glared at it for a moment, then hit the answer button. "Operations. Kerry Stuart speaking."

"Good evening, Ms. Stuart." Alastair's voice was cordial.

"Evening, sir," Kerry replied. "How's Texas doing?"

"About the same as it usually is, this time of year," Alastair replied. "Getting on to Christmas."

"Yeah." Kerry perked up a little. "And close to Dar's birthday." She leaned forward. "You're going to send her a card, right?"

A little chuckle came down the line. "Oh, I'm sure she'll get a few of those. So, how are things there?"

Kerry sighed. "Slow going," she admitted. "Dar's been at it all day, and to be honest, what she's doing looks like so much hex gibberish to me."

Alastair sighed as well. "Kerrison, Dar's been hex gibberish to 90 percent of this company for fifteen years, so don't feel bad." He paused. "I'm getting a lot of pressure on this."

"Mm."

"It's not that anyone doubts what we did, but I got a call from the JAG's office today. They're considering filing a reckless endangerment lawsuit against us."

Kerry glared at the phone. "Those pissants."

The CEO chuckled dryly.

"I mean it," Kerry replied. "They know something's wrong there, and they're just covering their friends' starched olive very drab butts."

"Y'know, I think some of your shyness is disappearing," Alastair commented. "Must be Dar rubbing off on you."

"I'm not shy," Kerry reminded him. "I told Dar to kiss my ass, remember?"

"And she certainly did tak—" Alastair stopped abruptly. "Good heavens! I beg your pardon, Ms. Stuart."

Kerry blinked, also a little startled at the retort. "Uh, that's okay," she told him. "I kind of opened myself up for that, didn't I?"

Alastair chuckled. "I try to be good," he said. "Anyway, as I said, I'm under a lot of pressure, here, Kerry." He turned serious again. "They want a meeting tomorrow in Washington. I'm going to have Hamilton get hold of that JAG officer and shake him up a little, but I'd really rather not go into the meeting, ah..."

"In nothing but your boxers?" Kerry asked.

"He wears briefs," Dar's voice burred. "White cotton ones." She closed the door to Kerry's office and walked over to the desk, hitching up the leg on her khaki cargo pants before she sat down on the edge. "Hello, Alastair."

"Ah. Hello, Dar," the CEO replied. "Good to hear your voice."

One of Dar's dark brows lifted. "Why, you been listening to Eleanor again?"

"The Navy wants to sue us for reckless endangerment," Kerry told her.

A chuckle. "Oh, really?" Dar leaned on her good arm and addressed the phone. "Who did a bunch of unarmed IS workers endanger, Alastair?"

"I don't know. I'm having Ham handle it," her boss said. "Listen, Dar, I know you've been on this all day, but what's the word? Do we have something or not?"

"Alastair, this isn't an Internet search," Dar answered, a touch testily. "It's a fifty-gigabyte drive array that I'm having to reconstruct in hex, sector by sector."

There was a reverent silence following this pronouncement, as everyone gave the information its due respect.

"And?" Alastair asked briskly.

Dar sighed, and rubbed her eyes. "I'm not done," she said.

"But so far, so good."

Kerry got up and walked around the desk. She put her arms around Dar and gave her a gentle hug and a kiss on the cheek. "You are so my hero," she whispered in her lover's ear. "Can I be you when I grow up?"

Dar blushed, her tanned skin darkening appreciably. "I can't promise anything," she muttered.

Alastair chortled. "Will you let me know tomorrow? They want me on the carpet first thing Friday morning in DC."

"I said, I can't promise anything," Dar repeated. Alastair remained prudently silent. Kerry gazed confidently at her. Dar sighed. "I'll call you tomorrow after lunch."

"Right. Have a great night, Dar," the CEO agreed. "Night, Kerrison; nice talking to you."

Dar released the line and gave Kerry a look. "One of these days, I'm not going to be able to deliver him the River Nile in a coffee cup, and we're going to be totally screwed."

Kerry smiled and reached up to straighten the unruly dark locks. "You look bushed, sweetie."

"I am," Dar admitted with a nod. She blinked, then rubbed her eyes again. "Ow."

Kerry gently took hold of her jaw and tilted her head toward the office light. "Your eyes are all bloodshot," she informed her lover. "Hang on." She went to her desk drawer and retrieved a bottle of eye drops, then came back. "Hold still."

Dar patiently did as she was asked, watching the ceiling as Kerry administered the treatment. She blinked as the liquid hit her eyes, stinging momentarily as her lover wiped off the excess with a fingertip. "Thanks."

"No problem." Kerry capped the bottle. "These are designed for us, you know." She examined the label. "Imagine, an entire product line based around the IS industry."

Dar peeked at it. "Wonder if it's any different from garden-variety Visine?" She rested her chin on Kerry's shoulder.

"Probably not." A smile. "But I felt so virtuous buying it in Office Depot, along with that gel wrist pad I got you and my new trackball."

"Mm." Dar straightened and stretched her back out. "You order dinner?"

"Yep." Kerry looked up as her intercom buzzed. She reached around Dar's body and hit the key. "Yes?"

"Ms. Stuart, this is Security at the front door. Did you order something?"

"Ooh. Nice timing," Dar purred into Kerry's conveniently

close ear.

Kerry managed not to laugh. "Yes, thank you. I'll be right down." She released the button and turned, not moving away from Dar, so that they ended up nose to nose. It was too easy not to just lean forward the additional inch, so Kerry did and they kissed.

It was a very pleasant, sensual jolt that followed, and Kerry found herself enjoying it a lot. It chased away the stress and exhaustion of the long day and made her smile, especially when she felt Dar doing the same. "You know." She backed off a few inches. "I really like that."

Dar merely smirked.

"Stay here. I'm going to get dinner," Kerry said.

"No." Dar patted her cheek gently. "Let me. I need to stretch my legs. That chair in Mark's dungeon was made for a dwarf." She got up off the desk and headed for the door before Kerry could disagree.

Kerry exhaled. "That crumb," she commented to the empty room. "She just conned me out of paying for dinner, didn't she?"

Dar leaned against the elevator wall, watching the numbers count down. As it was after hours, the annoying music that usually played in the contraption was turned off, and she could hear the hum and shush of the mechanism as it worked.

"You're not even going to think about getting stuck in this thing, Roberts," she told her reflection sternly.

The elevator seemed to hesitate, as though it was considering stopping. Dar glared at the panel and narrowed her eyes. "Don't you even think about it," she rumbled in a low growl. "I'll take you apart and make you into a toaster."

The chastened device obediently kept moving.

Dar smirked at her reflection, her upper body encased in a crimson short-sleeved shirt tucked into her cargo pants. She reached the bottom floor and the doors opened, allowing her to exit into the large empty lobby. She walked across the marble floor and past the fountain toward the security station, where she could see a guard talking to a man in casual clothing.

At her approach, the guard turned. "Oh. Ms. Roberts." He blinked. "I thought Ms. Stuart was picking this up."

"Nope." Dar gave the deliveryman a brief smile and handed him her credit card. He swiped it efficiently in a handheld device and offered the receipt to her for a signature. She reviewed the bill, added a tip, and signed it. "Thanks."

She accepted the box of food, its spices already sneaking out and tickling her nose. "Back to the mines."

The guard chuckled. "Good to have you back, Ms. Roberts. We missed you."

Dar swiveled and regarded the man, whom she might have seen all of twice before. "Why?"

The man blinked at her. "Pardon me, ma'am?"

"Why the hell would anyone down here miss me?" Dar asked curiously. "Is there a rumor going around that I bring in doughnuts or something?"

The guard looked around, then took a few steps closer to her. "No, ma'am, but everyone knows that when you're here, no matter what happens, we're okay."

Dar studied him in mild surprise. "Everyone knows that, huh?"

He nodded. "Yes, ma'am."

"Interesting." Dar turned and made her way back to the elevator, supporting her tasty-smelling box with her good arm and balancing it with the other. She punched the button for the tenth floor and watched the doors close.

They ate in the ops center, with Dar leaning back in her uncomfortable chair, her feet propped up on the desk and her container of spicy chicken and rice nestled in her lap. Kerry was perched on a box of computer paper next to the desk, and Mark was sitting on an old mounting rack.

They were alone and it was quiet, the only activity around them in the operations control room itself just around the corner behind its secured door. At 8 p.m., the office building was emptied of its staff and only the computer support group was left to tend the servers and provide support for the other offices around the world.

Mark selected a pea pod, turned it around so the small end faced him, and took a bite. "This reminds me of the old days, boss."

Dar chuckled. "The bad old days, you mean." She deftly used her chopsticks to transfer some chicken to her lips. "I spent so many damn hours in this room."

Kerry looked around. "This room?"

"This used to be Dar's office," Mark supplied, with a grin. "I remember whatshisface, that John whatever-his-name-was, that used to be the CIO. Remember when he came in here and saw this place the first time?"

Dar snorted. "Oh, yeah. Took one look at the posters on the

wall and nearly laid a load in his pinstripes." She looked around
fondly at the small space, its walls at an odd angle due to the
room's position in the corner space. "Took one look at me and
hauled ass right back to Houston to sign my termination papers."

"Didn't help you had your favorite uniform on," Mark
grinned.

"It was after hours," Dar demurred. "I was going clubbing
after work."

Kerry had been watching them, her eyes moving from one to
the other like she was at a particularly interesting volleyball
match. "Was this during your rebellious phase?"

Dar waggled an eyebrow at her. "Definitely." She took a sip
of Thai coffee. "I had on biker boots with more chains dangling
from them than you'd see in two days at the Westminster Kennel
Club."

Kerry covered her eyes as her shoulders shook.

"Mm-hmm. Those were nice," Mark agreed. "I have a pair."
He chewed thoughtfully. "Without the chains. They get stuck in
my gears. But I think it was the muscle-T that spooked him
worse."

Dar chuckled and shook her head. "It's a mystery why the
hell I wasn't fired that week. What was it that time, the mainframes in Troy? That whole processing center went down, and
they dragged me into it right before I was leaving. Damn, I was
pissed," she sighed ruefully. "The bad old days. Things sure have
changed."

Mark looked up at his boss, who had removed her light jacket
and was slouched in her chair in a short-sleeved top and cargo
pants, with hiking boots parked on the desk's surface. "Uh, yeah."
He tilted his head and studied her. "You make a lot less noise
when you move now."

Kerry almost snorted soup out of her nostrils as she burst into
laughter. Mark started chuckling, too, at the expression on Dar's
face.

"Hey!" Dar gave them an injured look. "I did grow up,
remember?"

"Sorry, Dar," Mark apologized. "I know it's a different world
now, but I miss those days sometimes." He looked contrite. "I
didn't really mean you look like a teenage punker anymore."

"Mmph." Dar appeared mollified. "Yeah, I do, too, sometimes," she admitted. "Long days, but we had some good parties,
didn't we?"

Mark nodded, sucking on the end of his chopstick. "The night
you guys were stuck in that hospital, we had the television in here.

Sixteen of us crammed in here most of the night watching."

Dar fell silent, concentrating on her container. Kerry watched her face for a moment, then picked up the conversational ball where it had fallen and rolled between her feet. "That was a pretty scary night," she said. "I don't remember a lot of it; the details are really blurry."

"You had a concussion," Dar stated quietly. "It's probably best you don't remember most of it." She picked out more chicken bits and ate them. "Just a lot of smoke, and loud noises, and heat."

They ate in silence for a moment. "Were you scared, boss?" Mark asked suddenly.

"You bet your ass I was," Dar replied without hesitation. "Anyone with half a brain cell would have been." She glanced up at him. "Why?"

He shrugged. "Just curious. I know I was scared pissless just watching the coverage," he replied. "You guys pretty much just got to that room, then busted out, though, right?"

"Right."

"No."

Dar looked at Kerry, who had replied negatively. One eyebrow lifted. "No?"

"Well..." Kerry leaned her head back against the wall, "I remember the explosion." She looked off into the distance. "I remember waking up and hurting."

"Dislocated shoulder, right?" Mark commented.

"Yeah," Kerry nodded. "Dar put that back all right, then we had to crawl out of where we were and through this little tunnel." She looked at Dar, who was busily decimating her chicken and studiously avoiding everyone's gaze. "It collapsed on us, and we almost died."

Mark stared at her. "No shit?"

Dar looked up. "Thought you didn't remember details," she remarked wryly.

"I just remembered that," Kerry murmured. "Jesus Christ, Dar. You saved us." She stared at her lover in bemusement. "How in the hell could I have forgotten that?"

The pause was awkward this time. Mark cleared his throat. "Shit like that happens with concussions, I guess. That's what I've always heard."

Kerry felt her arm hairs lift as the memory cleared and she pictured the image of that tiny space with its smell of concrete dust and their sweat and blood as the wall pressed in on them. She could almost feel the labored heaving of Dar's back under her weight as her lover struggled to breathe and the sudden, distinct surge as her body had arched, ready to break them out of their prison.

And in that moment, Kerry remembered with eerie clarity now, she'd had no shred of doubt that Dar would do just that. "Yeah," she agreed with Mark's comment. "I guess it does. Glad I finally shook that memory loose, though," she said with a conscious lightening of her tone, on seeing the tenseness in Dar's shoulders. "Anyway, it was an experience I never want to repeat. I was never so glad of anything as I was to put my feet on the ground after they rescued us."

"I bet," Mark chuckled, getting up from his seat. "Hey, I'm going to grab a Coke, want one?"

"Sure," Kerry agreed. "Dar?"

Dar nodded. "Sure."

Mark slipped out the door, leaving so quickly it almost seemed like an escape.

Kerry waited a moment, then stood up and walked over to where Dar was seated. "Hey."

Dar looked up at her from under dark brows and slightly shaggy bangs.

Kerry knelt. "He's not very subtle, is he?"

It was the right approach. Dar's lips tensed, then curled into a wry smile. "No," she drawled softly. "He's not." She put her food container on the desk and rested her chopsticks on top of it. Then she leaned on her chair arm and gave her lover her undivided attention. "So."

"You didn't tell me about that." Kerry put a hand on Dar's arm and rubbed her thumb against the skin of it. "You told me about the wall, and the window, and the children, but not that. Why?"

Dark eyelashes fluttered closed over Dar's eyes. "Maybe I didn't want to remember it," she said.

Kerry thought about that as she watched Dar's face. "Okay." She leaned forward and brushed her lips against her lover's. "I can buy that," she readily agreed, saving her thoughts for a later time. "But thanks."

"Anytime," Dar replied with a smile. "Now go back and finish your dinner so Mark can skulk back in here safely."

Kerry stuck out the tip of her tongue, but got up and resumed her perch. "What's the next step," she consciously raised her voice a little, "on the data restoral?"

Dar laughed silently. "Once I finish the structural rebuilding, we have to run data patterns to make sure the damn thing actually works and I didn't put a piece back in wrong."

Like a genie, Mark appeared in the doorway, carrying three cans of soda. "Hi." He gave them a cheerful look. "I'm back." He handed around the cans. "Damn AC's going goofy again, Ker. I think they need to change those filters."

Kerry sniffed. The air held a distinctly musty scent. "Son of a—" She sighed. "What is that, the fourth time this year? Where did they get the AC plant for this building, Dar, Sam's Club?"

Dar sighed. "You can't lay that one on my doorstep." She resumed eating her chicken. "One of Alastair's fishing buddies' long-lost fourth cousins twice removed got the contract on this building, and I've had nothing but trouble with it since we moved in."

Mark shifted. "You thinking of going somewhere else when the lease is up? I heard rumors."

"Maybe," Dar admitted. "I've got a couple of proposals on my desk. West Broward's got the best one, and they're promising me everything, including a private elevator and my own alligator."

"With a view of the Everglades?" Kerry teased. "I thought you liked the one you have."

"Gotta be a down side," Dar admitted. "And yeah, I do, but I'd be willing to give it up for someplace I don't have to have maintenance on three days a week."

"West Broward? I like it," Mark approved.

Kerry pointed a chopstick at him. "You live there."

"Gotta catch a break sometime."

"Maybe the rest of us don't like dodging possums on the way to work."

Dar rolled her eyes. "Can we wait until I pick a spot to start this debate?"

Dar peered at the screen and studied the algorithm. "Okay." She typed in a command and viewed the results. "I think that does it."

Kerry leaned on the back of her boss's chair and looked. "It's done?"

"Yeah." The dark haired woman rubbed her eyes wearily. "What time is it?"

"Two," Kerry supplied, shifting as she reached around and started a gentle massage of Dar's shoulders. She'd tried to get her lover to quit for the night some four or five hours before, but had no luck. "Dar, your neck feels like a suspension bridge."

"I bet." Everything ached. Dar wished she could sneak in

another round of painkillers, but it had only been two hours since the last set, and her stomach was already queasy from the medication. The throbbing in her arm was so bad she almost couldn't feel the pressure from Kerry's hands, though the warmth was definitely noticeable through the fabric of her shirt. "Mark!"

"Yeah?" Mark stuck his head around the corner. "I've got the links set up here. Hang on. You done?" He came into the room dragging several large cables behind him. "You wanted a patch directly into the big box, right?"

The IBM mainframe ran a custom program designed by Dar herself and was isolated from the rest of ILS's giant network. It could analyze the structure of a database design and take it to pieces; she'd used it on many occasions to locate not only holes in a newly acquired company's databases, but also hidden defects that could cause problems during integration.

"Right," Dar murmured. "I think I got it back together."

Mark cocked his head. "You think?"

She shrugged. "Far as I can tell." In truth, her eyes would no longer focus on the screen, and she'd been going by instinct for the last little while. "Let's find out."

Mark and Kerry exchanged glances. "Now?" the MIS manager queried. "It can wait 'til the morning, boss."

Eyes closed, Dar merely shook her head. "Not with Alastair booked on a flight at 1:00," she disagreed. "If we don't have anything, we need time to get our asses covered."

Another exchange of glances. "Well, it'll take me a little while to get all the connections secure and the ports configured," Mark temporized. "You wanna to take a break for a few minutes?"

"Sounds good," Kerry agreed quickly. "How about a cup of hot chocolate?" She tweaked Dar's ear. "I've got a tin of dark Godiva upstairs."

Hmm. Dar didn't feel like resisting the offer. "Okay." She slowly got up and stretched, wincing at the audible pops. "Jesus, I'm getting too old for this."

Kerry rolled her eyes out of Dar's range of vision. "C'mon, grandma. I'll race you up the stairs." She put a hand on Dar's back and gave her a gentle shove toward the door. They ended up, however, at the elevator, which was obediently standing open awaiting them. "Ah, our chariot," Kerry remarked. "Unless you'd really rather walk."

"Nah." Dar ambled inside and pressed the button for the fourteenth floor. She leaned against the wall while the elevator rose, then followed Kerry out as the doors reopened. "Wish it was this quiet all the time." She glanced around at the dim corridor, empty of even the cleaning staff by this time. "I think they vacuumed up here tonight."

Kerry wrinkled her nose at the scent of carpet dust mites clawing through the air. "Yum. Remind me to talk to the cleaners about using HEPA filters in those damn machines, will you?" As though in retaliation, her body expressed its displeasure in a sudden sneeze. "Yeesh. Listen, go on over to your place. I'll make up the hot chocolate and bring it over, okay?"

"Okay," Dar agreed quietly, turning to her left and heading toward her office while Kerry turned to the right. She swiped her keycard in the outside lock and pushed the door open, then continued on through her outer office and into her inner one.

It was very quiet inside. Her PC was turned off and just the wall rim lighting was on, leaving the office mostly in starlight. Dar stood inside the door, then glanced to her right and decided the couch looked pretty good. She dropped onto it, then swung her legs up and lay down, stretching her body out fully with a sense of weary relief.

It was a good choice. The cool leather warmed to skin quickly, and she let out a soft groan now that she was alone and didn't have to put on a good front for the troops. It wasn't as comfortable as her couch at home, but it was a damn sight better than that office chair, and the cool quiet of her surroundings soothed the ragged edges of her temper.

After three days of lazing around at home, you'd think I'd have more energy than this. Dar scowled up at the ceiling. She hadn't slept so much since the last time she'd broken her leg and they'd given her Percodan for the pain. All right, so it was two in the morning and they'd been here since seven, but so what? Used to be she could do thirty-six or forty-eight hours running and not feel this worn out.

Yeah. Dar had to laugh at herself. *Back in the days when you used to live on Jolt and Hershey bars and you never went home because there was nothing there to go home to.* She gazed out the window at the stars. *Isn't it nicer now that you're a grownup with a life?*

And someone to share it with?

She never even heard Kerry come in. The touch on her arm startled her, and her eyes popped open to see her lover crouched next to her, holding a steaming cup in one hand. "Oh. Sorry."

"Don't be." Kerry put the cup down on the end table and smiled. "I almost didn't wake you up."

Dar gave her a puzzled look. "I wasn't sleeping," she protested. "Was I?" She rolled up onto one elbow and captured the mug, taking a sip of the sweet chocolate. "Mm."

Kerry patted her arm. "Well, you were giving a pretty good impression that you were. Maybe you were just resting your eyes, hmm?" Her lips quirked.

Dar's quirked back. "No, I was sleeping," she admitted. "My head's killing me. I should just pack it in and go home, but I really want to see what we've got in this thing." She took another sip, then set the mug down, licking her lips appreciatively.

"I know," Kerry said. "Tell you what, why not just sack out here while Mark does his thing? A nap couldn't hurt you, could it?" she suggested.

Dar studied her as a slow smile edged its way across her face. "You know something, Stuart?"

Kerry blinked at the address. "Uh...what?"

"You're a pretty damn good Ops VP."

Confusion colored Kerry's expression. "Um, thanks," she replied hesitantly. "What got me that compliment?"

"Your engineering of a very slick maneuver that ended up with my ass on this couch."

Kerry pointed a finger at her own chest. "Me?" Her green eyes widened innocently.

Dar smiled. "Don't give me that sweet Midwesterner routine, short stuff." She extended a hand lazily and gave her lover a poke in the belly. "Yes, you."

Kerry's smile went from innocent to seductively triumphant. "Yeah, that was pretty slick, huh?" she chortled softly. "But I wasn't lying. There's the chocolate to prove it," she pointed. "I just know you."

"Mm." Dar wriggled into a more comfortable position and sighed. "Yes, you do." She closed her eyes. "Don't try to lengthen this by running a redundant loopback test on those ports, okay? Just wake me up when we're ready."

Kerry's eyes twinkled gently. "You got it, boss." She got up and took a seat in the chair next to the couch, cradling her own mug in her hands. Mark would take, she knew, about an hour to get things ready, regardless of how long it actually took to connect the systems together. By then, maybe the nap would help, and Dar would be able to take a few more aspirin. Kerry sighed. She didn't like it. She wished they were home, but she knew how important this was to Dar, and pushing her to slack off wouldn't be either appreciated or heeded at this point.

She just hoped the results were worth it.

"Is that it?" Kerry watched the monitor. "It's all ready?"

Mark pulled his head out from under the console and grunted. "Yeah," he agreed tiredly. "You know what, Ker? I think I'm the one who's getting too old for this crap. I used to be able to do all-nighters. Not anymore."

The blond woman chuckled wryly. "Yeah, me too." She leaned against the machine. "I hope this is worth it, or it's going to be one very long day tomorrow."

He nodded. "Yeah, but you know we won't really know for a few hours, right? The first run will just tell us if Dar managed to pull something out of that mess intact. It'll take the program about five, six hours to parse through everything and spit out a report."

Kerry stared at the screen. "What do you think?"

Mark fiddled with his pen, then shrugged. "Hard to say. If anyone could, it'd be Dar, but I think she was fighting this one." He glanced at Kerry. "That knock on the head still bugging her?"

"A little," Kerry admitted. "I think it's a little of everything. She's stuck between everything hurting and not wanting to take the pills for it because they knock her out," she said. "Just being in pain exhausts you."

"Well, the first stage'll just take a little while," Mark said. "Ten minutes, maybe."

"Ah." Kerry hadn't known that. "Good," she nodded. "Then we can all go home after we start the run, right?" Nap or no nap, Dar needed to go home and rest. *Hell,* Kerry rubbed the back of her neck, *I need to go home and rest. I'm bushed.*

Mark sat down on the desk. "Well, theoretically, yeah," he agreed. "But I dunno, Ker. This whole project's got my heebie-jeebie meter spiking to max. I don't want to leave this thing running by itself. I'll stay here and watch it." He glanced around. "I keep expecting some dude dressed in black camo to come out of the walls and zap me."

The darkened building was a little spooky, Kerry had to agree. What if the people whom they suspected figured out they might have kept some information? Would they try to get at them? All sorts of wild scenarios started to play out in Kerry's mind. What if they really were smugglers? What if they were connected with someone really bad, like the Colombians?

"Kerry?" Mark leaned forward and waved his hand in front of her eyes. "Yoo-hoo."

"Huh?" She blinked. "No, I was just thinking. What if you're right? What if these people do try something? It's not like we're set up for airtight security around here."

"You think they will?" Mark asked nervously. "For real?"

"They were shooting for real back there," Kerry stated. "I don't know." They stared at each other uneasily.

The floor creaked outside, making them both jump. "Shit," Mark squeaked. "Shut the door!"

Kerry felt her heart rate double and she turned, realizing that the door opened outward and she'd have to go out into the corridor to pull it shut. "I think we're letting our imaginations get out of hand," she stated, "but maybe that's not a bad idea." She edged toward the door, peering out into the darkened area beyond. "No one could get in the com center, right?"

"Uh..." Mark's nostrils flared. "Not like your average Joe Delivery Boy, no, but I'm sure the military has all kinds of crap to get around our security."

Kerry paused in the doorway, looking out. It was silent, desks and chairs crouching dumbly in the gloom. Nothing moved. Kerry suddenly became aware of a dark, looming object near the ops center door she didn't remember being there earlier. She stared at it.

Was that breathing she heard, or was it just the AC? She took a step out, and her eyes seemed to detect a motion from the still object. "Mark," Kerry tried hard to keep her voice steady, "come here." She reached for the doorknob and heard a creak. A hand touched her back and she yelped, then scrambled for the door.

Suddenly, the entire ops center came alive in a shocking blast of fluorescent light. Kerry slammed herself backward, knocking Mark flat on his ass behind her, and swung the door shut with startling violence.

She threw the deadbolt on the door and got back away from it, not trusting even the reinforced steel. "Shit."

Mark had crawled out of her way and ducked behind the desk. "You know, they never mentioned this in MIS 101," he muttered. "Let's call the cops."

"Good idea." Kerry joined him behind the desk and pulled out her cell phone.

They heard a sound on the other side of the door and froze, staring in horror at the lock.

It started to turn, a low rasping sound that ended in a distinct, harsh click as the bolt retracted.

The door opened. They ducked behind the desk. A voice split the silence.

"What in the hell are you two doing?"

Kerry lifted her head and peeked over the desk, her body almost dissolving in relief as she recognized the powerful tones.

"Oh." She managed a wan smile at her lover. "Hi, Dar."

Mark started laughing in nervous relief. "Shit."

Dar entered the room and pushed the door open, crossing over to them and taking a seat on the desk. "Do I want to know what just happened?"

Kerry got up and dusted herself off. "Overactive imaginations," she admitted with a sheepish grin. "We started wondering if—Well, anyway, there was a noise outside, and I looked, and I saw something I didn't recognize..." She walked to the doorway and peeked out cautiously. "Ah." Her eyes found her threatening intruder, now masquerading as an innocent, if covered overhead projector nestled in the corner. "Sorry. I was about to come wake you up."

"Mm." Dar was amused. She watched Mark stand up and brush himself off. "If we're done playing *Miami Vice*, can we run the test now?" She'd woken a short time earlier and had spent a few moments splashing water on her face in the bathroom, resulting in a state of reasonable alertness.

Mark blushed, then started up the interface. "All yours, boss." He rubbed his butt cautiously. "Damn, you've got a hearty forward block on you there, Kerry. Ever think of trying rugby?"

Kerry just laughed. "Sorry. I just wanted to get the door closed."

Dar stepped around the desk and sat down, flexing her hands a little before she accessed the program files and started the analysis running. She reviewed her command line, then hit enter and folded her hands together calmly, watching the screen.

Not much was going on. A little asterisk in the corner spun. Lights on the black box indicated it was being accessed by the mainframe.

"How long should this take?" Kerry asked quietly.

"Depends," Dar said. "It's a fairly complicated structure." She watched the screen tensely. "A lot of things could have gone wrong. One glitch in the line during transfer and the entire matrix can get thrown off. Without every key in place, the whole thing—" Dar stopped and stared at the console, which was now blinking a result at her. "Damn."

Structure Valid.

Mark let out a whoop. "Hot damn is right." He slapped the desk, making both of them jump a little. "Boss, you rock!"

Dar was frankly very surprised. She cocked her head at the screen as though not quite believing what it said. Given the complexity and her own state of scattered concentration, she'd had her doubts as to whether she'd gotten all the sequencing right. It had seemed more and more likely, as the night wore on and she'd had to redo her actions more frequently, that she'd made a mistake and would have to start all over again. In fact, she'd been pretty damn sure of it.

Well, apparently she wasn't as decrepit as she'd imagined. "That's good news," she remarked calmly. "Now the hard part starts." She rapped her head with her knuckles, then assembled what she wanted to do and typed in a second command to her system. "Go."

The asterisk returned, but this time Dar slumped back in her chair and relaxed.

"Now we wait, right?" Kerry perched on the corner of the desk. "To see if we have anything."

"Right," Dar agreed. "We wait." She paused and looked around the office. "Listen, no sense in all of us sticking around."

"No," Kerry agreed. "Mark said he'd stay and watch."

Dar had opened her mouth to continue and now she closed it, giving them both a dour look, realizing she'd been outflanked. "If I didn't know better, I'd suspect I'm being coddled."

"Nope," Mark jumped in. "I figured once this sucker runs and barfs up the results, you're the one who gets to figure out what it means," he said. "So the least I could do is watch the pretty lights flash for ya."

Dar looked at him, then at Kerry, who looked back at her with a gentle smile. "Okay." She dropped her hands onto the chair arms and pushed herself to her feet. "C'mon, Kerry, let's get a couple hours' sleep." She turned toward Mark. "Want me to double lock the doors?" she teased with a rakish grin. "I think I heard some phantom chicken men outside."

Mark cleared his throat. "Nah, I'm fine. G'wan."

Dar nodded. "Thanks." She lifted a hand in a half wave. "Call me if anything doesn't look like it's going right."

"Will do." Mark settled in the chair Dar had just vacated, and leaned back. The door closed behind them, leaving him in peaceful silence.

Being home felt good. Kerry scrubbed her teeth industriously, turning as she felt a warm body nearby. "Hfero, Chirf," she greeted her pet, who was standing up on her hind legs, peering into the mirror with Kerry.

"Argorf," Chino barked, very glad to have her family home.

"What are you guys doing?" Dar wandered into the bathroom behind her and snuggled up, putting her arms around Kerry's stomach. "Giving her pointers, Chino?"

Kerry spit out her mouthful of toothpaste. "No, she's showing me you didn't quite get all the blackberry sauce off her face." She pointed at the mirror. "How on earth did she get into the refrigerator, Dar?"

"Opposable paws." Dar picked up one of the Labrador's feet and examined it, getting a kiss for her pains. "Glad you didn't leave that container of pasta sauce on the bottom shelf." They'd come home to find purplish blobs everywhere and a suspiciously meek-looking dog trying very hard to appear innocent with a face covered in jam.

"Bad girl," Kerry scolded their pet. Chino cupped her ears and folded them downward in an expression only a Labrador could come up with, looking soulfully at Kerry all the while. "Ooh...you think you have me so fooled, don'cha?" She had to laugh at the hopeful tail wag. "Spoiled brat."

Dar chuckled and rested her chin on the top of Kerry's head, hugging her and swaying a little. "Mm...bedtime for nerds?"

Kerry spent a moment just absorbing how wonderful it felt to have Dar hugging her. Then she turned around in her lover's arms and the sensation trebled as she slid closer and returned the hug. "Mm." She took a breath filled with the scent of clean cotton and Dar's distinctive smell. "Definitely bedtime for nerds." She took a step forward and guided Dar toward the waterbed, tumbling onto it with a sense of exquisite relief.

Dar immediately curled around her, capturing her in a net of long arms and longer legs, creating a warm nest she snuggled into, letting out a pleased murmur of contentment.

Dar reached over and turned the light off, ignoring the clock, which reminded her it was after four. Then she resettled her arm over Kerry, who squiggled closer and sighed, warming Dar's chest with a minty scented breath. The still-nagging aches faded, and she closed her eyes as her body relaxed at last.

What would the analysis come up with? she wondered drowsily. She'd thrown the dice on capturing the data she had, hoping it would deliver to her the mechanism they'd been using to move around the funds that she'd seen in the accounts. But what if it didn't? Dar felt Kerry's breathing even out and slow, becoming deep and regular as her partner fell asleep. Curiously, she found herself unconsciously trying to match it.

She thought about that for a moment, then returned her attention to their problem. Or at least, that's what she'd intended to do. But sleep snuck up on her, ambushing her best intentions and taking her out before she could form another thought.

Chapter
Twenty

"Morning." Kerry gave Mayte an apologetic look as she entered, closing the outer door behind her. "Sorry I'm late." She shifted her laptop case to her other shoulder. "Anything blowing up that I should know about?"

Mayte smiled at her. "There is nothing that I know of. Mamá said there have been some messages for *la jefe*, but it is nothing too serious."

"Good." Kerry opened the door to her office and went inside, circling her desk and dropping her briefcase behind it. She collapsed into her leather chair and nudged the switch on her PC, leaning back and watching as it booted.

Late or not, she hadn't gotten nearly enough sleep. Her eyes were sore, and she could feel a heaviness in her head that made her hope she wasn't coming down with something.

Her phone rang. With a sigh, Kerry sat forward and answered it. "Yes?"

"Hello, Kerry." Eleanor's voice sounded a touch on the smug side. "Did you forget our meeting?"

Oh, pooters. Kerry rested her head on her hand. "Not exactly," she said. "We were here on a project until almost four last night. I just got back in."

"Four?" Eleanor replied. "Good grief, woman. I can't think of anything fun I'd like to do until four in the morning, let alone anything involved in work."

"Yeah, well, you know how it is."

"No, and I've got no urge to find out," the marketing VP said. "Well, how about a reschedule for tomorrow?"

"Fine." Kerry rolled her trackball and studied her schedule, now displayed on her fully booted PC. "How's 3:00? I've got two reviews to do in the morning."

"3:00 it is. Try not to sleep through this one, huh? Though I hear the company's worth it." Eleanor chuckled, and hung up.

Kerry had to think about that for a moment before she groaned and let her head hit the desk with a soft thump. Then she got up and trudged around the desk, snagging her coffee mug and heading for the door.

Mayte's desk was empty when she passed it, as was the hallway when she ducked across it to the little kitchenette that served the fourteenth floor. She went to the cappuccino machine and started some milk frothing, studying it as the coffee poured out of its nearby funnel. The scent itself made her perk up a little, and she breathed it in, trying to extract some alertness from it.

"Well, well!" Clarice entered with her own cup. "Everybody was wondering where you were."

"Really?" Kerry was very aware of the ragged edges of her temper. "They could have done something out of the ordinary, like ask my admin."

"Where's the fun in that?" Clarice chuckled. "Not that anyone blames you, Kerry."

One, two, three. "Blames me for what?" Kerry asked with studied innocence, pouring her coffee into her steamed milk and stirring it gently.

"Sleeping in," the black woman explained with a grin. "Not with that bedmate."

Kerry turned and looked at her. "Clarice, that's inappropriate," she stated quietly.

Clarice's eyes narrowed slightly, and she let her cup drop to the counter with a slight bang. "Oh, sorry," she said. "Here I thought what you two were doing was inappropriate. Silly me."

There weren't numbers high enough for her to count this time. Kerry walked over and got into Clarice's space, mustering up as much attitude as she could, given her sleepless state. "That's also inappropriate. One more time, and I'll put it on your record. You want that?"

Clarice studied her in silence for a short time.

"Do you?" Kerry repeated.

"No, I don't."

"Dar and I keep our personal lives out of the office. Why don't you try doing the same thing?" With an almost verbal snap of her fingers, Kerry turned and walked out, stalking across the hall and jerking open her door to continue inside.

Fortunately for both of them, Dar's reflexes were not quite as burned as Kerry's were, and she caught the cup of hot coffee as it went flying from the blond woman's grasp as they collided. "Whoa!"

"Crap," Kerry exhaled. "Sorry."

Dar carefully handed her back her cup, with only two lonely drips. "S'all right. Wasn't your fault—you had no way of knowing I was in here," she added reasonably. "So what put a barracuda in your shorts?"

"Grr." Kerry walked to her desk and put the cup down. "Just a personnel problem." She sighed. "Your friend Clarice."

"Ah." Dar scrubbed a hand through her dark hair. "I'll take care of it. I'll transfer her to the Nome office. Give me a minute." She started back toward the inner corridor that connected their offices.

Kerry intercepted her. "No. No, Dar, this is my problem. I'll handle it."

Her lover eyed her. "Point of fact, Kerrison, this is actually my problem, and we both know it," she disagreed.

"Actually," Kerry went and sat down at her desk, "it's really her problem, but she's my employee and I've got to deal with it. I'm not going to run away from another issue." She spun her trackball. "How's the data dump coming?"

Dar studied her, deciding if she should accept the change of subject. She walked over and perched on the corner of Kerry's desk, reaching out to take her hand and tugging a little to pull her around so they were face to face. "You deal with it," she said. "But if it gets to be too much, you come to me, Kerry. I'm the reason she's being a bitch to you. It's not your fault."

The blond woman pulled their joined hands over and kissed Dar's knuckles. "I appreciate the offer." She rubbed her cheek against the back of Dar's hand. "And I'll remember it."

"Okay." Dar ruffled her hair. "The data dump's going, but it's taking sixteen forevers," she admitted. "I hope we can get something out of it, or this is going to be one big expensive waste of time."

Kerry grunted softly. "Do you want to get something, really, Dar?" she asked in a quiet voice. "Sometimes proof is not all it's cracked up to be."

Dar looked at her. The blond woman's face was pensive, and the weight she carried on her shoulders from the choices she'd made was evident to her partner's watching eyes. Without a word, Dar leaned over and gave her a kiss, then a brief hug, before she stood and headed back to her own office.

Kerry reached up to touch the spot where Dar's lips had been, and found a smile somewhere. "Kiss my ass, Clarice," she announced wryly. "Just kiss my Republican WASP ass."

It was dark outside, and the MIS office was very quiet. Only one light was on, in the small office that once had been Dar's and was now temporarily again as she worked on her database project.

She leaned back in her chair and propped one knee up against the desk, reviewing the screen with tired eyes. An entire screen of characters faced her, white letters on a dark background that didn't change no matter how many times she read them.

With a soft curse, she got up and stretched out her back, careful not to jar her shoulder as she circled the tiny room with weary, slightly rocking paces. Finally she stopped and gazed at the wall, studying the spidery traces of the network diagram—her network—that was tacked up in all its glory.

Her cell phone rang. Dar turned and leaned against the wall, unclipping the instrument from her belt and answering it. "Yeah?"

"Hello, Dar!" Alastair's voice sounded, as always, resolutely positive. "How are things going?"

"Lousy," Dar admitted.

"Ah." Her boss cleared his throat. "No luck, huh?"

Dar gazed at the computer, aware of being balanced on a knife of decision. After a moment, she inhaled, aware of the sting as the knife cut her. "Wish I hadn't had any," she said. "It's all there, Alastair."

All there. She'd been wrong. Uncle Jeff had known, and more than that, he'd used knowing to buy Chuck his boat. There was no way to hide any of it—and Dar had in fact been more than a little shocked at herself for wanting to.

"Ah." Alastair absorbed the information and the silence that followed it. "Well, we knew it wasn't pretty, Dar," he said briskly. "But we did what we got paid to do."

"Yeah," Dar agreed quietly.

Another silence ensued.

"But?" Alastair ventured.

"But what's the price for it, Alastair?" Dar asked. "There's a lot of dirt in here a lot of people, very powerful people, won't want dumped into the sunlight. What about us?"

"Us?" Alastair asked. "As in you and me?"

Dar snorted, walking across to the desk and plopping back down into her chair. "Us as in the company. Thirty percent of our contracts are with the government, Alastair. You want them all pissed at us?" She looked at the screen, reaching over to scroll her mouse down a few clicks. "Is it worth it?"

This time, it was Alastair who was quiet for a span. "Y'know, I don't think I ever thought I'd hear you say something like that, Paladar," he said. "Don't tell me you're getting soft in your old age."

A faint, brief smile crossed Dar's face. "Maybe." She exhaled. "Or maybe I just don't want to bury old friends today."

"Ah." The CEO acknowledged her reluctance. "Well, the company can stand the glare, Dar. We just did our jobs. The brass can be upset at the results, but not the methods, and given your natural bias, they can't even fault the process."

"Bias?"

"C'mon, Dar," Alastair said. "At any rate, I know I can leave this decision in your hands, and I want you to know—whatever you decide, I'll back you a hundred percent."

Gee. Thanks. Dar tipped her head back and regarded the ceiling. "Gee, thanks," she repeated audibly into the phone. "You have a nice day too, Alastair."

Her boss chuckled briefly. "I know how you feel, Dar," he said. "Had to sit in your seat once myself, and it's not easy." His voice grew more serious. "But that's why they pay us the big bucks, lady. You know it and I know it. So you just make your best decision, and we'll take it from there."

Dar accepted the mild rebuke with a slight nod of her head. "Yeah, I know," she acknowledged. "It's just been a long week. Maybe Kerry was right after all; I was too close to this."

Alastair gave that statement its due and proper regard. "Or maybe you've just swallowed a few too many painkillers," he suggested. "Sleep on it, Dar. Don't choose now. Just go home, relax, and wait for sunlight to make your decision."

Dar's sensitive ears caught the sound of the elevator doors opening. "Good idea," she said. "I'll do that, Alastair." She cocked her head, listening for Kerry's distinctive walk and smiling when she heard it. "I'll let you know what I decide."

"Right-o, Dar," Alastair said. "G'night."

"Night." Dar watched as Kerry's figure filled the doorway of the small office.

"Say good night to Kerrison, too," Alastair's voice added, before a solid click indicated the line cutting off.

"W—" Dar looked at the phone in startlement. "How in the hell did he know you were here?"

"Ahh." Kerry looked as tired as Dar felt. She entered the office and dropped into the chair across from her boss, unbuttoning the top button of her shirt and loosening the collar as she did so. "You smiled when you saw me. It makes your voice all different."

"It does?" Dar responded in a slightly amazed tone.

"Yes, it does," Kerry said. "How's it going?"

Dar sighed. She propped her head up on one fist and looked across the desk at her lover. "I need a hug."

Kerry got up and circled the desk. "Nicest request I've had all day." She willingly perched on one arm of Dar's chair and wrapped herself around her lover, giving her the requested squeeze. "How's it going?" she repeated, glancing across to the monitor.

Dar threaded one arm under Kerry's knee and let her head rest against the blond woman's chest. "I recovered the data," she answered, after a brief pause. "Alastair says it's up to me to decide what to do with it."

Kerry exhaled, resting her cheek against the top of Dar's head. "You going to decide now?"

Dar shook her head.

"How about we go home, then? I'm pooped," Kerry said.

"Okay," her lover agreed.

They sat there in silence for a little while, only the soft squeak of the chair audible as they rocked gently together.

"Wanna go get some ice cream?" Kerry finally said. "I canceled my meeting with the group tonight. Just too much stress of my own to deal with theirs."

Dar perked up a little. "Mm."

"That little parlor on the beach? You, me, and a sundae?"

"Oh, yeah." Dar finally smiled. "Lead on. I'm right there with you."

After Dar carefully locked down her data, they got up and left the room, shutting the lights off. Arm in arm, they walked to the elevator, leaving the problem temporarily behind them.

The parlor was busy, but they found a table near the back windows and settled into it. Dar half turned in her seat and leaned her back against the window, easing her arm onto the table for support.

Despite the crowd, a server wound her way over to the table immediately and presented herself, giving them both a big smile. "Hi guys! Tough day?" she asked sympathetically. "Haven't seen you in here in a few weeks."

Kerry gave the girl a wry look, acknowledging there were worse places to be a regular at. "We've been swamped," she agreed. "Two of the usual."

"You got it." The girl scribbled something on her pad. "Want a couple Cokes while you're waiting?"

"Sure," Kerry agreed, leaning back and extending her denim-covered legs as the girl left. The parlor was a simple place—tile floors and formica tables lending it a cafeteria look, along with fluorescent lighting that did not flatter it any.

But the ice cream was rich, and completely overindulgent, so when they visited they dismissed any lack of décor as merely incidental. Kerry actually liked its plain functionality. It reminded her of a small corner drug store she and her sister used to frequent on their way home from school, with its cracked vinyl stools and chipped counter. They'd gone there enjoying the illicit thrill of it, knowing if their parents found out, they'd both be punished in a heartbeat.

Made the sodas taste better, she'd always sworn. The memory brought a smile to her face, even after all this time.

"What's so funny?" Dar asked, her fingers plucking idly at the paper napkin on the table.

"Life, sometimes," her partner responded. "I was just thinking how in my life, whenever something was supposed to be bad for me, I went right after it," Kerry added. "Ice cream sodas, chocolate, beer—"

"Me." Dar snuck it in craftily.

Kerry looked at her, then laughed. After a moment, Dar joined her as they both enjoyed the moment together. "Yeesh, how true that is." Kerry wiped her eyes. "Me, the Midwestern Republican rebel."

"You forgot Christian," Dar reminded her, reaching casually over and capturing Kerry's hand.

"Ah, yes." Kerry twined fingers with her. "Twelve years of orthodox indoctrination just so I can sit here in South Beach holding hands with you." She rolled her head to one side and regarded Dar. "It's funny, though. One of the things they try so hard to teach you is to do 'the right thing.' What they never tell you is how to know what that is."

Dar nodded somberly. "I know what you mean."

Kerry leaned on the table a little. "Dar, you don't really feel sorry for those guys, do you? I mean, yeah, they were friends of yours once, but remember being in that hospital, okay? And remember how all of us almost got in a lot of trouble because of them."

The waitress returned with both their sodas and their ice cream. She set them down, and the women applied themselves to the serious business of eating for a moment before Dar decided to answer.

"I know they're wrong, Ker," she said, licking a bit of hot fudge off her spoon. "But yeah, I do feel sorry for them. Maybe I wouldn't have at one time in my life, but I do now, and it's your fault."

"My fault?" Kerry looked up in surprise, getting the words out around a mouthful of banana split.

"Your fault." Dar dabbed a bit of whipped cream on Kerry's nose. "You gave me back my conscience," she said. "Now I have to make peace with it before I have to go do what I need to do."

"Oh." Kerry ate a bit of chocolate ice cream. "Is that a bad thing?"

Dar tapped the spoon on her lower lip, a thoughtful look on her face. "No," she decided, shaking her head and spearing a cherry. "Just a damned inconvenient one sometimes."

Ah. Kerry reflected on that. Life was damned inconvenient sometimes, if she thought about it. She just had to take the good with the bad, and make her best choices. She sucked on her straw and nodded a little to herself, almost feeling a sense of reconciliation with one of hers.

Almost.

The sun peeked slowly over a lightly ruffled gray ocean. Across an almost empty beach, a seagull wheeled, searching for a little breakfast for himself.

Dar sat near the shore, leaning against a half-buried, mostly dead tree, and watched the bird circle. Beside her sat her briefcase, on which she rested one elbow as she dug idly into the sand with her bare toes.

It had been a long night for her, lying in the darkness with Kerry's warm body pressed against hers as she went over and over her options; how they might play out, and what the consequences could be. She'd finally gotten up and showered, dressing as a sleepy Kerry nuzzled her back and wishing the day was already over with.

She'd then come out here, to this beach, to let the cool morning breeze clear her head. It was the same beach she'd come to the night she'd almost fired Kerry, the same beach she'd been coming to for years when she needed a few minutes to ground herself, here within sight of the vast Atlantic that had been her playground since before she could really remember.

Maybe that's why she'd always been so damned sure she belonged in the Navy. Dar sighed. Even as a young child, there had never been a doubt in her mind that one day she'd be out there, living on the sea just like her father. It had been a world she'd been completely comfortable with—a world she'd been proud to be a part of.

Nowadays, it was considered a little old-fashioned to be patriotic. Dar ran her fingers through the grainy sand, plucking out a bit of dried coral and examining it. Her father was, though; once upon a time, she had been, too.

Now? Dar's lips pressed briefly together. With a slight groan, she pushed herself to her feet and shouldered her briefcase, walking slowly across the sand to the beckoning waves. She kept going until the water covered her feet, the incoming tide washing over her legs up to her rolled up pant legs, bringing with it the clean, tangy scent of the sea.

A bit of seaweed wrapped itself around her ankle, its touch a little prickly. Dar gazed off into the dawn, letting the onshore breeze blow her hair back as the sun lit up the waves.

Kerry sat at her desk, cupping her hands around a steaming mug of hot tea as she watched the sun rise through her window. She looked up as a knock sounded on her door, a little surprised. "Come in."

The door opened and Mark stuck his head in. "Morning, Kerry."

Kerry's blond eyebrows lifted. "You're here early."

"Yeah," the MIS manager agreed. "You, too."

"C'mon in," Kerry repeated. "Dar's on a plane up to DC, so I thought I'd get in here and get some stuff done before the phones start ringing."

Mark entered and crossed the mahogany carpet, settling in the seat across from Kerry's desk. "Did she get what she needed from that array?"

"I think so," Kerry said. "Now she's just got to decide what to do with it. Sticky political situation, you know?"

Mark nodded. "Yeah. Speaking of." He folded his hands together and rested his chin on them. "You figured out what you want me to do with Brent?" he asked.

"Is he here?"

"Yeah."

Kerry exhaled. "Okay, send him over. I'll talk to him," she replied. "Maybe we can get some communication going. I..." Another sigh. "It's really too bad, because he's a good tech."

"Yeah," Mark agreed. "He's just got some weird hang-ups,"

he said. "And talking about that crap—someone else is talking shit around the place."

Kerry covered her eyes with one hand. "Karnak says 'Clarice.'" She opened her fingers and peeked at Mark. "Am I close?"

"She's a bitch," the MIS manager stated flatly. "I didn't like her when she was chasing after Dar the last time, and it pisses me off that she's walking around here spouting crap."

Kerry leaned back in her seat and sipped her tea. "Don't hold back, Mark. Tell me how you really feel," she remarked wryly. "I know. It's really taken me by surprise, because I always thought she was a good worker; never had a problem with her before."

Mark looked slightly uncomfortable. "She really had a thing for Dar," he said. "Everyone knew it. Dar finally called her on it in a big meeting we had. Big time."

Ahh. Kerry winced. "She didn't mention that part."

"You know Dar." Mark half shrugged. "Clarice finally got over it. I don't blame Dar, but it was pretty public and I guess now Clarice feels like, well, shit, after all that crap, and now—"

"Now us." Kerry nodded. "Yeah." She sighed again. "And that puts me in a really awkward position. But I guess I have to do something about it, huh?"

Mark looked around carefully. "You could just tell Dar," he said in a low voice. "Let her handle it. After all, she's, like...in the middle of the whole thing."

Yes, she could tell Dar and let her handle it. But Kerry's whole being resisted that, and in her heart she knew she'd lose a lot of respect for herself if she backed down on this one. "She's offered," she told Mark. "But the woman works for me, so it's my call."

Mark didn't look surprised. "Okay," he said. "I'll send Brent over." He stood up. "Lots of luck."

"Thanks." Kerry shook her head as he left. Feeling the tension creep up her back and knot her stomach slightly, she turned her chair and looked out over the water. It was a great view, she reflected, and it fit the spacious office to which her position entitled her, but along with those perks came the responsibility of making the hard choices. She had a much better understanding now of how Dar had come to be the way she was, as a leader.

Leaders had to step back and see the big picture. For the greater good of the company or sometimes just because of hard dollars and cents reasons that fell within their areas, they had to make decisions that hurt individuals. "What would you have done, Kerrison, if you'd had to integrate a half-rate little software development services company with mostly mediocre employees and a pissant ops manager who told you off?" She drummed her fingers on the arm of her chair. "Damn, I was lucky she liked me."

Another knock at the door interrupted her musings. Kerry gazed plaintively at the horizon. "Luckier sometimes than others, however." She said, "C'mon in." As the door opened and Brent entered, she turned her chair and put down her cup. "Hello, Brent," she greeted. "Sit down. Let's talk."

Warily he walked over and took a seat, edging back as far away from her as he could. "If you're gonna fire me, could you please do it quick?" he said. "I wanna miss traffic."

Kerry sighed. It was going to be a very long day.

Dar glanced around as she walked through the Pentagon, feeling a bit conspicuous even though her civilian dress blended in with that of a good percentage of the workers. She'd called Gerry from the airport and he was expecting her, but she felt a curious sense of reluctance as she walked down the austere hallway.

She recalled the last time she'd been here, picking up the government contracts that had, in the end, allowed her to salvage Kerry's former company and permanently piss off the regional sales manager she'd upstaged. A smile appeared briefly, and she squared her shoulders as she opened the door to Gerry's outer office and gave his admin a nod.

The woman smiled at her and pressed a button on her phone. "General, Ms. Roberts is here."

"Is she? Great. Send her in." Gerry's voice boomed through the intercom.

Dar walked past the woman's desk and opened the inner door, entering and closing it behind her as Gerry put down the folder he'd been looking at and came around the desk to meet her. "Morning, Gerry."

"C'mere, girl." He opened his arms and enfolded her in a hug. "First things first. How's it having your daddy back?"

Dar put down her briefcase, forgetting about its contents for a moment. She returned the hug. "Awesome," she replied simply. "When are you going to come down and visit? They've got a boat they'd love to show off to you."

"Ah, munchkin. You got no clue how glad I am." Gerry rubbed her back and gave it a pat. Then he pulled back and looked at her, shrewdly reading the expression on her face. "Bad news, eh?"

Dar nodded.

Gerry exhaled, releasing her and stepping back to perch on

the edge of his desk. "Well, you tried, Dar. Can't fault you for it," he said. "Did a damn risky thing. I'm glad no worse happened."

Dar picked up her briefcase and laid it on his desk, releasing the locked latches and opening it. She lifted out a thick sheaf of papers secured with a binder clip and dropped it on the blotter pad. "Don't thank me yet."

"Eh?"

"It's there." Dar closed her case after removing a square box and putting it next to the paper. "Hard and digital copy." Her eyes lifted and met his. "I got all of it out of there."

Gerry was visibly stunned. He slowly got up and circled his desk, sitting down in his chair and staring at the paper. "Did you?"

Dar put her case on the floor and sat in the visitors chair across from him. She leaned back and folded her arms, exhaling for a long moment. "I took a copy of the computer core before they came in and trashed the place," she said. "I was able to reconstruct it."

Gerry was silent for a long while. He pulled the stack of paper over and turned it around, flipping through a few of the pages. "Huh," he finally murmured. "Dar, you skunked me. I figured I was going to have to bat my way out of a bunch of starched shirts looking to hang me for hiring some civ company who didn't know their butts from a deck mop."

Dar's face twitched slightly. "You hired the best," she said quietly. "You got what you paid for." Aside from the knowledge of what the information represented, Dar couldn't deny a bit of pride in herself for doing what most people would have considered pretty damn near impossible. It had been, by anyone's measure, a brilliant piece of reconstruction.

The general nodded slowly, pursing his lips. "Can't argue with that, my friend," he said. "But now I've got a whole 'nother kettle of fish I've got to deal with."

Dar nodded. "I know." She folded her hands. "Wasn't what I expected either."

Gerry got up and paced behind his desk, visibly disturbed. "Damn it," he said. "This'll blow out all over the damn place. Papers'll have a damn field day." He snorted. "Congress'll have a damn field day with me, after that last mess."

Dar simply sat and waited, having gone over the same issues all the way during her trip up from Florida. After a minute, however, she cleared her throat. "Can't you handle it under the table?"

Gerry looked at her. "Once, sure. Now? Forget it. More leaks in this place than in my wife's noodle strainer." He sighed in disgust. "Well, let me get the legal folks in here. Sit tight." He picked up the phone and dialed a number.

Dar drummed her fingers on one knee, just wanting it all to be over.

"It just ain't right," Brent muttered.

Kerry rested her chin on her hands, gazing at him with wry exasperation. "Brent, it's not really any of your business, you know?"

"That ain't so." Brent kept his eyes on the edge of the desk. "Not when you big shots just parade around, pushing it out in everybody's faces. It's not fair."

There was, Kerry acknowledged, a grain of truth in what he said. "Look, Brent," she sighed, "Dar and I do our best to keep our private life private. I'm sorry I wasn't thinking when I came into Ops that night, and that's my fault. I made a mistake."

Furtively, he peeked up at her. "That's right. It's wrong."

"Love is never wrong, Brent," Kerry said. "I'm sorry if that doesn't mesh with how you were brought up, but you know, it doesn't mesh with how I was brought up, either." She got up and circled her desk, watching him edge back nervously. "Sometimes you just have to learn to live with things. My question to you is, can you live with this? Because if you can't, and you continue to do things like spread false rumors about me or about Dar, then you can't work here."

"I didn't spread no false nothing," Brent protested. "All I said was you were meeting with some guy after dark here. It was true!"

"Why would you even tell anyone that?" Kerry queried.

"'Cause you were touching him all over! What was anybody supposed to think?" Now Brent was righteously upset. "Wasn't me who said all that other stuff," he added. "Go and find that other stuck-up woman, that one from Chicago. She's the one who told everyone you was—I mean, she said about cheating and all that. I just said what I saw."

Ah. Some of the pieces clicked together. Kerry felt a slow burn of anger start. "You mean Clarice?"

"If that's what her name is, sure," Brent said. "She heard me telling one of the techs, and then she was off and yabbling to everyone. Thought it was one big joke."

Kerry walked to her side table and poured herself a glass of water, more to give herself a chance to think than because she was thirsty. "Okay." She turned, leaning against the table as she sipped from the glass. "But that doesn't answer the question. Can you do your job here or not?" *One problem at a time, Kerry. One problem at a time.*

Brent slid a bit lower in the chair. "I don't want no trouble." He averted his eyes again. "I do a good job here."

Kerry returned to her desk and seated herself facing him. "That's right, you really do, Brent," she agreed. "You're one of the best techs we have, and that's why I was so disappointed about what happened. I like you."

Very slowly, his eyes lifted to meet hers.

"I don't want you to leave. But I also don't want you to be so uncomfortable around me, or around Dar, that it makes you crazy," Kerry continued, in a gentler voice. "So you think about it, and you let me know, okay?"

Brent was silent for a moment, then he finally nodded. "All right." He got up and scuttled around the chair. "I got stuff to take care of."

"Thanks for coming by, Brent." Kerry dismissed him. She waited for the door to close behind his stocky form, before she let her eyes narrow and her fingertips drum on her desk. "That," she spoke aloud, "was the easy one." With deliberation, she got up and headed for the door.

Dar stood with her arms folded, looking out the window of Gerald's office. Behind her, the general was hashing over her data with a tall, constipated-appearing major from the military legal office. The major wasn't happy. Gerald wasn't happy.

Hell, I'm not happy. Dar observed a black-and-yellow bird settle onto a branch outside, its mouth opening in song she hadn't a chance of hearing.

"Ms., ah, Roberts."

Dar turned to face the major. "Yes?"

"The security group that reviewed the base reported back to us a very different story than what you present here," the major stated. "We found some small infractions, yes, and my office was preparing administrative sanctions against the base commander, but nothing close to what you are alleging."

"I," Dar stated flatly, "am not alleging anything. I'm just an information services professional who is tendering information to you. If that information looks bad, that's not my fault."

The major watched her warily. "We found no indication of major offenses at that base," he repeated. "There was no hint in any of their systems of any of this."

"Exactly why I asked Paladar to retrieve the records," Gerald interrupted him. "Figured if there was anything dicey, butts would be covered post-haste." He tapped the report. "Now, Ted, let's call spades spades. We got a problem here."

The major looked even more constipated. "General, I'm sorry, but I have to call these 'facts' into question. I refuse to believe an entire intelligence team could have failed to find even a hint of this." He threw his hands up. "This could all be fabricated!"

Both of Dar's eyebrows shot up and she started forward, pausing when Gerry put a calming hand on her arm. "What would be the point in that?" Dar demanded.

"Well, Ms. Roberts, your company has a certain reputation to maintain." The major gave her a smug look. "Busting the Navy would certainly put a shine on your cap, wouldn't it?"

"Easy, Dar." Gerry put his arm over Dar's shoulders. "This nitwit in a starched suit has no idea who he's talking to."

"Sir!" the major protested.

"You listen here, youngster." Gerald rode over him. "Dar and her people didn't risk their hides to get this stuff out for the likes of you to pooh-pooh it. Now, this's the real stuff. I don't like it, you don't like it, and believe me if you don't believe her, Dar doesn't like it. But there it is, and now you, sir, have to deal with it. Go kick some kiester and stop wasting my time."

"Sir," the man rested his hands on the table, "let's just think about this for a minute."

Dar straightened and circled around to the other side of the table. "If I didn't know better, I'd say you just didn't want to blow their little scam. You in on it?"

The major stood up dead straight, his jaw clenching. "How dare you."

Dar lifted her hands and spread them out to either side of her. "Government has a certain reputation to maintain, doesn't it? Appropriations? Budgets? Scandal's always bad for the expense account, isn't it?"

"Dar." Gerald gave her a warning look. "Now, I know Ted here just wants to cover our butts. Don't blame him. Once he gets a look-see at all this, I know he'll do the right thing." He turned and stared directly at the major. "Isn't that right, Ted?"

The major glared at Dar.

"Ted?" The general stepped between them. "You know as well as I do, it's no good trying to stuff this bilge under the bunk. Didn't work last time, won't work this time. Just bite the bullet and get moving on it."

After a moment, the major nodded. "You're right, sir," he

answered quietly. "I just hate to see it. We've come so far since..."

"I know." Gerry sighed. "Always an ass dropping crap when you least expect it." He half turned his head. "Pardon me, Dar."

The major picked up the stack of paper and the box next to it and tucked it all under his arm. "I'll get to work on it right away, General. Don't you worry." He ignored Dar, turning his back on her and walking directly to the door, opening it, stepping through, and closing it with sharp precision.

Gerry sighed, and sat down on the edge of the table. He glanced at Dar, who was still visibly steaming. "Can't really blame him, munchkin. He's third-generation Navy, and you know how we get."

"He's a first-generation jackass," Dar replied. "Can he even read?"

"Now, Dar," the general chided. "He's a good legal guy. Give him a chance. Once he goes through all that, he'll step up to the plate, don't you worry." He added, "He didn't know you were one of us."

The room went still for a moment, and Dar heard those words as though they were crystal shards falling on the tile floor. She drew in a breath, and when she exhaled, she knew herself for a different person. Her voice, however, remained casual. "I'm not."

"Eh?"

"One of you," Dar said, looking him in the eye.

Gerry didn't know what to answer to that. He blinked for a minute, then he shook his head. "Well, like I said, don't you worry, Dar. We'll take care of it."

Was she worried? Dar considered. She'd turned over what she'd found to the proper authorities. Was it her problem what they did with it? She sat down in one of the leather chairs and exhaled. "Sorry."

Her old friend got up and walked over, sitting down in the seat next to her. He patted her knee. "No, it's me who should be sorry, Dar. I owe you a big apology."

Dar gazed at him from under dark lashes. "For what?"

"Asking you to go out there," General Easton replied in a quiet voice. "Contract's one thing. I should have known this was more than it seemed. Risking you wasn't on my battle plan, Dar." He shook a finger at her. "Especially if you were hurt, you little polliwog. You should have told me that."

"It turned out all right." Dar stretched carefully, avoiding stress on her shoulder. "Guess I'm done here, eh?"

Gerry studied her for a long moment, then nodded. "Just leave it in our hands," he assured her. "You go on back home and take some rec, hear?"

Dar got up and brushed her jacket off. She extended a hand to him. "I will," she said. "Let me know when you'll be in my neck of the woods, Gerry."

"Certainly will, Dar." The general took her hand and clasped it. "I've got a handful of other bases I'd like you to check out, but let's wait for the feathers to fall on this one for a month or so, eh?"

"Yeah," Dar agreed. "Be in touch."

She picked up her briefcase and shouldered it, then made her way out of the office, turning and giving Gerry a half wave before she left. He smiled and waved back. Dar closed the door with a sense of guilty relief and headed out to the outer corridor.

There. Glad that's over. Dar walked through the busy halls, her progress noted only by a few quick glances, most of them merely interested in the tall, dark stranger in their midst. Dar granted her ego the right to preen for a moment, then she turned and headed out the door to the street.

It was cold, and she paused to zip her jacket up before she made the trip out to the parking lot and got into her rental car. She set her briefcase on the seat next to her and closed the door, starting up the engine before she exhaled, gazing back the way she had come, at the massive building.

It seemed to her, as it always did, a bland facade full of dusty secrets.

Dar sat back and thought about that. She'd never been a conspiracy theorist, truthfully. She accepted that sometimes the government didn't tell what they knew, and she accepted that sometimes the government didn't know its ass from a hole in the wall. It was made up of people. Having a treasury seal on your paycheck didn't make you any smarter or more capable than anyone else, and Dar reckoned that in a general sense she hired more capable people than the establishment did—and paid them better to boot.

So. Did she really trust the major? Dar gazed at her own hands, curled around the steering wheel. Ringless, they were long fingered and powerful, and she flexed them once or twice as she pondered the meeting she'd just left. "Should I really care?" she asked herself aloud. "Let 'em do what they want with that damn stuff. I'm out of it."

With that, she put the car into reverse and backed out of the spot, sliding on her sunglasses to block the rich rays of the setting sun that angled in and highlighted her face.

Kerry found her way out to the small balcony on the four-teenth floor. It overlooked the ocean, and a cool breeze counter-acted the retained heat of the sun in the stone bench she dropped down onto. Her body was tired, and she rubbed her neck to relieve the stress, closing her eyes against the throbbing headache that had snuck up on her after her conversation with Brent.

The sun had dropped behind the building on its way to set-ting, and she laid her head back against the wall, allowing the sound of the waves, distinct even this far up, to infiltrate her senses and bring their own kind of peace to her.

Dar used this spot, she knew, and after a few visits up here she understood why. Even in the heat of summer, the wind kept the temperature bearable; now, nearing sunset, it was a good place to be even when the day wasn't as troublesome as hers was today.

She wished Dar would call. She knew her partner had been very upset when she'd left, and not hearing from her all day was adding to the stress from the dozen or so problems she was work-ing on as well as the personnel issues that were now cropping up.

Her eyes opened when she heard the door latch work, and she looked over to see Clarice emerge onto the balcony. Kerry men-tally articulated a curse she was sure would surprise the other woman, then wrestled her manners into place and merely gave her a polite nod.

Clarice opened her mouth to speak, but she was forestalled by the sound of Kerry's cell phone ringing.

Saved by the bell. Kerry unclipped the instrument and checked the caller ID. A smile crossed her face at the readout, and she flipped the phone open with a sense of mildly vengeful relief. "Hey, sweetie."

She could almost hear Clarice's teeth grinding.

"Hey," Dar drawled softly. "Why are you outside?"

Kerry extended her legs and crossed them at the ankle. "How did you know I was?"

"I can hear airplanes. I assumed you hadn't gotten into model racing while I was gone."

The droll response made Kerry chuckle. "You know, I didn't even hear 'em. How's it going?" She made a point of ignoring Cla-rice, who went to the railing and looked over.

"Eh," Dar replied in a verbal shrug. "I gave Gerry the info, he gave it to some jerk in JAG. I get the feeling it might end up lining the president's secretary's birdcage before long."

"Mm," Kerry murmured. "That's a shame, after what we risked for it," she said. "So are you coming home now?"

"Yeah."

"To hell with them, then."

There was a brief silence. "Everything okay there?"

Kerry's eyes went to the stiff back facing her. "Everything's peachy. I'm going to clean up some garbage, then pack up my gear and take off. Can I interest you in a midnight cruise?"

"Mmm." Dar purred in response. "For that I'd climb to the top of the Washington Monument and flap my way home without the plane."

Kerry grinned in pure response. "See you soon, sweetie." She paused, her green eyes distinctly twinkling. "I love you."

"Love you, too," Dar replied. "See you in a bit."

Kerry folded up her phone and put it back in its clip. Then she leaned back and spread her arms across the back of the stone bench, taking possession of it, the space around it, and the situation she could feel brewing between her and Clarice.

She'd felt guilty about Clarice, she'd realized, because of what had happened over Thanksgiving. But now she realized she could no longer hide behind that guilt in dealing with the woman.

Clarice turned and looked at her. Kerry gazed coolly back.

"You know what, Kerry? I think—"

"Shut up," Kerry interrupted her in a quiet, yet carrying tone.

It caught the black woman by surprise, and she hesitated.

"I did you a favor and found you a place here," Kerry said. "And you repaid that by being as obnoxious as you could possibly be to me and undermining me with my staff."

"You didn't do me any favors," Clarice snapped back. "That was Dar."

"No, it wasn't," Kerry replied. "If it were up to Dar, you'd be in Nome." She got up and leaned against the wall, minimizing their height difference. "So you'd better decide if you want to keep on like you have been, because I'm losing my patience with you."

"You think you're so hot just because you're humping her—"

Kerry refused to get angry. "No, you think just because she and I are lovers, that gives you the right to attack me because Dar wouldn't sleep with you."

Clarice stared at her. "I guess she just likes white bread."

"Actually, she likes raisin toast with cream cheese," Kerry told her. "And you can pick up your severance check next Friday, in Personnel."

"What?" The woman's jaw actually dropped. "You are not firing me."

Kerry pushed off the wall and squared her shoulders. "Yes, I am," she informed Clarice. "For insubordination after a verbal warning." She paused. "It's in the handbook."

Clarice was visibly stunned. "You're joking."

Kerry shook her head. "I'm not."

"You can't fire me. I'll sue your ass!" The woman's voice rose in shrill anger. "I'll haul your ugly ass into court, and I won't have to work a day the rest of my life!" She stepped forward, her hands clenching into fists.

Kerry stood her ground, even though Clarice topped her by several inches. Adrenaline rushed through her body, washing away the ache and the exhaustion. Without her realizing it, her own hands curled into loose fists also. It brought on a sense of almost confusing power and she stepped forward instead of backward, her body responding to a fight-or-flight reflex in a completely unexpected way.

Fight? Her?

"It'll make a very interesting case." Kerry's voice rose. "I'll enjoy hearing your justification for your documented insubordination." She added, "Maybe Dar'll testify how she had to push you out of her office the last time."

"Bitch."

Kerry smiled grimly. "Sometimes," she said. "When I have to be." She took a deep breath, but half turned as the door opened. Mark's head poked out, along with that of a security guard.

Kerry wondered yet again if their MIS manager was some kind of clairvoyant. "Nice timing," she complimented. "Keith, please escort this lady from the building. She's been terminated."

The security guard edged around Mark and came out onto the balcony, obeying her without question. "Yes, ma'am." He gave Kerry a respectful nod, then said to Clarice, "Please come with me, ma'am."

"You have not heard the end of this, whorebait," Clarice hissed. "I will see your ass in court."

The guard took her to the door and they disappeared. Mark closed the door behind them, sliding out onto the balcony to Kerry's side. "Whoa, chief. That was radical."

Kerry felt her knees shaking. She went over to the bench and sat down before she fell down, letting her arms fall to rest on her thighs. "Son of a fucking bitch."

Mark's eyes widened.

"Yes, Republicans curse." Kerry lifted a shaking hand to her head and tried to catch her breath. It hadn't quite worked out how she'd planned, and she could only imagine the round of e-mails that would have to start between her, Mariana, and Hamilton Baird, ILS's legal council.

Mark sat down next to her and handed her a lidded cup with a straw sticking out of it. Kerry took it, surprised at the chill that stung her fingers and caused condensation to run down the outside. She sipped gingerly at the straw and was rewarded with a mouthful of chocolate milkshake. "Mm."

"I saw you guys out here," Mark said. "I figured it wasn't a cool thing. Brent ran down and got that from the shop. He said you guys talked."

Kerry sucked down another mouthful. "We did."

"So...he's going to be okay?"

She nodded. "I think so."

Mark looked out over the water, and then back at Kerry. "I'm really glad you fired that bitch," he said. "Because I was getting ready to, like, do something radical to her driver's license record and get her ass arrested for something really gross."

Kerry exhaled. "I'm not sure it was the right way to do it," she admitted. "But it's done. I guess I'll deal with the fallout."

And she would, she realized. In a series of decisions whose repercussions would probably be with her for a long time to come, it was just one more she had to come to terms with.

She thought it was the right choice.

Time, of course, would tell.

Dar paused at the stoplight, casting her gaze at the bulk of the Capitol building while she waited for the traffic to flow again.

Suddenly a familiar figure appeared, accompanied by two younger men. Dar blinked, surprised at the coincidental presence of Roger Stuart at just the same moment that she was passing the spot.

Obeying an impulse she didn't stop to analyze, Dar swung the car into a parallel parking spot and shut the engine off; then she opened her door and got out just as the senator reached her car.

They stared at each other for a moment, then the statesman relaxed slightly, watching her warily as she approached. "Roberts," he murmured, inclining his head a trifle.

"Hello, Senator," Dar found herself saying. "Mind if I have a word with you?"

It was obviously the last thing in the world Roger Stuart expected. He hesitated, watching her intently with his cold, green eyes, then he shrugged. "Go to the office. I'll meet you there," he instructed his aides, who were watching Dar with equal suspicion.

"Sir—"

"Go on," Stuart instructed sharply. He waited for the men to reluctantly retreat, then turned back to Dar. "Well?"

Why the hell am I doing this? Dar wondered. *I can't trust this man further than I could pick up that car and toss it. What the heck am I doing?*

And yet...

"I'd like to give you something," Dar said. "It's information I obtained from a naval base in Florida."

The senator looked at her as though she'd grown a second head. "Excuse me?"

"You heard me."

"What's this all about?" Stuart asked, slightly intrigued despite himself. "Why are you bringing this to me? Is it a trick? Another one of your machinations?"

With a sigh, Dar turned and removed her briefcase, taking a second copy of the data from it and handing it over. "No," she said briefly. "Look at it. If you think it's worth your attention, do something about it. If not, chuck it. I don't care."

The senator let his eyes fall to the top page. "What is this?" He picked up the cover sheet and examined the summary. "I don't know what you ex..." He looked up at Dar sharply.

"I gave it to the military's legal department," Dar said evenly. "I think it'll end up in a shredder. Now I'm giving it to you. I've done my patriotic duty, so whatever happens, the ball is in your court." She turned and tossed her briefcase into the car.

"Why me?" Stuart asked curiously, half his attention still on the summary.

Dar looked at him. "You're the only senator I know," she said, then her lips quirked. "Not to mention, the only one I'm related to."

Sour lemons had nothing on the face she got for that claim.

"Kerry's fine. She thinks of her family a lot. Call her sometime." Dar got it all out, then she got back into her car and started it, rolling up the window and pulling out without a backward look.

Dar felt a weight she had hardly been aware of lift off her shoulders. Now she could go home.

She hoped there would be ice cream at the airport.

Roger Stuart stood on the sidewalk, watching the car disappear into the distance. His hands curled around the papers, and after a moment, he tucked the sheaf under his arm, straightened his coat lapels, and started off down the street with a determined stride.

Chapter
Twenty-One

The boat bobbed lightly up and down on the waves, a round moon painting a pure cream stripe across the black waters. On the stern, a small table was set with candles and crystal, the remains of a light supper evident.

Kerry lifted her glass and extended it. Dar touched hers to it without comment, and they both took a sip.

"Long week," Dar said after a quiet moment.

"Very," Kerry agreed. "Glad it's over."

Dar got up and reached out, catching Kerry's hand and pulling her up. They walked to the padded benches and sat down together, Dar enfolding Kerry in her arms. The ocean rocked them gently, cradling them as the tide moved outward, tugging against the boat's anchor.

The sound of the land was completely absent out here. Only the waves rustled and the rigging softly clanked in the wind, and the city was a blur of light on the horizon that seemed remote and unimportant.

Kerry closed her eyes and drank in the scent of the sea. The breeze blew against her, and she could almost feel the tang of salt in it as it brushed across her skin. She let it take away the stench of the day's stress as she leaned back against Dar and soaked in her partner's loving warmth instead. "You think I was wrong?"

Dar was quiet for a bit. "No," she answered finally. "You were actually more tolerant than I'd have been."

"I kind of pushed her into it," Kerry admitted. "She heard me talking to you on the phone."

"Did you say anything you wouldn't have if she hadn't been there?"

"Mm, no." Kerry sighed. "But I keep thinking there should

have been some way for me to turn that around. To come to an understanding with her."

"She wasn't thinking with her brain cells, Ker," Dar said pragmatically. "Ovaries don't generally do well on their SATs."

Kerry chuckled wryly. "I guess."

"No guess." Dar rested her chin on Kerry's shoulder and blew lightly in her ear. "No regrets. You did the right thing."

Kerry leaned her head against her partner's. "Thanks, boss."

Dar bit her ear, then licked it, making Kerry jump slightly. "I love you," she murmured. "We have something in common now, y'know."

Kerry enjoyed the sensation before the words percolated through it. "Only one thing?" she asked, tilting her head back and kissing Dar on the lips.

Dar let the kiss linger, then she rubbed her cheek against Kerry's. "Another thing. Now I know what it's like to do something because it's the right thing, not because it's what I want."

"You mean, with the Navy?"

Dar nodded. "It was a club, one that I really wanted to belong to once upon a time."

Kerry hugged her.

"And then at some point in this, I realized I never would have belonged even if they'd taken me," Dar continued softly. "I never would have been one of them, Kerry. Never. Not and been true to myself."

No. Kerry kissed her again. "You might have ended up like Thunderbuns," she sighed. "I'm glad you didn't."

"Me, too," Dar agreed.

Kerry slowly unzipped the pullover Dar was wearing, exposing her chest. She planted a kiss on her partner's collarbone and put the day behind her. Tomorrow would bring what it would, but the important thing was that they'd face it together.

"Hey." Dar nuzzled her neck. "You mad at me?"

Huh? Kerry paused in mid lick. "Oh, about my father?"

"Mm-hmm."

"Um, no." Kerry found herself smiling slightly. "It'll be interesting to see what choice he makes."

Dar pulled her down onto the padded bench, unzipping her shorts. "Yes, it will." She heard the chuckle of the sea behind her. "Some other time."

Some other time. Kerry released herself to the moment, responding with abandon to Dar's touch. God had brought them together—and left them together for His own, good reasons. Now she could accept that and take whatever came next without fear.

No matter what it was.

Dar cradled Kerry's head, and their lips met as their bodies tangled together in rhythm with the motion of the sea.

The moon smiled benignly on them, ready to light a path home, not realizing it wasn't needed for two souls already there.

Other titles by *Melissa Good*
available from
Yellow Rose Books

Eye of the Storm

Eye of the Storm picks up the story of Dar Roberts and Kerry Stuart a few months after the story *Hurricane Watch* ends. At first it looks like they are settling into their lives together but, as readers of this series have learned, life is never simple around Dar and Kerry. Surrounded by endless corporate intrigue, Dar experiences personal discoveries that force her to deal with issues that she had buried long ago and Kerry finally faces the consequences of her own actions. As always, they help each other through these personal challenges that, in the end, strengthen them as individuals and as a couple.

Available at booksellers everywhere.
ISBN: 1-930928-74-2

And coming in 2003
from
Yellow Rose Books

Thicker Than Water

At the beginning of this sequel to *Red Sky at Morning,* Kerry
Stuart is forced to acknowledge her own feelings toward and
experience with her folks as she and Dar Roberts assist a teenager who is jailed after being tossed out onto the street by her
parents when they find out she is gay. While trying to help the
teenagers in the church group adjust to real world situations,
Kerry gets a call concerning a family emergency. Upon hearing
from her partner, Dar leaves during a major corporate crisis to
go to Michigan, determined to support Kerry in the face of grief
and hatred.

Melissa Good is a well-known writer of Xena fan fiction. She lives in Southern Florida with her dogs and computers. Her web site is www.merwolf.com.